winds of morning

By the same author

HONEY IN THE HORN

HARP OF A THOUSAND STRINGS

BEULAH LAND

winds of morning

H. L. DAVIS

wm
WILLIAM MORROW
An Imprint of HarperCollins*Publishers*

HarperCollins books may be purchased for educational, business, or sales promotional use. For information please e-mail the Special Markets Department at SPsales@harpercollins.com.

A hardcover edition of this book was published in 1952 by William Morrow and Company.

FIRST WILLIAM MORROW PAPERBACK EDITION PUBLISHED 2015.

Library of Congress Cataloging-in-Publication Data has been applied for.

ISBN 978-0-06-241318-5

15 16 17 18 19 OV/RRD 10 9 8 7 6 5 4 3 2 1

Marvel not that I said unto thee,
Ye must be born again.
The wind bloweth where it listeth,
and thou hearest the sound thereof,
but canst not tell whence it cometh,
and whither it goeth:
so is every one that is born
of the Spirit.

—Saint John, III, 7, 8.

chapter one

BACK in the year 1926 or 1927, or maybe both, there was a propertied young man named Ross Tunison living up the Middle Columbia River whose father, after a lifetime of self-sacrificing toil and manipulating government land entries, had left him thirty thousand acres of grass and hay land fronting on both sides of the river between the upper end of the big sand dunes and Indian Rapids, all outfitted with cross-fences, feed camps, barns, bunkhouses, lambing sheds, and enough sheep scattered around the draws and gullies and waterholes to patch perdition a mile and lap over. Young Tunison looked like an ideal man to handle such an inheritance, for he did not drink, gamble, run after women, collect fancy automobiles, or tinker with stock or real estate promotions, as wealthy young men of the middle 1920's mostly did. He didn't even use tobacco, and he had never owned a suit of store clothes in his life, though he could have had them tailor-made in carload lots if he had wanted to. His one weakness, which broke out on him after the old man died, was a passion for profits acquired by chicanery and underhandedness, in preference to money gained honestly. Men who had worked for him claimed that he occupied his idle moments by stealing loose change out of one of his own pockets and sneaking it into another, merely to keep himself in practice. There was probably some personal spite back of that rumor, but he did own a ten-thousand-gallon whisky still back in the hills that supplied half the bootleggers in the country, and a ferryboat that ran stolen cattle across the state line after dark, and a fifteen-bed hookshop nestled in the rimrock on the Washington side of the river where wandering stockmen could disencumber themselves of their money without having unfavorable reports circulated about it among their families and creditors. Usually his enterprises ran along profitably without any trouble, but sometimes one or another of them would begin to threaten trouble for him. When that happened, he would back out and throw himself into the sheep-raising business as if his salvation depended on it, putting his hired hands to a round of harrowing, road-grading, fence-stringing, tank-mending and weed-pulling that would have made his place one of the sightliest in the country if he had carried it out far enough. Since he only worked his men in sight of the main road where passers-by could see him at it, the actual improvements he got in didn't amount to much.

He was in the heat of one of his land-improving spasms one early spring when I was tending to some routine paper-work for the sheriff's office in the sand hills up the river. It started over a trifle: an itinerant rodeo performer claimed to have had a wallet stolen in his rimrock resort, and took a couple of shots at the furniture in protest. The girls cooled him off by applying a portable sewing machine to the back of his head and dropping him out the window, and a lawyer in town put him up to sue for damages on the strength of his resulting cuts, abrasions, lacerations, and mental anguish. It was the kind of scrawny little ten-cent cat fight that the whole country had come down to in those years, after its earlier start at more hopeful things, but it happened on the far side of the river, so the only part of it that lapped into my territory was young Tunison's splurge of zeal for sheep ranching, and his determination to protect his ancestral estate against the families of Indians that came down from the high country every spring to dig camas root in the bottoms close to the river, where it matured earliest. The Indians didn't hurt his land any, and the camas, being mildly poisonous to livestock in its flowering season, was actually better dug than left growing, but he threw off four or five of their camps anyway, to show the public how much the responsibility of land management weighed on him. Then he took it into his head to try something showier, and sent one of his foremen to rough up old Piute Charlie Spencer's camp a half-mile outside his property line, on the ground that its dogs were killing his sheep.

Except for Piute Charlie, who was close to eighty years old and doddering so his joints rattled, there was nobody in the camp except squaws, which may have been the reason he picked it to show off on. It was swarming with Indian dogs, as those camas-digging camps generally were: sharp-muzzled curs, frowsy and yellowish, that might have been mistaken for a last year's litter of coyotes except that they were dirtier and surlier. The squaws had herded them all inside the tents when they sighted the foreman's wagon heading their way, guessing what he was after. Dogs occupied a kind of special bracket in an Indian camp: too high to be killed, but never quite high enough to be fed. There were none in sight when the foreman drew up in front of the dirty canvas pole tents, but the squaws brought them out three or four at a time when he threatened to climb down and go in after them. They swore with every installment that there wasn't another dog left, and then hauled out three or four more when he made as if to back his wagon into the tents and flatten the whole camp for them. He shot from his wagon seat, probably for fear some of the squaws might club him from behind if he got down, and several of the loose curs dodged and cross-angled so it took him several shots apiece to finish them. When he got the last of them laid out, a squaw spread back the tent flap to show him that there were no more, and discovered that one of his cross-angle shots had gone through the tent wall and hit Piute Charlie, who had been lying in his blankets under the influence of some patent painkiller he had been taking for his rheumatism, or whatever had been hurting him that week. It was one load of medicine that gave him his money's worth, for the effects of it never wore off. The foreman's bullet took him almost between the eyes. When the squaws looked in at him, he was stone-dead.

Probably none of them felt especially sorry for the worthless old wart hog; a man who could hide out swigging painkiller while they were being hazed around by one of Tunison's gunmen deserved to have some kind of trouble land on him, so the stray bullet only evened things up. They wasted no time in mourning for him, and though a dead man and the man who had killed him were not exactly steadying company to have around at such a time, they managed as capably as anybody could have. The older squaws circled the foreman's wagon to keep him from leaving, and a couple of the younger ones struck out across the rocks to the railroad flag station where I was waiting to catch a ride back to town on a work train that was out spraying oil on the sand dunes to keep the spring winds from blowing them across the tracks.

The two young squaws spoke a sprinkling of English between them—none of the older ones could speak anything except their Pakiut dialect—and they explained about the shooting on the way back down the trail to the camp. It was a mistake to let them reel off the whole story without rustling up somebody else as a witness to it, but there weren't many people around, and it would have been impossible to make the squaws hold it all back till I found somebody. There was a section boss at the flag station, but he was too drunk to witness anything. I had come out to serve a divorce complaint on him, and he had so much trouble getting even that through his head that I left it stuck down his lamp chimney, alongside a trackwalker's note about some loose horses on the track at mile-post forty-six that looked to be at least three days old. He had enough discouraging news ahead of him, without piling any witnessing job on top of it. I left him to his dreams, and let the squaws clatter out the particulars as they led the way down through the rocks to their camp.

The camp squaws were still holding Tunison's foreman circled in his wagon when we got there. I recognized him, though I didn't know him. He was from out in the desert somewhere around Fort Rock or Silver Lake. His name was Sylvester Busick, and he was supposed to be part Indian himself, a quarter or three-eighths or something. I didn't know any more than that about him, and nothing against him except his looks, which he couldn't help, though it wouldn't have hurt him to try.

He looked heavy-featured and grouty and a little foolish when we pulled in, and all the squaws started gabbling at us in Tenino that they had kept him from getting away, though he denied that he had thought of such a thing, and there was no sign that he had tried it. The front wheels of his wagon hadn't been turned, and the tracks indicated that his team had been standing in the same place for upwards of an hour. He didn't object when I put him under arrest, merely remarking that he was ready to leave almost any time. His horses had been getting fidgety and hard to hold, and he was uneasy for fear some of the younger bucks might come in from the camas digging and decide to stir up trouble with him. It wasn't that he was afraid of any of them, or all of them put together, as far as that went, but he didn't want to get mixed up in any fight after what had happened already. One Indian down in a day was enough, he thought. The country couldn't stand too much improving all at one time.

He talked willingly enough about the shooting, but nothing he said was worth anything. He had convinced himself that he had not shot Piute Charlie; somebody else had, he thought, probably under cover of the rumpus he made in cleaning out the dogs. Plenty of the squaws had it in for the old man, and squaws weren't particular how they settled their grudges as long as there was no risk about it. One of them could have sneaked into the tent from the back with a camp gun, and then sneaked out again and put it back where it belonged without even being missed. Even from the wagon, he pointed out, the bullet mark in the old man's forehead showed considerably larger than the bore of his rifle; almost twice as big, he thought. He offered to wait while I took measurements on it, but I couldn't see that it would prove much. Those little .250-3000 bullets were built to open out when they touched anything, and his had gone through a double fold of heavy tent canvas on its way in. For that matter, it could have ricocheted off a rock or a digging bar inside the tent before it finally hit, though I didn't argue the point out that far. I climbed into the wagon behind the seat and said the coroner's inquest would do any measuring that was needed, and that we had better move out. If any of the squaws had shot Piute Charlie on a grudge, there was no telling when they might start thinking up a few against us.

THAT was all the persuading I did. There was no gun-in-the-ribs routine, or anything like it. It wasn't that I felt lenient toward him. Any man who went caving around shooting up an Indian camp on government land and trying to blame the squaws for the mess he had made deserved to have several guns poked into his ribs, and maybe a few points south too, but it wasn't my business to see that people got what they deserved, and I wasn't sure that I had any right to make an arrest for the shooting at all. I was underage and without authority to do anything except serve some divorce papers, and there were Indian police around the country who usually tended to cases involving Indians, when they got around to it. But the squaws did look mean, and an arrest looked like the best way to head off trouble with them. Busick was not too far behind them in mean-favoredness—long-armed and scowly, with a big grayish mouth and no eyelashes—but he sized them up and started his horses without arguing back. He didn't begin arguing till we got out of range of the camp and raised sight of the road that led down to Tunison's ferry landing. Then he broached the notion that we ought to hunt up Tunison and tell him what had happened before we went on into town. It wouldn't take long, he explained, and Tunison could telephone the sheriff and have lawyers and character witnesses and bail all arranged for by the time we pulled in.

It wouldn't have been unreasonable, under ordinary circumstances. The trouble was that Tunison was out with a crew of men stringing fence wire on one of his hayfields across the river, and crossing to find him would mean crossing the state line. Taking a prisoner into another state would mean that his arrest didn't hold any longer, and if he took a notion to stay there it would take extradition proceedings to get him back. Busick swore solemnly that he would scorn to take advantage of any such low-down technicality, and that when he had finished laying his case before Tunison he would hit straight back to the ferry without looking either to the right or the left; but I still felt uncertain about legalities, and he had shown a little too much shiftiness in trying to blame the squaws for the shooting for me to risk any more on him. I tried to let it down on him easy by explaining that it was late, the sheriff was out on a murder case in the hills, and Tunison would get word of the shooting from his herders before evening anyway; but he was harder to reason with than he had been among the squaws muttering and fingering loose rocks out of the sand and taking side glances at Piute Charlie lying dead in his blankets. Instead of recognizing tactfulness, he let on to be insulted at having his word doubted, got loud and high-tempered about his rights, and finally branched off into a harangue about the country being run into the ground by a bunch of big-headed understrappers who went around lording it over the taxpayers on the strength of their political pull or something, the Jesus only knew what.

He got his voice up to a yell before he was through, but the road may have had something to do with that. It was nothing but an old Indian pole trail, and he had to talk loud to make himself heard above the clatter of the wagon. He hunted out all the rough places, knowing they would be rougher on me in the back of the wagon than for him in the seat. I held on and didn't answer him back. There were hard losers everywhere, and arguing with them only encouraged them. We jounced through sand hills and across rockbreaks, and edged onto a rise of ground streaked with new grass. Off to the right was where the river swept into the upper rapids. The water was sharp black, capped in the lifts with dazzling white foam and jostling at the edges with grayish blocks of drift ice, that sometimes grazed each other and flung darkish clouds of powdery spray into the sky like dust from a dynamiting. At a distance, the churning ice and the overhanging spray made it look like a place where some tremendous work was going on. In its time it had been. There had been steamboats once, driving upstream with soldiers for the Bannock and Piute and Blackfoot wars, and once there had been pioneers running the swift water down between the cliffs in their calked wagon beds without knowing where they were going to come out, and once long fur pirogues had passed with loads of peltries on the long haul across the continent to York Factory on Hudson's Bay. There had been Lewis and Clarke, Captain Bonneville, Grant, Sheridan, Crook, Gibbon, Chief Joseph, Looking Glass, Oytes the Dreamer, Smohalla . . .

Nobody lived along the river now except section hands, some squatters in deserted shanties and grounded woodscows, the whores over at Tunison's establishment, and a few of his herders when the grass was up. One of his sheep camps came into sight as we bumped across another rise: a camp wagon drawn up beside a little creek with spots of green watercress showing between heaps of dead rye grass and patches of glare ice. There were no sheep in sight; nothing but a couple of broom-tailed horses grazing up the sidehill, and a skinny-looking girl in a faded pink dress hanging out clothes on a line stretched between the wagon and a clump of willows in the creek. It was too far to make out much about her. She was bareheaded and sunburned, her dress was one she had outgrown, and her hair was streaky-looking, part blonde and part darker. She was fourteen or fifteen, I judged; that was the age when girls' hair usually started darkening. She shaded her eyes toward us and lifted one hand as if waving, though I couldn't be sure whether it was that or whether she was only wiping her clothesline before draping her wash on it. Busick took no notice of her, but he stopped orating about his rights. She waved again and called something. We couldn't make out what she said, though her voice was so shrill that the horses on the sidehill stiffened and looked up as if somebody had shot at them. Busick half-raised one hand at her, and whacked his team with the lines and drove on. When we had turned down into another rockbreak out of sight of her, he limbered up and said she was his daughter. She was around fifteen, he thought, though he couldn't be sure about it without doing some counting up. He refused to concede that it was any hell of a place to leave a girl of that age alone in. He said it was as safe as any, and maybe safer. Besides, she was used to it.

"She's lived around places as wild as this one ever since she could crawl," he said. "She'll be around wilder ones before she's through, too. Before the month's out, if things work out the way they ought to, I've got a deal on to manage a big place back of South Junction, and when it's settled we'll be on our way out of here. There ain't anything worth hangin' around here for; everybody orderin' you around every damned minute."

Still, I thought, there was Piute Charlie lying dead up the river among the dog carcasses. He hadn't been worth much, but he was worth still less with a bullet through him. The law didn't take worthlessness into account much, anyway. "We'd better drive across to that sheep camp and tell your daughter what's happened," I said. "This business might hold you up longer than you expect. She oughtn't to be left out there all by herself without any idea what's become of you."

It wasn't that she counted for anything. She couldn't be much for looks if she had lived around sheep camps all her life, and if she could stand being stuck out on a naked gravel flat with nothing but her thoughts and her old man's dirty laundry for company, she was welcome to it. The only thing was that a man under arrest had a legal right to let his relatives know about it, and I wanted to give him everything he was entitled to. It didn't dawn on him that he was being treated considerately. He took it for sentimental weakening, and said, with a side glance at me to see how it took, that he guessed we had better let it go.

"It's late, and we ain't got too much time," he went on, parroting the rigmarole of excuses I had put up for not crossing the river. He had them down almost word for word. "We want to make it to town as much before dark as we can. The sheriff's out on a murder case somewhere back of South Junction, and court's in session and everybody's busy with that, and we don't know how long this side trip of yours will take us. She'll hear all about what's happened, anyway. Some of the herders will pack word to her about it before the day's out. . . ." There was something in his mimicking that wasn't quite right, but he dropped back to his ordinary tone of voice before I could decide what it was. "I wanted to ferry across and tell Tunison about this. It wouldn't take any longer than goin' across to that sheep camp. There's a road over to where he's at, and there ain't none over there. If I can't report where I want to, I won't report to anybody."

"You don't want to leave your daughter over there by herself without any word at all, do you?" I said. It was a mistake to argue with him, but it was hard to resist doing it. "You don't know whether the herders will bring word to her or not. There's no grass up and no sheep in sight. They may not get down this far for a month yet. She won't dare to leave without knowing what's become of you. You don't know what might happen to her."

That gave him an opening. He spraddled down on it like a hawk. "Anything that happens to her you'll be to blame for," he said. "Nothing would, if you'd do like I wanted us to. I wanted to ferry across and tell Ross Tunison about this. He could telephone his lawyers, and have bail all fixed up for me by the time we got to town, and I could be back out here before morning. I could leave this rig at the feed yard and come out on the train, and she wouldn't even know I'd been gone anywhere. You couldn't do that, though. Oh, no! There wouldn't be enough law in it to suit you. You wouldn't have no chance to swell around and give orders. All right, she'll stay out here by herself. If anything harms her, I'll take it out of you. I'll do it as soon as I git this Indian mixup off of my hands. What's your name?"

I told him what it was: Amos G. Clarke. I offered to stamp it in his hatband if he didn't feel able to remember it. "You can leave your hat on while I do it, too," I said. I wasn't afraid of him. "You're liable to have this Indian mixup on your hands longer than you think. You talk like shootıng that old buck wasn't anything. He's dead, ain't he?"

"You're bound you'll pack some squaw's devilment onto me, ain't you?" he said, grabbing at the chance to run that one through again. "All right, if you think you can make people believe it, go ahead and try. I'll settle with you for that, too. Yes, and for havin' to lay in jail overnight, when I could be out on bail if we'd done like I wanted to. You'll have enough to answer for. You'll answer for it, too. To me. Don't you forget it."

chapter two

HE STOOD to lay up in jail a lot longer than any overnight, but there was no use making a point of that, so I let him talk on to suit himself. He went over the whole round again, blaming the squaws for his awkwardness with a gun, trying to rake up sympathy on account of his daughter, harping about wanting to ferry across the river to see Tunison, and winding up with another round of threats. None of it amounted to anything. Ferrying across the river wouldn't have got him out of staying in jail overnight, no matter how much bail he could have raised. He couldn't post bail without a preliminary hearing, and we wouldn't get to town in time to have one before morning. I let him ramble, and watched the river where it spread out below the big rapids. The Hasslers' ramshackle old woodscow was still grounded at the edge of a backwater among some scrub willows where the ice hadn't reached. Old Mrs. Hassler was out on deck, scattering wheat to a couple of dozen chickens bunched on the sand bar under the prow. It made a restful picture, the light touching her white hair as she hove the handfuls of grain, the white and red hens jostling together on the dark sand, the old man Hassler tipped back in his chair asleep behind her, with his hat pulled down over his eyes and a shotgun across his knees in case any wild geese strayed within range. It was against the law to shoot wild geese within a mile of the river, but Mrs. Hassler was supposed to have killed a couple of men when she and her husband ran a roadhouse during the Canyon City gold rush, so game laws probably didn't hem them in much. They lived by stealing salmon from the company fishwheels when the run was on. How they managed the rest of the time nobody knew, but they looked peaceful. Their old workhorse was grazing lichens in the rockbreak a few hundred yards from us. He moved from one spot to another with a curious crowhopping gait, as if he was sidehobbled, though there were no hobbles showing on him. When we got closer, we saw that he had a strip of green rawhide fastened to each of his forefeet, with the loose ends dragging back so that he stepped on them whenever he moved faster than a cautious shuffle. It was a trick the Piute Indians used with horses they were breaking to ride; when the horse tried to act up, he got his hindfeet mixed with the loose ends of rawhide and threw himself. By the time he had learned not to act up, the rawhide was worn and suppled into a fair grade of dry tan leather. The Hasslers' old plug didn't need breaking. They were working the trick on him mostly for the leather, probably, though it made him easier for them to catch.

The Piutes always used green cowhide in their tanning

operation. The strips on the Hassler horse looked like something else; the underside looked whiter, and the hair was not any color that cattle usually came in. We got to arguing about what it could be, and Busick stopped the wagon, insisting that it might be cowhide, after all. Some breeds of cattle were dark bay, he thought; Guernsey or Alderney, he wasn't sure which. It was a relief to find something we could argue about that didn't matter to either of us, and we strung it out while the old horse worked toward us, trying to make out what we had stopped for. Finally he got within a couple of dozen yards of us, and it was plain enough that the strips were green horsehide. They hadn't been peeled off more than a few hours, either; they were limp and heavy-looking, the underside was pulpy and iridescent, and the hair on the upper side was hardly even scuffed. Busick fingered his chin meditatively, and remarked that old Hassler appeared to have been having an attack of running off at the shotgun. Nobody with half-sense would shoot a trespassing horse for the pelt. Skinning it out was more work than the thing was worth. "It was some stray pack plug from one of them Indian outfits, more than likely. Yes, sir, some old Indian pony's what it must have been. Them Indians is all over the country this time of year, and they all act like they owned everything in it. Robbin' clotheslines, and butcherin' stray calves, and gittin' drunk. I don't know how that girl of mine will make out, all alone amongst 'em."

He was trying to talk away from something, blaming the dead horse on Indians and putting in such a mortal heave to drag in his daughter again. The Hassler horse shifted a couple of steps, and one of the rawhide strips tilted up sideways. There was a brand on it. It was a little rumpled and hazy, but it was plainly the same as the brands on Busick's wagon horses. That was it, then. The dead horse had been his, and he was afraid the Hasslers might slap a claim against him for trespass charges. I remembered the trackwalker's note stuck down the section house lamp chimney back at the flag station, and decided to try a little leading along.

"The Hasslers ain't shot any horse," I said. "You don't shoot horses with a shotgun. There's been a bunch of stray horses reported on the railroad track at mile-post forty-six for the last three days. Some train must have got one of 'em, and the Hasslers found it and took the pelt. The owner could put in a claim on it, I guess, if he wanted to. He'd have to prove that it was his, but there's a brand on one of the strips. You can see what it is, if you look close."

He looked close, though he probably didn't need to. The idea that a train might have been mixed up in it perked him away up. He could put in a claim against the railroad, instead of having the Hasslers put one in against him. "It's one of my horses, it looks like," he admitted, as amiably as if he hadn't barely got through trying to deny it. "I've got a bunch of 'em in a draw below here, on the far side of the railroad track. I brought 'em down from my homestead when I let it go on a government mortgage. They scatter around sometimes, I guess."

I asked him to point out the draw when we raised sight of it, and asked how many horses he had brought down. He said, still sociably, that there must be around forty or fifty.

"Mixed stuff, some good and some rough," he added, slapping the team into motion with the slack of the lines. "I didn't take time to grade 'em out. There was some right-down horses amongst 'em, though. Some of 'em would fetch right at three hundred dollars apiece, if I worked on 'em a little."

That looked like doing some promoting for his claim

against the railroad company. I told him that if he was counting on any three hundred dollars for the horse that had got killed, he had better slow up. "There's a herd law in this county. You can't turn a bunch of rough horses into these breaks and expect to collect fancy damages when a train hits one of 'em. The law says there's got to be a herder with 'em."

"There is," he said. "There's a herder with 'em. You don't think I'd shove 'em out here loose and then walk off and leave 'em, do you?"

"It's supposed to be a man," I said. He had rung his daughter in on everything else, and you couldn't tell. This time he crossed me up. He squinted his naked-lidded eyes good-naturedly, and said the herder with his horses was a man.

"Yes, sir, whiskered and full-grown and some over. He's camped right with the horses, too. I pitched the camp myself, and it's square in the middle of 'em. I can bring him into court to swear to it, if I need to."

It sounded reasonable, but not very plausible. "A herder for fifty head of rough horses would cost around a hundred and twenty-five dollars a month and keep," I said. "I don't know how much Tunison pays you, but it can't be enough for you to pay out that kind of wages. Not and have anything left. The horses wouldn't be worth it, anyway. You can't collect any three hundred dollars from the railroad for a blamed scrub pony. You'll be lucky if they pay you thirty."

He studied on that, and admitted that Tunison didn't pay anybody enough to do any splurging around on, and that maybe I was right. The railroad company always had high-priced lawyers on tap to beat down people's claims. "The horses is worth something, though. They might not sell for much, but they're worth holdin' onto. This herder I've got don't come as high as some of 'em. The truth is, I ain't been payin' him anything."

I asked what was wrong with him. Something had to be, by the looks of it. Busick said there wasn't anything special; nothing to speak of, anyway.

"He's old, and kind of notional sometimes. He don't git around as lively as some of 'em, maybe. He's as good as anybody you could hire around here, though. They'll all throw off on you when they can, no matter how much you pay 'em. He's conscientious, that's one thing about him."

He explained about it while the wagon bumped on. The old man had wandered into the horse camp from a westbound local that stopped to take on water at the mile-post forty-six tank. He had been riding day coaches all the way from Missouri, or some such fastness, and he was tired and fretty and looking for something to keep busy at. He was used to working with horses, or claimed to be. He didn't show any hefty familiarity with wild cayuses hot from the sagebrush, but he appeared willing to learn, so Busick turned the camp over to him and left. He hadn't mentioned wages at the time, and the subject hadn't come up since, so it seemed better to let things ride along.

"If he likes working for nothing, it's his own business," I said. "It's about what he's worth, at that, if he can't keep his horses off the railroad right-of-way. The only thing is, he may not want to talk wages for fear you'll throw him out. He might be broke and not have anywhere else to go."

"He ain't broke," Busick said. "Not Pap Hendricks. He's got enough to git out of here on any time he feels like it, and there's plenty of places he could go right around here, if he was a mind to. He used to live in this county back in the old days, and he's got children littered around all over it. Most of 'em are well off, to hear him tell it. Some of 'em are, I know blamed well. He'd sooner herd horses out here."

"For nothing?" I said. And out in those godforsaken dunes and rockbreaks, and with horses he knew nothing about and was too stiff and old to handle properly. There were Hendrickses scattered around the county, and some of them were well off, or supposed to be. The murder case the sheriff was out on had to do with a daughter of the family. Her husband had been shot in his ranch house by some Greek roustabout from the railroad in the dead of night, and his estate ran over a quarter of a million dollars, according to the neighbors. It was hard to figure out why the old man could want to isolate himself from a wad like that, if she was his daughter. Or maybe not, either. He might not have heard about it, or he might not want to see how much the high country had changed since he had left it. His children must have changed, too. He might be hesitating to find out how much they had changed, and trying to nerve himself for it by watching the rock flats and the dunes and the river. The country along the river must be pretty much the same as when he had seen it last. It never changed much. Busick slapped the team with the lines again, and said it might sound a little out of the ordinary, but Pap Hendricks wasn't an ordinary old man. He had reasons for what he did, generally.

"He don't want to be around any of his children, for one thing. He don't even want 'em to know he's out here. He can't stand any of 'em. That was the reason he left here to start with. He had a big row with 'em about some fool thing or other. I don't know what it was, but they beat him down, so he told 'em they could all go plumb to hell, and then he picked up and scattered. That's as much of it as I could git out of him. He don't want anything to do with 'em, anyway."

It was about as might have been expected: not wistful contemplation of unchanging nature at all, merely senile vindictiveness over some old family squabble. "If he don't want to see any of them, what the hell did he come out here at all for?" I said. "Why didn't he stay where he was? They wouldn't have bothered him there."

"He's notional," Busick said. "He's got some ideas in his head about the country out here; things he'd laid out to try when he was here the first time, and didn't git around to. I don't know what they are, and I ain't any too sure he does. He don't talk about 'em much. Yonder's mile-post forty-six. His camp's over at the edge of the hill yonder, off to the right. It's up the draw, so you can't see it from out here. There's an old hay road turns up to it past a couple of old Greek bread ovens. The draw opens out right past 'em. He's keepin' the horses off the track better than he did. I don't see a one."

There weren't any in sight, that was the truth. "They've broke through a fence somewhere else, probably," I said. "You can't expect an old man like that to hold a herd of rough horses on a starvation pasture all by himself. He sounds touched in the head, anyway."

"He ain't touched in the head," Busick said. "Not Pap Hendricks. You ain't ever seen him, so you don't know anything about what he's like. He's got as much sense as anybody in this country. More than most of 'em. He's got things figured out better than most of the people around here ever will have."

"Maybe that's what's the trouble with him," I said. It was an aimless remark, with nothing back of it. As Busick had said, I didn't know what the old man was like. Still, there was something to it as a general observation. There were places where having more sense than other people got a man rated pretty much the same as being touched in the head. Busick drove on without taking it up one way or the other. He roused out of his musing after a mile or two, and inquired why I hadn't favored driving over to tell old Hendricks what had happened, the same as I had wanted to shove in on his daughter and blat the whole thing out to her, but I refused to waste any more steam arguing with him. The point wasn't important, anyway. The horses couldn't be left where they were, no matter what happened. Somebody from the office would have to come out and haze them down to a corral in town, or somewhere. Old Hendricks would be turned loose to take care of himself, if he was able, and if he wasn't, there was always the county to shoulder such responsibilities. I said it didn't matter, and we drove on toward town. We turned into the main county road for the last half-dozen miles, but it was not much of an improvement. The cold spring had frozen out a lot of winter wheat back on the ridges, and the road was all cut to pieces by ranchers trucking out new wheat to reseed with. There were long stretches where the mud dragged the wagon bed, with a shuddering rasp like an old sow scratching herself under a kitchen floor.

Nobody could have made much time through a wallow like that, so we didn't strike town till almost dark. The lights were beginning to come on in the store windows when we turned down the main street. Busick's horses had never seen lights at night before, and the plate-glass fronts coming ablaze and reflecting in the puddles under their feet set them to rearing and plunging all over the street, and sometimes up on the sidewalks. It was a help, in one way. It kept back the pack of store clerks and poolroom hangers-on that usually collected around to ask who had been arrested and what for and when it had happened and all about it. Some of them managed to edge within speaking-distance, but they didn't stay long. We stampeded through them without injuring anybody of consequence, and turned into the alley behind the courthouse where the lights from passing cars wouldn't glare on the horses. Busick snubbed them to a locust tree with a doubled picket rope, and we went around to the sheriff's office.

COURT was still in session upstairs. Some lawyer was blasting away at a closing argument, and the sheriff's office was empty except for the old jailer. He was nursing his feet on the desk, wiggling his white eyebrows over a paper-backed novel, and eating kidney pills out of a tin can, and he announced languidly that the sheriff had telephoned in from South Junction about a couple of attachments to be served the first thing in the morning. He complained indignantly over being called on to fix sleeping quarters for another prisoner so late, but he always took it hard when he had to do any work, so I didn't pay much attention to him. I sat Busick down in a chair, stood his rifle in a corner out of his reach, and got on the telephone to complete the formalities required in arresting a man for homicide. I called the district attorney, and explained the case and argued him into making out a set of commitment papers. I called the coroner and explained it all to him and described where Piute Charlie's camp was so he couldn't miss it. Then I called Tunison's lawyers and explained it to them, and turned the telephone over to Busick so he could tell them his side of it.

It was not an improving form of labor, exactly. The district attorney and the coroner both wanted to know things I had been in too much of a hurry to find out, and telephones always threw me off a little, anyway. Back when I first came to work in the sheriff's office, some Mexican had telephoned in to report a knife fight among some sheep shearers up the river. He was too excited to remember any English, and I got called in to talk to him because I had picked up Spanish in tagging fleeces for the Mexican shearing crews when I was younger. I had never talked over a telephone before, and one of the deputies remarked lightly that English was the only language it was built to carry. Loading it with a lot of chili lingo might make it do something it wasn't supposed to; explode, maybe. I didn't quite believe it would, but there was a lightning storm along the line somewhere, and it did sound threatening enough to be a little scary. A man is better off being scared of small things than of big ones, maybe. I had never got used to telephoning, anyway, and it was something of a consolation that Busick didn't make out especially well at it, either. He yelled and argued and threatened, and finally hove the receiver back on the hook and turned around with his back planked against the wall.

"They say they can't do anything till morning," he said. "The damned Bible-backed, louse-bound pack of pups! If they'd got word from Tunison earlier, they might have, but now they can't. I'd be out of the whole thing by now if we'd done like I wanted to. Well, that's another crow I've got to pick with you when this is over, and it ain't the only one. You held a gun on me when we come in here from the wagon. You didn't have any right to. I ain't done anything to be threatened with firearms for."

That was one that the lawyers had put him up to, probably. "I didn't threaten you," I said. "It was your own gun. What did you want me to do, leave it out in the wagon for somebody to steal?"

He lifted his arms, and went on mumbling while the jailer searched him. "It don't matter whose gun it was. You ain't got any right to march a man through a public street with a weapon in his back when he ain't done anything. I didn't try to git away from you. A man's supposed to be innocent till he's proved guilty, ain't he?"

That was the last out of him for the time being, anyway. The jailer opened the big barred door and called down to the other prisoners to show him where to sleep, and then swung it shut behind him and drew the solid iron door in front of it so we couldn't hear his griping. We packed his watch and pocketknife into an envelope and tagged his name on it, and the jailer went back to his novel and his kidney pills, one pill to every three pages. He was a slow reader, so the pills didn't hurt him much. I got down a file hook and hunted out the two attachments the sheriff had telephoned in about. They were small stuff; some grocery bills that a little hole-in-the-wall lunch counter was trying to duck out on. There were three or four other attachments that looked more interesting, but the sheriff hadn't said anything about them, so I put them back on the hook and went out to take Busick's team down to the feed yard for the night.

THE feed yard would have sent up a hostler to take the team down, if I had asked for one, but feed-yard hostlers were not very reliable at handling half-broken horses in the settled part of town. One of them undertook once to ride a bad stallion down from the courthouse, and got taken into a spasm of bucking through a crowd of country housewives waiting in front of a hydro-electro-therapist doctor's office with samples of their urine. The samples got mixed up while they were scrambling for cover, and some of the ladies complained afterward that they had got doctored for things that other ladies had wrong with them. Nobody could decide who to sue for it all, but it caused considerable ill-feeling, and there was no use risking anything like it again. I kept to the back streets to avoid the store windows, and the horses paced along as brisk and steady as a waterwheel, thinking they were starting out for home. It was a temptation to let them keep on going, just to see where they would end up, but the road out of town was piled full of automobiles bringing farm families in to the moving-picture show, and the miles of their headlights looked like too much trouble to risk, after what had happened during the day. I turned in at the feed yard and handed the lines to one of the hostlers. Then I borrowed a couple of blankets from the harness room and climbed up into the haymow to sleep.

It was lonely, but having too little company beat hell out of having too much. There had been lonely people up the river, and none of them had appeared to mind it: the section boss, the skinny girl hanging out her wash by the camp wagon, the Hasslers on their woodscow, Pap Hendricks in his horse camp; even Piute Charlie. The people to be pitied for loneliness were the ones who were afraid of it and struggling to get away from it: the farm families from the ridge bucking in through hub-deep mud to feast their fancies on the new seven-reel feature with Gloria Swanson, or maybe it was Bebe Daniels. Busick still had me worried a little. For one thing, four of the attachments on the file hook in the sheriff's office had been against his fifty-odd horses camped up the river opposite mile-post forty-six. They were for things like hardware, blacksmithing, harness and saddlery, and a couple of them ran pretty steep: three or four hundred dollars apiece, it looked like, though I hadn't taken time to add them up. What it meant was that he was hanging out a pack of scrub horses as bait for his creditors to grab, and keeping his valuables across the river out of sight till they had made their swoop. It wasn't an unusual trick, except that most people who tried it didn't get that far with it. He was smarter than I had sized him up to be.

The other thing was something that had struck me on the way into town, when he was parroting off the excuses I had given for not crossing the river. One had been about the sheriff being out on a murder case; back of South Junction, he had said. The sheriff actually was at South Junction, only I hadn't said so. I hadn't even known it. I wouldn't have known it at all if he hadn't telephoned in from there to the jailer about serving the two small attachments. Busick had known it all along. He was smarter than I had thought, and he knew more than I did about what was going on. It eased the irritation of that to reflect that he was in jail for a while, at least. A man as underhanded as he was deserved to be in jail.

chapter three

THE sheriff's trip to South Junction hadn't brought in much, it turned out. He hadn't found out any more about the murder than he had known to start with, and he hadn't found hide or hair of any murderer. The victim was a wealthy young stockman named Farrand, whose father had run an overnight freighting station on the old military road before the branch railroad came in. The old station buildings were half a mile back from the South Junction railroad depot, where an outfit train of Greeks was at work surfacing track. The main house was as big as an ordinary country hotel, but Farrand and his wife lived in it alone because he had grown up in it and didn't like to change. They were getting ready for bed in one of the upstairs rooms late at night when they heard a knock at the front door. His wife was already undressed, so he turned on the hall lights and went down to see who it was. She heard the door open and heard him say something, and then a shot. She ran downstairs in her nightgown, and saw him lying dead in the middle of the hall about ten feet from the door. A young Greek from the railroad gang was standing almost in the doorway, holding a rifle; there was a long gash across one side of his forehead, she noticed, and blood dried down his jaw that flaked off when he talked. He motioned her back, saying something she couldn't understand, and took a bead on Farrand as if to shoot him again. She screamed and struck at the rifle so it shot into the floor, and then dodged through the door and ran for the tall rye grass between the house and the railroad track.

That was the last she saw of him. He came running out into the dark after her, and she jumped down into a ditch and hid, covering the white of her nightgown under some dead tumbleweed. She heard him wallowing back and forth through the dead rye grass for three-quarters of an hour, sometimes only a few steps from her hiding place. Finally he got tired and left, and she climbed out of the ditch and trudged barefooted and half-frozen through the dark to the depot, where there was a light showing. The night dispatcher let her in, and telephoned the sheriff her account of what had happened as soon as she was thawed out enough to tell it. Considering all she had been through, she got it tolerably clear. That was because she was of pioneer stock, the sheriff thought. He was of pioneer stock himself, the first white child born in Pissant Bottom, or some such locality, and he credited much of his success in life to it. Her description of the young Greek was painstaking—medium height, slender build, dark hair and eyes, smooth-shaven—the only trouble being that it covered at least half the young Greeks in the United States, and a lot of non-Greeks besides. She had only seen him for a few seconds, after all, and she could hardly have been expected to turn out any masterful job of word painting on him, considering the circumstances.

He hadn't touched anything in the house, apparently, and though Farrand was carrying several hundred dollars in cash in his pocket, he had left it undisturbed. The whole case would have sounded a little fanciful, except that the Greek foreman at South Junction admitted having him on the payroll, after considerable hedging and stalling, and had dug up his name from it. It was Steve Addareous, which was something to know, though not much help in hunting for him. All Greeks had half a dozen names apiece, and switched from one to another whenever they felt restless. Still, they did keep track of one another, and since the young Greek had not shown any knowledge of English, the sheriff planned to trap him by posting all the Greeks along the railroad to hold him and report in if he came wandering around.

He picked me to do the posting. There wasn't much use in it. Those railroad Greeks knew what all the Greeks in the country had been up to, without being told, and they didn't like having an irrational murderer running loose any better than anybody else did. But the sheriff stuck to his plan; he didn't have ideas often, so he clung all the more stubbornly to the few that did hit him, and I spent the next four days riding freight trains and gas speeders up and down the main line and two or three sagebrush branches, explaining the case to Zographoses and Androcopouloses and Pappasses all the way from the steamboat landings on the Columbia to the snow line back in the Burnt River Mountains. They all agreed to send in word if any young Greek came wandering around, though most of them didn't act as if they took much stock in the Farrand woman's account of the shooting. It didn't sound quite like any Greek species of devilment to me, either. Still, there were all kinds of men in those big work gangs, and she had no reason to lie about it. I had to argue it out with them on that basis everywhere I stopped, and it was tiring.

Busick's trial was already going on when I got back to town. It was the last case on the docket for the court session, and the regular deputies were all busy hauling convicted prisoners down to the penitentiary, so I couldn't hang around the courtroom to hear any of the other witnesses. I answered the usual rigmarole of questions from the district attorney, and told what I had seen and what the two young squaws had told me on the way from the flag station to Piute Charlie's camp. Busick's lawyers did some cross-examining when I finished, but it wasn't as hostile as I had expected, merely some things they wanted to clear up about the different languages spoken by Indians along the river. I got the best of them on that. I led them into a long explanation about exactly the shades of difference they were trying to find out about, and then admitted that the only thing I knew about any of the Indian languages was the word *squinchum,* which raised a snicker and made them look a little foolish.

They decided not to try anything more on me after that, so I went downstairs to relieve the jailer at keeping watch on the sheriff's office. There were a couple of Indian police in the hall outside the courtroom as I came out, close-herding six or seven squaws who were waiting to be called as witnesses. They were from Piute Charlie's camp, though I didn't see the two young ones who had talked to me. I didn't pay much attention to them except to note that, as usual, they were taking turns using the men's urinal. Nobody was ever able to explain how squaws could get any satisfaction out of a structure so ill-adapted to the requirements of their sex, but they always preferred it; maybe it was the novelty of the thing, or maybe a few minor inconveniences made them feel more at home.

The jailer was beginning to fidget and paw gravel by the time I got back downstairs. He had to bring the prisoners' lunch from a Chinese restaurant halfway across town, and it usually took him around two hours, except when the restaurant struck a wild streak and sent up something the men could eat. Then it took him longer. He groaned his shoes on and left with the grub baskets, and I sat back and thought about squelching Busick's lawyers on Indian languages. It had been a good thing; it had stopped their cross-examining, and they might have tapped me in one or two shaky spots if they had kept on. But it was nothing in itself: a dryish little dab of back-house comicality that the courtroom hangers-on had snickered at because, in a place like that, they hadn't been expecting comicality at all. It was nothing to feel triumphant about, not that there were any heftier triumphs to look forward to. I had worked for the sheriff two years, nearly, and there was nothing to look forward to except more of what had been already: serving attachments, writing out tax receipts, arguing with slow-minded section bosses and deranged sheep herders, watching the jail fill with prisoners before every court session and empty out again afterward, and reveling sometimes in the exultation of plastering a defense attorney with a comeback that would set the crowd to tittering at him.

It was no better anywhere else in the country, either; tagging fleeces for the Mexican shearing crews hadn't been any better, or timekeeping for the railroad. Men were born, they grew up and worked at what they were thrown into, they spent half their lives struggling to acquire children and the other half trying to get rid of them, and they died for no reason except that they couldn't hang on any longer. They never had any clear belief about either their living or their dying. Chief Joseph's Indians had died at Yellow Creek and the Lolo Pass for something they believed in. Piute Charlie died because a whorehouse he had never heard of got shot up by a wandering rodeo hustler he had never seen. Farrand died because a lonely young track snipe had his head addled by more sex than he knew what to do with. They were both martyrs, in a way, but it wasn't easy to figure out exactly what they were martyrs to: the country, maybe, or civilization; or maybe nothing.

The regular run of courthouse business went on. Two or three dry farmers clumped in and paid their back taxes; a couple of razor-backed women left a package for one of the prisoners; a lawyer brought in a set of attachment papers on a barber shop; the trial upstairs drowsed along, and men kept passing the door on their way up to it. Most of them were from town: the harness-shop bookkeeper, the owner of a hay warehouse, a clerk from the hardware store, old Tillery from the wagon shop out by the stockyards. They might be curious to see how the trial was going, though there was nothing about it worth listening to, or they might have been called as character witnesses. They could hardly do much testifying in behalf of Busick's character after the trick he had played on them with his scrub horses, it seemed, but they kept on passing: a cashier from the bank, a department-store collector, Tunison's range boss from across the river. Busick's daughter came down the corridor behind them. She started to follow them upstairs, and then dropped back and looked in at the sheriff's desk and the handcuffs hanging on a nail above it. She read the sign on the door, hesitated a couple of seconds, and came in.

She was as scraggly and sun-cured as she had looked hanging out clothes in the sheep camp up the river, but at least she hadn't made it worse by slathering ornaments and flurrididdles on herself. Her dress was new and starched so it would have stood alone, besides being one or two sizes too big for her, but it was plain brown gingham, or something of the kind. Her hair was tied at the back with a raveling from it, and she had a man's sheepskin mackinaw draped over her shoulders like a cape, with some old thorn brush twigs tangled in the fleece of the collar. She had on black ribbed stockings, and there was bran smudged on one breadth of her skirt where a horse had nudged her. It was anybody's guess whether she was trying to look grown-up or trying not to. She stared at the big iron jail door, and edged back and glanced out into the corridor as if half a notion to leave again. I decided to help the impulse along.

"If your father's name is Busick, his trial's on upstairs," I said. "You can go on up, if you want to. The courtroom door's open. You can't miss it."

Instead of making up her mind, she changed it. She turned and came over to the desk. "That's my father, all right," she said. "My name is Calanthe Busick. I know how to get to the courtroom. I've been up to watch the trial a couple of times already. It wasn't anything except some old lawyers droning at each other. I thought I might wait down here awhile. They'll bring him back down here when they're ready to turn him loose, won't they?"

The lawyers had been giving her their customers' treatment, I judged, or maybe the sheriff had. He came apart easy when girls were around. I couldn't see how it was doing her any kindness to string her along, whoever had done it. "They'll bring him back here when they're through with him, I guess," I said.

"They'll do that, whether they turn him loose or not. They might not get through with the trial today. Some of these trials drag along for a week or more."

She looked me up and down. The sun, in tanning her face darker than it was meant to be, had bleached her eyes paler. There was almost no color to them at all. "You're the one that arrested him," she said. "You rode behind him in the wagon past the sheep camp. I remember. You don't think they're going to turn him loose."

"It ain't what I think, it's what the jury thinks that counts," I said, trying to make it easy on her. "You can't tell what they'll do. There's been a man killed, and they might feel obliged to do something."

"My father didn't kill anybody!" she said. A couple of men passing the door halted and looked in, and she moderated her voice a little. "You think he did because you brought him in. You think the jury will find him guilty, just on your say-so. You don't care what happens to him, as long as you show up all right."

"I arrested your old man to get him away from a pack of mad squaws," I said. "I had to bring him in, because that's the law. What I think about it don't make any difference. These jurymen don't ask me whether to find a man guilty or not. They do as they please, and they don't care what I think. Neither does anybody. That ain't what I hired out here for."

She looked me up and down again. "You testified against him," she said. Then she laid her mackinaw over the back of a chair and sat down. "You had to, I guess. Besides, it won't do you any good. That's what they said, anyway. . . ." I wondered who had said it, but she changed the subject before I could ask. "If you're not hired out here to think, what are you hired for? Have you caught the section hand that killed Mr. Farrand up at South Junction yet?"

"He wasn't a section hand," I said. It was curious how people could live in sight of a railroad for years without discovering the difference between section hands, who presided over the disintegration of one particular section of track, and extra gangs, which moved around patching up the whole line before it was too far gone to run trains on. "We ain't caught him yet. We expect to before long, though. We've been shorthanded, and it always takes a little time."

It wasn't quite as empty as it sounded. It took the most unwavering steadiness and self-control for a man to stay hidden from a county-wide search very long, and nobody with even the commonest self-control could have been capable of the Farrand shooting. She didn't have her mind on it much, anyway; she was listening to the drone from upstairs.

"I hope you do catch him," she said. "I certainly hope you do. I'd be scared of a country where anybody like that was running loose, and we're moving up to that Farrand place as soon as we can. It's all settled, I guess. My father's signed a contract to manage it, so he couldn't back out now."

Her father had hinted at something of the kind, I remembered, on the way down from the Indian camp. It seemed curious that he could have closed the deal while he was in jail, but his lawyers might have handled it for him. I said it sounded like a big thing, and that she needn't be afraid of the country. "Your father said you'd never been scared to stay out by yourself, no matter how wild it was. He said you'd lived around sheep camps ever since you could walk, or something like that."

"We've lived in a lot of 'em," she said. "That's where his work's been, and you have to move from one to another. I don't like it, though. Someday I'll have a house, like these in town. If this new contract holds up for a year or two, we might have enough to buy one: a small one. We might buy one right here in town. That's what I hope we can do."

"I hope you make it," I said. A picture of a man like Busick staking hollyhocks behind a white picket fence was a little hard to hold together, but it was her for it. "You don't need to be afraid of anything bothering you up at South Junction, anyway. We'll have the wild section hands all weeded out and put away by the time you get moved in."

It was meaningless, but she sat back and looked at me, and drew her hand lightly across her face, as Indians used to do at something unexpected. "You think it'll be a long time before we can move up there. You think they're going to send him to the pen. It isn't because you hope so. You think they'll have to. Is that it; is that what you really think?"

"What I think has got nothing to do with it," I said. "I told you that once. I don't know anything about what they'll do. Neither will anybody, till the trial's over. It wouldn't do any good to tell you what I think. I don't even know how the trial's going. I've been out of town nearly the whole week. . . . All right, then. I think the jury will find him guilty."

She took it better than I had expected. Still, the real question with her was not what would happen to her father. It was to find out what I thought would happen. Knowing she had got the truth on that took some of the tension off her. She let out her breath and unclenched her fingers. "I knew you had something like that in your head. I could tell by looking at you. I can tell about some people. . . . How long do you think they'll send him away for?"

"It'll depend on how they feel, I guess," I said. "The judge might parole him, or give him a suspended sentence, or something. Involuntary manslaughter is seven years, generally. They'll count some time off for good behavior."

"Not with him they won't," she said, studying it over. "Seven years. I don't know what I'll live on all that time. Sheep herding is all I know much about. Nobody'd hire me for that, I guess. I might get married."

She made it sound like practically nothing; merely grab an ear on one of Tunison's roustabouts and murmur, Hey, big-and-ugly, if you're not doing anything this afternoon, let's get spliced. "You'd have to have permission from the probate court," I said. "You'll have to have that till you're of age, if your old man ain't around. They might not give it to you. Not for a while yet, anyway."

I tried to keep it from sounding personal, but she worked it out. "Do you mean I'm not old enough to get married? You know a lot about it, don't you? How does the probate court find out what I'm old enough for, anyway?"

"I don't know anything about it at all," I said. It seemed safer to change the subject before she blurted out something about herself that might embarrass her to remember when she grew into better sense. "There's other things you could do besides herd sheep. You could cook, or wait tables, or something."

She said she supposed so, as if the argument had lost interest for her. "I won't, though. It's hot and sloppy and ugly, and I don't know enough about it. I don't have to work that hard to live. I can go across the river and work in the house Ross Tunison runs over there. He said I could, any time I wanted to. He's got other girls working in it, and they don't mind it."

Anybody would have sworn she was serious about it, she was so offhand and practical sounding. "No, I don't suppose they do mind it," I said. "That bunch of buckskin-bellied old sluts would work on a snorting pole in a stud-horse corral if they could get enough out of it to keep them in whisky. And morphine. Half of 'em are drunks and the rest are hopheads. That's how they keep going; they're too drunk and gowed up all the time to know what's happening to them. Do you know what they're like? Have you seen any of them? Do you want to look like they do?"

She didn't act much impressed, merely mildly interested and a little pleased with herself. "It looks like it would have to be either that or get married. I'll see, anyway. You know a lot about those women, it seems to me."

"We've had most of 'em in jail here, off and on," I said. She had only brought the subject up to see what kind of a rise it would get. I should have seen that to start with. "Go ahead and get married, if you can get around the probate court and there's anybody around that Tunison outfit worth having. It's no business of mine what you do. Go ahead and do as you please."

"There's nobody around Tunison's outfit," she said. "I don't want anybody from up the river. I want to live here in town. You like it, don't you?"

It wasn't what she said, but there was a stir in her voice, a feeling of double-edgedness, or something of the kind. It dawned on me what she was working up to, and that she had been working up to it almost from the beginning. She had reason enough to feel worried about her future, but it wouldn't do to let her think she was roping anybody in. "It's all right as far as it goes," I said. "I'm not here much except when court's on. Mostly I work out in the back country; sheep camps and places like that."

There was a hubbub of voices from upstairs, chairs scraping

and spittoons clattering. The court was taking a recess. A couple of farmers came in to look at the delinquent tax list. She got up and picked her mackinaw off the chair. "I'm used to sheep camps," she said. "I don't mind them. Not as much as some people would. You'll be here awhile longer, anyway?"

"Till court's over," I said. I had an uneasy feeling, watching her out the door, that she was leaving disappointed. It wouldn't have been strange, since I had sidestepped all the leads she threw out—all except the one about Tunison's offer of employment, at least—but it hurt a little to think about. I tried to shed it off by remembering some of the things she had told me. Somebody had told her my testimony against her father wouldn't do any good; his lawyers, probably, but why were they so allfired sure it wouldn't? And there was the contract her father was supposed to have signed to manage the Farrand place, which was even harder to figure out.

She could hardly have made it up out of nothing, and she had no reason to lie that elaborately anyway. What made it a problem was the timing. Farrand wouldn't have dreamed of hiring anybody to manage his place for him; he supervised everything himself, from checking abstracts of title to slopping the hogs, and liked doing it. So Busick's contract could only have come up after his death. But when Busick spoke of it on the way down from the Indian camp, he hadn't been dead much over thirty-six hours, and his wife was supposed to be still prostrated from the shock. It might be that her pioneer stock had come through stronger than usual, or maybe Busick had merely been counting some of his chickens before they hatched. It might even be that he had lied, but he wouldn't have picked that to lie about without some reason. One thing it did explain was how he had known the sheriff was at South

Junction; he had picked up word of the Farrand shooting, and drawn his own conclusions. Clearing up that much was something.

COURT took up, and the hubbub in the upstairs hall died down. The two farmers finished scanning the delinquent tax list and left. The old G.A.R. court bailiff tramped downstairs and came in, muttering to himself, and began poking around in the drawer where confiscated firearms were stored. I asked what he thought he was doing, and he explained that the sheriff had sent him down for some prisoners' property.

"That stuff you took off of that Busick, the night you brung him in, if you must know," he said. "The sheriff wants it up in the courtroom. It ain't here."

"It's in the safe, where it belongs," I said. "What does he want with it, and why couldn't he come for it himself? You're supposed to stay in the courtroom when a trial's on, ain't you?"

"I don't know what he wants with it," he said. "It ain't any of my business; evidence, maybe. He couldn't come himself because he was talkin' to some lawyers. The jury's out, so I didn't have anything to do, so he sent me. He said to tell you some of them attachments has been settled up. You ain't to do anything with 'em till he gits down to go through 'em."

I gave him the envelope with Busick's things. He tramped out with it, and I sat back and tried to figure out what it was wanted upstairs for. It couldn't be any use in the trial. If the jury was out it couldn't be put in evidence. It meant something, because it had to. Maybe the sheriff's message about the attachments meant something, too. I went over to the file and looked through all the attachments in it, and then came back to the desk and sat down again. There was something up, for certain; it was probably simple, if only I could make the different parts fit together. The trouble was that the more I found out the more complicated it got. There had been four attachments against Busick in the file the night I brought him in. Now there weren't any; somebody had taken them all out. The jailer came creaking in with the prisoners' lunch, and went to his quarters to recuperate. Voices clattered and chairs scraped upstairs, and the sheriff came in and closed the door behind him.

"I sent up that stuff of Busick's," I said. "What did you want with it?"

"I thought I'd better give it back to him up there," he said. "I figured there might be trouble if he run into you down here. He's a bad actor, or thinks he is. What's happened upstairs ain't apt to improve him any, either. The jury's turned him loose."

He nodded, and then nodded again. I realized that I was still staring at him. An acquittal was the one thing that hadn't struck me as even possible. The things I had found out were beginning to move together into some kind of pattern: not quite clear yet, and too late anyway. Maybe it had been too late from the beginning. "They turned him loose, after what I testified, and with all those Indians to back it up?"

"They didn't back it up," the sheriff said. He sat down, stuck his pistol into a pigeonhole of the desk, and sighed. "We couldn't locate the two squaws that told you about it. The lawyers got 'em drunk, I expect, or Tunison did. That bunch you saw upstairs all got up and swore there wasn't a squaw in the whole camp that could talk English. You'd said you didn't know any Indian lingo, so that fixed it."

"The jury thought I lied about those two squaws, then," I

said. "Did the flat-headed old bastards think I'd get up in court and lie a man into the penitentiary, just for something to do?"

He shook his head sympathetically. He was kind-hearted enough, when it didn't involve any serious outlay. "That's what it'll look like on the book. The jury probably didn't think about that part of it. Them merchants up there had more to do with the verdict than the witnesses did, I expect, but that ain't supposed to show. Well, that's law for you. It don't help any to fly off the handle. You git used to things like that."

"It'll take me a long time," I said. I thought back to Piute Charlie lying dead in his tent among the rocks with the squaws ringed outside it, and of getting the Busick girl to believing her old man would be sent up for killing him. It was easier to remember how Piute Charlie had looked, but she stayed in my mind even when I remembered him the most clearly, even the folds in his blankets and the grains of sand gleaming in the wrinkles of his hands. Her name was Calanthe.

"What did the merchants do that ain't supposed to show?" I said.

chapter four

Exploring into the real ins and outs of a community like that is something like taking a deep look into a waterhole out in the desert. You can ride within a few feet of a desert waterhole every day for a year without ever actually seeing the water at all, only the things it reflects: sky, willows, snakeweed, tules, rye grass, maybe a few circling snake doctors and a bird or two. But when you get down to drink from it and lean close, the reflections disappear and the life under the surface becomes visible: water bugs, tadpoles, minnows, dwarf crawfish, pin-point molluscs, naked roots, red water weeds, thread grasses. The mere shadowing out of some surface images that never really existed opens up a whole new world as active and populous as your own, different from anything in it and still part of it.

The sheriff had lived in the town and the country around it

close to sixty years. He had started himself off in business as an urchin by peddling three-dollar Indian ponies at the steamboat landing to prospectors heading for the Canyon City gold rush for from eighty to a hundred dollars apiece, and he had kept up his interest in local commerce ever since. He leaned back with his eyes half-shut and talked along musingly about the water bugs and molluscs that might have been lurking under the surface of Busick's acquittal. Old Lycurgus Stonacre from Rail Hollow, the jury foreman, was a director in the town bank; the bank was managing the finances of the hay warehouse and the hardware store till they could pay off their delinquent bills-of-lading, and Busick owed money to both. If the jury turned him loose he might pay it; if he went to the pen they would lose it and be that much farther from ever getting even with the board. Banks loved justice and revered law, but they couldn't stay in business on delinquent bills-of-lading.

Besides that possible influence, another juror had been Cap Bassett from Chicken Springs, and he had a daughter who kept books for the blacksmith shop and was engaged to the blacksmith's eldest son; and not a minute too soon, either, by what some of the old women were telling around the sewing circles. And there had been Deacon Gault, who lived by renting a couple of old waterfront store buildings to some Chinamen for a hop joint and fan-tan parlor and was afraid the merchants' association might have them condemned as firetraps if he made anybody mad; and Honest John Dimmick from Axehandle, who was in debt to every merchant in town and would vote for anything that would keep them off his neck a little longer, and somebody else who pastured his cow on the wagonsmith's vacant lot, and so on with all the rest of them. There were relationships and intermarriages and outstanding obligations and tieups with co-operatives and fraternal orders all the way down the whole jury list. What it came to was that a lot of the merchants had thought collecting some back bills was more important than being vindictive about a case of accidental manslaughter, and the jury had let them have their way about it, not to be unaccommodating.

"I suppose the attachments against Busick's herd of horses got worked into the deal somewhere," I said. "There was four on the hook, and now there ain't any. He didn't have enough money to pay 'em off, did he?"

"The lawyers rigged up some kind of an adjustment about 'em," the sheriff said. "He give up his title to the horses, and he's to have his wages paid through the bank. The bank will hold out so much a month and pro-rate it amongst all his creditors. It's slow, but it's better than they'd ever have got out of him in the world if this hadn't come up. You done 'em that much of a favor, anyway."

"The district attorney could have told me those two young squaws hadn't showed up to testify," I said. "Ten to one he got something out of it himself. Maybe the bank handed him some of its collections to handle."

"I've known it to happen," the sheriff said tolerantly. "They'll hear from him, more than likely. You could have found out about them squaws yourself, if you'd been a mind to. All you had to do was go up there and look. Or you could have asked them Indian police that brought 'em in. They'd have told you."

He was as mild and unaccusing as a last-year's circus poster, but the facts spoke for themselves. I could have found out, and I hadn't. It was no excuse that there had been too many other things to think about. There were always too many things to think about when court was in session; a man was supposed to take that for granted, and allow for it. "I didn't have time to get up there," I said. "They ran the trial off like a dose of salts through a tall Swede, and I've been busy with people coming in here all morning."

He rolled half a dozen silver dollars in his palm, which was a habit he had. Then he stood them on edge and eyed me across them. "What people? What did they keep you busy at?"

I couldn't see what that had to do with it. There had been the usual run of people wanting the usual things, the . . . No. He meant the Busick girl. Somebody had told him about her. He was right. She had come in at about the time the defense testimony was beginning. She had stayed talking during the exact time when the squaws were being put on the stand to swear that I had lied like a tombstone. It must have been when the last one had finished that she got up and left. I had thought she looked disappointed. If she did, it was probably for thinking what another fifteen minutes alone with me might have got her—the fillings in my teeth, maybe, or the combination of the safe. The dress two sizes too big and the black wear-ever stockings had been to drum up sympathy. They had certainly paid off. There was no use cockering up excuses about it; there weren't any.

"All right, it was Busick's daughter, and she played me for a hoosier," I said. "I got the short end of it all the way round, and I deserved to. Maybe it ought to have been worse. A jury verdict of perjury don't sound like quite enough, somehow."

The sheriff clacked his stack of dollars together softly, and said it wasn't as disastrous as all that. "They didn't intend that verdict to count against you. Somebody's bound to git hurt a little when there's one of these things to straighten out, and you laid yourself wide open for it. Nobody'll notice it much. The only thing is that this Busick's loose again now, and he might hold you to blame for this whole business. The lawyers said he was packin' a rock in his hat for you. There might be trouble with him if he runs into you around town."

"He won't have to run into me," I said. "He can catch me at a slow walk, any time the notion strikes him. I hope he tries it, only I heard he was fixing to leave for South Junction to manage that Farrand place, and that he had a contract all made out and signed for it."

The sheriff riffled his coins and looked pitying. "Heard from who, that girl of his? I thought it sounded like her. Who's to sign any contract on the Farrand place when Farrand's dead and his wife's sick in bed, with a doctor and a pack of her relations takin' care of her? Who'd want anybody like Busick to manage a place like that, anyway? That girl's a bad influence on you. We'll have to put you out some place where she can't git at you for a while."

"She's no influence on me at all," I said. He was working up to some assignment forty miles from nowhere; I could see that sticking out all over him. It was all right with me. I could do without Busick and his daughter without a pang, and the town too, as far as that went. "I'd as soon work out in the back country as not, as long as people don't think it's to dodge trouble. I don't want to do any more chasing around after that South Junction Greek of yours. There's no use in it. It only scares him so he stays hid. He might show up somewhere if you let him alone."

"You won't have to chase any Greeks," the sheriff said. "I'll tend to that young gentleman myself, as soon as we git cleared around a little here. Nobody'll think it's to dodge trouble, either. You'll have plenty of that on your hands with what I've got lined up for you to do. It's to move them horses of Busick's back to some headwaters in the open country back of the Indian reservation; or some place where there's room for 'em. They can't stay where they're at, and he's give up his title to 'em, so they're up to the county to tend to. He said you knew where they was camped. There's a herder with 'em that might be some help to you."

That was it, plain and unenticing. As between one kind of trouble and another, there were points in favor of staying in town and having a run-in with Busick. "Those horses are wilder than antelope, and there's close to a hundred miles of wheat fields between here and enough open land to turn 'em out in," I said. "The herder that's with 'em is a broken-down old tramp named Hendricks that beat his way out here on some freight from the East and took up tending camp for his board. He used to live out here, and he's got children scattered around the country that he can't get along with. He's childish and doddering, and he's more apt to need help than be any. He'd let the horses run loose all over the railroad right-of-way when I was up there."

That was shading the truth a little, but it didn't matter. The sheriff shuffled his stack of dollars thoughtfully, and said that if horses could be trailed down from the upper country they could probably be trailed back to it. "You can keep along the breaks of Camas River with 'em, and they won't bother anybody. The winter wheat's all froze out up there anyway, so what can they hurt? And if the herder's as bad off as you say, we ought to—Hendricks. There's several families by that name. They ain't all related, though. Hendricks; yes. He had a place out on Burnt Ridge when the dry farms first come in, and then he pulled out and left. There was some scandal back of it, or people claimed there was. He mistreated one of his daughters, and the neighbors had to interfere, or something. That was how they told it, anyway. It might not be the same man. What did he look like?"

"I didn't see him," I said. It probably was the same. Things happened like that sometimes. First they would take a streak of running bad, and then they would turn around and get worse. "What if I was to decide not to have anything to do with the blamed horses, or him either?"

It was merely glancing at possibilities, and he dealt with it on a strictly hypothetical basis. "You'd be out of employment, more than likely. Temporarily, maybe, but you can't tell. Everybody would figure out that you'd been fired, and they might think it was on account of that perjury business and put you on a sort of blacklist. You wouldn't gain by it, any way it come out. We've got to git them horses moved somehow, and the old man too, if he's as bad off as you say he is. Maybe he ain't the one that used to live on Burnt Ridge. Even if he was, he's an old man, and he can't stay camped up the river without anything to live on."

His reasoning was persuasive, especially the part about the perjury business and the possibility of being blacklisted. He knew that town. I said the job looked more inviting than it had, but it would be a long one. Keeping a herd of rough horses together in those river breaks would be bad enough. Having a rickety old man to look out for would make it two or three times worse. "What do you want me to do with him, turn him out along with the horses when we hit open country?"

"You said he had children scattered around," the sheriff said. "If he's rickety and old, it's up to them to look out for him. Find some of 'em that can stand to have him around, and leave him with 'em. I'd git started right away if I was you. Take a couple of pack horses from the feed yard, and take along something to eat. He's been up there by himself for a week, and he might be short by now. Have you got money enough to run you?"

I said it would do unless old Hendricks turned out to be persnickety, and went over to the confiscated weapons drawer and got out a pistol that had caught my eye when it first came in: an almost-new service model .38-44, with squared sights and honed trigger and a shoulder holster. Deputies weren't supposed to make free with confiscated firearms, but the sheriff was not in a rigorous humor. He merely inquired if it wasn't a little fancy for horse herding, and what I expected to use it on.

"Road agents and grizzly bears and one thing and another," I said. "I might scare up that young Greek of yours somewhere. I'll take him along for company if I do. He might be an improvement."

It wasn't for road agents, though, or for the young Greek, or for fear of meeting Busick on the way out of town. What I felt uneasy about was old Hendricks. Everything that came to light about him sounded more and more as if he was touched in the head, and I had been up against too many head-sprung sheep herders to feel easy around such specimens. I deserved some hard luck for letting myself be taken in by a bunch-grass girl, but a man had to draw the line somewhere.

THERE were places even then where a man riding out of town with a couple of pack ponies towing along behind him would have been considered a sight worth calling the children to see, but in that country such things were looked down on as something a youth turned to after failing to qualify as a service-station attendant or a store clerk, so I kept to the back streets and rode hunched over, to avoid starting wild rumors. Out on the river road it was better. The sun was cold and paling with afternoon, and there was a sharpish wind from down the river, but it didn't cut deep, and it helped to keep the horses shoving along. There was nobody on the road. The flock of pigeons out by the railroad yards drifted back and forth overhead, watching for wheat spilled from the boxcars. The river showed steely roils of slick water that gleamed as if floating the light downstream with them. The willow catkins bordering the rip track were already in bloom and shedding pollen down into the slough water among the cattails and tules left over from winter. The Cherry Creek branch freight rolled past, its car roofs white with snow from some late storm up in the sagebrush, the sides of the cars streaked and spattered dark where it had melted and dripped down during the run.

It didn't make the upper country look like an enticing locality to be starting for with an ownerless horse herd and an aged man. Snow was always a possibility back on the high plateaus at that time of year, and trying to move loose horses through snow was almost as tall an order as trying to prevent them from moving till it melted. Still, neither that nor anything else could ever be counted on as a certainty in those latitudes, and there were evidences of spring to set against all the remnants of winter: the willow catkins against the snow on the car roofs, half-open leaf buds beading the mahogany thickets with bright green against the old patches of coarse water-colored snow in the shady places back of them; a cock pheasant blazing out into the light from a thicket of old cockleburrs against a long echelon of wild geese coming in from the high wheat fields to their wintering ground in the sloughs. A month earlier, the sky would have been streaked with flocks of wild geese all the way back to the horizon. Back during the winter, a locomotive ran into a big flock of them that had settled down for the night on the railroad track, and piled them under the drive wheels so deep they stalled the train. Now there was only the one flock in sight, and it was a small one, and a much longer flock of red-winged blackbirds went past up the river, heading for their summer nesting grounds, flying so low their wings almost touched the water; and the wild currant bushes were beginning to bloom, though there was white glare ice still on the puddles a few feet away from them. The signs could be read either way. It did no good to read them at all. The weather in that country paid little attention to signs.

The road I had brought Busick in on forked off across the railroad track and struck down into the sand hills along the river. The two pack horses broke the tedium by trying to turn into it, but I yanked them back and held to the old county road skirting the hills on the upper side of the railroad. They settled down to the dejected shambling gait that horses affect when they don't know where they are going. Not knowing a great sight more about it than they did, I settled down to noting familiar landmarks as the scenery sidled past: a willow thicket where I had hidden once with a gunnysack full of illegal wild geese to let some cars pass, and instead of passing they pulled up squarely opposite the thicket while the people in them had a family row. It lasted nearly an hour, and I almost froze waiting for them to get it settled and leave. There was an old foot trail down across the rocks to the river where the youngsters from town used to go to shoot carp, which various suburban truck gardeners bought up for fertilizer; and the gravel wash below an old Indian graveyard where beautiful red and black arrowheads washed out after a rain, and where a town youngster once got his hand caught in a coyote trap while investigating the bottom of a badger hole, and lay helpless and suffering for three days before a searching party found him. Three days. An old man whom nobody knew about could lie longer, if he had taken sick, or if anything had happened to him. . . .

Well. Beyond that was the railroad siding where I had once put in a couple of months timekeeping for a track gang of green Chinamen who could speak only Cantonese and lived entirely on rice. They always stampeded to the top of the highest hill in sight whenever a train went past, and had to be rounded up and herded back to work like a flock of turkeys; like fleas in a cigar box; like wild horses. Herding wild horses would be harder. The Chinamen had at least been worth the trouble, or so the railroad company imagined. Wild horses weren't worth anything; they were almost as hard to reason with, and they could run faster. The sheriff probably felt sentimental on the subject of horses because of his early associations with them. Nobody else would have considered them worth wasting a deputy's time on, though that might not be worth very much, either, under the circumstances. . . .

Thinking about such things did no good. There were other landmarks: the backwater of a slough in which the town youngsters had once found an old river squatter drowned, with eels swarming over him. There had been nothing evil about it. It was merely the spring run of eels up the Columbia, and he was in their way; he had fallen into the slough and drowned merely because he was old and half-blind. Old and alone, and with nobody around to keep tab on him. . . .

The wind had dropped, and the sun had gone down. It was useless trying to dodge foreboding by raking up old associations; they merely circled around a little and came back to it. Old Hendricks might have taken sick; something might have happened to him; he might be dead. That there had been no signs of horses loose on the railroad right-of-way meant nothing; they might have strayed back into the hills and left him, or he might have struck out with them to hunt better pasture and got himself lost. There would be the job of finding his camp, maybe in the dark, and lifting the tent flap and lighting matches to look in, and seeing the lank old hands stiffened on the rumpled blanket, the same as it had been once already.

It could be the same as it had been with Piute Charlie. One of those in a week was enough. I leathered the horses into a jog, watching the draws above the road for signs of smoke. Spring smoke clung close to the ground when there was no wind, and a small campfire would send out enough to be visible even in the dark, but there was none, and the lights of a passenger train ramming past in the final heat of its run from Chicago blinded me so completely that I would have ridden past the landmarks Busick had described if it hadn't been for the two pack horses. They crowded forward while I sat blinking and dazzled, and turned off the road into a dark field of dead wild sunflowers, and the saddle horse followed and moved up to his rightful place ahead of them. I let them go, to see how it would come out, and after they had clattered through dry sunflower leaves for a quarter of a mile the ground opened out and revealed a trail and the two Greek bread ovens beside it, exactly as Busick had described them. They were nothing but rounded-off heaps of rough stone, about half as high as a man, with an opening at one side where the fire was raked out and the bread shoved in to bake. It would have been hard to pick them out at any distance against the grayish sidehill if the horses hadn't helped out.

The trail held on into the draw for a couple of hundred yards, and then joined a dim old wagon road bordered by the remains of a barbed-wire fence. Most of the wire was broken and tangled, and the ground in places looked as if the posts had been worked loose and pulled out. The light was better than it had been nearer the river, because of the higher ground and the reflection from the dead grass up the slopes. The tracks of unshod horses were plain in the road, though they all looked to be several days old. Ahead, I saw why there were no new ones, and why no horses had been loose on the railroad track for a week. The draw was closed between two steep rockslides by an improvised two-wire fence, strung with rusty wire on crooked sticks and old pieces of broken fence post, and hung with gunnysacks and scraps of dirty cloth to make it visible in the dark. There was a wire gate across the road, and a man was squatting beside it, pounding a bent nail into the gatepost with a rock. He had his back turned to the road, and his pounding was too loud for him to hear the horses in it. I pulled up short, and felt for the pistol under my arm, waiting for him to finish and stand up.

The pistol was not because he looked suspicious, merely that he was completely unlike anything I had been expecting. Even crouched down with his back turned, it was plain that he wasn't an old man, but a young one, and not even an American. I had worked around too many sheep-shearing crews not to know a Mexican when I saw one. Nobody else would have carried a blanket folded over one shoulder like a *sarape*, and have been able to pound on a nail with a rock without having it slide off. He threw his rock away and got up, and, as if further evidence of his nationality might be needed, drew the blanket up around his face so it covered his mouth and nose. Only Mexicans ever stood off the chill in that manner. They had a theory about it, something to the effect that a man got cold from the air he took inside him instead of what stayed outside, so that the real remedy against sharp weather was to warm it before it was breathed in. A lot of them admitted that it was simple-minded to believe such a thing, but they all did it.

The young Mexican seemed harmless, at least. There are not many occupations more innocuous and absorbing than stringing barbed-wire fence by hand with no implements except some rusty nails and a rock. I dropped the pistol back into the holster and rode up on him. He looked around hurriedly, and pulled the blanket almost up to his eyes and backed against the gate. Then he drew away from it a little and drew the blanket down again.

"*No entiendo inglés, señor,*" he said. He made a sort of nerveless mumble out of it, without waiting for me to say anything. He was from some sheep-shearing crew, all right, I could tell it by his clothes. Lanolin may be a boon to the human complexion, but it doesn't do much for a pair of overalls. Knowing where he had come from and what he had worked at made it almost as if I knew him.

"*Pues quien se lo habla?*" I said. "*Hay una parada de caballos sueltos por aquí, verdad?*"

He backed a step, and felt behind him for the gate, staring. You would have expected him to be pleased, finding somebody he could explain himself to, but he showed no signs of it. He acted more as if he was being raided. "*Sueltos?*" he said under his breath, as if trying to figure it out. "*Caballos, sí. Están por allá, por la . . . Sí, por allá.*"

His voice trailed off, as if the strain of cerebration had valved off all the pressure from behind it. I kept after him, so he wouldn't have time to do any deep thinking about it. "And the old man that's herding them?" I said, still in Spanish. "*El viejo? Está por allá también?*"

I didn't take him up fast enough, or else he got his thinking done in spite of me. "*No sé,*" he said. "*Creo que no está. Ya no hay nadie.*"

Hauling out the law on him was not quite the ideal treatment for his case, but it was too near dark for any campaign of patience and kindly understanding. I dug out a deputy's badge and poked it at him so he had a clear view of it. "There's been an old man herding loose horses here, in this *cañada,*" I said, making it slow and distinct. It wouldn't do to go too fast with him. Those people could only grasp one thing at a time, and their vocabulary even in Spanish didn't generally run much over two hundred words, as compared to the average school-trained American's seething repertoire of two hundred and eleven, including dirty ones. "I've brought him some supplies, and I've got orders to deliver them to him. If he's not here, it's because you've got rid of him somehow. Either I find him, or I'll haul you down to the *cárcel* and lock you up till you tell what's happened to him."

It may have been the badge, or it may have been mentioning the supplies, but he backed up and began unfastening the gate. "*Está, sí*" he said. "*Allá á la vuelta, por los árboles. Tiene un jacal allí: un jacalito, sí.*"

He was better stock than I had figured him to be. The ordinary border riffraff wouldn't have called a hut a *jacal;* they called it *mocál.* Knowing about small things helped in handling those people. I put the badge away and picked up the reins. "There's no sign of a fire," I said. "Is he sick?"

He got the gate down, and held it for me to ride through. "*Triste, no más,*" he said. "*Preocupado. Ruega mucho.*"

I rode through and left him to put the gate up again. The pack horses had lost patience with the halt, and it took some jockeying to stop them from shouldering and biting at each other. I had wanted to ask the young Mexican about his "*ruega mucho,*" which didn't sound quite sensible—"ruega" meant "he prays," as near as I could recollect—but when I looked back he was gone. Probably he hadn't the faintest realization how lucky he had been in trying his stalling on somebody familiar with his language and at least some of his national peculiarities. Any of the other deputies, anybody else at all from that part of the country, would have shotgunned him off to the calaboose on suspicion, without wasting time arguing with him or even trying to understand what he was arguing about. It would have been no more than he deserved, but it was a satisfaction to think how much trouble and inconvenience a little knowledge had saved us both. There were times when learning things seemed merely another form of time killing, like collecting arrowheads or rattlesnake rattles; a little more dignified, but not a notch better as far as usefulness went. It was encouraging to know that there was a difference, after all.

THE horses turned onto a trail across the creek bed and into a stand of cottonwoods and black locusts that looked to be the remains of some abandoned timber culture. It was dark under the trees, but in the open ground there was still light enough to make out a stock pond, a patched-up corral with a lank horse in it, the half-wrecked scaffolding of an old windmill. A gray tangle of dead sweetbrier grew out from among the scattered timbers and up one side of a gray pole shanty, windowless and open on the side facing the corral. It had to be the *jacalito* the young Mexican had spoken of, since it was the only one in sight, but the opening was dark, and though some boulders were piled together for a fireplace outside it, there was not even a smoulder of fire visible. I pulled up at the edge of the cottonwoods to look the layout over before risking it out in the open, and then sat still and listened. There was a man's voice coming from the shanty. It did sound as if he was praying. I tied the horses back among the cottonwoods and went carefully toward the shanty on foot, trying to hear whether it was anything that could be interrupted or not.

There was probably considerable truth in the doctrine that prayer never hurt anybody. Sheep herders drove themselves crazy at it sometimes, maybe, but they usually didn't have far to drive, and for most people it was at least harmless, if not actually beneficial. I don't know why it was such a bone-loosening relief to discover, when I got in hearing range, that he wasn't praying at all. He was only having an argument with himself. It sounded at first as if he was getting a little the best of it.

. . . "No. You can make it sound like everything was gone to hell all you please, but that ain't all of it. Not by a goddamned sight it ain't. There's more to it than it looks like there was, and you know it. I've got a rattle or two left in my old tail yet, by God! It ain't all in my head, either. There's other people that thinks the same thing. A man wouldn't trust a herd of his horses to any damned old broken-backed dodderer that fell off of a freight train down by the water tank. That greaser kid wouldn't waste all his fence buildin' and night herdin' on some helpless old puke that wasn't worth a whoop in a rain barrel. No. Them men's got sense. They can size a man up. They know whether a man will do right and see a thing through or not. This ain't any run-down and wrung-out country, like some of 'em. I've lived all over it. I know as much about it as they do, yes, and maybe more. Let me have time to git straightened out here, and I'll—"

He stopped. There was a sound of water dripping somewhere, and the far-off whistle of a train. A night swallow flitted over the pond, dipping so low it left dark ripples in the reflection of the sky. A bird moved in the tangle of sweetbrier. A horse clattered a rock far up the draw. I wondered if he was finished. His arguments toward the last had sounded a little forced; not the result of any real conviction, but as if he was trying to drum belief into himself by uttering them out loud. He began again.

"Yes, you're a mighty smart man, ain't you? Layin' here in this christly boar's nest cacklin' over what you've laid out to do, and not doin' a lick at that or anything else. You're lippin' full of big seven-hundred-dollar ideas, anybody can see that. Keen as a brier, you are; all fixed up to raise hell and put a block under it, and where have you got to? You've got horses dependin' on you, and people dependin' on you, and all you can do is lay here and hoot at yourself. Is that all you're good for? Name of God, if you can't give them what little help they need, how do you ever expect to do anything for yourself? You don't think that'll be any easier, do you? If you do, I feel sorry for you; yes, sir, I feel sorry for anybody that's as far gone as that. I feel for you, Pop, but I can't quite reach you. . . . All right, then, why don't you give up and git it over with? That's how you'll end up anyway, that's how it'll come out, that's where you're headed right now. If you had any sense left, you'd admit it. What are you good for, what can you do that's any use to anybody, answer me that!"

It was enough. I backed away and circled back to the cottonwoods, feeling a little ashamed of having eavesdropped on him and considerably relieved at what it had brought out. He was nothing like the kind of case I had imagined; not quite as moderate in his expressions as some people might have approved, maybe, but a man who could line up both sides of the truth about himself wasn't very likely to have anything wrong with his sanity. He was in the clear on that as long as the see-saw between the two sides kept up. The time to look out for derangement was when one side got the best of it and threw the weight all one way. Doubt and uncertainty could deprive a man of his reason in time—though paresis had more to do with it in that country, generally—but as long as they continued to work in him he was safe. The surest sign of insanity was a state of certainty about everything. Old Hendricks might be troubled in spirit, but he was not touched in the head.

The darkness among the cottonwoods was as black as the bottom of a mine shaft. I would have had trouble finding the horses if one of them hadn't let out a nicker. It was loud enough to carry to the shanty and a half-mile past it, and I was a little afraid the old man might conclude from it that I had been prowling on him. Still, it was one way of warning him that somebody was coming, and it might have sounded merely like strange horses nickering to the horse in the corral. Evidently it had, for when I rode up in front of the shanty he was out starting a fire in the outdoor fireplace. It had got so dark that without the light from his heap of cottonwood twigs it would have been hard to make out what he looked like. The blaze showed him to be tall, smooth-shaven and rawboned, with a stiff bush of white hair raked back from his forehead like the old pictures of Andrew Jackson. His eyes were deep-set and pale gray, though so nearly colorless that they reflected the firelight from under his brows like a bobcat bayed in a hollow log.

"Climb down and rest your rig," he said, laying on some bigger sticks. He didn't sound as if there were any dark thoughts within a hundred miles of him. "I'll have supper rustled before long, or something that looks like it. We ain't got much, but you're welcome to what there is of it, as the little boy said to the schoolteacher."

Right at the beginning seemed a good time to find out how much of a rattle he did have left in him. "I'm from the county sheriff's office," I said. "I've brought you some supplies to fill in with, and I want to talk to you about some range horses you've been running up here. They've been loose down on the railroad, and there's been complaints about it. You're responsible for them, ain't you?"

He wasn't as spirit-broken as he had made himself out when he was alone. He didn't back and fill, or try to blame the horses on their owner, or mention that he had been herding them for nothing. "I guess I am," he said. "I'm the herder for 'em. They did git away from me a couple of days last week, but they're all bunched back here now, and the draw's fenced so there won't be any more trouble with 'em. A stray Mexican kid put the fence in for me; maybe you noticed it. These supplies you've brung, are they from anybody named Busick? It's about time, if they are. We've been runnin' on wild goose and China pheasant here till my belly's startin' to sprout pin feathers."

Wild geese and pheasants were both protected by law that season. Still, a man had to eat, and if there wasn't anything else . . . I tried him with another lead. "The things I've brought ain't from Busick. He's had a little legal trouble on his hands, and it's been taking up all of his time lately. How much has he been paying for a herder here?"

He could have told me it was none of my business. It would have been reasonable enough if he had; a man was entitled to his pride. He merely told the simple truth about it, as if it didn't particularly matter. "He ain't been payin' me anything. The only thing we agreed on was my keep, and he ain't . . .

What's this legal trouble he's got himself into? Has he . . . It ain't anything he could go to jail for, is it?"

"He's all clear of it now," I said. It seemed off the subject to add that he had gone to jail, at least for a little spell. "The only thing about it is that you're not working for him any more. He's thrown up his title to these horses. You're entitled to a work lien on 'em, so they're yours if you want to claim 'em. They might be worth it, if there was somebody around the country that could furnish you pasture for 'em for a while—some relative, maybe."

He glanced up, and laid a couple of sticks on the fire. "I've got relatives around the country, if that's what you're hintin' at," he said. "A whole grist of 'em, children and grandchildren and every other damned thing. To hell with all of 'em. I knowed them horses couldn't be worth anything. I knowed there'd be something wrong with anything that Busick had any hand in. That's why he wasn't particular who he got to herd for him."

"You don't have to take 'em," I said. "If you do, we'll have to move 'em back where they've got open country to run in. It'll be hard work and a hard trip. No horses are worth much right now."

He said he supposed not, and stood up and looked down at the fire. "Goddamn it, though, why ain't they? There's some good heavy-set horses in this bunch here, and it took work to round 'em up and trail 'em all the way down here. They ain't useless. There's work right around here they could be put to, if anybody wanted to take a little trouble with 'em. Hell, there's always use for horses! All right, by God, I'll claim 'em. We'll move 'em back to open country whenever you want to start. They'll be better off out of here, anyway. Climb down and unload your packs. That greaser kid's night herdin', or he'd help you, and I've got to fix supper. It'll be ready by the time you're finished, if you can stand pheasant stew."

"You'd better let it set and fix something from the packs," I said. He had mentioned being sick of pheasant. "You ought to be ready for a change by now."

He looked at the packs as if he was on the point of agreeing. Then he turned away from them and said no. "No, I'll be damned if I do! Me and the kid put in half a day bushwhackin' this pheasant with an old sheep-herder rifle, and if we don't eat it tonight it'll have to be throwed out. I won't stand to see work wasted like that. Another bait of it won't kill us. We'll git to your victuals when it's gone."

I got down and took off the packs, feeling easier in mind than I had all day. He was better than I had expected, no matter how much scandal his onetime neighbors on Burnt Ridge had circulated against him. He was more restful to be around than the people in town had been; or the people on Burnt Ridge, either, as far as that went. Some of them had principles, probably, the same as he did, but the difference was that he wasn't afraid to live up to his, even the little picayunish ones that hardly seemed worth living up to all the time. I could understand why the young Mexican had stopped in to help him with his fence building and night herding, even without being able to understand a word he was saying. I wouldn't have done it, but I didn't have any trouble at all understanding how the young Mexican might. . . . Old Hendricks brought the stew bucket out from the shanty and set it on the fire, and propped a cake of bread up on one of the rocks to warm.

"This greaser kid that's night herding for you," I said. "Do you think you can get him to come along with us? He'd be a help, if the horses are used to him."

"He'll come, I guess," old Hendricks said. "There ain't

much else he can do. He had a pay check that he didn't know what to do with, and I promised to git it cashed for him. I ain't done it yet, and he can't go anywhere till I do. To tell the truth, I don't know what to do with the blamed thing. He claims it's wages he earned, but it don't look to me like anything a man could cash. Here, see if you can make anything out of it."

He dug it out and handed it over, and I held it to the firelight. It wasn't a pay check, but a railroad identity slip which could be exchanged for a pay check on presentation at the railroad's main office. It was the kind of thing always given to track snipes who quit the job before the payroll had been sent in. The amount was thirty-eight dollars and twelve cents, and the name on it was Estéban d'Andreas. It seemed a little stylish for a youth in the young Mexican's state of life, but he had signed it himself, and had even got it spelled right. I gave the slip back to old Hendricks, and explained the difficulty about getting it cashed.

"It's not on any of the railroads around here, anyway," I said. "It's on the Santa Fe, and they don't run any line this side of San Francisco. He'll have to take it down there to get his money on it, I expect. I can explain it to him if you want me to. I can talk his lingo."

Old Hendricks studied the slip by the firelight, and shook his head over it. "I ought to have noticed that myself, if I'd had any brains," he said. "I ought to have remembered that there was more than one railroad in the country. I ain't as smart as I thought I was, that's the trouble. I don't know whether you'd better explain it to the kid or not. He's got to dependin' on me here, and I hate like hell for him to find out that I'm a damned fool. A kid like that's better off if there's somebody he can depend on. . . . Damn it, no! Don't tell him anything. I promised him I'd cash the blamed thing, and I'll do it if I have to dig up the money myself. Leave it the way it is. If he asks you anything about it, tell him you don't know. It'll be easier on both of us."

It would be easier on all three of us, I thought, since leaving the identity slip uncashed meant that the Mexican youth would stay around and help out with the horses. We did need his help. I didn't bring that up, because it was plain that old Hendricks hadn't thought of it. He was thinking of the youth needing somebody to depend on, and maybe, at the back of his head and without admitting it, of himself. He needed the kid as much as the kid needed him. It helped him to hold up to have somebody around who depended on him.

chapter five

THE noise of a late-lingering flock of wild geese going out to its day's feeding in the wheat fields woke me the next morning. The sky was already beginning to fill with light, and there were a few cold yellow sun streaks on the high ridges, but it was still too dark in the camp to make out anything except the pond and the shapes of a few leafless bushes patterned black against it. The sky's reflection in the pond water made the darkness around it deeper and more impenetrable. The cold bound down like rawhide contracting, and scythed up through the cracks in the floor as if the straw and dead leaves old Hendricks had spread down for bedding didn't count in the least, though they may have slowed it down a little. The air felt frosty, but it was impossible to be sure till I reached one hand outside the shanty and felt the hoar frost, deep and bristly and searing cold, on a pile of old boards.

As usual in such places, the first appearance of light in the sky touched off noises. Animals began wandering in to the pond to drink, and the horses in the corral roused up and moved over to the near fence to watch them. Horses could see in the dark. They were ahead of me on that, but the sounds were plain enough, and the animals around a waterhole in the early morning were always pretty much the same. The laws of the Medes and Persians would have looked like a flea on a hot griddle in comparison to the solemn and unimaginative regularity of wild animals in that country. Some cottontail rabbits came and drank. A couple of porcupines came and drank. A family of skunks came and drank. A covey of grouse came clucking down from the cottonwoods and drank, and were followed by something that sounded like a deer, though it was not deer country. Then a big waterfowl of some kind hit the pond with a splash that scared everything else away and made the horses shy back from the fence with a thudding of hoofs and rending of fence poles that always sounded as if they were tearing the corral to pieces and always turned out, when you got up and looked, not to amount to anything at all.

The waterfowl rose after a minute or two, and flapped away to the north: a wood duck, maybe, or some lone snow goose that had got left behind by the main flock and was hurrying to catch up. The ripples in the pond smoothed out again. The light overhead was strengthening steadily, swelling the sky out like a bubble being blown thinner and thinner. The darkness outside the shanty changed from black to a wavering gray, like a river fog at nightfall. There was light in it, but it was no easier to make out objects in than the full dark had been. The pond was no longer bright and sharply outlined; it looked like merely a place where the dimness had worn threadbare. Some quail whistled from the cottonwoods, and went suddenly still, as if something had startled them. The horses in the corral moved restlessly, and one let out a loud whinny. A rock clattered, something splashed in the pond, and I could see that there were horses crowding down to it and drinking. They were coming down from the dead-grass pasture on the ridge. There was not enough light to see what any of them looked like, merely their bulk as they came out of the grayness and stretched down to drink from the pond. Behind me, old Hendricks finished hauling on his shoes and went out, wrapping his bedding around him like a toga, to start a fire. He walked lightly, as if the cold hadn't crippled him any, old though he was. His kindling caught and flamed up, and he turned to reach some heavier wood from the pile and saw that I was getting fixed to join him. He dropped some boards on the fire and got up.

"Well, yonder they all are, as big as life," he said. "It's funny how a man is. Here I put in all last week swearin' to God that if I ever got the dratted brutes off my hands I never wanted to see 'em again, and then I laid awake most of last night stewin' for fear they might have stampeded on us, or got stole, or something. It don't look like any of 'em had, but they might try to stray when we hit new country with 'em. By God, there ain't many places left in the world where a man as flaxed out and stove up as I am can come into a herd of livestock overnight, and I'd hate to lose any of 'em right at the start. If Busick's give up his title to 'em, that brand he's got on 'em won't count any more. Maybe we ought to counterbrand 'em before we strike camp. By God, this is a morning with feathers on its legs, ain't it?"

I let that go as it stood. It was a morning, for what it might be worth, and putting counterbrands on fifty full-grown horses without any branding equipment was more of an order than I had any authority to tackle. "It would take too long," I said. "You've got no brand to put on 'em. Even if you made one up, it wouldn't count unless you had it registered with the county clerk. We'd have to have a branding iron made in town, or else use a running iron. It would take us a week to get done with it either way. There's not feed enough to carry these horses another week here, and they're not worth that much trouble."

Old Hendricks set a bucket of water on the fire and looked sideways at the pond. "We could put on hair brands," he said. He was set on showing off his ownership somehow, and he was away behind the times. Hair branding had been a device resorted to in the old days by horse thieves. It was not really branding at all, merely crimping a horse's hair into a brand pattern by scraping it with a sharp knife blade so that, when finished, it appeared as if curled back from a brand scar. It was painless and plausible looking, but there were drawbacks. The pattern vanished completely when it got wet, and it was five times as much trouble to put on as an ordinary iron brand was. Old Hendricks turned back from the pond and stirred the fire with his foot. "Hell, it don't matter," he said. "It would be foolishness to waste time brandin' all them horses, and it wouldn't be right anyway. This country's treated me right, the same as it always does anybody that meets it halfway, and I got no right to haul you in on a brandin' job that wouldn't mean a damned thing when we got it done. It's this property business that's the trouble with me, I can see that. Property can make a plumb idiot out of a man if he ain't careful."

"We could put hair brands on a few of 'em, if you want to see how it'll look," I said. "Five or six wouldn't take long. We can pick out some that are scrawny and not too rambunctious."

His reasonableness had seemed to call for at least that much of a compromise, but he wouldn't have it. Once he got a case worked down to its underlying principle, he played it straight through. "I wouldn't waste two minutes of my time on it, or anybody else's," he said. "It wouldn't mean a damn thing. Everybody would know it was childishness, and that I was back of it. Right's right, and there ain't any halfway business about it. I've done enough halfwayin' in my time, and I'm through with all of it now. You're wrong about them horses, though. There ain't any right-down rambunctious ones in the bunch, and no scrawny ones, either, except that they're all gaunted from poor feed. Look 'em over when the kid gits 'em strung out. You'd better tell him to drop off and eat before we pack up, if you can handle his lingo. I've been havin' to swing my arms at him when I wanted anything."

The Mexican youth sat on his horse at the edge of the pond, waiting while it drank. He kept his blanket bunched high against the cold, and he had fixed a pad of gunnysacking with a halter rope cinched around it for a saddle. He nodded when I translated the message, and rode out to head the horses down the draw as they left the pond. Old Hendricks was right about the horses. They weren't anything like ordinary range ponies; not skimpy little cat-hammed Indian cayuses at all, but square-built American farm stock, with solid shoulders and bone structure and even some space between the eyes for a few brains, if a man wasn't too exacting. The explanation was simple enough, when it was worked on a little. The war boom had infected the country with a fever for tractor cultivation, and the introduction of tractors had resulted in all the regular farm horses being turned out into the sagebrush to run wild. Some of them had the marks of old harness galls on their shoulders, and a few still had nail marks in their hoofs where they had been shod, though travel and rock pastures had fixed that for them long since. They were better than I had expected, even if they weren't worth owning.

"They oughtn't to be hard to handle," I said. "Some of 'em have been worked. They made money for these back-country scissorbills when the boom was on. This is what they get for it: turned out to rustle or starve. It's a great country we've got here. Fair treatment's the watchword."

Old Hendricks said stiffly that there were bound to be a few natural-born thunder mugs anywhere. Property ownership had raised his spirits in spite of him. He acted as if any criticism of the country was a reflection on him personally. "I've seen 'em splurge around like this when I was runnin' sheep out here in the old days, and I've seen 'em bawl their heads off about it afterwards. There'll be fair treatment for these horses before I'm through with 'em, I'll promise you that. Does that blamed kid know he's supposed to come in and eat before we pull camp?"

I said he did if telling meant anything. The truth was that country-raised Mexicans didn't bear down much on breakfast: a bun and a few swigs of half-burned coffee usually covered it for them. "How did he ever get signed on here?"

"The same way I did, or right close to it," old Hendricks said. "He got throwed off of a freight train down at the water tank. I was down there tryin' to run some of the horses off of the railroad track, and he come over and took a hand at it. I was mighty glad he did. One man can't do much with a bunch of loose horses."

"It's funny you didn't know enough Spanish to talk to him, if you used to run sheep out here," I said. "All the shearing crews have always talked it, and most of the herders used to be Mexicans or Basques."

"I never got around to learnin' it," old Hendricks said.

"Some of the kids got so they could handle it. Kids pick up things like that. And a hell of a lot worse ones sometimes, too."

That was heading the conversation into ticklish territory. The sheriff's instructions to dump him on some of his progeny probably didn't hold any longer, since he appeared able to look out for himself, but it was safer to have some understanding about it. "You said you had children scattered around the country. Maybe we ought to hunt up some of 'em, if it won't take us too far out of our way. They may not even know you're out here."

The Mexican youth rode past and dismounted to wash his hands at the spring. Old Hendricks watched him absently. "You're damned right they don't," he said. "They don't any of 'em know where I'm at, and they wouldn't thank anybody to tell 'em. All they'd think was that I needed help, and it would scare the livin' peewallopus out of 'em to think they might have to furnish some. I don't need their help."

"Some of them might need yours," I said. "I heard Busick say something about one that might. She had her husband murdered out at South Junction last week. Some crazy young Greek from a railroad gang did it. She's been laid up from it ever since, and she's got a big place on her hands and nobody to run it for her. It's the old Farrand place. Her husband's name was Farrand."

The Mexican youth helped himself to a piece of bread and coffee in a tin can, and went back with it to his horse. Old Hendricks said he remembered the Farrand freight station. "It was back in the big cove above the Upper Camas River. This would be the old man's son, I guess. I don't know which one of the girls was married to him, though. There was some that hadn't got married when I left here. I never heard who any of 'em got married to. They figured it wasn't any of my damned business, and they was right. One thing I can't git through my head is how a thing like that would lay any of 'em up for a week. It don't sound like 'em. You say this Farrand left a big outfit?"

"It's supposed to appraise at about a quarter of a million dollars," I said. "It wasn't the killing that laid her up as much as the way it happened. It was in the middle of the night, and she was alone. This Greek shot her husband almost in front of her, and then tried to rape her. She ran outside and hid in a ditch to keep him from finding her, and then walked to the railroad station and got help. She was almost froze when she got there. That was partly what laid her up. She was scared half to death, though."

"I can imagine," old Hendricks said. There was no sympathy in his voice. It sounded slow and thoughtful, and a little shaken. "Yes, I can imagine it. It must have been enough to lay anybody up, havin' to hide outdoors at night, as cold as it's been, and then walk through the dark barefooted and with nothing on but a nightgown. Have they caught the Greek that done it?"

"Not the last I heard," I said. His imagination was vivid. I hadn't mentioned her nightgown or her being barefooted. "The sheriff's out after him. The trail we've got to take the horses over will come within a couple of miles of the Farrand place, if you want to stop in."

He picked the coffee bucket from the fire with a stick, and stood holding it. The steam from it made a sort of veil before his face. "I'll have to see about it. Maybe we ought to, if it's close to our trail. I don't know what for, but there might be something. I might be some help. I hate to git into it, but maybe I ought to. There might be somebody out there that needs help. I'd better find out, I guess."

"You'd find out which one of your daughters it is, anyway," I said.

He moved the coffee bucket so the steam blew away from him. There was a hardness in his face that made me wonder whether I hadn't been right about him in the beginning. The old cuss could be dangerous, if he took a notion. "I know which one of 'em it is," he said. "I know which one it is now, good and well. By God, if I didn't know another damned thing in this world, I'd know that! That's one reason I'd sooner not git mixed up in it. We'll see. I wish you hadn't told me about it. Hold your cup, and I'll pour some of this gumboot juice into it. We've got to git packed and git out of here."

Packing didn't take long. Except for the groceries I had brought and a small pile of bedding, there were only a few cooking utensils to pack, and we had canvas packsacks, locally and inaccurately called *alforjas,* so there was not much to it except dropping things in and roping them down. There was no tent, but that didn't make much difference. It would have been a nuisance to handle, especially if it got rained on, and there were old homestead shacks spaced out every few miles along the Camas River breaks that would do to hive up in if a storm hit us. We saddled up, and drove the pack horses ahead of us down the draw to overtake the herd. The Mexican youth had taken down several panels of his fence to let the horses go through. We helped drive them past the wire, which some of them were nervous about crossing, and he rode on ahead to turn them up the river when they cleared the mouth of the draw. It began to dawn on them that they were being taken somewhere after they had got past the fence, and they kept closed up and moved along without even needing to be prodded. Old Hendricks reined up at the flattened fence panels, and looked back.

"I was prayin' the Lord for something to git me out of here a couple of days ago," he said. "Yes, by God, and as late as yesterday night. Now I hate like hell to leave. I wish we didn't have to. A man never knows. Maybe he's better off not to know. . . . This saddle of mine's a hell of an out for these times, ain't it?"

It was a little bit dated: an old split-seat army castoff that had been rigged with a high knob-ended horn and a cantle board reaching clear up into the small of his back. The horn, besides being of a model that went out with the free silver agitation, was sprung about three inches to one side so it looked as if the whole saddle was tilted. His sheep-herder rifle, which was tied under one stirrup leather with some ravelings of rope, was a rusty-looking .44-40 that must have been the last word in firearms back around 1876, reinforced in spots with baling wire. His horse was a cumbrous-footed old hide rack with a humped nose and prominent hip joints that worked up and down like a railroad block signal when he walked. I remarked that he might have found something sightlier in the herd than that. He said one advantage about being old was that things like looks ceased to matter.

"This old skate was easy to catch. That's the big item when you're my age. He matches the saddle, anyway. I found that in an old hay shed up at the head of the draw. The rain had warped it forty ways from Sunday, but I limbered it out. It'll carry me all the places I want to go. Yes, and some that I don't, the way it looks now. Damn it, a man can't stick his head into a place without gittin' things piled on him to fix. These horses, and the kid's pay check, and now this business out at the Farrand freight station. Well, right's right, and it don't do any good to dodge around it. The country's still here, anyway, and we'll have a few days that other people can't mix their hell into."

He had some things to learn about what had happened to the country since he had left it, I thought. Some of it was still there; a lot wasn't. There was no use telling him that. He would find it out for himself soon enough, and it might be better to let him. Maybe the other people's hell that he had taken it on himself to fix would seem less forbidding by comparison.

We trailed up the river along the edge of the low hills, letting the horses pick what grass they could find as they went. The Mexican youngster rode ahead because his night herding had got them accustomed to him, and we followed along behind to keep the tail-enders from straggling too far in search of feed. When the big poplar-grove bordering Camas River came in sight, we turned south through some Indian allotment lands bordering the hills, and kept to the high ground till it dropped off into Camas River canyon. There were some fences in the way, but the country was ridgy and broken, so they were not much hindrance. Wherever there was a gully, the fence builders had saved posts by stringing their wire straight across from ridge-top to ridge-top and drawing it down to the low ground by weighting the middle with a big rock. Crossing it meant merely taking the rock loose and driving the horses under the wire when it hoisted up in the air. We crossed half a dozen fields of winter wheat that had been frozen out and left standing, dead and yellowish-brown and unhealthy looking. The horses tried to graze it at first, but it was too much like musty mattress stuffing for even their appetites, and they gave it up and hurried along through the acres of brittle deadness without bothering to look at it.

There was one field where somebody had made a start at reseeding, and had given it up after two or three rounds because the low ground was too wet for a tractor to work in. He had left his seed drill and tractor standing on the edge of a plowed-over gully. The tractor had three of its wheels dug into the soft ground almost out of sight, and the fourth slanted up in the air like a man gesticulating for help after a well had caved in on him. The tractors of those years appeared to have been designed for use out on the prairies. They were too unwieldy and topheavy to stand up to the light soil and steep slopes of that foothill country, though nobody discovered it till almost everybody had bought them. Old Hendricks sidled his horse over and nodded at the one iron wheel poking dumbly up at the sky.

"It looks like somebody had got enough of them things already," he said. "There'll be a lot more of 'em like that before long, you wait and see. All it takes is time."

There was no way of telling whether the tractor's owner had got enough of it or whether he had merely got enough of work, but it showed that old Hendricks was feeling in better spirits, and there was no use starting an argument with him. I said that all anything took was time, only a lot of things took too blamed much of it. He rode for a while thinking, and then came up with another one.

"There used to be bunch grass all over these ridges," he said. "Belly-deep to a horse, some of it. I freighted wool through here three or four summers. There was a freighters' camp where we crossed Buck Creek, and a stand of big alders for a couple of miles both ways from it, and prairie chicken thick enough to write your name in, and deer. It ain't like that now, I guess."

I said it wasn't likely that anything was. We had already crossed Buck Creek. There hadn't been much about it that he would have noticed. It was merely a chain of naked mud holes at the edge of a wheatfield, no different from a dozen others we had crossed except that the mud was deeper and juicier. There were no alders, no deer, no bunch grass, no prairie chickens. Civilization in any country meant shifting the balance in favor of people. That was its business. Where people had to live, other things had to die. Someday all other forms of life would be exterminated, and there would be nothing left anywhere but people. Then humanity could settle down with a happy sigh to revel in its triumph. There wouldn't be much of anything else left to do.

"It's always bad when you start a trip like this," old Hendricks said. "It gits better. I've done enough of it to know. I've hatched out some humans that I'd take back if I could, but you never know about 'em till it's too late. It always looks for a while like it was worth tryin'. One thing my old man used to tell me was that you didn't git game with the bullets that stayed in the gun. You have to shoot blind and risk it sometimes."

"If that's the best he could do with his advice, he'd better have kept it," I said, to take his mind off any depressing analogies. "He might have got somebody shot."

"He might have, for a fact," old Hendricks agreed. "Come to think of it, I wouldn't be surprised if he did. Maybe it'll turn out that he . . . No, there ain't any use lookin' that far ahead. To hell with it, we're headin' for somewhere new, and that's enough. New country puts an edge on a man."

WE held south between the wheat fields and Camas River canyon for four days, making around fifteen miles a day and camping wherever night caught us. There was wind along the breaks, but it stayed clear, the waterholes had not blown dry yet, and the horses herded without much trouble except to keep them from drifting down into the canyon. The wind was cold enough to keep them bunched close, and the rockbreaks had tufts of old grass spaced out far enough apart so they had to keep moving to keep eating. We didn't talk much. At night everybody was too tired to think of anything to talk about, and talking against the wind during the day was too much work to be worth it. Sometimes old Hendricks moved his lips as he rode, but nothing was audible when I edged close to listen, so I edged away again and left him to have his argument out with himself undisturbed.

A storm hit on the afternoon of the fifth day, as we were clearing the wheat fields and entering a long gravel flat grown up to sagebrush and juniper, with blackish outcrops of rim-rock poked out into it like headlands in a gray sea. Like most storms in that country, it began with the wind letting up close to the ground and blowing so hard in the upper air that the hawks had to beat their wings to stay in one place. Big cloud banks came driving up from the west, coloring the ridges with clots of shadow that looked blackish-purple against the sunlit places and then streaking them with splotches of sunlight that looked coppery-yellow against the shadows. Across the wheat country to the west we could see half a dozen places where it was already raining, some blurred dark with it, others blank white with faint rainbows wavering over them. There was a washed-out old wagon road a mile back of us that led down to an abandoned ferry station on the river. I hurried ahead and helped the young Mexican turn the horses back toward it. A yearling coyote jumped out from behind a bush while we were getting them turned. There was a six-dollar bounty on the ratty brutes, so I pulled up and threw a couple of shots at him before he made it to the shelter of a rockbreak. One missed him a country mile because my horse fidgeted while I was letting it go. The second would have nailed him right in the middle of a jump, except that he was digging for cover so hard he didn't take time to jump. I looked around and saw old Hendricks watching me. He had swung his horse to face the oncoming rain, and he had taken off his hat to let the first drops spatter on his face.

"By God, this is something like it!" he said. "To hell with people's troubles! This here's something new for you, the way that rain stomps along the wheat fields, and three rainbows all in sight at the same time . . . No, by God, there's four! You can't expect to hit anything with that pistol off of a horse that's standin' still. He'll always shift his feet or do something to throw your aim off. Put him to a canter before you shoot. Then you'll know what he's goin' to do next."

I held the pistol out to him. "There's four shots left in it," I said. "I've got extra loads, so go ahead and show me. If you can hit anything off of that old plug at a canter, you belong in a circus."

"I ain't as good at it as I used to be," he said, and took the pistol and eased off the hammer to test the pull. "I hope we don't scare that kid to death with all this bangin' around. He's gun-shy sometimes. Well, watch the white mark on that rock yonder."

He thumped his old mount to a lope, and let go the four shots at the rock as he went lumbering past it. The young Mexican pulled up and looked back, but I waved him to go on, and then rode over to see what the rock looked like. The white mark had four lead splashes in the middle. Old Hendricks handed the pistol back and reined around to follow the horse herd. "She's light in the barrel, but she handles easy," he said. "Hell, I've seen the time when I could wipe the drip off of a man's nose with a thing like that. Where are we headin'; down into the canyon?"

"Down to the river," I said. "There's an old ferry down there, and some empty sheds and a fenced pasture. It ain't been lived in for years, so we may have to patch it up some, but it'll beat laying out a storm up here."

"I remember that old rope ferry," he said. "An outfit named Waymark owned it and the land alongside it. If nobody lives there now, maybe somebody ought to. What's to hinder me from movin' in with the horses and holdin' it down? There used to be enough wild hay on that river flat to run a bunch of horses like this the year round. If nobody's usin' it, why ain't it open land?"

"It's been reconveyed to the government," I said. "They bought back the patent, and it's being held in reserve for a water-power site, or something. Nobody's supposed to use it at all. We can sneak a few days on it till the storm's over, but you try to move any bunch of horses in on it to stay, and you'll land in the cooler."

He fingered his reins, and pulled his hat down tight. "It used to be like that back in the early days," he said. "My old man used to tell about the times when you wasn't supposed to take any government land unless you paid for it. People moved in and took it anyway, and they kept it, too! By God, I knowed there was places where a man could still git started in this country, if he wanted to bad enough!"

"Maybe there are, but you'd better not try it here," I said. "You can't make much of a start anywhere from inside a jail. The place is all run down, anyway. The buildings are all caved in, and the hayfield's run to weeds."

"Somebody ought to try it, just to show 'em," he said. "If I didn't have this family business on my hands to settle, by God, I would! We'll see what it looks like, anyway."

The rain was coming closer, beating a grayish spray into the air as it hit the ground. He prodded his horse to a trot, and we went shouldering and thumping down the old ferry road into the river canyon.

chapter six

THE old ferry road was steep and slippery, and the switchbacks were angled so sharply in some places that a man could almost spit down the back of his own neck in rounding one, but the horses were anxious to keep ahead of the rain, and they held to a shuffling trot that kept the Mexican youth glancing back anxiously for fear they might run over him. Old Hendricks, having talked himself out of a set-to with government conservation policies by bringing up his family responsibilities, stood off brooding over family responsibilities by telling about the Waymark outfit during the years when the ferry had been in operation.

The Waymark family had consisted of three sons, all studious by nature and each a sort of specialist in his own field of investigation. The eldest had devoted himself to studying about wars, and knew all about every military campaign from

Alexander the Great down to Coxey's army, or whatever passage-at-arms happened to be raging at any given time. The second son knew all about horses. He could call off every racing record and every blood line that had even been catalogued, and pour out statistics about Pacolets and Double Brimmers and Steel Dusts and Brimmer and Printers till people waiting to take the ferry would sometimes swim out to it to get away from him.

All their specialties accomplished for them in the long run was to separate them permanently from the place their old man had wrung from the wilderness for them to live on. The one who knew all about wars got a job teaching history in some small midwestern high school, and the one who knew horses wound up as a harness maker in a prune town down the Coast. It did seem something of a comedown for both of them, though it enabled them to keep in touch with their chosen subjects while avoiding the disillusioning realities that might have come from wading in close. The third son made out better, against everybody's expectations, because his besetting interest was women. The ferry station was too far from any big town to permit him any wholesale philandering, but from the age of thirteen on he pestered around all the women within riding distance till some of them took to carrying sawed-off hoe handles to stand him off with. It got to be so much of a joke that most of them were ashamed to be seen with him, but when he was seventeen he fell desperately in love with a homesteader's daughter back on the ridge, and organized a courtship that included all the conventional forms of demonstrativeness and a whole deck of new ones. He went around glowering and refusing to eat or speak, stationed himself scowling outside her front gate every day for weeks on end and beat her father over the head with a fence picket when the old gentleman tried to make him leave; followed her around town glaring and muttering, hid in the grass outside her house and threw rocks at it all night, and once, when she refused to tell him where she was going in her best clothes, tore most of them off her and chased her back into the house with a knife, fanning her bustle with it at every jump, and weeping piercingly between threats to cut her heart out and stomp on it.

"I'd like to have been around about then," I said. "I'd have seen that he had something to bawl about. Didn't she have brains enough to put in a complaint against him?"

"She wasn't any intellectual prairie fire, I guess," old Hendricks said. "Still, what did she have to complain about? He loved her, and he showed it. You couldn't expect her to git aggravated about that, could you?"

"I've seen court judges that would have," I said. "He picked a blamed peculiar way to show his affection."

"You've got a few things to learn yet," old Hendricks said. "Love can hurt like hell. When people like that git hurt, they want to git back at whoever's responsible for it. She was responsible for it, so he got back at her. He was logical, that's all. Damned fools generally are, if you track it back far enough. She married him, so you can't say it didn't git results. It must have rained here earlier today, the way this road acts."

"It's not dried out from winter yet, I guess," I said. "Marrying him wasn't the end of it, was it?"

Old Hendricks held on uneasily while his horse slid fifteen feet in the red mud, and said the marriage had been more like the beginning than the end of it. "They moved down here to the ferry, and the old man Waymark moved into town and left 'em to run it, but they couldn't git leveled off, somehow. It was a love match right from the start, only it turned out that she couldn't stand him. She finally run away with some peddler from a street carnival that got hung up at the ferry for a week or two. But he left a wife of his own, so young Waymark took up with her, and they got along as well as if he'd courted the stuffin' out of her to begin with. A man never knows what's good for him; a woman, either, I guess." He pulled his horse up at sight of the river, after a dizzy slide in the mud that almost threw the old skate headfirst. "Them old sheds down there ain't the Waymark ferry station, for God's sake! Hell, what went with the house? They had a big white house with three floors to it!"

"It burnt down," I said. "The way they tell it, the woman was on a big drunk and got snakes in her boots, so she got to throwing lamps at 'em and set the place afire. It burned with her in it, but maybe she didn't mind. It saved her from having to sober up. There's some of the old timbers over in that stand of dead brush, but there's nothing much about 'em. They're old scorched timbers, that's all."

It was dreary to look at: dull gray sheds, dim gray trees, stone-gray river. Even the horses looked wraithlike, plodding across the colorless gravel flat toward it. Old Hendricks moved sideways in his saddle, muttering something to himself. "Yonder's the old road down to the landing, all right," he said. "There's the old wash house. That clump of cottonwoods up past the bend of the river is where the big spring comes out from under Burnt Ridge, and that must be the old Ibee Powell homestead, across yonder where the patch of trees is. It don't look like there was anybody on it, either. What become of young Waymark?"

"He drowned trying to move some sheep across the river," I said. "A sheep got crowded off the ferry, and he stepped in to throw it back. The water wasn't deep, but it's colder than whaley all summer, and it was blazing hot overhead. So he got a cramp, and the current took him downstream hellity-split, and that was the last of him. Women didn't hurt him much, when you go to count up. His downfall was work."

"Some people ain't made for work or women either, I guess," old Hendricks said. He picked up his reins and stirred his horse, and we rode on down the slope, both horses skidding in the mud at every step. "The old man Waymark was a hand for work. He fought every blamed thing there was to git this place started: snowslides, drought, cholera, floods, no roads, Indians a couple or three times, and he worked on it every minute he was awake afterwards. He put in this road and built the ferry and the landings and the old house, and cut and hauled all the timbers for everything himself. What good did it do him? What good did it do anybody? What did he git out of it?"

"He got a harness maker and a high-school teacher," I said. "There's worse things."

"By God, there is, you're right about that," he said. "I ought to know it if anybody does, but that ain't enough for what he went through. It don't take all that work to git harness makers and high-school teachers, damn it! I don't know what use there was in it."

"If he kept at it, he must have liked it," I said, though the reasoning seemed a little hurried. "Would it have been any better if one of his kids had got elected to Congress?"

"He'd have thought it was, more than likely," old Hendricks said. "It would have been the same thing, though. He got swindled, somehow. He put in more than he took out. By God, you can feel it raise up and hit you when you look at the place! Hell, I wouldn't have it now, you couldn't give it to me! The quicker this storm lets up so we can leave, the better it'll suit me. Look at the stubble move up on that point!"

The rain was reaching close. We rode on down, and dropped the packs off in the old wash house where there was a rusty stove and part of a floor, and then helped work the horses across the fenced pasture to a wrecked hay shed at the far end, where there was a little shelter from the rain beating sideways. We left the pasture gate open, because the grass was better outside, and the storm driving downhill would keep them from straying far. Horses hate traveling against a storm. It was dark before we finished, except for the radiance that shed from the river as the air over it began to darken. Old Hendricks kept looking back at the old ferry station, but several times, when I had pulled back to dodge his horse sliding, he glanced up at the corner of high stubble slanted against the sky that he had pointed out as Burnt Ridge.

A MAN can understand something of what a high-country spring storm is like by having to lie out and let one hammer on him, but the way to reach the deepest knowledge of its ferocity and blundering spitefulness is to listen to it from inside a house at night, with forty or fifty dumb animals left out in it that have come to depend on you for help and protection, and to be completely powerless to help them. During the worst of it, when the old wash house swelled and contracted with the wind like a blue-bellied lizard on a stump and the rain roared like a ninety-car train on the roof shingles overhead, we merely sat and listened and thought what it must be doing to the horses. In the lulls, the Mexican youth turned his face away from the lantern and slept. I fed broken pieces of flooring into the stove and listened for sounds of the horses above the dripping from the roof, and old Hendricks trudged back and forth between the one dirty window and the wall opposite, trying to work the saddle cramp out of his joints. He glanced out the window every few rounds, though it was too dark outside to see anything.

Finally I broke his rhythm by uttering a few cuss words because the roof drip was too loud for me to hear anything else. I hadn't intended it to take effect on him, but he came and sat down by the lantern and said part of that drip never would let up while the world lasted, and that the rain had nothing to do with it. It was from a fight a long time ago between a couple of Ibee Powell's sons: his son and one of his two stepsons, rather. It was over a girl who ran a rural telephone switchboard over at Elkhead. They had both taken the notion to go calling on her, and they made a race of it from the Powell homestead down to the ferry. The son got there first, having the faster horse, and got the ferry started across with him, which should have given him a good three-quarters of an hour head start, and maybe more. But the stepson, instead of waiting for it to land and come back, jumped his horse into the river and swam across, pulling even with it as it touched the landing. They both rode ashore together and fought it out with their knives on horseback, and the stepson got the worst of it, his horse being worn down from fighting the river current. So he fell off, wounded in fifteen or twenty different places, and crawled up into the wash-house attic and bled to death. The people at the ferry went on hearing his blood dripping overhead after he had been taken away and buried.

"You mean it hasn't let up since?" I said.

Old Hendricks said it had let up once, but only for a little while. The son rode on to Elkhead after the fight was over, and paid his call on the switchboard girl in what might be called triumph, though it scared her halfway back into her last year's birthday, because he had undergone an ungodly amount of whittling himself. The town doctor patched him up so he could ride home, but somebody bushwhacked him on his way down to the ferry and blew him almost in half with a shotgun, so it was all pretty much for nothing. The drip in the wash-house attic did let up for several months afterward.

Most people thought it had let up because the bushwhacking had been the work of old Powell's surviving stepson, and that he had done it to even up for his brother, but there was no way of proving it, and his mother swore in court that he was not only incapable of such a terrible thing, but had spent the entire afternoon holding her yarn for her in the living room, except for a scant fifteen minutes when he was out feeding the young turkeys and changing the water in the canary bird's cage on the back porch. So he was let off clear, only to perish tragically a few months afterward by accidentally shooting himself through the head while practicing spinning a six-shooter in front of his bedroom mirror. There was some legal inquisitiveness about that too, since the wound, from its location, could scarcely have been self-inflicted except by a contortionist, but the old lady came to the rescue again, and deposed on oath that there had not been a soul in the house at the time of the shooting except her son and herself. Old Powell had been cutting wood up Rail Hollow eight miles away, she testified, and the news that there was one more vacant chair in their family circle had struck him so completely of a heap that he was almost a broken man even yet. The drip in the wash-house attic started up again after that, it was noticed, and it was still going on, now that the ferry was abandoned and the Powells gone from their homestead for good.

"It's funny to look across from here and not see their light," old Hendricks added. "They wouldn't have one this late at night, but it kind of looks empty. Nobody's on it now, is there?"

I said it was vacant. The doctor in Elkhead owned it. He had foreclosed on it for his bill, which was what happened eventually to half the homestead land in the country. "Old Powell was a call boy down at the railroad yards for a while; stoop-shouldered and scrawny, with watery eyes and pampas-grass whiskers that feathered out when he walked. Nobody knew much about him except that he'd come off of a homestead somewhere. He didn't look as if he'd ever been within forty miles of a killing. You can't blame him much for doing it, I guess. Nobody wants his son's murderer camped around the house living off of him. You can't blame the old lady, either. The old man did kill her son, probably, and she lied like hell to get him out of it. Still, what good would it have done to let 'em hang him, when he was the only man she had left? She used to traipse down to the railroad yards every day with his lunch, I remember. She looked harmless enough. They both did, though, so maybe it didn't mean much."

"They was both alike," old Hendricks said. "Fluttery and cowed as a couple of stray pups, both of 'em. They used to stay indoors with all the blinds pulled down when it come time to mark calves. They couldn't stand to look at it. Right's right, but maybe there's sides to it sometimes. Maybe she loved him."

"I used to see 'em together," I said. "She treated him a whole lot more as if she didn't think he had good sense. It would work out the same, I guess. A woman nowadays don't want a man she can love. He might take an unfair advantage of it. She'd sooner have somebody she can despise. It's almost as much fun, and she can keep things under control easier. . . . That noise overhead don't sound to me like any drip. It's more like some roof stringer warping in the damp, or something like that. I'll bet I could find it if I took the lantern up there."

"You could find something, I expect," old Hendricks said. "It would take time, and you'd git dust and spider webs all over you, and you wouldn't gain anything by it. I'd sooner you didn't. It's one thing in this country that's stayed the same as it was, and I'd sooner you'd let it alone. It's late, and the rain's stopped. Maybe we ought to turn in."

It was almost morning. The window had turned grayish, the shapes of trees showed against the white patches in the river, and a bird chirped a few times experimentally. There were a few stars out between the clouds, but the absence of ground mist showed that the rain was not over with. "We might as well wait till daylight and see how the horses came through," I said. "There'll be another storm before long, and we can sleep then. There won't be anything else to do. You didn't tell what became of the switchboard girl all this Powell trouble started over."

Old Hendricks glanced at the young Mexican asleep back of the stove, and dropped his voice a little. "There wasn't much about her," he said. "She circused around the country awhile, and finally had a baby. She didn't want to own it, so she pulled out and left it hid under the bed. Her landlady heard it bawlin' and got it out, and they brung her back to make her tell who'd got it. It didn't do 'em any good. She blamed it on some gospelin' old hay binder back on the ridge with a family of his own. It was pure cussedness. He'd never had anything to do with her, or much of anything to do with, by his looks. She'd got to be as brassy as hell by then. Havin' men killed over her and showin' off in court went to her head, it looked like. She made all the trouble she could, and then she left. Nobody ever heard what become of her."

It was one chapter of local history that I couldn't help out with, but something in his tone did strike me: a strained casualness, as if it was costing him an effort to hold back some bitterness. "Who was this hay binder she blamed it on?" I said.

"Some dried-up old Bible banger from up in the breaks; I can't call back what his name was," old Hendricks said. "It wouldn't mean anything, anyway. If he ain't dead by now he ought to be. It wasn't me, if that's what you're hintin' at. By God, no! That's one thing I'm clear of, anyway."

"Still, a thing like that could have happened to anybody," I said. "I thought it might have had something to do with your leaving here."

He turned to the window and looked out at the graying sky. "That wasn't it. I never had any truck with the damned trollop, and you couldn't have hired me to. Hell, I wouldn't piss on a strap like that if her clothes was afire! Someday I'll tell you what I left here for, maybe. It wouldn't be any use now. You wouldn't have anything to go on except my word, and that wouldn't be enough. A man's word ain't worth fishguts without something to back it up. There's daylight enough for us to see what the horses look like, if you want to try it."

"We don't both need to go," I said. "There'll be mud and wet brush, and it's liable to start raining again. The horses ain't worth that much. You'd better stay here and keep the fire up."

It never did any good to argue at him. He got his hat and crowded himself into his coat. "The fire'll last. A man ain't much account if he can't look after his own livestock. If they ain't worth anything, that's all the more reason. There won't be anything back of it but solid sentiment. This is a place where people live up to their sentiments if it kills 'em, so it'll fit right in."

"They don't any more, I guess," I said. "Times change. You ought to know that."

He held the door open for me. "I do know it, damned good and well. Times do change. People don't, though. Step easy, or you'll wake the kid up. We don't all three of us need to go."

We went out, leaving the young Mexican asleep back of the stove. There had been times during the night when it sounded as if the whole place was being ripped to gun wadding, but the only damage visible was a few half-dead trees broken down in the thicket around the ruins of the burned house, and some dead branches torn off and flung against the broken-down fence. The river had changed color a little; it was not blackish, as it had been when we looked at it from the hillside, and not roily, as lowland rivers always were after a hard rain, but milky green, like snow water that has thawed too fast for the air to separate from it. The current was swift, but it held to its ordinary level as if the torrents of rain flooding into it had all been beneath its notice. One thing about those rimrock rivers was that wet and dry seasons never raised or lowered them. When there were floods, the surplus seeped out into the crevices of the rimrock, sometimes hoisting the water table fifty or sixty miles away, and when there was a drought it seeped back again. The rivers always ran the same.

There was no sign of the horses in the pasture where we had left them. It was blind work hunting for them, because the rain had washed out all their tracks, but old Hendricks finally located them in a stand of willow brush on a gravel flat below the old house. They had picked it because it was free from mud, probably. The brush didn't reach high enough to be any protection from the wind, there was nothing for them to graze on, and they were soaked and shivering with cold, but there were none missing, and they showed no signs of drifting or scattering. Several of them nickered when we looked down at them, but they didn't move, so we left them to stand it out, as they had doubtless done often enough before.

The sun came out for a little as we started back past the old burned house, and some grouse flushed in the tangle of dead brush and old fruit trees around it. They didn't fly more than a half-dozen yards, so I got out the pistol and picked up a rock to toss in after them. Old Hendricks stopped to watch, and I offered him the pistol, since he had done better with it than I could. He refused it, and said that even if we shot a grouse, getting it out of the thicket would involve getting soaked to the hide and scratched all to hell, and that it was not worth it. I argued back that it would be a change from salt meat, and he reminded me that he had run a pheasant diet into the ground down in the horse camp where I first found him, so the prospect of upland poultry didn't exactly put him in any flutter of anticipation. Then he looked at the sky, shut one eye and looked at the river, and led the way down to a rock flat directly below us, where a little side trickle of water spilled into a pool about half the size of an ordinary bathtub. He held out his hand for the pistol, motioned me to keep quiet, and shot into the middle of the pool. The report rang ungodly loud against the rocks, and rattled back and forth between the walls of the canyon like something falling down a long flight of stairs. The pool swelled, whitened, and lifted itself as if about to stand on end. Then it settled, and a two-pound trout rose to the surface and floated, stunned and helpless, to the shallow at the edge. Old Hendricks flipped it out into the rocks, and gave back the pistol.

"That's one old trick that still works, anyway," he said. "I used to shoot into this hole and pick a trout out of it every time I come past here. They was always about that size, too. I'd never git but one, but I'd always git him."

"It's about the only place in the whole river where you could these days," I said. "The rest of it gets trout planted in it the week before the season opens, and they get fished out the week after. We ain't supposed to catch 'em, anyway. They're put here to attract tourists. Tourists help business."

Old Hendricks picked the trout up and finished him off with a rock. "I didn't catch this one; he was floatin' around helpless, and I put him out of his misery. You can talk all you want to about how this country's got all the stretch worked out of it. There's places in it that ain't been worked at all. The trouble with young sprigs like you is that you don't git out and look for 'em. All you do is set around learnin' laws about what you ain't supposed to do. You wouldn't have believed a man could fetch trout out of this river with a pistol if I hadn't showed you. By God, though, maybe I oughtn't to have done it. If the kid heard it up at the wash house, it's probably scared him blue-legged. We'd better go see. Damn it, I ought to have remembered that he was as gun-shy as hell!"

We hurried up the old road from the landing and looked. The Mexican youth was outside, hurrying uncertainly toward some bushes on the uphill side of the pasture fence. He was coatless, bareheaded, and empty-handed, and he kept peering nervously back over his shoulder, stopping sometimes to listen. It was plain to see that the shot had scared him badly. Any ordinary dog fight or neighborhood squabble could bring a Mexican out of doors without his shoes or shirt or even his pants, but only the most mortal terror could ever scare him into the open without his hat. He stopped after we had yelled at him for three or four minutes, and stood wavering back and forth like an Indian getting trance-struck in a ghost dance. We had to go over and bring him back to the house between us through the start of the rain, since he couldn't make up his mind about coming in out of it himself. Inside, we showed him the trout and explained about the concussion produced by firing a pistol into a confined body of water, and about the foolishness of streaking it for the tall weeds every time a shot sounded anywhere in the neighborhood. It not only subjected him to unnecessary wear and tear, but it left the camp wide open to anybody who might feel like looting it.

"Yes, and he left that old rifle of mine layin' out where anybody could have walked off with it, and there's the horses," old Hendricks said, when I translated the admonition back for him. "Hell, he'd be meat for any horse thief that come prowlin' around him. All you'd have to do would be to sneak up and pop a paper sack behind him, and you could run off every horse we've got while he was scatterin' for the brush. Tell him the next time he hears anybody shoot, to come out and see who's doin' it and what they're up to, and to bring that rifle along with him. It ain't here to hang over any spinnin' wheel. It's to use on anybody that needs it. Tell him that."

"You're liable to land him in trouble, putting him up to run loose with a gun at anybody that shows up around here," I said. "You don't know what he might do. He's not very heavy on sense, and he scares easy."

Old Hendricks' pride in having shown his old-time prowess on the trout ran too strong in him for any counsels of moderation to take hold on. "I didn't say anything about runnin' loose with a gun at anybody that showed up," he said. "I said for him to bring it out if he heard anybody shoot, or if anybody tried to run off the horses. He don't need to use it unless there's something to use it on. Maybe he won't scare as easy if he knows it's here for him to use when he needs it. Tell him what I said, anyway, and be sure he gits it through his head."

I translated it as he had laid it off. It was a little risky, considering how apt the Mexican youth was to follow any advice literally and unimaginatively, but there wasn't much chance that he would ever need to act on it, and he did need something to put a little sand in his craw. We built up the fire in the rusty stove and got breakfast: the trout, with pan bread and middling bacon, boiled potatoes, dried peaches, and water cress wilted down with vinegar and hot bacon grease. If a man wanted to start a career as a glutton, there could be a lot worse ways of doing it.

When we had finished, old Hendricks rolled up in a corner and went to sleep. I could have done the same thing without any effort at all, but I waited till he had dropped off, and then got the old wire-bound rifle and laid it between the edge of my blankets and the wall; not hiding it, but arranging it so nobody could lay hands on it without waking me up. The young Mexican looked questioning, and I explained that I was only making sure it was in a safe place in case he dozed off or had business outside; it was there for him to use if there was any use for it. He murmured, "*Aprovechar, sí,*" and went back to looking out the window at the rain. It was coming down hard. The beating on the roof woke me up once, but then it leveled off into a rhythm as regular and restful as sleep itself.

It let up about midmorning, and the silence that followed it woke me as sharply as a hundred trumpets could have done. The storm was breaking up; a light wind was blowing scattered tags of cloud across the sun, and vapor was blowing from trees and bushes and old buildings like wefts of down from a bull thistle. I dropped back to sleep, but it was not as deep as it had been with the rain covering it. The young Mexican woke me at the end of a half-hour or so, squeezing his hand on my shoulder like a child working the whistle on a rubber doll.

"*Vienen gente,*" he half-breathed. "*Afuera, sí. Ahí vienen.*"

I threw off the blankets and got up. It was two men, by the sound. They were coming up from the landing, talking about the mud; the wandering sort of pointlessness that overheard conversations usually run to. There was nothing especially inviting about having visitors show up, but there was one encouraging thing about it. In spite of old Hendricks' admonition, the young Mexican hadn't tried to get out the rifle. As near as I could judge, he hadn't even thought of getting it out, and he had not thought of hitting for the brush to hide, either. It was something to know that he could use his judgment on occasion, and that he had some to use.

chapter seven

THE visitors were two youths of not much over high-school age, one blocky and heavy-featured, the other stringy and shrill-voiced and a little pop-eyed. They were from some wheat ranch up the ridge, as near as I could gather. They didn't volunteer their names and I didn't recognize either of them, but they kept tossing out allusions to the ridge and its residents, calling them all by their first names, old George and old Sime and old Vence and old Jake, as if a show of familiarity with the neighborhood might enhance their own importance before strangers. They were afoot, and one of them had a pump shotgun. I suspected they had brought it along to use on the grouse in the old fruit-tree thicket, though they insisted that it wasn't for anything special, merely in case they jumped something. They kept trying to figure us out, talking aimlessly along about the country they had come through and what the rainstorm had done to it, and how a lot of cars had got in trouble trying to make it across the ridge before the road had time to drain off, and the kind of special talents that were required to drive those ridge roads in wet weather. Finally, so that they wouldn't overstrain themselves making guesses about us, I told them where we were from and what we were doing. They quieted down at that, and came out with what was bothering them. They had heard some shooting a little before the storm opened up, and they had heard it again on their way down the canyon. They wondered whether it had been us, and if we had been shooting at coyotes, and if we had got any. It wasn't that they wanted to pry into other people's business. The only thing was that they had several coyote dens all marked and posted to dig up and collect scalp bounty on as soon as the whelps were born, and they were afraid we might have knocked over one of their female coyotes before her time.

It sounded trifling, but it was worth being concerned about. Coyotes whelped ten or twelve in a litter sometimes, so the difference between shooting an expectant female and waiting till she had achieved maternity could amount to sixty or seventy dollars. I explained that we had shot a few times, but only at a mark to try out a pistol. They looked a little doubtful, so I showed them the pistol and described the shape and location of the rock old Hendricks had shot at. Then, to keep them from spreading word all over the country about where we were camped, I told them we were moving out as soon as we could; maybe before evening, if the trail dried out enough.

"You'd better scout that ridge out good before you try to take any bunch of horses across it," the heavy-featured one said. "There's places up there in them sand washes that'll drop a horse plumb out of sight after a rain like this."

"Or a car either," the stringy one said. "Yes, sir. Old Ves

Busick tried to git across in a pickup truck with all of his stuff in it, and she's kicked herself off of the road into a sand wash right now, and buried plumb up to the tail gate. He come over to our place afoot to telephone for a tow car from town, but you couldn't git any tow car up there with the road like it is now. So then he struck out to git help someplace else, and his truck's still there and inchin' right on down. It'll be plumb out of sight before night, and he won't ever know where it went down at unless his girl stays there to show him. I guess she'll have to, though. She said everything they owned was on it."

"She wouldn't if she didn't want to," the heavy-featured one said. "She's kind of scrawny, but I could arrange to sleep her for the night if she caught me in the right humor."

"I could too, if I wasn't a married man," the stringy one said. He couldn't have been much over eighteen. "There's drawbacks to everything, it looks like. Old Ves could have got the truck through all right, only he didn't know anything about handlin' it. It wasn't any good, but you give any car full power when she starts to drill sideways in that mud, and she'll kick herself off of the road every time."

The heavy-featured one agreed that he was right, and recalled several similar cases from his own experience, and they wandered off into a discussion of different makes of cars and the kind of handling needed by each. They could have pursued the subject the rest of the afternoon, probably, but old Hendricks headed it off by remarking pointedly that we had to start pulling camp if we were to get started out before evening. They got up to leave, and the stringy one remembered something else that had been bothering him.

"You ought to know something about laws if you work for the sheriff's office," he said to me. "What I'd like to find out about is, I've got a lot of property comin' to me from my grandmother's will. My old man's got ahold of all of it, but she didn't will it to him. She willed it to be divided up amongst all of his children. That was a long time ago, when they didn't know how many children he'd have. He didn't have any but me, and he's too old to have any more now, so all the property's mine under the will, only he keeps hangin' onto it. Is there any way in the law that could make him do what the will said?"

I said it might run into complications. The case would require a lawyer, and would probably involve hauling his old man before the probate court to establish whether or not he was sexually impotent. The stringy youth looked a little appalled at the idea, and said regretfully that he guessed it was out.

"I thought there might be some way to do it without gittin' me mixed up in it," he explained. "I don't know why there ain't. It's mine, and it ought to belong to me, and my wife keeps peckin' at me about how we ought to have it while we're still young enough to have some enjoyment out of it, but I wouldn't want any legal fight over it. I wouldn't want to make the old man mad at me. He's vicious when he's mad."

"Your wife'll be all right as long as you can keep her in magazines," the heavy-featured youth said. "Order her a couple more bales of *True Love Stories* and *Real Life Romances*, and she'll last."

"What was your grandmother's name?" old Hendricks said. "Where's your old man's place at on the ridge?"

It was so unexpected that the stringy youth had to take a couple of seconds to think before answering. He said the name was Millstead, and the place was up on the peak of the ridge, about three miles off west of the main road.

"It's straight west from where old Ves Busick's got his truck stalled," the heavy-featured one put in. "You'd better not try to take them horses up there till it's dried off a little. You'll have to camp 'em in mud, and the grass is all beat out of sight, and they're liable to mire. You might lose some of 'em."

"We'll see how it looks," I said. There were more important things to think of. "We could stand to lose a few of 'em, I guess. They wouldn't be much loss, the way horses are these days."

They both stared at me, though I hadn't said anything very surprising. The stringy one got hold of himself first, and said they wouldn't hold us up any longer. They had only wanted to find out about the shooting.

"I wouldn't try that ridge if I was you, though," he added. "Stay away from the washes if you do. Keep to the rocks. They're hard on horses' feet, but it's better to bring 'em in sorefooted than not at all."

They left, looking back several times as they picked their way along the rocks to keep out of the mud. Old Hendricks watched them till they pulled out of sight, and then brought his saddle and saddle blanket from the wash house. "So he's a Millstead," he said, and laid the saddle on a board and spread the blanket over it to air out. "I used to know 'em. That grandfather of his could squeeze a nickel till the buffalo on it got the nosebleed. He got his old woman to divorce him and take all their property so his creditors couldn't attach it on him, and then they went right on livin' together. Yes, sir, they didn't even put up the pole between 'em. And yonder goes what he done it for: that washed-out little whistlepecker. By God, it makes me feel better about some of mine! No, I'll be damned if it does! Mine ain't a lick better. Some of 'em are meaner, and some's bigger louts, that's all."

"You oughtn't to say that about 'em till you've seen 'em," I said. "What have you got those lead ropes out for?"

He was too steamed up to bother answering that. He tossed the ropes across his saddle, and brought out a gunnysack with a little grain in it. "Did you hear 'em talk about puttin' property notices on coyote holes? Ain't that an out for you? Hell's fire, they'll be earmarkin' bullfrogs and grasshoppers around here next!"

I explained about coyote holes being valuable, and brought up the lead ropes again. "You've not got 'em to catch a horse with, have you? We can't pull out of here till the country dries out a little. You ought to know that. I thought you only talked it up to those young squirts to get rid of 'em."

"I did," he said, and looped one of the ropes neatly on his forearm. "This is a little trip of my own. I'll have it over with and be back here by dark. It ain't anything you need to bother with, it's . . . Hell, you might as well know about it! I'm goin' to pick out a couple of the herd horses that's been worked, and take 'em up to the ridge and pull that Busick truck out of the mud for him. There's some collar and hames sets in the tool shed that'll do for harness. They're old, but they'll hang together long enough for that."

"You can't do it!" I said. "You don't know how much of a job it'll be, or how long it'll take. I'm not supposed to let you go augering around the country with these horses like that. They're in my custody. So are you, as far as that goes. How did you take such an idea into your head, anyway?"

He coiled the other rope, and said it was one of the notions that struck him sometimes. He never knew where they came from, exactly. "It was the way that little fizzle-ended squirt told about it that gouged me, I guess. That girl settin' up there on a truck that's droppin' into a mud wash with everything she owns on it, and he acted like it wasn't any more concern of his than two stray dogs a-courtin'. His grandfather was the stingiest old pup that ever went dirty to save soap, but there wouldn't have been anything like that in his time. He'd have had everybody on the place up there helpin' to unload things, and a big fire goin' to dry 'em out, and a hot meal ready, and a couple of teams harnessed to pull the truck out, and anything else he could think of. I've seen him do it. He ain't here to do it now, so I thought I'd do as much of it as I could for him. You're welcome to come along if you want to, but that's the most I can do for you. I can't help you any with this custody business of yours. Not till tonight, anyway. I'll be back then."

There wasn't much that I could do about the custody business, either. It would be idiotic to threaten him with a gun when we both knew I wouldn't use it on him. Throwing and hog-tying him would be ridiculous, especially since the young Mexican would only cut him loose the minute my back was turned. The reasons he had given for wanting to pull the truck out seemed lame and insufficient, but it was a case where opposing his foolishness looked more foolish than falling in with it. "I wouldn't mind going with you if it was anybody but Busick," I said. "He's got it in for me, and I'm supposed to keep away from him. He's a bad actor."

Old Hendricks faced around and beaded me with his eye, waiting. There was nothing to do except come out with the whole story. I left out all except the high spots, but they didn't add up to anything very flattering. He let out his breath when I had finished, and shook his head. "Old Piute Charlie," he said. "Lord, I wish I had a dollar for every time I've rolled the worthless old reprobate out of the road when he was too drunk to crawl out himself. It's something to know what become of him; yes, and to know that somebody else around here can be as big a damned fool as I am. I don't know but what you're a bigger one. You're supposed to know better, and I ain't. You won't have any trouble with Busick. Them kids said he wasn't with the truck. They said he'd gone to find a tow car."

It was a hard one to turn down, having Calanthe that close and being able to ride in on her with assistance in her time of need and act strictly impersonal about it. Chances like that didn't come every day. Still, there was Busick to think of. "He might have got back by now. Or he might come back while we're up there."

"He won't if you'll stop arguin' and git started," old Hendricks said. "We can make sure of him, though, if you're still uneasy about him. Let me take that pistol of yours, and I'll guarantee that you won't have any trouble with him. You've seen what I can do with it."

I took the pistol off, trying to think what could come of it. The whole thing still looked a little dubious. "It's not that I'm afraid of him. The only thing is that I'm supposed to keep away from him. That's the main reason I got sent out here."

Old Hendricks slid one arm out of his coat and looped the holster over his shoulder. "You've missed the point of the whole business," he said. "You'll be all in the clear if he don't bother you, and I'll tend to that. You're supposed to stay out of trouble with him, but I ain't. I'll see that he behaves himself if he shows up, or I'll fix him so he'll have to. I wish you wouldn't blat it out to people that you've got me in custody, or anything like that. They might think I've done something to git arrested for, and you never know who they'll turn out to be. You done it before them two young squirts that was here, and I could swear from the first minute they started talkin' that one of 'em was my grandson."

"But you didn't let on, or say anything!" I said. "You didn't act as if there was anything about 'em, and you said . . ." His grandson must have been the heavy-featured one, the one who hadn't given his name. And if old Hendricks was sure of him, there had been no reason to say anything; and if I had led them to think he was under arrest he wouldn't have wanted them to know who he was. I said I was sorry, and he said there was no great harm done.

"He was a lout; you could tell it by his looks," he said. "And not honest enough to hurt him much, either, the way he shifted around when they was leavin'. I don't give two hoots about him, but there's some others around that we might run into. Some of these days I'll show the whole pack of 'em, but it won't hurt to be careful for a while yet. You'd better tell the kid we're leavin'."

It may have been the meeting with his grandson that had got him set on going, I thought; wanting to do something to make up for the poor figure he had cut, maybe. It was the only reason I could think of, unless it was his pride over the trout still working in him, and it didn't look like pride. It was more the headlong stubbornness of a man who has resolved on doing something foolhardy and is afraid somebody will point the foolhardiness out in time to keep him from it.

THE youths' forecast about the difficulty of taking horses up the ridge turned out to be accurate in general, but considerably hind-side-to in detail. They had dwelt far too lightly on the first half of the route, and a little too ominously on the rest of it. The old road out of the canyon was bad enough when we came down it, but the rain had made it as slippery and as yielding as soap. Climbing it on horseback with two unshod horses leading behind was a desperate process of scrambling up ten feet and trying not to slip back more than nine; of working to keep all the horses moving without letting them crowd close and slide into one another; of fighting them around the gullies and mud slides they had crossed in coming down and wanted to cross again going back; and of trying to keep an even pressure on the lead ropes without drawing hard enough to bring on a general tangle when a horse fell down. They fell several times, and once a led horse slid thirty feet downhill on its side and refused to get up till we climbed down and lifted on it to help. It struck me to reflect, as we wallowed in the red mud, straining over it and dodging its hoofs every time it floundered, that we were going through all this for a couple of people for whom neither of us had the slightest reason for wanting to do anything, and that neither of us had so much as hinted at the possibility of calling it off and going back to camp. Old Hendricks didn't owe Busick or his daughter any favors; the long end of the singletree was on the other side, if it was anywhere. I owed them even less. We got the horse on its feet and boosted it back to the road and inched on, taking no time to rest so there would be none to think what we were doing it for.

The horses were winded and steaming when we finally struggled out onto the rock-flat above the canyon, and old Hendricks allowed them a ten-minute cooling spell before shoving on. He was so tired himself that his hip pockets were dragging his tracks, but he didn't do much resting. During most of the halt he walked around examining the horses, moving his lips soundlessly as he had done when we were trailing up through the frost-killed wheat fields in the wind. He spent a couple of minutes inspecting the old collar and hames sets he had rummaged out of the shed down at the ferry, and once he climbed on a rock and looked across the flat at the scrolled and intertwined patchwork of green winter wheat and dark summer fallow and gray scab land lifting against the sky to the south.

"Yonder's the ridge," he said. "That patch of white rocks off to the left used to be Juniper Springs. Them telephone poles must be where they've got the road now. We'll head straight across to it. That'll keep us clear of the sand washes them kids talked about, and it'll save us some time."

"It won't save much," I said. "There'll be more fences to cross. Every one of those wheat fields has got one around it, and we'll get in trouble if we cut 'em. There's not that big a hurry about the blamed truck, is there?"

"There's a whole swad of things besides the truck," he said. He looked across the flat again, and went on as if to change the subject. "A man gits back to a place like this, and he thinks that maybe now he can use his time to do what he wants to. He can't, though. There's always other people's troubles waitin' to swarm onto him, no matter how long he's stayed away. It's like yellow jackets around a nest after a bear's tore it up. They'll set around it for months, waitin' for somebody to come along that they can jump on and sting for it. They never try to go after the bear that done it to begin with. We can cross them fences easy enough. We won't have to cut 'em, the shape the ground's in."

Something had turned his mind on his daughter at South Junction, I thought. It looked like reaching a long way out for something to feel despondent about. She had been through a trying experience, but a quarter-million-dollar estate was not exactly a crushing addition to her afflictions. "People that get themselves into trouble ought to get themselves out," I said.

"You don't have to shoulder it for 'em. Nobody knows you're back here, so what difference does it make what you do?"

"It don't make any, I guess," he said. "No, it don't make any. That's what's hard to take about it. A man as old as I am ought to have himself sized up close enough to know what he can stand, but anybody's liable to overlook something. Nobody else knows I'm back, but I know it. Well, let's poke ahead a ways. Maybe it won't turn out as bad as it looks. I'll show you about them fences."

We cut straight across the flat, aiming for a point about four miles off where the line of telephone poles crossed the peak of the ridge. Fences began to come up at us when we left the rocks, but we skirted some of them by following the tongues of scab rock between the cultivated fields. The ones that couldn't be skirted were easier to handle than they had looked, because of the rain. The posts loosened easily in the wet ground, and when there was a place that had to be got through we merely pulled one out and laid it down flat, wires and all, till the horses had crossed, and then stuck it back in the hole again.

Skirting fences brought us out on the main road a half-mile below the point we had aimed for, but we picked up the marks of Busick's truck the minute we turned into it. It was hard to understand how he could have undertaken to drive a loaded truck on such a road after a heavy rainstorm, unless he wanted to find out how much he was capable of standing. The roadbed had been carefully graded out all the way up the ridge, with a high crown in the center and wide drainage ditches on each side, in preparation for hard surfacing. But the hard surfacing had been put off during the bad weather, and the road had been left with a topping of the same light soil we had been pulling fence posts out of all the way across the flat. The rain had turned it into a foot-deep layer of slime, and the tracks of the truck went wandering back and forth through it in crisscrosses and zigzags and sinuosities as if the driver had been trying to see how much of it he could track up and how many different patterns he could make in doing it. There were places where he had gone sideways, and places that looked as if he had taken the wheels off and rolled them one at a time, and places where he had churned along with one wheel in the road and the other three in the ditch, and one torn-up stretch where he had slid completely off the road and had corduroyed a ramp out of fence posts along a wheat field to help in getting back on it.

Studying the tracks and figuring out what maneuvers they indicated was so absorbing that we didn't notice the truck till we were within a hundred feet of it. It was dug down and plastered with mud so deep that there wasn't much of it to notice. The rear end had gone completely out of sight, and the muddy ditchwater was lapping a couple of feet up on the tarpaulin that had protected the load against the rain. The front end had made out better; the wheels were sunk almost to the top of the rims, and the battery had probably shipped more water than it should have, but the motor was still clear. Calanthe was nowhere around. She came half-running through the dead rye grass and scrub willows along the edge of the wheat field as we stood sizing up what would have to be done. She knew us before she got within talking distance, but she was too much out of breath to show surprise or embarrassment. Her dress was muddy where she had crawled under the fence, her hair had some twigs and dead grass tangled in it, there was a smear of mud on her cheek, and she was flushed with hurrying and prettier than I had thought she could be. It was the truth that some girls looked best when they tried to the least.

"I saw you crossing the field toward the road," she said. "I was afraid you wouldn't turn up this way, so I ran to see if I could head you off. I tried to call to you, but I couldn't get near enough to make you hear. Then I saw you turn into the road, and I knew it was you, and I was afraid you'd ride on past before I could get back, so I . . . We've had some trouble with our truck. I guess you can see that. I saw that you had a work team with you, and I thought maybe . . . There's a tow-rope under the seat—a long one. It's part of an old derrick rope. I can get it out for you if you need it."

"We can git it if we need it," old Hendricks said. He was not far from acting downright hostile toward her. "You'd have to wade belly-deep in that mud to reach the seat, and what would you look like afterwards, or don't you care? If you don't, there's other people that might. Stay where you are and git yourself dried out."

She looked hurt and surprised, and after all the times I had hoped something might happen to cut her feathers for her, I was sorry. "We can get things out of the truck easier than you can," I said, tempering it down a little. "How did you know it was us, if you were so far away you couldn't make us hear you?"

She started to answer, and then glanced at old Hendricks and changed it to something different. "I'll tell you the truth—I recognized the horses," she said. "They're some my father let go. I helped trail them all the way down to that camp on the river, so I know all of them. I knew you'd been sent out to take them somewhere, so I knew it had to be you. My father's gone for a tow car, if he can get one out here over these roads. I don't know how long it'll take him. He didn't want to leave me out here alone, but the truck's got all our things in it, and somebody had to watch them. He thought he could get somebody from one of the ranches to come down and stay with me till he got back, but I wouldn't let him. The people around here are not much company, and I don't mind being alone sometimes."

She was talking to fill in the silence, mostly, though part of it was probably something she couldn't help. Women left alone on a country road with a stalled car invariably felt compelled to reel off a rigmarole about how the man of the outfit had fought like a bay steer against leaving them out there unprotected, and how they had finally forced him to swallow his chivalry and go anyway, gazing back in manly anguish as he took his reluctant but necessary departure. I had seen bankers' wives do it, and shop girls, and dance-hall trulls. I had seen migrant women from a crop camp put up the same story, word for word, when their old man was laid out in a strawstack not fifteen feet away, too drunk to flap an eyelid. It was a sort of automatic reflex to which the whole sex was subject, seemingly. Old Hendricks announced that we would need the towrope from the truck, and rode his horse into the mudhole and reached it from under the seat before I could offer to do it for him. It was a way of keeping out of the mud that I wouldn't have thought of, right on the spur of the moment, but since one of us would have to wade in and hitch it to the truck before we could start work on it, I couldn't see that he had saved much. I offered to take the rope in and do the fastening, but he held onto it.

"I can hitch it on without gittin' in the mud," he said. "You couldn't; that horse of yours has got too much life in him. This old skate'll stand wherever he's put, so him and me'll tend to it. You're doin' more good where you are than you could anywhere else. Stand your hand and keep on at it. I'll let you know if I need you."

He took up a couple of notches in his cinch, rode back into

the mudhole beside the truck, and dropped one end of the rope back of the front wheel. He hooked his heel back of his saddle cantle and leaned down and looped it over the axle. Then he rode to the opposite wheel and did it again, almost stood on his head while he looped a series of hitches underwater, and straightened up and came riding out, all thronged up with triumph, though he was so dark-red and windbroken that it seemed open to doubt whether keeping his feet dry had been worth risking apoplexy for. He dropped the rope end as he rode past, and I got up to bring the workhorses within reach of it. He waved me away again, and set his eye on Calanthe.

"You'll have to steer your truck when we're ready to pull it out," he said, still with a curious harshness in his tone. "Right now, I don't need either one of you. You'd only be in the way, so stay where you are. When there's anything you can help with, I'll tell you."

We sat on some rocks in the sun while he dragged loose a fence post and rigged it to use as a singletree, and Calanthe began talking again, eager and low-voiced, though it was nothing especially confidential, merely about the people on the ridge. Most of them were newcomers: renters or men who had bought wheat land at eighty dollars an acre during the boom and were trying to pay out on it now that it was down to thirty. She knew the Millstead youth who had been down to our camp at the ferry; he was married to a girl from some crop camp who had never seen an ordinary toilet till the night of their wedding, when she tried to take a bath in one and got herself stuck in it. They blew in so much of the old man's money touring the country on their honeymoon that he had cut them down to exactly enough to live on, with a warning that there would be no more unless they got out and earned it. So young Millstead spent his time figuring out ways to augment his allowance without bowing to tyranny by working, and she spent hers lying in bed reading trashy magazines and waiting for him to think of something. As to the heavy-featured youth old Hendricks had thought might be his grandson, his name was Asbill, but he might be related to the Hendrickses; there were still some of them around. He had been married twice, anyway, both times before he was old enough to vote. One was to a woman twice his age, who left after papering the country with bad checks. The other was a traveling tent preacher's daughter who turned out to be not quite right in the head, and wrote amorous poems which she threw out of an upstairs window to anybody who happened to be passing. Some of them were funny, though not intentionally. She finally had to be sent away to a mental hospital, and the heavy-featured youth was being kept close to home so he wouldn't get mixed up with any more like her, or worse. The Asbills had made out well in the wheat boom: over a hundred thousand dollars from one year's crop, people claimed. They had a daughter who worked at waiting on tables in an ice-cream parlor in town. She made barely enough to live on, but she preferred it to living out on the ridge with them. The ridge was not a place that women took to much, unless they were new to it. Some of the newcomers' wives liked it. Most of the girls who had been raised on it couldn't stand it.

"You look as if you'd stood it well enough," I said. "It hasn't hurt you anywhere that shows, anyway."

She colored up, though I hadn't intended it as a compliment, and said she had never really lived on the ridge. "My father's worked over in the breaks a few seasons, and I kept camp for him. That was enough, too. We'll have a place from now on where we won't have to camp around any more. There's a house goes with it. I'll have one in town someday, and we won't have to sit out on a rockpile to talk. Don't go yet. You're not in any hurry, are you?"

I sat down again. "Your father claims he's going to take a shot at me because I threw him in jail," I said. "That's what he was telling around town when I left. I didn't know but we might run into him up here, and that he might take a notion to try it."

"He won't—he knows better than to try anything like that around me," she said, and set her chin. "He knows that if he tried it on you, I'd . . . He won't, anyway. He's done too much of that already. That's why we've had to move around so much, and live in camps. We're out of all that now if he can behave himself, and he's got to. He knows it, too, so you needn't worry. He won't bother you."

"I'm not worried about him," I said. Old Hendricks had the team hitched onto the towrope, so I got up. "I'll go where I please, whether he likes it or not. If you're out at South Junction, maybe I'll see you again."

"Maybe you will," she said, and held out her hand to be helped out of the rocks. "If you want to, if you . . . He'll like it if I tell him to. He'll have to. I'll look for you."

We set to work to pull the truck out. It was more of a project that we had counted on. The ground was too soft for the horses to get a solid hold in, unshod as they were, and the truck wheels had settled into the mud too deep to budge. We tried it till the ground looked as if hogs had been rooting it, and then Calanthe rode a saddle horse out to the truck and broke the wheels loose by starting the motor and spinning them. She stayed in the seat to keep the motor running and steer, and we hooked both saddle horses on ahead of the team and hauled the truck out, giving it everything we had and almost capsizing it as it plowed through the dirt fill up to the road. We put the fence post back in its rightful place, stowed the towrope back under the seat of the truck, and got the horses ready to travel. Calanthe held out her hand after we had mounted, but mine was smeared with mud, so I let it go at repeating that I might see her again.

"Don't forget," she said. "My father won't be around much in the daytime. I'll look for you." She looked up at old Hendricks. "If my father was here, he'd want to pay you for all this. He'd have to pay anybody else for doing it, so it's . . . If there was some place where we could find you, we'd . . ."

The sternness of his look upset her. She gave up and stood silent while he glowered down at her. "You can tell your father he don't need to bother about any pay," he said. "Or about where to find me, either. If he can behave himself and stay out of trouble for a while, that'll be all the pay I'll need."

He rode past her, and the horses all turned in after him. I looked back when we had gone a couple of hundred yards. She stood looking after us, shading her eyes with one hand. She raised the other and waved good-bye, and old Hendricks shook the horses into a trot and held it till we had dropped her from sight. It was near the end of a mile before he said anything, and then it didn't come very close to what must have been running in his mind.

"The road's dryin' out fast," he said. "It'll be in fair shape to travel by evening, if it keeps on like this. I was thinkin' that there's an old Indian trail down to the ferry that's better than that old washed-out wagon road. It's the one them kids come down this morning. It takes down a rockslide into the canyon, and then along the river for a couple of miles. It's rough, but it'll beat hell out of all that mud. Maybe it don't make much difference to you whether there's mud or not, with the work that girl done on you still to wear off, but it does to me."

"If you think it'll be better than the road, let's take it," I said. "I don't see what the girl's got to do with it. She didn't do anything except talk. She'd have talked to you, if you hadn't barked at her every time she tried to."

He raised in his stirrups to watch a car coming up through the rock flats toward us. It was a good mile off, and taking its time. Once it skidded halfway around, but that it could keep moving at all showed the road was drying. "We'll turn off about a half-mile below where that car is," he said. "It'll skirt us around the fences. That girl wouldn't have been the same with me. She'd have been different with you if I'd hung around. You ought to know that, if you've got any sense. I thought you didn't like her? Wasn't it her that rigged it so you had to leave town?"

"She didn't rig it, I guess," I said. It was better to be inconsistent than unfair. "I thought she'd lied a little, but it turns out she didn't. She don't lie much; not enough to hurt, I guess."

He rode silent for a minute, watching the car creeping toward us, and asked what I had suspected her of lying about. I told him about Busick being retained to run the Farrand holdings, and he sat back and said something under his breath. "Well, the Jesus wept!" he said aloud. "Well, the Holy Ghost and General Jackson! Now, what in the name of Godamighty do you suppose that means?"

"It means the Farrand woman wants him to manage the place for her, I suppose," I said. "I don't see what else it could mean."

"Like hell!" he said. "Her want a man like that to run a quarter-million-dollar outfit for her? You don't need to tell me. I know a damned sight better. There's more than that back of it, if there's anything to it at all. Maybe that girl was runnin' another whizzer on you. No, hell, she wouldn't do that, not the way she was rubbin' up to you!"

"They're on their way out there now," I said. His reasoning was too low to deserve notice. "That's what she said, and I believe her. She didn't have any reason to lie about it."

"Not a speck," he agreed. "If she said the Farrand place, that's where they're headed. She wouldn't steer you wrong on it, after all the trouble she took to git you lined in. She's no fool, if she does act like one sometimes."

I said she hadn't acted like one around me, and we pulled off the road as the car drew even with us and stopped. It was a service truck, equipped with chains and a hoist and inscribed with the name of a crossroads garage down on the flat. The driver leaned out and asked if we had heard of anybody having trouble up the ridge. A telephone call had come in along in the forenoon about somebody needing help somewhere along the road, or near it. He hadn't got the directions straight; the connection was sputtery from the rain, and whoever was calling had talked in some foreign accent—Indian, he thought, or something like it. All he had managed to make out was that somebody was hurt or in need of help, and he had decided to drive out and investigate, in case help really was needed. We told him about Busick's truck. It was the only case of help being needed that we had heard of, and it was all straightened out now. The foreign accent over the telephone was hard to account for, but Busick might have got somebody to call for him, or something. The man wiggled his ignition key thoughtfully, and said that was probably it, and he was glad of it. He had fought enough mud for one day, anyway. If it was for nothing, all right.

"I've got my hard-luck clothes on this week, I guess," he said. "Everything's turned out wrong. We had three carloads of brand-new farm tractors all ordered, and these wheat farmers signed up to buy every last one of 'em the minute they got here, and this morning comes a telegram from the factory that the government won't make any more farm loans to buy 'em with. That fixes us. We're out of business right now, if we had sense enough to know it. You're lucky you've hung onto your horses. Plenty of places around here didn't. Give me a boost till I can get turned around, will you? This truck holds the center of the road solid enough, but she slips sideways when she's close to the shoulder."

We climbed down and helped him to turn the truck and start it back the way it had come, and then remounted and rode along in its tracks as it drew out of sight ahead of us. Old Hendricks fell silent, keeping his eyes on the chain prints in the mud as if they were some trail he was being paid to run out, and moving his lips in another soundless dialogue with himself. He was so absorbed in it that he rode past his old Indian trail without seeing where it turned out. He nodded and reined back when I pointed it out, and then dropped into his dialogue again. Once or twice he scowled, and once he half-smiled to himself, though there was no humor about it. It was more as if he was triumphing over something, or over somebody.

He shook off his reflections after we had scraped through a wild-cherry thicket and topped out on the rock flat again. It was high ground, and we pulled up and looked back at the road. A long knoll covered with green winter wheat shut off the ridge where we had left Calanthe and the truck but the rest of the road was visible all the way down to the little crossroads from which the garage truck had come. Half a dozen children on horseback moved along it, going home from school. They rode slowly, to keep their horses from slipping in the mud, and at times seemed scarcely to move. They looked small and lonely, crawling across the big swell of grain land that shook against the skyline as the wind stripped streamers of black and green and gray from it, held them flapping for a second, and then dropped them back into place again. Old Hendricks watched for a minute, and then touched up his horse and moved on.

"Yonder went horses," he said. "They've got some left around here."

He was brooding over what the garageman had said, by his tone. "Some places keep one or two old plugs to drive the cows in with," I said, to keep him from looking on the dark side. "They're run-down old corral stock, mostly, and worthless for work. The kids ride 'em to school when the roads are like this. They're not much good even for that, but they're safe, and it's probably better than staying at home."

He allowed that it might be, without giving it much thought. "A man don't like to build up too high all at one clatter. There's liable to be a call for work stock around here yet, then? That garage hand sounded like he expected there'd be one."

"Some of these places will need 'em when plowing starts," I said. Talking about it appeared to brighten him, so I followed it up. "Not yet, maybe. Most of these ridge outfits don't have feed enough to carry extra horses on now. But there'll be pasture later on, and they'll have their summer fallow to plow and harrow, and their harvesting to get ready for. If they've had three carloads of tractors shut off at the factory, they'll have to fall back on horses for it. That bunch of yours might be worth counterbranding, after all. It might save some arguments, if there's any demand for 'em."

"Maybe we ought to do it," he agreed. He seemed down in spirit again, maybe on account of something I had said, maybe because of his thoughts. "It might be a good thing, I don't know. I had it settled there wouldn't be any sale for horses for three or four years yet, and I thought I could hold 'em back in the timber somewhere till the market brisked up. Me and the kid could have run in strays from the brush, and built 'em up into a real herd. I don't expect there'll be many strays runnin' loose in the brush now, if there's any market for 'em."

"None that anybody'd want, I guess," I said. "These half-section wheat ranches can use fifty or sixty head apiece in the work season. That ought to clean 'em out of the brush fast. You'll make a profit out of the bunch down at the ferry, that's one thing. Anything you get out of them's yours. The county pays me, so I've got no claim on 'em. They didn't cost you much."

"My time's all," he said. "The Lord knows that ain't worth a gillywhiffet in a whirlwind. Whatever they sell for will be all clear. If they fetched four bits apiece, it would be like findin' it in the road. The hell of it is, I hadn't planned to sell 'em. I'd planned it out to hold onto 'em. The kid's good with horses when I'm around to watch him. It would have been something for him to work at. There's some countries that never will let a man do what he wants to. I'll git used to it, I suppose. You can git used to anything."

There was no reasoning that would touch that kind of spirit.

Anybody else would have been feeling thankful over the prospect of making money out of some old castoff horses that hadn't cost anything except a little herding. He took it as if he had expected something of the kind any time he felt like reaching out for it, and was disappointed because it had happened in so much of a hurry. It was a kind of temperament that went with the country, maybe. There had been a freighter up the river once who laid out on his smokehouse roof all night with a gun to catch one of his wife's admirers, and when the admirer didn't show up he flew into a temper at her because he had had all his trouble for nothing. Arguing with people like that never got anywhere. I let old Hendricks alone. We rode on down a shallow gully past an old watering trough ringed around with scrubby wild-plum bushes, all gray and leafless, and then down the narrow rock cleft by which the trail led down into the river canyon.

It was hard traveling, that part of it was no campaign slander. The cleft dropped between two sheer cliffs, not over twenty feet apart, and the space between them was slid full of loose gravel in flat plates and sharp-cornered chunks about the size of a windfall apple. There was no room between the chunks for a horse to step, and stepping on one started eight or ten square yards of them all sliding and rolling together, clattering and scraping and banging between the narrow rock walls like a dozen steam drills running full-blast under a tin roof. It was useless trying to ride the horses down such a place; they had enough work merely to keep their feet under them and keep going, so we dismounted and followed along behind. Halfway down, the slope steepened so we could hardly stand up on it, but the horses by then had discovered how to manage it without wearing themselves out. Instead of trying to walk with the rocks moving and shifting underfoot, they merely started a patch sliding, set back and coasted on it till it stopped, and then moved on and started another one to coast on. Not many animals are smarter than a range horse, when he is left free to figure things out for himself.

The rockslide fanned out near the bottom of the canyon, and we followed the trail in the half-darkness through a thicket of wild gooseberry bushes and into the dead grass and scattered rock outcrops along the river. We mounted without taking time to rest, and turned down toward the ferry, letting the horses nose out the trail because it was too dark for us to see it. The clattering of the rocks down the steep slide had been so numbing and incessant that the river seemed moving in the dark without any sound at all, though we could feel it jarring and twanging under us when the horses crossed solid rock. Finally we began hearing it, and old Hendricks opened up again.

"I've made up my mind about the horses," he said. "I won't sell 'em. I had it planned that I wouldn't, and I'll be damned if I'll switch around for any blamed market! If I have to counterbrand 'em, I'll do it. Probably I'll wish I'd sold 'em before I'm through, probably I'll want to kick my tail end till my nose bleeds for hangin' onto 'em. I would anyway, so it don't make any difference. That's how you come out of everything when you're my age. No matter which end you take, you git the worst of it. You come out of it with a girl. What do you think of her?"

"She's all right, I guess," I said. It was hard to figure out what he intended to live on while he carried on his horse raising back in the hills. Maybe he hadn't figured it out himself. "There wasn't . . . She's all right."

"Not many girls would have worked to rustle help the way she did, runnin' across that plowed ground after us, and wantin' to wade in after the towrope," he said. "Most of 'em would have folded their hands and waited for somebody else to do it all. She's got her eye set on you."

"She wanted somebody to talk to, that was all," I said.

"She picked what she wanted to talk about, I noticed," he said. "All about where you could find her, and the house she was goin' to have in town some of these days. She'll have one before she's through, and you in it. You'll be pushin' a lawn mower and weedin' the flower patch and shakin' out parlor rugs to beat cats a-fightin'. Drive down to work at the store every morning, the same as the rest of 'em, and don't forget a quart of milk and two loaves of bread, and git back early so you can string the sweet peas. I can see you now."

"I talked to her because there wasn't anything else to do," I said. It was a colorless-sounding prospect. It was not as forbidding as he had intended it to be, that was the irritating part of it. "I wouldn't have talked to her at all, only you didn't want anybody to help you with anything. That was all there was to it, and all there ever will be, probably. There's nothing wrong with her; I don't mean that. She's all right. I've seen a lot worse that thought they were better, but there's nothing about it to make that much out of. I might not see her again at all. Maybe I won't. I've got nothing to go to the Farrand place for. I don't think I will."

"I don't think I will either, by God!" he said. "A man's got rights of his own." He rode for a while in silence, and then took it up from a little farther along. "I've still got that pistol of yours. I'll keep it till we git to camp, as long as I've got it harnessed onto me. You won't need it before then. . . . You ought to see her again, though. She's a good girl, and she likes you. You don't strike many like that, and they'll git scarcer when you're older. Her old man won't be any trouble, if that's what you're afraid of. I said I'd see to it that he didn't bother you, and I will."

"I'm not afraid of her old man," I said. It was the third or fourth time that the possibility had been brought up, and it didn't improve with wear. "I don't need any help to stand him off. If he thinks he can make anything out of . . ."

The horses had raised their gait almost to a trot as it dawned on them where we were headed. One of the work team broke into a trot so his lead rope slacked, and let out a loud whinny. Before the echo had time to clatter back from the canyon wall, a horse answered from the dark between us and the river. A little farther off, another horse snorted inquiringly, and there was a sound of hoofs as a half-dozen others moved up from the low ground to see who we were.

"Why, thunder, they're ours!" old Hendricks said. He was in better spirits; a man generally is, when he has come to a decision about anything. "What in damnation made 'em drift all the way up here? The feed's better down by the old orchard than it is up here, and they must have walked right past it to git here. Maybe the kid brought 'em up. He might be out with 'em now, the way they're scattered around."

It looked as if that was it. The horses wouldn't have left a fair pasture below camp for a poor one above it without somebody behind them, and they appeared to be spread out in small bunches among the grass strips, when their ordinary instinct in a strange place would have led them to bunch. There was no sign of the Mexican youth, even when we called, but he always rigged some kind of cover for his night herding, and the river might have kept him from hearing us; or he might be asleep again. It all reasoned out naturally enough, whichever it was, so it was no surprise to find the old wash house dark when we rode up to it. There was nobody around it, the ashes in the stove were cold, and the youth's blankets were gone.

Those were signs that could have meant anything, but a more reassuring one was old Hendricks' rifle. It was still laid out between my blankets and the wall, as I had left it. The youth's rope bridle and the gunnysack pad he had been using for a saddle were on the floor back of the stove, though that didn't mean much either way. He always rode a horse out to his night camp when old Hendricks was around, and could ride better than old Hendricks could, but something about old Hendricks' presence was necessary for him to do it. When he tried it by himself, the meekest old pelter in the herd would fight, buck, strike, rear and fall backwards, and almost rupture its fool self trying to tear him apart and scatter the pieces. It wasn't that solitude undermined his horsemanship. Its effect was on the horses. Not many riders could have lasted out the pitching spasms those old herd plugs put him through when old Hendricks was not around to back him up. So he had given up trying it when he was alone, and his saddle pad and rope bridle on the floor signified no more than a silent acknowledgment of his limitations.

We settled it that he was out with the herd, and built up a fire and got a skimpy supper and turned in. It didn't take long to get to sleep. There was something about being back in the old wash house that was like a homecoming. The sound of the river was part of it, and the blood drip in the attic overhead, and the wind stirring the old trees down the road, and old Hendricks' breathing. Silence is not restful if it is strange; sounds are, if they are familiar. There was a restfulness about the wash house, and it stayed on after I had gone to sleep.

Old Hendricks was gone when I woke up. It was late morning, and I got up and hurried breakfast to have it out of the way. Some Indians came riding down the old road and drew up at the door as I was eating; a buck, three or four squaws, and a string of pack ponies. They didn't call; they merely sat their ponies and waited. They didn't even talk among themselves, which meant that they had something serious to bring up. I left breakfast unfinished, and went out to see what it was.

chapter eight

CLALLUM JAKE was a Columbia River Indian by residence, though he was heavier-built and more dignified than river Indians generally were. He lived most of the year on an Indian allotment sand spit that stuck out into the Columbia a few miles above the mouth of Camas River, where he operated a seining ground during the salmon run, with the help of four or five squaws of varying ages and uniform homeliness. He was a hard-working old buck, and usually hung up from ten to a dozen tons of salmon in a season. He was also a sharp trader. Instead of selling his salmon to the cannery at some starveout price, he preferred to home-dry and peddle it to the upper-country Indians for such raw material as deer hides and the pelts of winter-killed sheep, which his squaws tanned and converted into genuine Indian-beaded buckskin gloves, moccasins, belts and handbags. Knickknacks of that kind found a ready and profitable sale at tourist stores and curio shops around the country, besides supplying the squaws with something to do so they wouldn't be tempted to start fighting among themselves.

Nobody knew anything precise about the relationship subsisting between Clallum Jake and his squaws. Some public-spirited people in town had tried to find out about it from the squaws a few times, but the squaws knew only a few words of English, all brief and forceful, so the investigation had never got far. Clallum Jake had escaped it himself, being too dignified in appearance to be questioned about his domestic eccentricities by a set of town busybodies who might not have stood up very well under any searching inquiry into theirs. He could understand English moderately well when there was anything in it for him, though he usually professed ignorance of it to be on the safe side. He had no language of his own, or none that anybody could pin him down to, having wandered into the plateau country in the early days from somewhere down on the Coast, where all the native languages were different. In his trading with other Indians, he relied partly on his squaws and partly on a scattering of English mixed with Chinook jargon, the simplified mixture of mispronounced French, Indian, Russian and Eskimo that had once been the universal trade lingo among western tribes all the way from the Bering Straits to the California line.

One Coast Indian trait that had stayed with him was clumsiness with horses. In spite of the fifty-odd years he had been riding, he still rode like a shirttail full of rocks, but with an air of weighty deliberation that made it look as if he was doing it in fulfillment of some plan too deep and far-ranging to let the general public in on. There was not much romanticism about his looks, but there must have been some sparks of it in him when he was younger. His first appearance in the country had been at the time of the old Piute wars, when he rode in to the old Kirkbride toll bridge on the Lower Camas River astraddle a half-foundered scrub pony, with an Indian girl hanging on behind him. He explained that she was a chief's daughter from the Willow Creek Snakes, that they were running away to get married, and that all the Willow Creek men were out trailing him to kill both him and the girl if they got close enough. He thought he could outdistance them if he could drop the girl somewhere and lighten his pony's load that much, but he was determined not to leave her. Life without her would be no more than a slow death anyway, he said, and if he couldn't save her it was better for them both to perish together and have it over with.

The Kirkbrides were sympathetic and prompt with help. They fixed the young couple a hiding place under some hay in the barn, stood off the Willow Creek war party when it pulled in, headed the chief to the wrong end of the haymow when he insisted on searching it, and finally got rid of them and sent the relieved lovers on their way with a couple of fresh ponies and a note to the nearest justice of the peace, who was so moved by their story that he could hardly bring himself to charge anything for marrying them. Every year from that time on, as long as the Kirkbrides held onto the old toll bridge, Clallum Jake always showed up after his salmon season was over, bringing a pack pony laden with salmon and Indian beadwork as a token of his gratitude to them.

He kept it up for over thirty years, which seemed a long time for any gratitude to last. After old Kirkbride had died and his wife had moved away, some of the neighbors got to nosing around and discovered that the runaway marriage to the Willow Creek girl hadn't lasted past its first six months. Then she had not only run away with some young high roller from the Idaho Bannocks, but had chopped Clallum Jake lopsided with a salmon knife before sloping out on him. The discovery did not detract in the least from the sentiment that had prompted his yearly tribute to the Kirkbrides. That had clearly been gratitude, only nobody could decide exactly what he had been grateful for. It may have been the experience. He had profited by it, if the assortment of squaws lined up behind him was anything to go on. He reined his pony's head up and said, "*Klahowyam,*" when I came out of the wash house, and they all fidgeted and clacked at him, wanting him to get down to business. He started like a lawyer, laying out his points before explaining what they had to do with anything.

"Him Joe Klikamuks, him got *tenas* camp *sahalé yawa matlié,*" he informed me. "Up-river, *wek-saya* steam train. Got *hiyu* hoss, got kids, got *kloochman, hiyu* stuff. *Sapele mamook;* make wheat. *Hiyu* dig, *hiyu* work, *kakwa* sonomabitch."

He paused. The squaws murmured, "Aaaaaaah-nah!" approvingly, like a church congregation intoning responses. It was clear enough, in a general way. Some Indian named Joe Klikamuks was camped up the river to plant spring wheat near where the railroad cut across a corner of the reservation. He had his hands full with work, and his camp was small and overcrowded. "All right," I said. "What about it?"

He silenced the squaws with a look, and went at it again. "Two white boy come him camp *taholké.* One boy big, bmmmmmmm! One boy skinny, eeeeeeee! Skinny boy, him go. Big boy, him stay: him feel bad like hell, *mamook kwolt.*"

It was getting a little deep for me. The two boys weren't especially hard to account for, from his description, but I didn't know *mamook kwolt* at all. He saw that he had lost me, and took another try at it. "Two boy come Joe Klikamuks camp," he explained patiently. "One boy big, one boy skinny. Skinny boy, him go; Big boy, him stay: him *hiyu* sick, make holler, make bawl, oooowoooowoooo! Bad like hell; *kokshut*."

"Why couldn't you hunt up his folks and tell them?" I said. "They could get a doctor for him, if he's bad off enough to need one."

They conferred again, and Clallum Jake moved up a little more of his English. "Him say no," he said. "No got. Him sick like hell, *hiyu* holler. Joe Klikamuks got little camp, got hoss, kids, *kloochman*, *hiyu* work, white boy sick. You go?"

"I guess so," I said. The urgency of the case was clear enough. Upper-country Indians were afraid of deaths. If the sick boy should die, Joe Klikamuks might feel obliged to move out. "How far up the river is it?"

They held another council on that, and agreed that three handbreadths of the sun up the sky would about cover it. Clallum Jake measured them up from his hat brim, and threw in a couple of extra fingers so as not to seem small about it—two hours, maybe a little more than that. "You go," he said. The squaws all reined their horses around simultaneously, like a flock of wild ducks wheeling. He picked up his reins. "*Kopet*. We go down-river."

"Have a nice trip," I said. "Try not to fall in."

They rode away, and I went back in the wash house to finish breakfast. There are not many things more disillusioning for a man to look back on than his own feelings. It was hard to understand how a place so bedeviled with reports of people in need of help could ever have seemed restful, how coming back to it could ever have seemed like any kind of homecoming. It was true that Calanthe and her truck had not been strictly in line of duty; the likelihood was that old Hendricks had helped her out because he wanted an excuse to look over the country he had once lived in. There was nothing to regret about it, but it hadn't been as serious as Clallum Jake's report of the two boys up the river appeared to be. From his description, they sounded like young Millstead and young Asbill, though if they were, it left a lot of things still to clear up. One was what they were doing on horseback up the river only a few hours after they had come down to the ferry on foot. Another was why young Asbill had intruded himself into an overcrowded Indian camp overnight instead of going home where he belonged, especially if he was as desperately sick as Clallum Jake had made him sound. There had been one phrase of Chinook jargon about him that I hadn't understood. Old Hendricks came in as I sat thinking back over it. He carried a yellow and red poplar leaf in his fingers, and had something clenched in his hand. There was an ash-colored ridge around his mouth.

"I've been up to look at the horses," he said. "The kid's gone. Sloped out on us. I hunted the whole place for signs of him, and he ain't anywhere. I found this."

He opened his hand and laid a cartridge shell on the table—a black-powder .44-40, old-fashioned and straight-sided, the same caliber as his old rifle. It had only been fired a few hours. The chamber scores on it were bright and fresh, and the smell of burned powder was still strong in it. "We'd better see if your rifle's been shot," I said. "It was right where I left it, and I supposed . . . What's the leaf for?"

He held it out and studied it. "It was close to where somebody'd got on a horse. He'd had trouble at it, by the tracks. The ground was all tore up, and there was . . . Look it over."

He dropped it beside the cartridge shell, and went over to inspect his rifle. I turned it over, half-watching him. It was as bright-colored as a flower, brighter than poplar leaves usually were so late in the year—daffodil-yellow and poppy-red. I picked it up for a closer look, recalling that poplar leaves didn't usually turn spotted when they shed, and the red spots cracked and shed off little dry flakes between my fingers. I had always thought that blood turned dark when it dried, but the red spots were dry, and they were blood. Old Hendricks finished levering the cartridges from his rifle, counted them, opened the breech and sniffed it, and closed it again. He loaded the cartridges back into the magazine and stood the rifle in a corner.

"It's been shot," he said. "There was five cartridges in it; all I had. Now there's four, and the powder smell's as strong as a shootin' gallery. Well, what it looks like is that somebody tried to run the horses off yesterday while we was gone. There was two of 'em, by the tracks. They drove the whole bunch up the river to where we found 'em last night, and they was tryin' to separate some of 'em when the kid come out with the gun and took a shot at 'em. Then they got scared and run. He hit one of 'em, by the signs, and then he got scared and pulled out himself. That's the best I can make out of it. He ain't hurt himself; if he was, there'd be some signs of it here, or else he wouldn't have brought the gun back and put it away. One thing about it is that if the horses is worth stealin' they're worth something. I'd like to know where he went to, though, and I wish to God I had my hands on the pesky thieves that tried to jump him like this."

"You don't think it could have been Indians?" I said. There was no use overlooking the possibility. "There's a camp of 'em eight or ten miles up-river, at the edge of the reservation, and they've got some spring wheat to get in."

"No Indians made the tracks I seen," he said. "Indians don't have their horses shod all around, and they don't wear shoes;

they wear moccasins. An Indian don't git on a horse from the left-hand side. He gits on from the right. I don't know who they was, but there wasn't anything Indian about 'em. Where did you hear about any Indian camp up the river?"

"Some Siwashes came past with a pack train," I said. It was narrowing down too close for much doubt to be left, but there were still a couple of points to make sure about. "If you remember that much about Indians, you might remember some of their jargon. Have you got any idea what *mamook kwolt* is? And are you related to anybody up the ridge by the name of Asbill?"

He was quick at putting things together. He went to the door and stood looking out, repeating the phrase over to himself in an undertone. "He was my grandson, all right; my next oldest daughter . . . So that's it! Where's he at now? Did them Siwashes bring any word about him? Is he hurt bad? . . . Goddamn it, don't gawp like that! That Chinook jargon means he's been shot! Is he hurt bad, or did they say, and where's he at?"

"He's in the Indian camp up the river, and they said he was hurt bad," I said. Letting it out a little at a time might have been easier on him, but there didn't appear to be any way of doing it. "The Indians got scared that he might die on their hands, that's why they sent down word about him. I'm sorry about it. Some of it's my fault. He might not have thought of trying it if the horses had been counterbranded, and I talked you out of that. And when they were here I said something about horses not being worth anything, that if we did lose some it wouldn't matter much. They probably figured that if we felt that way about 'em, it wouldn't hurt to chase off a few for themselves. It must have looked like easy money."

It didn't help much. He looked out the door again. "When

you take what don't belong to you, it's stealin'," he said. "It don't make any difference what it looks like; stealin's what it is. You ain't to blame for it any more than I am; not as much. I was against brandin' the horses, after we'd counciled about it. I put the kid up to use the gun on anybody that tried to jump 'em. It was my idea to go up and help that girl with her truck and leave him here by himself. None of this would have happened if we'd stayed here. They wouldn't have tried anything on all three of us. Well, it's over with now. I'll have to go up to that Indian camp and see what kind of a fix this young nature's mistake has got himself into, I guess."

"I'd better go with you," I said. "A couple of knotheads like that oughtn't to be left loose, after the trouble they've made. I ought to arrest 'em, just for the looks of it. They've got it coming."

Old Hendricks dragged his saddle outside and turned it underside-up with his foot. "I'd think you'd have enough of arrestin' people for the looks of it, after the round you've been through," he said. "It's as much my fault as it is theirs. You don't hold loose cattle responsible for goin' through a hole in a fence. You hunt up the man that left the hole, and blame it on him. I'll be back along in the afternoon, if them Siwashes told the truth about how far it is."

"It's not much over ten miles up to the railroad, and the camp's closer, so they couldn't have missed it far," I said. I hated to see him start out alone. He looked strained and old. "You stay here with the horses, and I'll go. I ought to anyway, so the blamed little squirts won't think they've got away with anything. They deserve some kind of a shaking-out for this, no matter who left the hole in the fence. People ain't cattle."

He spread his saddle blanket out in the sun and picked up a lead rope. "You'd be surprised what people are sometimes," he said. "I have to go up there anyway. I want to see what's happened, and if it's them, and you don't need to. You couldn't do any good. It wouldn't help any to arrest 'em. There might not be anything to arrest 'em for. All we know is that somebody's been shot, and that he's laid up in an Indian camp up the river. We don't know how it happened, or where, or anything about it. I'll tend to 'em if they need it. I don't hanker to, but I will, and it'll be better for you to keep out of it. You hunt around and see if you can find any track of the Mexican kid. Bring him back here if you find him."

It was not much to look forward to, poking through rocks and bushes in search of a frightened young *chopo* who might not want to be found and might already be streaking it halfway across the next county. "Even if I found him, he might balk on coming back," I said. "He might think I wanted to haul him in for the shooting. Maybe I ought to, as far as that goes, and hog-tie him and hold him for the grand jury. You don't want me to do that, do you?"

He brought out his rifle and fixed a carrying thong around the stock. "If you have to, yes," he said. "Arrest him all you blamed please. I can take him away from you when I git ready, and he's better off here than runnin' loose on the county. It might do him some good. He's got to learn that when he lands in trouble on account of me, he can depend on me to git him out of it. Besides that, I owe him money. I've still got that pay check of his that I promised to cash for him. I'll be damned if I'll have him thinkin' I beat him out of it."

He traipsed out to catch up his horse. It was late, and I should have been getting things packed up, but it was hard to start. I sat at the rickety table, trying to think past all his explanations for himself and get down to some understanding of what really did keep his bull wheel turning. His talk about not hankering to go up to the Indian camp may have convinced him, but it didn't convince me. Actually, he was eager to go, not because young Asbill would be any improving sight to look at, but because the disagreeableness might relieve him of some heavier responsibility that threatened him, that he was afraid to put out of his mind and couldn't bring himself to face. His wanting the Mexican youth back was easier to figure out; he had skimmed close to the truth about that himself. It was merely that it helped his self-respect to have somebody depending on him. The uncashed pay check didn't have much to do with it. He may have thought it had, but what counted was his self-respect.

After all the arguing and mis-explaining, he didn't go up to the Indian camp by himself, as he had laid out to do. He came back from the horse herd leading both saddle horses, and explained that he had run across fresh foot tracks in some wet sand along the river. There was only one set of them, pointing upstream, and they had evidently been laid down by the Mexican youth, since nobody else had been up there alone and on foot. He was for following them to see where they led, but it didn't seem very likely that anybody running away from a shooting would walk out into some rock flat and sit down till the trackers caught up with him. It looked more as if he had decided to strike past the Indian camp for the railroad and grab a train out of the country. It looked like sounder strategy to pull camp and head there first, rather than to poke up the river searching out tracks and leaving the camp and the horses behind to tempt prowlers. For once, old Hendricks gave in to reason, and we got in the pack horses and packed and pulled out, bunching the herd horses out of the rocks and larruping them to a trot as we moved up the river.

There were two things that struck me as we were leaving the old ferry. One was as we turned past a clump of service berry bushes at the corner of the old pasture. A hen grouse flapped out into the sparse stubble with one wing spread out helplessly, trying to lead us away from her nest by pretending that it was broken and that she would be easy for us to catch. She crippled pathetically along trying to tempt us for fifty yards, and seemed downright despondent when we took no interest in her or her nest either. The other was that, looking back at the old sheds, I saw that all the dead tangle of plum twigs in the thicket around the burned house had started to put out white blossoms. Anybody would have taken oath twelve hours earlier that they were all dead. It appeared that none of them were. Old Hendricks glanced back to see what I was looking at. Ordinarily he would have taken it in and ridden on, maybe with some mumbling to himself, but this time he did his talking out loud.

"Spring's on our tails," he said. "Grouse nestin' and plum buds startin' to pop; that's two signs. When she starts to roll around here, she don't back up for anybody."

So I was right about him, I thought. Having young Asbill's butter-fingered bungling to tend to had relieved his mind of something that lay deeper—a flutter of sun on the surface of a rock pool concealing a trout at the bottom, the flash of raindrops along dry shriveled plum twigs that hid the buds rising. Only it was something he dreaded a little, I thought.

The ride up to Joe Klikamuks' grain camp took nearer four hours than the two that Clallum Jake had measured off for it, not that he had tried to make it sound easier than it was, but because of the horses. They were no trouble to manage; the cliffs shut them in on one side and the river on the other, so a little rock-throwing and slinging a rope at them sometimes was enough to keep them moseying. But they were tender-footed from the rocks and lank from poor feed, so we had to let them poke along and pick soft ground for their feet, with a halt every mile or so to graze tufts of old bunch grass up the steep side-hill where the sheep hadn't managed to kill it out. It was past noon when we turned a sharp angle of the cliff and raised sight of the Indian camp. It was half a mile ahead, across a long flat. Since the grass was better among the rocks, we left the horses to go on grazing it, turned the pack horses loose with them, and rode on for the camp unencumbered except for anxieties, which old Hendricks continued to bear easily, though he did frown over them as we got close.

The Indian camp could have come straight out of the old frontier-life chromos except for the collection of farm implements scattered around it: a couple of plows, two or three harrows, a drag to break clods, a seed drill, a light farm wagon with a striped beach umbrella stuck up over the seat. Three frowsy-coated ponies gnawed listlessly at some weedy hay in the back of the wagon, and four or five others were poking through an old chaff dump at the edge of the plowed ground, hunting for patches where spilled grain had sprouted. The camp consisted of four old-fashioned pole tepees set in a square, the crossed tips of the poles sticking picturesquely through the openings at the top where the fireplace smoke found its way out after half-suffocating everybody inside. A couple of hundred feet from the tepees, a small stick and blanket hut had been put up as a menstrual lodge for the women—a feature of Indian camps that the frontier chromos usually passed over in silence, though there were civilized communities that might have gained by adopting the idea, trimmed up with a few refinements such as light, heat, ventilation, and space enough for a human being to move around in.

It was unoccupied, by the looks. Some young men from the camp were repairing a barbed-wire fence not over thirty feet from it, which they would hardly have risked if there had been anybody in it. The squaws were at work around a fire in the space between the tepees; a girl of about sixteen, with a green silk headkerchief fastened with a high-school class pin, sat peeling young cedar roots to be woven into huckleberry baskets. She stripped the bark off with her teeth, and hung the peeled roots over a log to dry in the sun. A couple of young squaws were converting wild millet seed into meal in a wooden salad bowl with a rock, one grinding and the other pouring; an older squaw was cleaning water cress in a wooden candy bucket, and a middle-aged one kept vigil over a row of winter piñon cones laid out on a blanket where the heat from the fire could dry them out and release the seeds inside.

It was a busy scene, but there was no air of drudgery about it, because none of it was in the least necessary. Even at post-boom prices, the three-hundred-odd acres of wheat they were getting ready to plant would bring in close to ten thousand dollars, so the piddling with piñon nuts and millet grinding and cedar root stripping was merely a game they were playing at, maybe to prove to themselves that they could still do it, or maybe to keep from thinking of some set of real responsibilities that were harder. They all looked up as we rode into the space between the tepees, and then went on working again. Joe Klikamuks came out of the tepee at the far corner of the square, and lifted one hand in greeting, holding an open can of tomatoes in the other.

"*Na mika nanitch hapwho?*" he said cordially. He was tall,

middle-aged, a little overweight, and togged out for company: a high-crowned black hat with a fancy horsehair band, hair braids looped into a coon tail on his chest, a beaded belt a foot and a half wide, and shiny new rubber overshoes covering bright yellow moccasins. He addressed his Chinook jargon to old Hendricks and broke it down into a simplified version for me afterward, eating tomatoes out of the can with his fingers. "You come see boy, huh? *Hiyu* sick. *Kah memaloose;* maybe die."

"He's still alive, is he?" old Hendricks said. "*Na wake memaloose alta?*"

Joe Klikamuks said, "*Kaweke,*" and spread back the door flap and stepped inside, as if to prove that it was still safe. There was a small fire smouldering in the middle of the dirt floor, and a tumbled heap of blankets and rabbit-skin robes at one side with a man's naked arm poked limply out of the tangle. That was all we could see from on horseback. Old Hendricks dismounted and went in, and I climbed down and stood in the door, holding the horses and watching. It was young Asbill, sure enough. The young Mexican's shot appeared to have got him in the right upper chest, between the top rib and the collarbone. A white cloth that looked like torn-up underwear was bandaged around his shoulder and across the breast muscle, with the mark of the bullet showing through it. His eyes were almost shut, his face was flushed dark, and his breathing was heavy and stertorous. Old Hendricks stooped and touched the bandage, and then straightened up and came back to the door.

"If he sees you here, he's liable to think you've come to arrest him," he said, keeping his voice down. "We might as well kill him as scare him to death. You wait outside."

I led the horses back from the door and waited. After a

minute or two I could hear them talking, but I didn't feel slighted at being left out of it. There was nothing much about the inside of an Indian lodge except smells, and the rabbit-skin robes used for bedding sometimes sheltered various forms of insect life. I watched the squaws working, and they went on at it without letting on to notice. The cedar roots that the girl peeled with her teeth and hung out to dry looked exactly like the skinned tails of dead rats. The piñon cones drying on the blanket beside the fire burst open with a sort of paroxysmic regularity, like popcorn when it first begins to pop—a long wait with nothing happening, and then, when the squaw had given them up and let her attention wander, a sudden spatter of three or four letting go all at once, followed by another long lull while she swept up the scattered nuts and set new cones on the blanket. She didn't eat any of the nuts. Desert piñones were delicious to eat, but Indians seldom ate them, preferring to press out the oil and peddle it around the fancy grocery stores in town to be retailed as genuine imported Italian olive oil at a dollar and forty cents a pint. Joe Klikamuks came out of the tepee, stood in the door for a minute, and then went across to where the young men were patching the fence. Old Hendricks came out after him and came over to the horses.

"He's bad off," he said. "We think it missed his lung, but it's too close to fool with much. I got him to talk some. He lied considerable, but it must have happened about the way we figured it, from what he let out. I didn't want to sweat him too hard, the shape he's in. These Indians done the best they could for him—cleaned the bullet-hole and filled it with fir pitch to stop the bleedin'. It'll do for a while, but the bullet's still in him, and it's got to come out. I'll have to git him to a doctor, or else git one out here for him. There's an ambulance over at Crosskeys, the Indian says."

There probably was. Crosskeys was a sizable town—about two thousand people. Only, it was a good twenty miles away, and doctors and ambulances didn't make twenty-mile calls over dirt roads after a heavy rain for the fun of it. "If you get mixed into any doctor and ambulance business, you'll have to pay for it," I said. "Why not telephone his folks up the ridge and let them tend to this? You're not responsible for what's happened to him; they are, and they'll have to find out about it anyway, and they can afford to pay for it better than you can. They've got money enough to buy him all the horses in the country if they wanted to. I don't know why he took it into his head to try stealing 'em. They sold one year's wheat crop for a hundred thousand dollars a few years back, and it wouldn't hurt 'em to spend a little of it on him. They raised him, if you can call it that."

He conceded that. He was always ready to concede any point against him, as long as it didn't count. "His folks ain't here. I asked him about 'em. They're on their way out to some kind of a family powwow at South Junction, and they left him to run the place while they was away. They're all tryin' to git a finger into that Farrand estate, he thought. It sounds like 'em. They've cut off his credit everywhere so he can't run up bills on 'em, and he needed a little money to go courtin' with, so he figured that he could run off a few horses and raise it. That girl up the ridge that we helped out was what give him the idea, I guess. He asked about her a couple of times. He can't lay here with a slug in his craw till his folks git back from South Junction, anyway. It might be a week."

There was something in that; more than he brought out, maybe. If young Asbill should die where he was, the Indians would have to strike camp and leave till the infection of death wore off, and it would mean losing their wheat crop for the year. A ten-thousand-dollar wheat crop was a lot to throw away on superstition, but Indians couldn't help being Indians, not that they ever wanted to. They had to be taken as they came. You couldn't reason with sentiment. . . . So. He had been trying to raise funds to go courting Calanthe, after having been married twice already. So that was his trouble. I felt a stir of appreciation for the Mexican youth's marksmanship.

"I'll put him under arrest," I said. "That'll get him a doctor and an ambulance and anything else he needs, and you won't have to pay for it. The county has to pay medical expenses for anybody under arrest."

"I'd sooner you didn't," old Hendricks said, and then pointed it up a little plainer. "I'd sooner you didn't try to. He asked me if you'd come along to arrest him, and I told him no, so we'll have to work it some other way. I'll ride over to town and git the doctor and ambulance and whatever the hell else he needs. You can pace on down to the railroad and nose around for that Mexican kid. The Indian says there's a track gang at work this side of the tunnel; maybe they'll know something about him. You can come on to town afterwards. I'll wait for you at the feed yard."

"You'll pay for your doctors and ambulances," I said. He would have run anybody out of patience, handing out orders and brushing aside advice as if we were playing blow-the-feather at a social. "If they haul him to a hospital, you'll pay for that too. What's wrong with letting the county pay for it; ain't it expensive enough to suit you? What do you intend to do with the horses; leave them scattered out here in the rocks? Maybe you've forgot it, but I've got orders to see that they, to see that . . . You're not planning to sell 'em in town? To pay doctor bills for this no-account lunkhead that tried to steal 'em?"

He had it all settled with himself. It wasn't a plan or an intention; it was an approaching event. "I thought I'd turn off a few of 'em," he said. "The Indian says the feed yard in town is out buyin' some, and I can find out what the market's like. He's offered to send a couple of young bucks to help trail 'em into town, so they can steer the ambulance back here afterwards, if it turns out we need one. They want to git this whole business off their hands as quick as they can, so we won't have to pay 'em for it. Some of the horses ain't worth keepin', anyway. They slow up the whole bunch. We'll be better off rid of 'em."

It sounded business-like for a minute. Then the weak spots began to show up. "Horses that ain't worth their keep won't be worth anything to sell," I said. "Feed yards don't throw money away on worthless horses. You'll sell 'em good ones or you won't sell any. The money'll go for doctor bills and hospitals, and what will it get you? If you think it'll make that young flathead take you for a big-timer, you don't know the breed. All he'll think is that he's played you for a come-on. If you think it'll be something you can swell about to his folks, you don't know them either. All they'll think is that you're struck in the head, and that you need somebody to take care of you. Arresting him might scare him into behaving himself for a while—a few months, maybe. Every little helps."

He was patient, but he had his mind made up. "I don't care what his folks think," he said. "If you think I want to see any of 'em, your whang's out a foot. I don't, and I don't intend to, either. If you arrest this kid, he'll land in jail, and I don't want him to. It's too much to pay for a little dab of foolishness. Everybody gits into foolishness sometimes. You've done it, and so have I, and we're workin' out of ours without any harm done. That's the way it used to be with everybody, and that's how it ought to be now. What have you got to arrest him for, anyway? He's got himself shot, but you don't know how it happened, or where, or what about. That old gun of mine ain't anything to go on. There's guns like it all over the country; there's one in that Indian lodge that's the dead mate to it—same make and caliber and everything. You don't know a damned thing, and you can't prove a damned thing, so leave me to handle this, and go do as I tell you. It'll be better for both of us, and we'll feel better about it."

Feel, feel, feel. Orders, orders, orders. Too much was enough. I dropped his reins on the ground and led my horse around and climbed on. "You've got it all mapped out, ain't you?" I said. "All right, I'll find the Mexican kid for you. I'll bring him into Crosskeys for you. Then I'll haul him to the justice court and have him held as a material witness to this shooting, and I'll get a deposition from him about it, and I'll arrest this young saphead on that. If you're still around town when I get there, you can come over and watch me do it."

Ill-tempered or not, it did put him where he had to do the arguing. "You oughtn't to do anything like that," he remonstrated, as if gentling a wire-snagged horse. "You'd stir up a lot of trouble for everybody, and what would you gain by it? I oughtn't to have brung it up about that girl, but you don't need to rear up and ride bug huntin' about it. This kid can't bother around her, the shape he's in now. You'll cool down when you git her out of your head a little."

He probably intended that to be placating. It couldn't have missed farther. "She ain't in my head, and it's nothing to me whether he bothers around her or not," I said. "What I'll arrest him for is attempted horse rustling, and he's got it coming.

He'll be better off in jail than he is here, and so will everybody else. So will you. It'll keep you from piddling away all the money you've got, and to hell with how you feel about it."

I prodded up and rode out on him before he could think of anything else to argue back. A couple of hundred yards down the trail to the rocks where we had left the horses, it struck me to wonder what argument he would have tried if I had waited. I slowed up to see if he was coming after me, but he had ridden out to help herd in the Indian ponies from the chaff pile back of their camp; so I rode on without bothering any more about him, except to look back a time or two to see how he was coming along at it. There was no telling which horses in the herd he might take it into his head to sell when he got them into Crosskeys, so I caught up the two county pack horses to take along, so he wouldn't be tempted to dispose of them. We had dumped all the camp rig into the packs together, so I sorted out the part that was his and piled it on a flat-topped rock close to the trail where he would be sure to see it. Then I lined the pack horses out and struck up the river for the railroad, making a wide circle along the hills so as not to ride through the Indian camp again while he was still in it. I was through with him for a while, I thought, and it was a relief to be through with him—his streaks of wavering and obstinacy; his picking at undercurrents in other people's minds that were none of his business; his making familiar places strange by recalling things about them that nobody else remembered or wanted to remember.

A couple of miles beyond the camp, the trail took out across a long undulating grass prairie that lifted to a chain of scrub-timbered mountains, topped with towering black crags on which, in the old days, there had been bighorn sheep. It was a relief to look at the crags again as plain rock pinnacles against the sky, naked and waterless and lifeless, and not to have their reality colored over by reminiscences about how different they had been once, what the bighorn sheep had been like, what hunting them had been like, and what the people who inhabited the neighborhood then had been like and what had become of them. Looking at the crags as I had been used to looking at them, clean and uncluttered by old associations, was so much of a triumph that they didn't seem a familiar sight at all, but something entirely new, because I was seeing them for the first time with a full appreciation of their meaninglessness.

Rearranging the packs had taken longer than I had counted on. It was late when I raised sight of the railroad from a swell of the prairie, and since it would be dark before I could reach it, I decided to camp somewhere and let it go till morning. Then I decided not to go back to old Hendricks at all. If he liked running things to suit himself, he could run them alone and see how that set with him. He would be disappointed, maybe, but it would be some consolation not to have his grandson hauled off to jail, and a few days of uncertainty on that point might do them both good. A little pious sweating never hurt anybody.

There was a sheep camp down on the river where I could have put up for the night. It belonged to four brothers named MacGillivray, who leased that part of the Indian reservation for their spring pasture. But they could speak only Gaelic, and the one who kept their camp and tended to the cooking was blind. It was always a strain trying to keep cases on their *m'hoimbeachtheain* lingo while he worked with his eyes shut at peeling potatoes, carving meat and lifting hot kettles off the fire, always coming within an ace of cutting or scalding himself, and always managing to come out unscathed without knowing what a close call it had been, or even that it had been any call at all. It was too much like watching a sleep walker on the edge of a cliff. I let them go, and turned in at an abandoned stage station in a thicket of overgrown orchard a mile or so back from the river to camp till morning.

It was a kind of deliverance to spread down beside the old orchard without knowing who had set it out or what his character had been or what sentiments he had squandered his life's enthusiasm on. The moss-cankered old fruit trees were weighed down with dead wood and broken branches, and choked underneath by wild sprouts and vines and deer brush so dense that it looked as if a starved-down snake would have had trouble moving around in it. Yet the mud around the pool where the spring ran out showed tracks of bobcats, porcupines, coyotes, lynx cats, skunks, rabbits, grouse, quail, badger, chipmunks, and two or three deer, all leading back into the thickest part of the tangle. It was consoling to think that nature could take hold of an orchard that had been planted as an outpost against the wilderness, and, with scarcely an effort, turn it into a wilderness itself after all the wilderness around it had disappeared. It was evening up with humanity for some of its triggering with the designs of nature, and there was no reminiscence of humanity mixed into it.

chapter nine

A DRYING wind set in about dark and kept up all night; not hard, but steady, drawing through the naked branches of the old orchard with a monotonous droning rasp like the breathing of a lung-shot animal, broken sometimes by the convulsive flapping of dead leaves drying out and blowing loose from the sinks and swales in which winter had matted them. By morning, when it quieted, all the knolls and ridge-tops had dried to a pale dust color that stood out in stripes and brindles against the darker level of the prairie, and the black adobe mud bordering the pool where the spring ran out from the orchard was bulged and cracked open and tilted askew by the lift of new-sprouted grass seed buried under it by the winter freshets. A full-grown man could hardly have broken up that much drying adobe with a pick in a day's hard work, but a couple of handfuls of grass seed had been able to shiver it into scraps and shards that looked like an old Indian pottery dump, by merely pressing their sprouts against it to reach out to the light.

There was nothing else new. The orchard was dry, its twigs and branches unbudded and as hard and lifeless to look at as so many iron rods. The sky was clear but palish, with the stunned blankness that it always had after a dry wind. The horses were grazing close, picking old grass out of the brush tangle where it had been the least overpastured by sheep. There were no new tracks around the pool when I dipped water from it; no horse tracks at all, though even the drying mud would have registered them if the horses had been to water during the night. They hadn't; the wind and the dry pasture they were on must have made them thirsty, but they weren't used to watering at night, and horses liked regularity. They edged close and watched while I dipped the water bucket, and afterward, when I was finishing breakfast, the lead pack horse moved down to the pool and lowered his head to the water to try it. Instead of drinking, he touched it cautiously with his muzzle, and drew back an inch or two and snorted. I got up to look, and saw that the pool, which had been clean when I dipped from it, was roiled and muddy and flecked with scraps of dead leaves and torn grass roots: not only the pool, but the little waterfall that ran into it, and the whole spring-branch as far back into the orchard undergrowth as I could make it out.

It was possible that the mud might be from a deer moving somewhere back in the orchard; some horses disliked the smell of deer. But a deer would hardly have muddied the stream that much, and the pack horse had not sounded alarmed or distasteful so much as inquiring, as if the roiled water was merely something that needed to be accounted for. He refused to drink it, and kept sniffing it and blowing against it as if manufacturing ripples might help to lift the veil from the mystery. The two other horses watched from a distance, and would not come near enough to try it themselves. They needed to drink before starting out for the day, and since they plainly had no intention of touching the pool while it stayed muddy, I brought them in and saddled up and moved out, heading for the upper end of the orchard where the spring-branch came in. If the roiliness was from some animal moving in the orchard, the water above it would still be clean, and they could drink there, since they were so fastidious about it.

The orchard was laid out on a long fan of bottom land that narrowed into a shallow draw between two sharp ridges, spotted with scrawny sagebrush down the sides and topped with naked reddish clay and shaly gravel in which even the sagebrush had not been able to take hold. A soil too harsh and sterile for sagebrush to grow in didn't hold out much promise for anything else, but on the highest point of the ridge, and all down the naked slope where it faced the sun, there were rock roses in bloom. Some were as big as the palm of a man's hand. There were never any stems or foliage to rock roses, nothing but the flowers, their delicate apple-blossom-pink petals contrasting so startlingly with the coarse conglomerate they had emerged from that they had the look of having been torn loose from their stems and scattered on it by mistake.

In most places in spring, the scrawny and common colored flowers always appear first: gentians, grass flowers, cresses, rustweed, sorrel, all hurrying to make the most of their modest looks before the showier blossoms appear and blaze their lights out. With us, it was the showiest flowers that came earliest: rock roses, foxgloves, black and red bird bills, wild snapdragons, blue flags. At the bottom of the draw, where a cutbank held back the sun, there was a long grayish drift of old snow still unmelted, and the water from it ran down in a lacework of little streams to the creek through a grass swale crowded full of the pale-gold rock lilies that old settlers called lamb tongues: tall, delicate, cool-looking against the coarse watery snow, quivering with even the light stir of air that the horses made in walking past them. They came the earliest of all flowers except rock roses, and they came close to being the sightliest of all. Usually they grew best at the edge of oak timber, where the piled leaves held the winter snow water longest; it was the runoff from the snowbank that had led them to venture so far into open country. They were always the same wherever they grew. Even sheep herders turned their herds sometimes to keep from trampling them; there was one once who went trudging past a bank of them toward the end of a long day's drive, muttering to himself that it beat all hell how those blamed cockwallopers could grow out of the same dirt a man had to wash off of his feet every change of the moon, or worse.

There was a kind of empty feeling about looking at them alone. There was such a thing as seeing them too many times, with only the same things to think about them all over again. Two people looking at them together might have scared up something new to think about them. It would have been something different, at least.

One thing new did come up. I discovered why the spring branch had run muddy. A herd of wild horses had waded it a little above the snowbank. Their tracks were fresh in the wet ground, so fresh that in places the creek still ran roiled from them, and there was a dark swath through the lilies where a colt had walked up to examine the snowbank, and some scattered clods of snow where he had pawed the drift to see what it was. They had not been gone more than a few minutes.

Loose mud was still sliding back into the hoofprints they had left at the edge of the creek, and the wire grass up the slope beyond the lilies was beginning to spring loose from the damp gravel into which they had trampled it in leaving. Counting the colts, there must have been a dozen or fifteen of them in the bunch. There was a stallion with them; that was plain both from the number of colt tracks and from the care they were taking to keep out of sight. Wild mares and colts were inquisitive and moderately trusting when left to themselves. It was always the stallion that drove them into hiding and kept them there when strangers were around. The stallions were always worthless, but there was never more than one with a herd, and he would be easy enough to dispose of.

Counting him out as reducible to coyote bait, a dozen or fourteen mares and young colts would be well worth old Hendricks' time to corral, if he knew where to look for them. For a minute, thinking back on the rock lilies and a man's need of company sometimes, I had the thin end of a notion to head back to Crosskeys and tell him about them. But he was not exactly the kind of company that the case required, so I decided to hold a grudge against him a little longer, and keep on to the railroad as I had started out to do. The wild horses would keep anyway, since there seemed to be nobody after them, and if I could overhaul the Mexican youth and head him back, telling him about them would work out the same as telling old Hendricks, without nearly so much obstinacy and fittiness to put up with in doing it. I shook up the horses and turned back to the main trail again, heading for the railroad.

What I planned was merely to ride up the line, asking about the Mexican youth at the stations and section houses along the way. I had forgotten about the track gang the Indians had spoken of till I plodded down through the brush hills bordering the prairie, having trouble with the horses being stung a dozen or so times apiece by bees working on the new wild cherry blossoms along the trail. Below the wild cherry brush was a long slope of grassland reaching down to where the railroad made a wide curve along the river, and I could see the dingy red cars of the track gang's outfit train standing on a siding, the long line of raw earth that the men had cut through the dead grass along the right-of-way fence as a fireguard, and five or six handcars standing alongside the track where they were working.

It was close to noon, and the cooks at the outfit train were getting dinner ready. The stovepipe in the cook car was fogging coal smoke into the greasewood, and a couple of kitchen helpers came carrying something on a wooden stretcher up from a stone oven below the track. It was lumpy and heavy, and covered over with a sheet so it looked like a dead body, but I knew it wasn't. It was only the day's baking of Greek bread. It was the Greek track gang that had been working up at South Junction. I turned out of the main trail and rode down across the open grassland toward the siding. As long as there were inquiries to make, it was as good a place to start as any.

THE men of the track gang were in from work and at dinner when I got down to the siding. Some had already finished, and were lolling in the sun, arguing among themselves with a high-voiced fury that would have led a casual observer to swear they were on the verge of a stabbing, though it was probably not about anything of the slightest importance. Greek track workers always argued loudest and most passionately over some totally abstract quibble, like the difference between saying that a town was ten miles around and saying it was ten miles square, or why a railroad curve that was banked high on the outside for a train going one way didn't have to be banked equally on the inside for a train going in the opposite direction. They were mostly middle-aged men, heavy-built, grave-featured, and all bareheaded, conforming to the unwritten rule among track snipes that when a man had his hat off he was not working; when he had it on, he was on company time, no matter how little he might look it. They were not talkative with strangers, but one of them did loosen up enough to say that the foreman was still at dinner, and to point out the dining car. He offered to watch the horses, so I turned them loose in the grass below the track and went down the line of ramshackle old bunk cars, sun-faded and smoke-stained and gaping at the seams, and as cheerless as the gray-black greasewood slope behind them, to see what I could find out.

Dinner was almost over. The men were crowding out of the dining car in threes and fours, so I stood back to wait till the rush let up before going in. The cook, a dark fattish man in his middle thirties, edged into the doorway back of them and held up a plate and cup, beckoning at me with them like a child trying to entice a stray cat. Greek railroad crews were always reserved with strangers—the men passed without letting on to notice me—but they never allowed anybody, no matter of what race, creed, color or condition, to get past one of their outfit trains without being hauled in and fed, unless he was moving too fast for them to catch. There seemed no particular benevolence about it, merely a vague but profound feeling that human beings ought to eat, and that anybody who could be induced to do it must have a certain amount of humanity still washing around in him somewhere, no matter how mean and wild he might look.

When the men thinned out a little, I shouldered past them into the car. It was merely a worn-out boxcar with badly fitting doors and windows let into it, and a plank table running its full length where the men ate. There was a plank bench on each side of the table for them to sit on. The planks were worn smooth with use, and as hard as iron, so a meal was usually a sort of endurance contest to decide whether a man's appetite or his hind end could hold out the longest. The cook led the way to the end of the table, cleared a place for the plate and cup he had brandished at me, and went to bring back some of the dishes that had been taken out to the kitchen. The foreman was finishing his dinner across from me: a dark, close-featured man of about forty, smaller than most track-gang men, and more thoughtful-looking and self-contained. I hadn't expected that he would turn out to be anybody I knew, since all the other men were strange to me, but I knew him. I had put in three or four days once, back when I worked for the railroad, showing him about filling out report forms under some new union pay schedule. There had been mutterings from some of his men about his brusqueness and haughtiness with them, and a few guarded hints about some irregularity in his record on one of the Coast lines, but that had blown over, and since he attended to his work and ran his oufit with a low labor turnover and no accidents, nobody ever bothered to find out whether the Coast lines had liked him or not. He nodded as I sat down, nodded again when I explained about having some things to ask him, and pushed back his plate and got up. It was not manners to let a visitor start talking until he had eaten, whether he felt like eating or not.

"Sure, we'll talk," he said. "Eat your dinner first. Then we'll talk to beat hell. I don't know nothing, but we can talk. No hurry about it. I'll be outside. Eat your dinner."

He went outside, and the cook brought what there was: browned goulash, with turnips, carrots, onions, peas, greens, and all the assorted garden truck that Greek dinners always abounded in. As usual, there was no butter, the goulash had too much garlic in it, and the bread was delicious. It is curious that anything so inanimate as bread should be sensitive to its surroundings, but nobody who hasn't eaten bread baked in a stone oven can have any idea how good bread can be. The men had all finished eating by the time the cook got all his refections set out for me, and he and his kitchen helpers started clearing the tables, bantering among themselves in Greek as they clattered stacks of plates and sheaves of knives and forks and spoons. They appeared to have ganged up to tease one of the helpers, a tall young man with pale eyes and a large fluffy mustache, and some of their rallying didn't seem to set too well with him. Finally, when thc cook got off some sally that made the two other helpers almost die laughing, he flung his dish cloth at them, dumped a heap of knives and forks on the floor with an indignant crash, and tramped out to the kitchen, banging the table with his fist as he went, and refusing to answer when they called him to come on back. The cook went out after him, but came back alone, bringing a wedge of apple pie for dessert.

"We was make a leetle jokin' with that fellow," he explained, setting it in front of me. "All the boys, they makin' fun at that fellow now. He's go back to Greece to get married and live. So they make fun at him about it, so he's get mad. They make fun at him too much, maybe, but he's got it comin'. Makin' to get married to a woman back in Greece when he ain't never seen her. Goin' back to the old country to live on a farm she's got, and he come off from a farm in the old country to come here. Hah! You can't blame the boys to make fun, huh?"

I said it was hard to decide without knowing a little more about it. He took a look at the tables to see how much cleaning up was left to do, and hauled out the bench and sat down, bunching his apron under him for a cushion, to explain about European ways and traditions. It seemed that there was an acute shortage of marriageable men in Greece since Mustapha Kemal's army had done so much heavy weeding out on them in the Smyrna campaign. There were not enough men of any description to go around, but the ones most in demand for matrimony were those who had taken out United States naturalization papers. American citizenship graded a man higher in Greece than it did in America. It guaranteed him the privilege of settling down to live as he pleased without being subject to conscription for Greek military service. So all the marriageable girls in the country were out hunting red-eyed for any man who had it, and since the fluffy-mustached kitchen helper had got his final papers recently, his aged parents were being swarmed on by steaming young women angling to lure him back where they could get their hands on him.

Some of the young women submitted lists of their property, as an extra inducement, and the helper's parents had landed one bid from a brisk young widow of the neighborhood that had been too imposing for him to hold out against. She owned a farm, to begin with, with a whole nine acres in it, or maybe even nine and a half. Then there were several dozen olive trees on it, all in full bearing; and some grapevines; and a house with three rooms in it, one with a window; and sheds and outbuildings enough to patch hell eleven feet; in addition to two dozen sheep, several high-class goats, three cows and an eighth interest in a bull; three full-grown jackasses and another on the way; and imposing inventories of chickens, ducks, geese, pigs, and seven or eight stands of bees. The helper's parents had been completely swept off their feet by such a glittering lineup of assets, and the helper, whether impressed by it or sick of wrangling dishes, had written them that it was a deal. So he had signed some documents about it at the Greek consulate, and as soon as he had money enough for his passage he was going back to some half-civilized hill town back of Corinth to contract matrimony with a nine-acre farm, a house with one window, an assorted list of livestock, and a woman. She seemed to bear about the same relation to the transaction as the article of glass jewelry that came as a premium in a box of Cracker Jack, except that she couldn't be thrown away. That was what the men were poking fun at the helper for. He was touchy about it because he knew he deserved it. Most of them had got bids of the same kind, some better; all who had their citizenship papers, at least. They had turned them all down without even thinking about it, so they had a right to poke a little fun at him. Maybe they rubbed it in too hard, considering how touchy he was, but a man couldn't blame them much. He knew they were right; that was why he flew off the handle so easy. The cook bunched his apron under him again, and looked at the scarred wooden table, the dingy old walls covered with wrinkled paint and flyspecks, and the lifeless black greasewood on the slope outside.

"He's work in thees country nine years now," he said. "Yes, sir. I remember. He was come off the boat in New York nine years, he was work on a fruit cart in New York when he don't know no English except three-for-five-cents. Now he's got a job, he's in a union, he's a citizen, and what does he do? Throw it all away. For pigs and bees and jackasses, and in the old country where it ain't even civilized. You can't blame the boys, huh?"

"I don't know," I said. It needed a little getting used to. If there was anything in the men's way of looking at it, all the old schoolbook teachings about the joys of modest contentment were shot to wadding, and shining examples like the Village Blacksmith and the Miller of the Dee were left without a leg to stand on. Pigs and bees and jackasses had limitations, but they were something a man could depend on, and they had as much horizon as dishwashing in a track-gang cook car. It was true that the widow might not be any steal, but nobody could be sure of that, and there ought to be room on nine acres to dodge her if she was too monstrous. But there was more to it than that. The men on the track gang might not know much about schoolbook moralizing, but they knew well enough what kind of a prospect the helper was in for; what he would gain by going back, and what he would lose. If they thought he was making himself ridiculous, it was not for an outsider to gainsay them on the strength of the Miller of the Dee and the Village Blacksmith. They knew both sides of the case from firsthand knowledge, and they were not all stupid. The thing needed thinking out; there was no time for it, which was probably as well. I pushed back from the table, and said it was hard to decide who was right.

"I'd have to see the widow first," I said. "Maybe there's something wrong with her, if she has to bid that high to get married."

"Them Corinthias girls good-lookin' like hell sometimes," the cook said. "What difference? He's go back to farm in the old country for a woman, huh! In thees country, a man pays a woman money for overnight, and what is she? A bitch, huh? No good. In the old country, a woman pays a man cows, ducks, sheeps, and it's for all the rest of his life, and what does that make him? You theenk these boys go back for that? No, sir! You bet not! No more pie?"

I said I guessed not, and went out. The foreman was sitting on the steps of the office car, studying his watch every few minutes. The men were scattered out along the line of bunk cars, killing time while they waited for the signal to start back to work. Half a dozen of them were rolling *barbootie* dice on a push car for nickels; one was making a flute out of a hollowed-out length of elder, with three others watching and offering advice; a dozen or fifteen were grouped around the steps of a bunk car listening to a sharp-featured young man reading aloud from some Greek novel; four or five sat on one of the handcars arguing over the sporting section of an out-of-date newspaper. Two men were spaced off by themselves. One was a pulpy-faced young sprig in store clothes who sat on the end of a main-line tie, pensively knocking two rocks together. The other, a lank middle-aged man in patched overalls, sat in the grass against a fence post, twisting a tobacco plug absently between his fingers. They didn't look in the least alike, but they both looked out of place in a Greek track gang. Part of it was that Greek track snipes didn't wear store clothes or chew plug tobacco, but there was something else, an uneasiness about both of them that the other men showed no trace of: uncertainty, self-distrust, self-consciousness maybe.

What it was was hard to pin down, and probably not worth it. I let it go, and told the foreman what I had come for, about the young Mexican and what he looked like, that he was from some sheep-shearing crew, ignorant of English, easily scared, and supposed to be hiding out somewhere on the line to catch a freight out of the country. The foreman didn't take it quite as I meant it. I should have remembered that, though he could follow English well enough in short installments, too much of it all at one load was apt to mix him up. He took it that I was accusing him of concealing the Mexican youth somewhere around the train, and he slung sweat all over the place denying it.

"No Mex kids workin' on this gang, no, sir!" he said. "None been around this gang for months, weeks, a hell of a long time. We ain't seen none; I wouldn't hire none on this gang no more. You can look if you want to, but you won't find nothing. No Mex here any more; nobody but Greeks here."

Any more, he had said. It opened some unanticipated possibilities. "Do you mean you've had men on the gang that weren't Greeks? I thought the company employment office didn't send anybody but Greeks up here?"

"Most times, sure," he said. He appeared relieved at the shift of subject. "Sometimes that company employment office don't know. That fellow all by himself yonder, with the good clothes on—they sent him. He ain't Greek. He's a Cilician. How could anybody in that railroad office tell the difference? Most times they can tell. Sometimes they can't. These poor fellows get shipped up here, and they're broke and no place to go, and they want to work. We let 'em work. What the hell?"

It seemed fair enough. A railroad employment office couldn't be expected to know what a Cilician was; neither did I, as far as that went. "That long-coupled Johnny Appleseed playing with that plug of tobacco over by the fence don't look like any Greek, either," I said. "They didn't send him up here for any Cilician, did they?"

The lank man in the patched overalls was still trying to work a chew loose from his plug, though without putting much heart into it. Any of the men would have lent him a knife to cut it, if he had asked. "I don't know what that poor fellow is," the foreman said. "They come along the track sometimes, and they're broke and hungry. We give 'em their dinner, and if they want to work and make a few dollars, all right. There's work here for 'em. I don't try to figure out what they are."

He pronounced "figure" with an *n*, so it sounded like "finger." Curiosity stirred in me; not strong, but working in several different directions. I wondered whether the mispronunciation would affect his spelling of a name foreign to him, and why he had denied so emphatically to begin with that there were any non-Greeks on his outfit, and what nationality the Johnny Appleseed character by the fence actually was. It was all aimless; I didn't expect to find out anything. "Let's look at your payroll a minute. I want to see what kind of a name you've got down for him."

He brought the payroll, not with any great eagerness. "Maybe it ain't spelled right, I don't know," he said. "I ask 'em and they tell me, and I put 'em down the way they sound. You know how that is. A man can't get everything right. Sometimes they don't know how to spell their names themselves. That fellow's down at the bottom—number sixty-two. That's him."

There it was, laborer number sixty-two: Alozo Jekous. It took me a minute to get used to it. Then it began to clear up. The first name merely had an *n* dropped out; it was intended for Alonzo. The surname came harder; it didn't seem possible to misspell anything into Jekous. It took several stabs before I got it cornered, partly because it was so simple. It was Jenkins. There were no other names on the roll that looked misspelled from anything familiar. The notion struck me to hunt back a little and see if there had been any. "Let's see the payroll before this one," I said. Railroad payrolls were closed and sent in every two weeks. "There's a name on it I want to find out about."

For a minute, it looked as if he was going to balk on that. "It's the same as this one. It's got the same names, and they're spelled the same, and everything's the same. The only difference is the hours they've worked. You don't care nothing about that. I ain't supposed to let anybody see that payroll when I ain't here, and it's time to go to work. We ought to start now."

"You can take a couple of minutes," I said. "That's all I'll need. You can start your men for the handcars now, if you want to. I'll be finished with the payroll by the time they're loaded on. One name's all I want to look up."

He brought out his file copy, and stood holding it. "If it's the young fellow that had the trouble over that woman up at South Junction, you won't find out nothing from this," he said. "There ain't anything on it but his name and work number. Everybody's looked at that a hundred times already. Maybe I didn't spell his name right, I don't know. He didn't draw his time when he left, so it ain't signed anywhere."

I took the carbon sheets and ran back over the names—Pappas, Gatsis, Xanthous, Fasilis, Procopious. There it was: laborer number fifty-eight, Steve Addareous, with the space for hours worked ending in a row of *x's* where he had quit. The first name didn't look as if there was anything much wrong with it. There weren't many names that could be misspelled into anything resembling Steve, and it was a common name among the Greeks anyway. Addareous looked more promising. The foreman's habit of omitting *n* before a consonant might have had some effect on that. It might be Andrews. But then, if he could make Jekous out of a name like Jenkins, it might be something like Andrins. There was no such name. "This young fellow that had the trouble up at South Junction," I said. "Was he Greek?"

Sometimes a man could be inveigled into volunteering information that couldn't possibly have been smoked out of him by direct questioning, but the foreman was cautious. "I don't know what that poor young fellow was," he said. He made it sound as if neglecting to find out was one of his bitterest regrets. "Some kind of Greek, maybe. Maybe not. I don't know. They come here, they're broke, they're hungry, they got no place to go, we give 'em their dinner and put 'em to work; what difference does it make what they are? I got no time to find out about all of 'em. You know how it is on an outfit like this, reports to make out and train crews hollerin' about bad track and all that stuff. Sometimes I find out about 'em from the boys, but this young fellow didn't talk much. He didn't bother anybody. He was a good worker. Then he had that trouble, and he left, and that's all I know. He got a dirty deal with that woman up at South Junction, I know that. That shootin' wasn't his fault. It was hers. If they don't catch that poor young fellow, it'll be all right with me."

I looked at the name on the payroll again. Steve Addareous. It matched up somehow with some name I had seen before: on some other railroad form, when there had been other things to think about. Trying to clear it up did no good; there were still other things to think about. "If you know that much about the South Junction shooting, why didn't you say so when the sheriff was up here investigating it?" I asked. "When you've got evidence in a case like that, you're supposed to speak up about it. Nobody wants to cinch a man for a shooting he didn't have anything to do with. . . ." Out of nowhere, and for no reason, it struck me that the Spanish for Steve was Estéban. "That kid couldn't have been Mexican, could he?"

The foreman looked at his watch. It was past one, and the men were grouped around the handcars, waiting for his signal to pile on. He put the watch away without appearing to notice them. "I don't know what that kid was," he said patiently. "Mex, maybe. Maybe not. Some of the boys might know. I didn't tell nothing to the sheriff when he was up here because I didn't know nothing to tell. When you tell a sheriff anything, you've got to swear to it in a court. I can't swear to nothing. I can't go into no court, anyway. Them lawyers, they ask things about you that ain't any of their business, they look up your record and ask about it, they wave their arms and holler about these Greek foreigners testifyin' against people that belong here. I don't get into anything like that, no, sir! I ain't got any evidence, and I didn't say that young fellow didn't have anything to do with the shootin'. I said it wasn't his fault. It wasn't, either. I seen that woman with him. I seen how she worked on him. You can't tell that in a court for evidence, but when a man sees things like that, he knows something's goin' on. A man's got sense."

"Could he talk any English?" I said. It was mere curiosity; the shooting wasn't any responsibility of mine. The foreman once more cloaked his evasiveness under a show of regret, said he didn't know, and got up.

"He didn't talk it to me," he said, and held out his hand for the payroll. The men began crowding onto the handcars, ready to start. "He didn't talk much to anybody. Maybe to the boys, I don't know. He didn't draw his time when he quit. His pay check's up at the South Junction station now, I guess. He might need it if they catch him, poor fellow. I hope they don't. You'll be around here for a while?"

The name kept gouging at me: Steve, Estéban. "A day or two, maybe. I've got this young sheep shearer to hunt for, and

I want to post the train crews to look out for him. I'll . . ." Addareous, Andreas. That was it: Estéban d'Andreas. It had been on a railroad form, written in pencil; an identity slip. It had been . . . Great Christ in the wilderness! Could it have been the one old Hendricks had shown me? It didn't seem possible. What else could be? I gave the payroll back, wondering if my hand was as shaky as it felt. "Maybe I won't, either. I've got to get over to Crosskeys right away. I may not get back."

The foreman tossed the payroll into the car, and raised his hand to the men. One of the handcars backed up to take him aboard. "There's a water tank a couple of miles up where the trains stop. They draw their fireboxes on the side track. We got to keep the cinders shoveled off so they don't burn the ties. The boys could run you up there, if you want to look around. That sheep shearer might be layin' out up there to catch a train."

"I've changed my mind about him," I said. "I don't want him. If he can catch a train out of here, he's welcome to it. I hope he does. I've got to get over to town."

THE trail out of the Indian reservation to Crosskeys followed a little creek that ran through a steep-banked gully too deep to see out of in any direction except up. The banks were of earth, and the blackbirds had dug them completely full of little caves to nest in, like the tiers of mail boxes in a country post office. The willow buds were not open, but there were wild flags in the places where the sun reached, and yellow and black snapdragons where the water ran still enough for them to take hold. There was not the elation about finding them that there had been in past years; they marked off different stages of meditation, that was all. In places, the blackbirds were so absorbed in their nest building that I could have caught some of them by merely holding up one hand and grabbing it shut as they flew past. Finding out the truth about the Mexican youngster carried no sense of elation with it, either; only a sort of limp guiltiness for not having figured it out to begin with, before I knew him so well; and an uneasiness over how old Hendricks would take it.

It seemed a pity to dump such a load of bad news on old Hendricks all at one clatter, but there seemed nothing else for it. Such things couldn't be parceled out in easy installments. Trying to change or temper them down was apt to make them sound fictitious, and to put too much of the blame in the wrong place. Estéban had not been altogether to blame for the Farrand shooting, according to the Greek foreman's account of it. Holding back the woman's part in it would amount to saddling him with the whole thing. It might bear lighter on old Hendricks, since she was his daughter, but it would be unjust to Estéban, and it would be hard for anybody to believe who knew as much about him as old Hendricks did. I wouldn't believe it myself, from what I knew of him. No. It had to be the whole story, no matter how old Hendricks took it. It would be no worse in the long run than to let him string himself along with illusions and false expectations. A man had to take the country as it came. Nobody had compelled him to come back to it.

The creek gully shallowed and widened. Where it turned too heavy and gravelly for the blackbirds to dig their nesting caves in, the wild flags were coming into bloom, cream-white and long-stemmed and heavy-headed, everywhere that the ground lifted a foot or two above water level. In a few places, the bank had been broken down by horses coming down to water—

mares and colts, by the tracks. They were unshod, and there was no sign that anybody had been herding them. A few hours earlier, they would have been something worth noting down to tell old Hendricks about. With Estéban gone, bringing up any such subject would only look like taunting him. He couldn't handle a wild-horse camp all by himself.

One curious thing was that finding out the truth about Estéban made what I had already known about him seem not incongruous or contradictory at all, but completely clear and logical for the first time. If the Greek foreman had come anywhere near the truth, the Farrand woman had inveigled him into tending to a rat-killing job for her, and then had thrown it all on him and set half the country hunting for him on a charge of first-degree murder, among other things less capital but more aggravating. It was enough to make him timid and distrustful and self-effacing. The wonder was that he had held up as well as he had. I hoped they wouldn't catch him. For some reason, probably explainable if it had been worth the trouble, I didn't much want to see him again.

The creek turned back into the hills, and leveled off into a shallow runlet full of little waterfalls. The water was so cold the horses refused to drink it, but wild snapdragons crowded every shallow of it, flowering in spite of the cold. They had the place all to themselves; there were no birds, no horse trails, no sign of any other living thing. The masses of yellow and black blossoms jostling with the rush of water might have been all the life such a windstruck rock bench could stand all at one time, but there was nothing new about them. They came out exactly the same every spring, in the same places, and it was not a day for pausing to gape at wild flowers anyway. The Mexican youth's underhandedness had made it into a day for revising estimates. If his show of blank innocence had taken us in so easily, there was not much depending on the truth about anything. One after another, other things came to mind, fell apart, and recrystallized into something different because he had played simple on us and made it work. There was old Hendricks' plan for setting up a horse camp in the hills. It had looked moderately reasonable along in the forenoon; a little imaginative, maybe, but worth taking a stab at. Now it showed up as nothing but an old man's vaporishness; there wouldn't be wild horses enough to run a horse camp, and if they were worth catching there would be other people after them, and he was too old for such work. Old men had a weakness for overestimating what they could do, and for arguing for it so plausibly that it was not always easy to make the proper allowances and deductions.

There were the Greeks on the track gang. Most people imagined that their pulling ties and hacking fireguards for the railroad was some kind of escape from a harder and more poverty-stricken life in their own country, and it appeared that with a lot of them it was no such simple thing. They could have lived more easily back in Greece than where they were, and they had turned away from it deliberately, merely because it was easier, seemingly. For them, a life that offered a man enough to eat, a place to live, freedom from anxiety, and remoteness from the world's troubles, missed the whole point of human existence; and anybody who could prefer it to a round of surfacing railroad track in a blank corner of a measly Indian reservation was not so much misguided as comical and ridiculous. Railroading had its drawbacks, but there was something more to it than merely staying alive, and they were men with whom the extras counted sometimes more than the essentials. The country brought out such quirks in people—sentimentality, showiness, idealism. Old Hendricks selling off his best horses for money to squander on a worthless grandson; Clallum Jake carrying his offering of salmon and beadwork to the Kirkbrides every year in gratitude for a wife he hadn't seen hide or hair of in over twenty years—they were men as different in most things as human beings could be; but in rising triumphant over self-interest and common sense, they were all of a piece.

The trail turned off through the hills and struck down through a long sweep of grassland and rockbreak toward the county road. The sun was low, and the flat angle of light across the flat made it reflect the sky and the clumps of scrub juniper on the horizon like a lake. Revising estimates was not as easy as it had been along the creek. There were no birds or plants or signs of life to lighten the monotony. Featureless country left a man only his reflections to work on, and some of them were seated close to a nerve. We had been simple-minded to fall for the Mexican youth's pretense of clinging helplessness, but he had been worse. He couldn't be blamed for keeping the Farrand killing to himself, considering all the circumstances; but to conceal it under a show of limp dependency was carrying it farther than he needed to. A man who could act blank and innocent with a thing like that on his conscience was not to be trusted in anything. It was two-faced, conniving, contemptuous, insulting, treacherous. The Farrand woman was even worse than he was; not by much, maybe, but inveigling him into shooting her husband and then trying to get him hung for it was piling one treachery on top of another, and that was worse. It was painful to think that Calanthe at South Junction would be exposed to her on one side and Busick on the other, with no chance of getting clear of either of them. There was no way to head it off that I could think of. Old Hendricks might think of one. An old man's ideas were apt to be wild and vaporish, but there were times when they beat hell out of no ideas at all.

By rights, there shouldn't have been any estimate of Calanthe to revise, with so little knowledge of her to go on, but a streak of revising is hard to hold, once it clamps its tail down. One disillusionment can start a man raking back through things in his mind that may not need overhauling at all, like a fussy housewife scalding the entire pantry on the strength of one ant in the cooky jar. If there had been any scenery to look at, Calanthe might have been spared it, but there was nothing, so into the mill she went. She was pretty part of the time, and straightforward some of it. She had a habit of making everything she said mean two or three different things, but she was not underhanded in it. It was more a sort of eagerness, a straining to make every string draw because there wasn't time to pick them separately. Nobody else had that. There was no telling how deep it went or how long it would last. Seeing her twice was not enough to hand down any final judgment on. Both times she had been strained, hurried, anxious, not at all as she might appear to anybody who had known her a long time. Strain and uneasiness didn't last forever. When they wore off in her, she would be different—less tense and headlong, lighter in mind, happier, maybe more likeable, maybe more ordinary. Or maybe completely ordinary; not worth picking up in the road. She was not likely to run short of trouble at South Junction, that was one thing. Old Hendricks might figure out some way to get her clear of that. She had listened to him once.

The sun went down. What had looked like a lake with

junipers reflected in it turned into a pale mist and then faded to naked prairie. The horses stepped up more briskly, partly because of the chilliness in the air and partly because the town coming into sight across the wheat fields gave them something to head for. It stood on a rise, with no sky back of it; the timbered mountains to the west shut the sky off like a backdrop, but the concrete grain elevator and the leafless shade trees stood out sharper against the blackish haze of mountains than they could have done against forty skylines all rolled into one and welded. Lights were coming on—street lights, signs, store windows, the headlight of a train switching back and forth between the grain elevator and the stockyard loading chute, whether making up to pull out or setting out cars to unload it was impossible to tell. I lost sight of it for a minute, watching a little screech owl sitting a few yards from the road on a boulder labeled "Jesus Saves" in white block letters. The owl studied the horses without moving, and turned its head almost completely around to keep tab on them as they passed. A screech owl never turned its body to watch things circling it, only its head. Idle-minded old men used to tell little boys that they could make a screech owl wring its own neck by walking around it three times, but there was some catch about it. It never worked.

The shadows had spread down over the town when I looked back at it, and nothing was visible except the lights. Small flickers of light were even scattered out far beyond town, outside the yard-limit lights and in the willow flat back of the water tank, gleaming weakly like crumbled fox fire. That settled the question about the train. It had pulled in and was setting out cars to unload. A swarm of crop hoboes had come in on it to work in the back-country lambing camps. They always dropped off at the water tank outside of town, to dodge the company detective in the yards. The flickers of light were fires where they had scattered out to camp for the night. It was an odd thing that, though the crop hoboes never had any money, business in towns like Crosskeys always livened up when they began to drift in. Towns like Crosskeys could stand a little livening up, usually.

Some men were hunkered around one of their campfires back of an old billboard, a little off the road. One of them stood up and called something, probably wanting to know if lambing had started in the back country yet, or something of the kind. The horses moved on hurriedly, not wanting to stand out in the cold for a roadside conversation, and I let them. Crosskeys had been home once. I had ridden into it against the lights in the dusk more times than were worth counting up, though never before without wishing that some sleight-of-hand operation could turn it into something different for a change—Constantinople or Alexandria, maybe, or Winnemucca or Silver Lake or Hardscrabble. Scappoose would have done. Old Hendricks made it more worth coming back to, seemingly.

chapter ten

THERE was no zone of truck gardens and tin-can dumps and shanties separating the wheat fields from the town, as there generally was in such places. Where the wheat stopped, the town started. The oldest part came first—three or four unlighted blocks of weedy old picket fences and broken hitching racks, and teetery board sidewalks buried in tangled sweetbrier and littered with broken branches from the half-dead old trees masking a huddle of lank-fronted houses, paintless and broken-windowed, which were used sometimes by little boys as cover from which to bushwhack stray quail and sage rats when the wheat was ripening, and by youths and maidens for heavy smooching parties in warm weather. All the houses were falling to pieces—floors rotted, beams tilted and sagging, walls gaping black where boards had fallen off, and dangling patches of grayish lichens like scraps of dry hide on a horse carcass where they still hung on. Age added no dignity to buildings in that country, and not even any pathos. The pathos was in thinking that human beings had once had to live in them.

Under the street lights, beyond a vacant half-block piled with wrecked automobiles and rusty farm machinery, the shade trees were smaller and better kept, and there was a row of outdated wooden store buildings, false-fronted and dirty-windowed, housing an assortment of small enterprises that had crept in after the stores had moved down nearer the railroad. There was a hay, grain and poultry-feed store; a plumbing and tinsmithing shop; a Chinese laundry with a tong headquarters flanking it; a fortune-teller's studio; a meeting hall for labor union locals; a junk shop with a back-door trade in hides from illegally-killed cattle; and Stiffneck Hulse's run-down old poolroom, badly lighted and empty except for old Hulse asleep over his flyspecked cigar showcase in the front and half a dozen sheepmen huddled over a no-limit poker game in the back. The respectable businessmen of the town held their card sessions in a high-toned poolroom downtown, usually for stakes of twenty-five cents a corner, amid arguing and loud imputations that sometimes bred lifelong enmities. Old Hulse's establishment wouldn't have inventoried much over fifty dollars for everything in it, including stock, fixtures, lease, good will, and old Hulse's own wardrobe and prospects of eternal salvation. The sheepmen ran their game in the back without raising their voices or even moving, except to deal and rake in. There were times when sheep were around twenty dollars, and things were so prosperous that they had six thousand head of ewes with coarse lambs riding on one showdown. Easy come, easy go. A man who had it always had brains enough to get it back.

If things tightened up so he couldn't, he could always blame the government.

The town hookshop was around the corner from old Hulse's poolroom. It was no different from the other buildings except that the windows were heavily-curtained, with the entrance on the alley, screened from the street light by a tall box hedge. There was nothing special about it. Wheat-town straddling houses were all of the same pattern, like their customers. The woman who ran the place was rawboned and imperious, with a voice like a guinea fowl and a set of looks so hatchet-proof and forbidding that a man couldn't help wondering how she had ever disposed of the admirers she must have scared to death when she was taking an active hand at her calling. She could lie like a tombstone, which was a count in her favor sometimes; as when she brought my father home when he was dying from his stroke, and insisted up and down that he hadn't been in her place at all; that a couple of the girls had merely noticed him slumped down on the sidewalk outside, and she had feathered out to see if there was anything she could do; that was all. She couldn't let a man die in the street under her front window without trying to do something, no matter how respectable he was. She had already sent somebody for the doctor, but she helped to get him undressed and into bed, and only left when he showed signs of coming to, explaining that there would be enough for him to worry about without trying to figure out what she was hanging around for. He had been in her house, for all her denying it, or his seeing her wouldn't have made any difference. He had been desperate for company for a long time, probably, and age made him less particular what kind it was. Anything was better than nothing.

It had been a hankering for company more than anything else. He couldn't have afforded much of anything else by then.

With some people, loneliness binds harder the longer it holds on, like being tied down with strips of green rawhide in a drying wind. He held on after his stroke for six days, and they were all hard. Dying would have been hard enough by itself, but to die unnoticed and neglected in a place like Crosskeys gave the bitterness fourteen rattles and a button. There were times when his spasms of pain seemed actually welcome, because they dulled him from realizing what the place was and what he was in it. He had set store by people's notice as he got older and less able to gain it. His best chance for it had been spoiled years ago, back in the land-rush days, during a flurry of excitement over a supposed oil-well prospect in the slough below town. The merchants were circulating a subscription list for funds to incorporate and start selling drilling rights, and he had knocked it all in the head by discovering that what they had taken for a natural gas blowoff was nothing but a leak in the schoolhouse sewer. He did it to be helpful, probably, but it made them look foolish, and they never forgave him for it, though there wasn't much that they could do to him at the time. He was government land commissioner for the district, and his fees from land entries kept him independent of them while the homesteading stampede lasted. Afterward, it was harder for him. He was getting too old to move or change his calling, there was not much government land left to commission, and people's coolness began to count. Most of them had forgotten by then what they had to be cool to him about, but they kept it up out of habit. The worst of it was that he had not shown up their oil-well flurry to make them look ridiculous at all. He had wanted to be one of them, and took the wrong way of going about it. Worse men acquired standing among them without doing anything to deserve it, and without caring anything about it. He might have made out better if it had counted less with him. The intensity of his hankering made people uncomfortable around him when he got too old to hold it down.

They were right about one thing. What he had wanted was not worth all that hankering after. It was pitiful to think that he had spent so much of his life honing for something that amounted to so little. He should have known better, though it was some excuse that he didn't let it show much till he was old. Calanthe was young, and she was spending her life working and honing for the same thing. A place in town, standing, permanence, neighbors, a fence to string flowers on—that was the same lineup that he had wanted, and it was as far as her imagination reached. One life squandered on such an empty ambition was enough. Two would be a lot too many. There were other things more worth doing: some, maybe, anyway, if a man looked around for them. Opportunity beckoned in odd spots sometimes. Yes; like young Elzey Phipps inventing a rig to lift creek water to irrigate his family's alfalfa patch, which worked so well that he went to jail for diverting the flow of a mapped stream without a conservation permit. And there was some elderly sheep herder who claimed to have conquered the loneliness of desert herding by teaching a flock of magpies to talk, and carrying on long and improving conversations with them. He had to wring their necks finally for siding against him in a political discussion, he said, but it had at least taught him never to argue about politics with magpies, feathered or human; which was something gained, and there really were things a man could do. If old Hendricks could find one, nobody need give up.

The three horses turned off down a dark side street, with an open field on one side and the back entrances of store buildings on the other. The glare of lights from the main street made a quivering luminousness in the sky over the dark outlines of the buildings, and striped the road white wherever there was an opening between them. There was no other light for the horses to steer by. The feed yard was near the railroad track, between the freight house and the grain elevator. They had never been there, and its lights were blocked out by a long wool warehouse back of it, but they reached out for it almost at a trot, and turned down along the railroad track toward it as if reins and lead ropes were hung on them solely for trimming. The wind carried the smell of the other horses to them, probably. A switch engine was juggling cars back and forth on the siding, making too much noise for them to be heard if they had whinnied, but they raised a long trot when the gate came in sight. It was bad for pack horses to trot with loads on, but I didn't try to hold them in. Their eagerness meant that they had winded horses they recognized, and it could hardly be anything but old Hendricks' horse herd. It was a relief to know that he was still in town. It hadn't struck me at all before, but it seemed as if I had been afraid for a long time that he might have decided to strike off into the hills all by himself, maybe thinking everybody had abandoned him.

THERE was nobody in the feed-yard office except the night hostler, still reasonably sober though a little bleary and out of humor because the proprietor had gone out for an evening with the ladies, leaving all the work on his hands. He helped with the unsaddling, pointed out a hay shed at the far corner of the yard where old Hendricks spread down at night, and let the horses through into the feed corral, muttering to himself because it had to be kept locked against the hoboes who were in town for the lambing season. It was curious how casual the horses acted in joining the herd around the feed rack under the light. After all their crowding to get there, they shuffled listlessly past a dozen or fifteen of the herd horses, drove half a dozen others away from one end of the feed rack by kicking and snapping at them, and began picking up loose straw scattered on the ground from an earlier feeding as if it was some treasure the herd horses had been too coarse fibered to appreciate. They didn't even look up when I passed them on the way to the hay shed. Horses and women. Leave either of them alone with only a man to depend on for company, and they could develop an intelligence so quick and sensitive that it was uncanny to be around. Herd them back with others of their species, and they dropped instantly to a depth of dull pettiness and mental squalor that made a man wonder how he could ever have credited them with intelligence at all, or with anything nearer to it than an anxiety to outdo one another in low vanity and meanness. Calanthe would be the same among other women. She was no freer from their weaknesses than any of them. A man didn't have to spill a whole wagonload of marbles to find out which way a floor slanted.

The door to the hay shed was fastened with a twist of baling wire, and sprung partly ajar by horses trying to reach the hay through it. I edged inside without unfastening it or making any noise, and stood listening in the dark. Sounds carry better in the air when there is no light. The wind rattled a loose board. A mouse scuttled lightly along a beam overhead. A horse in a box stall through the wall stopped eating, stood listening for a minute, and lay down with a thump and a comfortable groan. Some straws cracked as the night damp expanded the hay bales. From somewhere back among them, old Hendricks started talking to himself. By the sound, he was taking up something the horses' movements had interrupted him in.

". . . It's a nice town, yes, sir, a nice town you've got. Kind of built up since I was through here last, but you can't hold back progress—not around here, anyway. Nope, I ain't from around here; got some horses over at the feed yard that we're shirt tailin' through to open pasture, that's all. One of my herders got stove up a little down the river, and we had to bring him in for some doctorin', and we fetched the horses along to try out the market, and one thing and another. There's always business that needs tendin' to, and these blamed herders nowadays is more trouble to look out for than the horses, by God! I'll swear, if it ain't one thing with 'em, it's a half a dozen! Well, they're young, and they've got to learn some way, I guess. The Lord only knows where they'd end up if I wasn't around to keep tab on 'em, but they've got it to go through. We was all young once. Yep."

He stopped. The loose board flapped twice, like a chairman rapping for order at a meeting. The horse in the box stall shifted heavily, and grunted. He began again, keeping his voice a little lower.

"They believed all that, didn't they, from the kind of a lookin' specimen you are? Yes, like hell! Do you think they didn't have sense enough to size you up when you was doin' all that windyin' at 'em? They're too simple for that, ain't they? They ain't got any better sense than to believe anything you tell 'em, have they? No, they wait around for people like you to come along and explain things to 'em, so they'll know what to think. They wouldn't know straight up from six bits unless somebody like you laid it all out for 'em, would they? What do you think they're sayin' about you now? If you'd told a little of the truth about yourself, they might have believed it about your herder gittin' shot up, but no, you couldn't do that. You had to do it up right, didn't you? A blamed rickety old fool wallopin' around with a clutter of scrub horses out of the county pound and blowin' about his business arrangements and his herders! Hell, it would take more herders that I've got to keep the . . . Who's down there? Talk up!"

I couldn't think of anything to say. Listening to him rip himself up the back had been a relief. A man who could do that still had his feet under him, at least, but to come out and say so would have sounded prying. He challenged again.

"There's somebody blockin' that crack in the door, and whoever it is had better start testifyin', or I'll . . . That hostler told me to keep you sheep tramps away from here, and, by God, I'll do it! Where's that gun of mine?"

He did have his old broken-backed rifle. I rattled the door, to make him think I had just come inside. "Don't you call me any sheep tramp," I said. "I'm an officer of the law, and I heard there was some flashy young buck named Hendricks selling off county horses down here. Come out and tell what you know about it, and maybe I can talk the court into being easy on you."

For a minute it sounded as if the lightness had gone over his head. "Sellin' horses?" he said, half to himself. "Why, hell, there ain't been any . . ." His rifle lever rattled, the hay rustled, and he slid down from the bales and felt in the dark for the pistol holster under my arm. "So it's you. I ought to have recognized you to start with, but a man's mind gits to runnin' loose sometimes, and there was the way you come at me about sellin' horses. I ain't sold any. They're all out there, right the way they was."

"Not sold any?" I said. "Wasn't that one of the things you came in here to do?"

He moved back and sat down on a loose bale of hay. He could see better in the dark than I could. The bale was completely invisible to me, but he planked down on it without a moment's fumbling or hesitation. "One of the things, yes," he said. "There was two or three. I left the horses here while I took the kid over to the hospital, and this feed-yard boss had four or five picked out and priced by the time I got back. His price was fair enough, I guess. So I took him up, and he went down to the bank for the cash, and I went back to the hospital to see about payin' the kid's doctor bills, and they've fixed it to charge his family for everything. They'd telephoned his folks at South Junction about it, and said they was well off and could stand it, and if I had any extra cash I'd better keep it to live on. So I came back here and called off the deal for the horses till I could work out some arrangement with the doctors. You can't do anything with 'em, though. By God, one of 'em wanted me to put in a bill to the kid's folks for bringin' him in! I told 'em to hell with 'em, and I didn't go back. I don't have to depend on puttin' in bills for my livin'."

"It wouldn't have hurt anything to put one in," I said, though I didn't blame him for not doing it. "It might have saved you from selling off some of the horses. You'll have a feed bill against 'em, and the longer you stay here the bigger it'll get. You've got nothing more to wait around for, have you, if you're through with the doctors?"

"A man hates to have a pack of strangers tell him what to use his money for," he said. "What I need and what I've got to live on ain't any of their damned put-in. I can turn off three or four of them stringy ponies to square the feed bill here. They'll cover it, and we'll be better off rid of 'em. I've been waitin' around for you, mostly. I figured you might want to rest up a day or two, as long as we was here. I've still got some settlin' to do about that Mexican kid before I leave."

That brought it up all in a pile, and there was no use shying around it. "So have a lot of other people, I guess. If you intend to hang around here running up feed bills till he's straightened out, you'd better get a rate by the month. I didn't raise any track of him down the river, and he's probably . . . Where's that railroad time slip he left with you to cash? I want to see the name on it again."

There was only the thinnest chance that I could have remembered it wrong, but it was better to be sure of the thing itself than of remembering it. Old Hendricks moved in the dark, reaching for it, and then stopped. "This is it, I guess, but what good will it do you? You can't read it in the dark, and we can't light any matches around this hay. I know what name's on it, if that's all. I ought to. I've done enough arguin' about it since this morning. It's Esteeban de Andreese. That's what it's spelt like anyway. I knowed before you got here that you wouldn't . . . What's the matter?"

"Nothing," I said. Estéban d'Andreas—Steve Addareous. It couldn't have matched much closer. "It'll keep. What was it you knew before I got here?"

"I knowed you hadn't raised any track of him along the river," old Hendricks said. "He wasn't down there. I know where he's at. He's here in town."

He knew he was springing something unexpected, but he couldn't have known what a wind cutter it was. For a runaway murderer to show up in a town so near the place where the murder had been committed sounded like insanity. It couldn't be much else, if he actually was the murderer. Maybe he wasn't. Maybe it was a clear conscience instead of insanity. There wasn't much difference sometimes. I wanted to see the actual name on the railroad time slip. It wasn't enough to depend on anybody's memory for it. "If he's here in town, he'd better get out as quick as he can make it," I said. "You ought to know better than to let him hang around here, in a town where everybody knows everybody else, and with stray foreigners getting picked up on suspicion all over the country. You don't know what kind of trouble he may get himself into. Maybe he don't either. It don't sound as if he knew anything."

"What he knows won't founder him, I guess," old Hendricks said. "There's some excuse for him, though. People won't notice him much, with all these sheep hoboes flockin' in. And he can't leave, even if he wanted to. He tried to, and that's his trouble now. He's in jail."

"You mean he's in jail here? Here in this town?" It was like hearing that he had gone to sleep drunk in the middle of a main-line railroad track. The Farrand woman's description of him was probably posted on the wall of the jailer's office not over twelve feet from the tank where he was locked up. If somebody from the Greek track gang got thrown in and recognized him. . . . "I'll have to see that time slip of his. I can take it outside to look at it. I want to make sure we didn't mistake the timekeeper's signature for his, or something. What did they lock him up for?"

He fumbled for the time slip again, and said it wasn't for anything desperate, merely equal parts of ill-timed smartness and idiocy. "He'd struck out to leave the country when he took off on us down at the old ferry, and he hoofed it in here to make sure of gittin' on a train. These sheep-camp hoboes always go down to the water tank to climb trains, because it's outside the yard limits. He didn't bother to find out about that. He jumped a freight right here in front of the grain elevator, and the yard detective yanked him off and hauled him to the cooler before he'd rode a hundred yards. That's what he's in for. Here's his time slip. I promised that hostler not to strike any lights around this hay."

I took the paper outside and examined the name, burning up three matches to make sure of it. One would have been plenty. It was the same as we had both remembered it; no amount of match-striking and squinting at it could change it by a syllable. I took it back inside and held it out in the dark, and old Hendricks picked it out of my hand and stowed it away.

"You can say he brung it on himself with his foolishness, but some of it was my fault," he said. "It was me that put him up to that shootin' down at the ferry. He wouldn't have pulled out on us if it hadn't been for that. And if I'd cashed this thing for him like I promised, he wouldn't have had to jump a freight to leave town on. He could have bought a ticket."

"You couldn't get that thing cashed," I said. "I told you that. It ain't a pay check, and it ain't on any railroad in this country, and he'd probably have got picked up on his looks if he'd tried to buy a ticket. They're watching all the railroad stations around here now. You don't need to blame yourself too much about the shooting down at the ferry, either. It wasn't anything new for him. He's shot people before, and he's an old hand at being talked into it. He's the buck that killed your son-in-law over at the old Farrand freight station."

He didn't start blurting a lot of indignant denials and objections, as I had expected. He moved in the dark, and said something in a whisper to himself, and then sat silent, waiting to hear the rest of it. I told him what I had found out down at the Greek outfit train, about the similarity in the two names and Greek peculiarities in spelling, and what the Greek foreman had hinted about the Farrand woman. He sat thinking it all over for a couple of minutes after I had finished. I couldn't blame him. It needed some thinking over.

"You don't know any of this for sure," he said. "You've put two and two together and done a lot of figurin' out, but you don't know."

"I'd as soon not know," I said. "I've told you what I found out. You can think anything you please about it, but I know what a jury'd think. That's what counts."

He moved a little. "Yes. I don't know, there ain't any . . . It looks like it might have been him, don't it? Yes. If I was on a jury and it come up like you've told it, I'd vote to hang the damned little two-face higher than you could shoot. A man couldn't do anything else. Everything's against him. Everything we know's against him. There was the way he come draggin' into my horse camp down in the sand hills along the river, when I . . . Well. That Greek track boss might have had the right line on the whole business, at that. There's trouble wherever there's people. You can't watch 'em all the time. You think he'll have a murder charge stuck onto him if he stays in jail?"

His change in tone at the last was a relief. In the dark, it was hard to remember that he was old, and his wandering half-sentences had been an uneasy reminder of it. "He's liable to," I said. "They might haul in somebody that'll recognize him, or he might blat out something to make them suspicious. They've got descriptions posted around that would fit him close enough to gamble on. He's in danger every minute he's there, and it'll be worse when he comes up for his arraignment. They'll want to know his name and what places he's worked and where he's been and all about him, and he'll be too scared to know what to tell and what not to. There's no telling what he might let out. He might have other shootings against him somewhere else."

Old Hendricks reflected, and said no. "He was as gun-shy as hell when we found him, so he couldn't have piled up too many of 'em. This one's all that counts, anyway. It'll be enough to work on, for a start. He ain't wasted his time; misspent some, maybe, but he ain't frittered away any. Damn these backboneless little pukes, anyway! The meeker they are, the more dangerous they are, it looks like. Hell, I don't know."

He was beginning to wander again. There was excuse enough. It wasn't only the young Mexican. His daughter was in it, too. He hadn't mentioned her. "It depends on who's hold of 'em how dangerous they are," I said, to stir him up. "What do you think we'd better do?"

The place was still as dark as the inside of a cow, but I could see him shoulder his thoughts to one side before he answered. "Git him out, I guess. If there's any way to do it. I wanted to when I seen 'em pull him off the train, and I worked my damnedest at it the whole afternoon. I argued with the jail keeper and the town marshal and the railroad detective and the city recorder, or whatever the hell they call him, till I was windbroke. I told 'em my horses was runnin' up a big feed bill and I couldn't move 'em without a herder to help me, and I offered to pay his fine or put up bail if they'd tell me how much it was. They all preached around about how I'd have to wait for the police court hearing and what a heavy docket there was, and that was all I could git out of 'em. I thought I might hire a lawyer, but I don't see what good it would do now. I didn't do it."

"It's a good thing you didn't," I said. "You've done too much the way it is. I could have got that yard bull to withdraw his complaint for two dollars and a half if you'd stayed away from him and kept your mouth shut. With all this hullabaloo you've raised about feed bills and wanting to move your horses, he may take some real buying off. It might run you a couple of hundred dollars. Do you want to go that high for somebody with a murder on him? It's ten to one he did it, too."

He took it without a quiver. "If he did, that woman put him up to it, and she's as deep in it as he is, so it'll be a kind of a family donation. I wanted to make one, anyway, to show that the old man had amounted to something in spite of 'em. If you have to go higher than two hundred, I can raise it, I guess. There's about that much in the feed-yard office that I can git. The boss left it in case I changed my mind about sellin' the horses he picked out. I'll have to hunt him up and have him write an order for it, and you can take it down and see what you can do with it. The hostler will know where he's at, I guess. You're sure it'll be enough?"

"More than enough, probably," I said. "I'll hold it down all I can. These whistling-post bulls don't generally come very high. If I was to run the bid much over two hundred dollars, he'd be scared to take it. I won't need to take it with me. You can bring it to the jail, and hand it over when they turn the kid loose. You won't need to hunt far for the feed-yard man, either. The hostler told me when I came in where he was. He's over at the whorehouse getting his cane varnished. Do you know where it is?"

Old Hendricks moved, and got up. "I can find it. I've never been in any of them places, and if you'd told me a couple of days ago that I ever would, I'd have called you a liar. Well, a man that never sees anything except what he wants to never learns much. You don't . . . You don't reckon they'll try any tricks, or poke any of their banter at me, or anything like that?

I could borrow a quirt from the office and take it along, if it would help to cool 'em down any. This old rifle of mine's too cumbersome to pack around a place like that, I guess."

The rifle would have been ridiculous as well as cumbersome, but it was true that those twist joints were generally a hangout for all the tinhorns and sharpshooters in the country, and he would have to arrange about drawing a considerable sum in cash and carrying it through a couple of dark streets down to the jail. It was better not to risk any shrinkage in transit. I took off the sheriff's-office pistol and gave it to him. "Don't pull it on anybody down at the whorehouse. Nobody'll banter you unless they're drunk, and it's better not to pay any attention to them. Starting a fight in one of those places can make trouble for people miles away sometimes. If anybody tries to follow you after you've got the money, see that he keeps his distance. If he tries to argue or crowd you, let go a couple at his feet. Count your money before you sign any bill of sale on the horses, and see that it describes the horses you've agreed to sell, so there won't be any argument about it later on. There's been complaints about this feed-yard outfit switching horses on customers, and it don't hurt to watch 'em. When you get the money, separate it into fifty-dollar bundles so you won't have to pull the whole wad to pay out part of it, and bring it on down to the jail. I'll probably be there ahead of you, but whether I am or not, don't let on to anybody that you've got it or what you're there for. Don't pay anything to anybody till I tell you to. Have you got all that straight?"

He said he guessed so. He was trying to buckle on the pistol holster one-handed without taking his coat off, and it took some yanking and straining to make it. "As much of it as I'll remember, anyway. I already fixed it so they can't switch horses on me. The ones we agreed on is over in the colt corral by themselves, and I cut a lock from each of their manes and tied it up in paper to keep. If there's any argument, we can match 'em back. I'll do the best I can with the rest of it. There wouldn't be much more rigmarole to it if I'd hired that lawyer, after all."

"He'd have strung you along for a week and hung a bill on you," I said. "You'd have this to go through anyway, the same as you've got it now. He couldn't do it for you, any more than I can. If I could, I'd . . . Look here, you don't have to do any of this at all. Nobody expects you to. Nobody'd blame you if you didn't. You won't get any thanks or credit for it. This is a lot of money you're fixing to throw away on other people's worthlessness, and you've worked for it. You're old enough by now to think about getting something out of life for yourself once in a while, instead of stewing about things you're not even supposed to know."

He got up and unfastened the wire on the door, and stood blocking out the light in the opening. "I've thought of it," he said, knotting the holster lanyard across his chest. "I've thought more about that than anything else lately. I know blamed well I won't git any credit for this. If I got any, I'd throw it back. But it would be worse if I stayed out of it, you ought to know that. It would be worse if I had to watch what happened afterwards. You know more about viciousness in places like this than I'd find out if I lived to be a hundred, but one thing you don't know is that what a man gits out of life don't count for a damn in the long run. It ain't what you git out, it's what you put in that lasts. Some of it lasts as long as you live, and maybe after you're dead, and it's the only thing that will. Maybe that don't sound like sense to you now, but you'll see the time when it will. . . . Well, here I go. If I git cinched for juvenile delinquency, I'll blame it on you."

He left, shutting the door behind him as if to head off any arguing back. The sounds that came through into the dark were of horses moving out of his way as he passed them, and his rattling the gate for the hostler to come and unlock it. I had forgotten that it had to be kept locked against sheep tramps. There was nothing in what he had said that would have been worth arguing out with him. He probably believed most of it, though some was not quite the truth. He could have gone about his business without having to watch how the young Mexican and the Farrand woman came out in their partnership. There were plenty of places out of range that he could have headed for, as easy as not. Still, having it on his mind would have been as much strain as watching it, so if it wasn't altogether the truth it came close enough to tingle. It was hard to decide about the rest of what he had said; that what a man put into life lasted longer than anything he got out of it. Was it the truth? It didn't mean much. He had said it might not, but that there would be a time when it would. Old men were always getting off prognostications like that, wait till you're as old as I am, heh-heh-heh, then you'll sing out of the other side of your mouth, you'll see.

It turned out to be the truth, anyway.

chapter eleven

ANY restless concourse of waters is apt to reach out an advance splash or two at a man's ankles when he is getting ready to pile into it. The hostler was waiting at the corral gate when I came out. He locked it behind me, held the key up in the light and wiped his nose with it thoughtfully, and said he had finally been brought to realize that there were things a man couldn't do alone. Things came up sometimes that needed to be done and couldn't be done without somebody to help. It sounded reasonable enough. I could think of one, right offhand. He drew himself up reproachfully and said that wasn't what he meant; he was talking about something serious. It had probably happened to plenty of people before, but it was the first time he had ever run into it, and he couldn't get it off his mind.

"The old man said you was a deputy sheriff, or something,"

he went on, jiggling the key back and forth in his palm. He was scrawny-featured and dusty-looking, a little undersized, a little bit drunk, and a little overly self-important at discovering that he had emotions. "That's what I need, I guess; somebody from the law. I'll swear, I don't know what to think of the women out in this country. The more you find out about 'em, the less you know; that's what it works out to. I've been livin' with a girl here in town for two years now. We had an apartment upstairs over the harness shop—nothing stylish, but we'd fixed it up, and there was room for the kids. She's got three of 'em. She never complained about anything. I couldn't tell but what we was makin' out all right. So I had to leave town for a few days, and when I got back, what do you think I seen when I got off the train? One of them squarehead freight handlers down at the wool warehouse drivin' around town in my car! She'd moved him in with her the minute I got out of sight, I guess. They're livin' in my apartment, anyway, and I'm out and injured. Cleaned down to nothing. I ain't got any car or any apartment or anything else. How does a woman figure, anyway?"

"Some of 'em don't, I guess," I said. The story was nothing new. It happened all the time in those places. "If she got you to register the car in her name, she can do as she pleases with it. What else did you give her title to? Your bank account?"

"Everything there was," he said. "The furniture, and an electric range and a new electric washin' machine that I hadn't any more than got through payin' for. I didn't have any bank account, or she'd have got that too. I loved the woman. That's what gouges a man. I thought I could go away somewhere for a while and git it off my mind, but it didn't do any good. You can't run away from it. The only way to have it over with is to face it out. That's what I've got to do. So I come back, and I've started in at it. You can see it on me, I guess."

It was hard to tell about him. He was strained and bereaved-looking, all right, but he was obviously taking pride in it.

"It don't look like there was much that anybody could help you with," I said. "You said something about needing help."

"It's my clothes," he said. "They're still up at the apartment; every thread I've got to my name except what I've got on. She sent word for me to come and git 'em, and I might as well do it, but I want somebody from the law to go with me. I don't want to go up there without some kind of a witness along. I don't trust her that far. She might claim I'd threatened her, or drawed a knife, or tried to beat up on her, or something. I wouldn't put anything past her now. I wouldn't want to trust myself around her, anyway. There's no tellin' what I might do. I loved the woman."

"I may not be back here in time to help you with that," I said. "I'll be busy downtown till past midnight, probably, and we may pull out then. You ought to have held out for getting married, if you thought that much of her."

"She didn't want to on account of the kids," he said. "That was how she told it, anyway. Their father sends her money for 'em, and she was afraid she'd lose it if she got divorced. She claimed she didn't believe in divorces anyway, but it was the money she was after. I can see through her now, for all the good it does. I loved her, that's the trouble. If I don't git them clothes, she's liable to throw 'em away. They're all I've got."

"She won't throw 'em away before morning, I guess," I said. "You can get somebody from the marshal's office then, if you want to. I'd lay off of that jug the rest of the night, if I was you. If she can claim you busted in on her drunk, you'll be in some real trouble."

He agreed that it was sound advice, and went thoughtfully back into the office, probably with no intention of following it. I went down the railroad track toward the station. Love—he was a victim of love, and enjoying himself at it. The chances were that he had a marriage of his own laid away somewhere, the same as she had. All the upstairs-apartment couples in the wooden-building part of town were married, but usually not to each other. Marriage among them was something to get through and be done with, and the faster and more inconspicuous the better, like vaccination. It never held them together. In the old days, all the law-enforcement offices in the country got a steady flood of complaints from women whose husbands had deserted them, all demanding plaintively to have the low-down skunk hauled back and made to support the children. No such petitions ever came in any more. The girls had discovered a preventive against desertion that beat all the prescribed legal and religious ordinances to a frazzle. Instead of marrying a man to live with, which had never worked as it was supposed to, they tickled his pride by offering to live out of wedlock with him, and then took title to his car and the electric washer and the furniture so he couldn't afford to abscond. It seemed almost too simple to be practical, but the results spoke for themselves. A man who couldn't desert his helpmeet without giving up his car was held down as solidly as if she had him nailed to the bedpost by the ears. When there was a separation, it was the woman who did the separating, and the man who did the complaining about it, for all the good it did him.

Customs changed. When one lost its efficacy, another came in to replace it, usually without anybody being aware of it. People changed a custom to avoid changing themselves, but they changed nevertheless, and the country changed with them, so gradually and effortlessly that only somebody coming back to it after a long absence could see how far the process had gone—new cars along the side streets; a new plate-glass front in the restaurant; new things in some of the store windows; new lengths of concrete in place of the old board sidewalks and picket fences; new girls grown up and old ones dropped out of sight; new potted palms in the lobby of the transient hotel fronting the railroad station; a bright new head-kerchief and a dozen or so new wrinkles on the half-drunk squaw waiting in it for some out-of-town roomer to get into bed with for the night. Nannie Annie—she had been at it for years. Nobody had any idea what her legal name was or what she lived on. A homesteader had once claimed to have seen her sober for part of an afternoon, but he had no witnesses, and it turned out afterward that he thought he was in Eastern Montana, so it was put down as probably the product of an overwrought imagination. Old residents used to claim that a man in Crosskeys couldn't qualify to vote until he had been through a round of dalliance with Nannie Annie; but that was only talk. Nobody would have gone through that much for a vote when there was so little worth voting for, and not much financial inducement.

There was nobody in the passenger section of the railroad station except the night dispatcher, getting ready to close up and go home. He had the waiting room dimmed down to one light, the ticket window locked and a time card hung over it, and a newspaper spread over his telegraph instrument and his eyeshade and a mail hoop laid reverently on top, like a sword and helmet on the bier of a fallen hero. He denied knowing anything about the yard detective, and denied it again a couple of times while he locked the safe and got his coat and hat on. Then he scowled at the clock, said it was none of his business now that he was off duty, and unlocked the baggage-room door and motioned me to go on in. There was a light in the far corner behind some piles of trunks and crates and rolls of bedding, and little spurts of low-voiced conversation interspersed with a subdued clattering. There was no mistaking the signs. A sound-effects expert couldn't have done better at creating background noises for a hideout crap game.

THERE were ten or a dozen men and one girl in it. They were squatted in a half-circle under a dirty old carbon-filament light bulb, rolling the dice across the bare floor toward an empty baggage truck on which the railroad detective sat watching, reaching down from time to time to gather a dollar from the pot before the winner raked it in. All the players straightened back hurriedly at sight of an intruder. Then, seeing that the detective merely nodded and hitched over to make room for me on the truck, they eased down and went on with their fun. They were something of an assortment: three or four lambing hands, two signal maintainers from the railroad, one of the baggage handlers, a traveling man for some typewriter company, the cook from an all-night hamburger stand, his apron kilted up under his coat like a bustle; a late homesteader named Nosker from the rockbreaks across the county line, blocky and wooden-faced and indifferent; his younger brother, spoiled and perky and overdressed, from somewhere around town; and a sallow young sharpie with a twitching mouth, shirt cuffs falling over his knuckles, and a twenty-dollar gold certificate stuck in the knot of his bow tie and flared out at the ends, from which he had acquired the name of Yellowback Kid. The girl was next to young Nosker. She was seventeen, maybe less; blonde and pretty, following the dice breathlessly and letting on not to see me. I had been in school with her for a while—Dodie Thorbourne. She was from one of the country's old families; her parents' wedding had made town history twenty years back—wedding-dress from Paris, diamond clips for the bridesmaids, three preachers, all the trimmings. It hadn't turned out well; her parents had taken to quarreling and sometimes fighting, and she had taken to the streets to get away from them, and now to this. She got the dice, laid down twenty dollars and had it covered by the traveling man and one of the signal maintainers, and shook out a seven. The detective reached down for his percentage before she could calm down enough to haul it in. Then he changed his mind and sat back indulgently.

"No hurry about it," he said. "She won't hang onto it long. It's a friendly kind of a game. I could haul the whole bunch in for it, but they'd only find some place else to do it, and maybe in worse company. This is quiet, and we don't allow anything rough. A little recreation never hurt anybody. Was there something you wanted to see me about?"

Dodie shot her forty dollars, lost it on her second throw, and pitched the dice away and put her arm across her eyes, pretending playfully to be grief-stricken. She had always been pretty. It had always been easy for her to tap friends of the family for a dollar or two so she wouldn't have to go home and listen to the quarreling. She had no more business in a baggage-room crap game than she would have had working on the section; but there was no use bringing that up, with all the bargaining still to do. It might be useless anyway.

"It's about a kid you pulled off of a freight down by the wool warehouse—a young Mexican," I said. "He's over in jail now. There's nothing against him but that, and it wasn't anything but ignorance. He don't know anything about company regulations. He can't even talk English. He'll be better off out of your way than hived up in jail, and you'll be rid of him for good."

The traveling man made a pass for twenty dollars, let it ride, and lost it to the hamburger cook. The Yellowback Kid gathered the dice in, performed a snare-drum roll with them in the hollow of his palm, and shoved out a fifty-dollar Liberty bond for his stake. Getting it covered took time. The detective watched for a minute, and then let it go temporarily.

"Down by the wool warehouse, huh? Uh-huh, I did pull a kid off down there, I recollect now. Damned little fool, antickin' around between them cars when they didn't have 'em made up yet. He could have got a foot pinched off in a couplin' block as easy as not. He was Mex, or something like it, so he must be the one. He can talk English, though. He talked it to me when I hauled him in, I know that. Not much, maybe, but enough to git around with. Come to think, there was an old mossback in here this afternoon hollerin' around about wantin' to git him sprung; threatenin' and stompin' and swingin' his arms and preachin' about some herd of horses he needed a herder to git out of town with. I didn't waste much time on him. You know how far anybody would git threatenin' me, I guess. I finally asked him which was the most important to the country, his horses or the law, and he hauled in his horns and left. He had sense enough to see what kind of a customer he was up against, I'll say that for him. . . . I don't know about this business of yours. The kid give me some trouble, arguin' and yankin' back and bawlin' around the street, and there's the law. People like us have to live up to it. It wouldn't look right to let him break it and git off scot-free."

"I didn't say anything about scot-free," I said. Dodie had

covered the final twenty dollars of the Yellowback Kid's Liberty bond. He rolled a five, and threw half a dozen times without turning anything that counted. "We need him for some business down the river; nothing much to it, but it'll save some trouble to get hold of him. I could get the city recorder to come down and put through his arraignment tonight, but it's late, and he'd gabble all over town about it. So I thought . . ."

The Yellowback Kid made his five. The detective reached down and removed a dollar from his winnings, and sat back again with a sigh.

"I told you I'd git it," he said. "If I'd raked it from that girl, she couldn't have bet even money, and it would have mixed everything up. . . . Well, this Mex kid. Business, you say? It wouldn't be some reward for him that you're tryin' to hoosier out on me, would it?"

"You've seen him; talked to him, too, you claim," I said. It was probably true. He had taken us in about so many things that one more hardly mattered. "Did he look like he could do anything that there'd be a reward out for? You said yourself he was a fool. There's no reward for him. If there was one, you could claim it anyway. You've got the record of your arrest, and you've got witnesses. . . . That girl's got no business in a place like this. You oughtn't to allow her in here. She's only a kid. I know her, and I know her folks."

The Yellowback Kid had his Liberty bond out again. Only part of it was covered. Dodie opened a little imitation-leather purse, shook it to show that it was empty, and leaned her head against young Nosker's sleeve, edging sideways to save the crease in it. "It's all gone, all empty," she said, pretending childishness. "If somebody don't put some more money in it, we'll be broke all to pieces. You don't want us to be broke, do you? And have to sleep in the trash barrel behind the hardware store, where it's all dark and cold?"

She wouldn't have used that tone to anybody in school. Young Nosker reached his arm around her, took the purse and rolled it between his fingers to spread the cracks in the finish. "That thing would fall apart if you put any real money in it," he said. "I'm broke, too. Buck, here, has got all the money. Maybe we can talk him out of some of it."

The elder Nosker half-opened his eyes, flipped a wadded-up twenty-dollar bill across to cover the Liberty bond, and dug down for his wallet. He had a new homestead across the county line, in one of the stoniest and most inaccessible scab rock and alkali outcrops in the state. Nothing grew on it except a few patches of weeds and salt grass along the creek, but he made the most of its possibilities. The creek water, though unfit to drink by itself, toned down the sharpness of rifle whisky, and marihuana was a weed. Everything had its uses, if a man looked far enough. His modest researches helped him to eke out a better living from his rockpile than most people made from ten times as much land in country ten times as fertile. He had no vices, and no interests that anybody could discover. His younger brother did his high living for him, and he took more satisfaction in that than in anything he did for himself. He sorted half a dozen more bills from his wallet and handed them over in a wad.

"This'll have to last you," he said. "She's run through a pile of them things for you tonight, and I don't carry the First National Bank around with me. I'd start figurin' how to git my money's worth out of it, if I was you. I don't like the way them dice is actin', either."

Young Nosker handed one of the bills over to Dodie. "I'll

get my money's worth, I guess," he said. "There'll be ways. Maybe we can think of some, if we work on it."

The dice rolled and stopped on nothing. Dodie reached down and picked them up. The Yellowback Kid leaned back, watching amusedly as she examined them, balanced one between her fingers, and rolled them in her palm. "They stop in the wrong places, that's all," she said, and tossed them back. "The night's young yet. You'll get your money's worth, if you know where to look for it, and maybe your money too. Watch and pray."

She sat back against him. The Yellowback Kid started rolling for a nine, and spattering all around it—five, eight, three, four, five again. The detective leaned back against the truck brace and half-closed his eyes.

"You don't need to be uneasy about her," he said. "There ain't much anybody can do now. Let 'em git started at this and then put 'em out, and they're liable to holler about it all over town and land everybody in trouble. You're safest to let well enough alone sometimes. . . . About that Mex kid; I've been thinkin'. My car's got to be overhauled—bearings tightened, valves ground, new rings, stuff like that. A man over at the garage will do it on his own time for a hundred and fourteen dollars, material and everything. It's worth every cent of it. I'll call it a hundred and ten, to make it round numbers, and if there's a reward on the kid you can keep it. If that ain't fair, I don't know what is."

"There ain't any reward, and you know it," I said. "I'll give you fifty dollars, and I'll keep still about that girl being here. She's underage, and this is bad for her. She'd be better off running the streets. A man can go to the pen for contributing to the delinquency of a minor; did you know that?"

"She'll make out all right," he said placidly, and shifted his feet to keep from interfering with the dice. They came on a long roll, spinning and tumbling slowly, and I watched the spots on them as they stopped almost under the truck. There was something odd about them; something that should have added up and didn't. I put my foot on them and turned one over: five, three, ace . . . The Yellowback Kid leaned forward, mean-favored and muscled up. There were two bright-red patches on his forehead, one above each eye. He started to say something to me, and then changed his mind and appealed to the detective.

"He's got to let them dice back in the game; he's got no right to hold 'em, and you've got no right to let him!" he said. "They belong back here; make him throw 'em back so the game can go on! You get your drag out of it, don't you? All right, then, make him turn the dice loose, and hurry up about it, or I'll . . ."

I waited to see if he would do any threatening. He didn't, so I kicked the dice back to him. There was nothing more to find out about them anyway. They were tops and bottoms, an old-fashioned cheaters' device used to make points with because the spots couldn't possibly add up to seven. He probably had a straight pair palmed under his shirt cuff to switch to for his opening throw. There was nothing special about it, considering the kind of gathering he was using them on. The only thing was that he had let Dodie examine them without letting out a peep. She had gone over them far more closely than I had, and he had smirked confidently through her inspection as if nothing could possibly be wrong with them. And she had not found anything wrong with them.

"You see how it is," the detective murmured. The game was under way again, noisily. "She ain't doin' bad. She'll do better at this than she could at anything else around this town. It won't damage her any. Not now. That's all over with. Since about four months ago, I guess it was. She learns fast, I'll say that for her. No arguments, no rough stuff, everything quiet and good-natured. If she can take them Noskers, who cares? Ill-gotten gains never prosper, and everybody knows where theirs comes from. . . . Look here, I can meet a man halfway that knows how to stay out of other people's business. I'll take in a little extra money here before the night's over. I'll count that out of the price I quoted you. Pay me eighty-five dollars, and I'll call up Cap Burgess down at the jail and pull back the charges against that kid. There's a phone over by the door. You can listen while I do it."

"Sold," I said. He would have come down to fifty, but it would have taken time, and the place was getting hard to stand—the stench of railroad disinfectant; the clutch of floor dust and dried spittle; the weak old light bulb frying scum from dirty hands on its hot glass; the players' faces like moldy bread, their fixed eyes like gouts of cold slime; a girl like that in the middle of it working as a capper for the shoddiest specimen among the whole pack of them, the filthiest, and having a good time at it. Four months ago it had happened; too late to do anything, better not to try anything, with the young Mexican still to be arranged for. Lost was lost; maybe he was lost too, but old Hendricks wanted him out, and that much was not lost yet. "I'll pay you the eighty-five dollars when I see the kid turned loose," I said. "If you want to come over to the jail and spring him for me, it'll be there. If you'd sooner not miss any of this, I can leave it with old Burgess to give to you. It'll be safe enough. I know him."

The detective reached down and took in a dollar from the game. "That'll have to be it, I guess," he said. "I'll be tied up here a couple of hours yet, maybe longer. I'll call old Burgess and fix it for you. Put the money in an envelope with my name on it, and have him put it in the safe to keep for me. You won't need to count it out to him. I'll trust you for that. Tell him what it is, though, so he'll be careful of it. I'll call him now, if you want to come over and listen."

"I'll trust you for that," I said. "If the kid's turned loose, the rest don't matter. I'd better write his name out for you. What do you want the money in an envelope for if you want the jailer to know what it is?"

He got down from the truck and shook out his pantlegs. "So if there's any kickback on it, or anything. If the money's in an envelope, he can swear he didn't see anything. You don't need to write any name out. There's only eight or ten of them hoboes that I've pulled in since court set. You can pick out any one of 'em you want, and the jailer'll turn him loose for you. What counts in this business is to see that the customer gits what he wants. You'll find that out when you've been at it as long as I have."

He meant well, but the street outside was a relief from him. There were probably youths doing time in the reform school for yielding to pleasures a lot less satisfying than the darkness was, and the sharp air and distant sounds, and the coarse grass underfoot, and the smell of damp greasewood and juniper in the wind. . . . Four months ago. That would have been early in the winter. Nothing much had been happening then; somebody in town might have spared time to find out what she was getting herself into and what could be done about it. Maybe they had hesitated for fear of hurting her parents' feelings—an old family with a long-established lumber business that had slowed up after the country stopped needing lumber for homestead buildings, sidewalks, fences, bridges, warehouses, trestles, hayracks, header beds. . . . Her home life was responsible.

People could say that and feel gratified at having something so convenient to blame it on. Calanthe's home life had been worse. She wouldn't have found any emotional stimulus in throwing herself away on a tadpole-skinning gambler. She wouldn't have thrown herself away on him at all, for that or anything else. Her hankering for respectability would have prevented her. It was her worst drawback; the hardest thing about her to stand; but it would have saved her, and with room to spare.

THE city hall was a square-fronted wooden building down an unlighted side street on the edge of the open fields, surrounded by dead tumbleweed and trailers of rusty barbed wire that had once been a fence. The basement, walled in with stone and barred at the half-windows, was the jail. The jailer's office was a badly-ventilated cubbyhole in the front, with a closed cell at one side for women prisoners and a main tank back of it for men. Both had the doors closed for the night, but they were still lighted, and Cap Burgess was whiling away his night vigil carving a floral design on a cigar-box top with the small blade of his pocketknife, swearing when he made a mislick at it. He took pains with his wood carving, which was mostly reproductions of floral designs from the oilcloth section of the mail-order catalogue. He also wrote poetry off and on, usually dirty in a few spots but not very good, and entertained himself by practicing music during the seasons when there were not enough prisoners in the jail to make an issue of it. The only tunes he knew all the way through were *I Wonder Who's Kissing Her Now* and an old dance tune that started off: *I had a little dog and his name was Bose; I cut his tail off hyass klose,* but he could play them on eighteen different instruments, including a Chinese flute, an Indian chicken-bone whistle, and a set of cow bells. His wife lived in one of the small houses on the far edge of town: a peaked, colorless woman, who chased young men around the pool-rooms and sometimes disappeared for several weeks at a time without leaving any word where she had gone or what for. His daughter was crowding thirty and still unmarried, not because she was unattractive, but because the marriageable young men in town could never feel sure how closely related to them she might turn out to be if the old lady ever took a notion to start belching things up from the past. Old Burgess took pride in being a family man and head of a household, but he showed up at home only once or twice a year, usually after carefully reconnoitering the premises to make sure nobody else was ahead of him.

"So you're back amongst us mud pullers for a spell," he said, and stowed his carving away under some old Salvation Army papers. "We heard you'd had a little misunderstanding down in the city, and kind of got the short end of it. Well, a little dodgin' around ain't anything to be ashamed of when a man like Ves Busick's out after you. You ain't the first one. There's plenty here in town that's tied into him and come out at the little end of the horn, and you've got a better excuse for hidin' out than they had. It's your duty to keep the peace. Stayin' out of a fight's a better way to do it than hangin' around where you might git into one. This is a civilized country. Fightin' ain't got any place in it. You done right."

"I didn't get the short end of any rumpus with Busick," I said. "I hauled him to jail where he belonged, that was all. I didn't dodge out on him, either. He's out somewhere in this country now, and I'd as soon run into him as not. The only trouble I had was with the jury that tried him. He owed everybody in town, and they turned him loose so he could get paid out. I don't know what kind of a civilized country it is where killing an old Indian counts less than getting your bills paid, but that's how they figured it. They don't even know for sure that he will pay 'em. They hope he will, that's all."

Old Burgess leafed through some dusty papers on a spindle, and said they had done the right thing. He could always switch ends fast when it came to proving that something or somebody was right. "The only way you can tell about anything like that is to try. If they lose, they won't be any worse off, and it'll show that they had confidence in humanity. It wouldn't do that old dead Indian any good to send him to the pen, and if he kills any more of 'em there'll still be time to handle him for it. What counts is to believe in people; yes, sir, in human beings. It shows your heart's in the right place, whether theirs are or not. Well, how're you stackin' up? You been gittin' any lately?"

There was no use asking any what. When a question didn't state an explicit object, it could only be about one thing. I said no, and asked if there had been any calls from the railroad detective or old Hendricks. He scrambled a paper loose from the spindle, studied some scrawling on a corner of it, and said the detective had called, but that old Hendricks hadn't been heard from since early in the afternoon.

"That's the name it looks like was wrote down here, so I guess it was him. He was in around three o'clock or so, chargin' around and blowin' fire through the seat of his pants about one of the prisoners he wanted put up for a hearing or bailed out or something. There wasn't anything I could do, so he stomped out and said he'd be back with a lawyer. He ain't showed up since then. There wasn't anything for him to holler at me about. I'd have turned the whole tank out for him if it was mine, and glad to. They haul these blamed drunks and high rollers and bums in on me, and I don't git anything out of 'em. The railroad bull said over the telephone that you wanted to draw out one of his, and you'd leave an envelope for him. Eighty-five dollars and pick out the one you wanted, he said. He's pricin' 'em a little steep, ain't he?"

"The same as usual, I guess," I said. "All he can get. I could have beat him down, but I didn't have time to argue with him. It's old Hendricks' money, anyway. He ought to be here with it before long. We want a young Mexican that's in for jumping a train inside the yard limits; name of D'Andreas, light-built, around twenty, kind of scared-acting. He can't talk much English; none, maybe. You've got him here, ain't you?"

He was straightening the papers on the spindle so the edges lined up. One was a bulletin about Steve Addareous. The description on it tallied almost word for word with the one I had given of the young Mexican. He kept me sweating for a minute, slanting it and turning it at different angles to study some pencil marks on the margin. Then he gave up and covered it with some other papers.

"Something my wife wanted me to do, and I can't remember whether I done it or not," he explained, pushing the spindle away. "To hell with it. These women will take up all your time with their blamed errands if you let 'em. They can't ever git it through their heads that a man's got business of his own to tend to. What was it you . . . Oh, yes, that Mexican. He's here in the tank, along with the rest of 'em. I don't know whether he can talk any English or not. He ain't talked at all since he got here; sets in a corner with his face to the wall, and that's all there is to him. He don't look like any eighty-five dollars' worth to me. Not but what the yard bull's right to hold him for that, if he can git anybody to pay it. These railroad detectives don't have any easy time of it. Hard work and responsibility and long hours, and you never know when one of these hoboes will pull a gun on you. Or a razor. Still, eighty-five dollars, I don't know. You could pay out the girl we've got in the women's cell for that, and have enough left over to show her a little night life with before she leaves town. It might tone you up."

"The eighty-five dollars ain't mine," I said. "What's she in for, and what is there to do around this town that would tone anybody up?"

"There's parlor games," he said. "Riddles and forfeits; and push-and-pull, or whatever they call it nowadays. It's the same in this town as it is anywhere else. Cats fight over it. A cat's the most intelligent animal there is. She ain't one of these old regulars. She's from out in the bitter-lakes country somewhere, and she's as respectable a young married woman as you'd want to see when she's home. She took a little trip down to the city to buy some clothes and knickknacks a couple of weeks ago, and blowed in all her money on the sights before she thought, so she come up here to see if she could make some of it back in the lambin' rush. She got a room at the transient hotel downtown and told the clerk she was open for customers, and she set her prices so low she had a land-office business runnin' for a couple or three days. They thought it was a fire sale, I guess. She had lambin' hands and Greeks and Chinamen packed into the lobby and lined up clear out to the railroad track, and there was some fights amongst 'em, and old Nannie Annie got jealous and turned her in for everything in the book. So the fine took more than she'd made, and she's got to stay here till her husband can come in and pay her out. He'll haul her back to the homestead out in them alkali flats, and she'll have to stay there. This may be the last outing she'll ever have in her life. It ain't any eighty-five dollars she's in for; it ain't much over sixty. You could scare up that much. We'd call it a kind of a bond for the evening. Git her back here by daylight tomorrow morning, and I'd give it back to you. I feel sorry for her."

"We've got some horses to get out of town with before morning, so I'd better not," I said. Feeling sorry for her didn't go far enough. It seemed a time to feel sorry for everybody. "If she was driving that kind of a trade before she got picked up, I wouldn't want to risk it anyway. I might fall in. . . . How does this husband of hers expect to get along alone with her on a godforsaken alkali homestead after what's happened? There won't be anybody else for them to talk to, and there won't be anything else for them to talk about. He sounds like a worse damned fool than she does. They'll probably kill each other before they're through."

"It won't hurt as bad as all that," old Burgess said. "I've seen cases like this before, and they worked out. You don't understand all you know about some things, that's all. That husband may sound like a damned fool to you, but he knows well enough what he's doin', and he's right. A man can't stay on one of them dry homesteads all by himself, and she'll be easier to keep around from now on. He can always throw this up to her when she gits a wild hair in her crupper, and it'll hold her down. It wouldn't be sensible for him to go experimentin' around with a string of other women when he's already got one that suits him. When you git hold of a woman that suits you, it's better to hang onto her, even if you have to strain a point or two to do it. Everybody's entitled to a misstep once in a while. We've both made 'em. It ain't for us to cast the first stone."

"I didn't say anything about casting stones," I said. "All I said was that they'd probably kill each other, and I'll bet they do. They might drive each other crazy first, but I doubt it. People don't go crazy unless they've got something to go with."

"They won't kill each other," old Burgess said. He sounded resigned. I hadn't realized before how nearly the conversation skimmed his own state of domestic misarrangement. "They'll git used to it. You'd be surprised what people can git used to when they work at it. Give and take, that's the secret. That's what married life is. There's something rattlin' the tumbleweeds outside. Maybe you'd better look. It might be your man with the money."

I went out and looked. Old Hendricks was waist-deep in a weed pile, yanking at something around his feet and muttering to himself between yanks. He had wandered around the building trying to find the jail door, and had got mixed up with a nest of rusty barbed wire that wouldn't come loose. I held matches while he untangled himself from it, and told him about the arrangement for buying the young Mexican out. He shook his feet cautiously to make sure they were clear, and handed over two bundles of greenbacks.

"There's fifty dollars apiece in 'em, like you said," he explained. "You got him off cheaper than I expected. These damned cutthroats around this town! I had to knock forty dollars off of them horses because that feed-yard pickpocket knowed I didn't have time to argue with him. Well, it comes out even; I lose money and you save it. Damn such a place, anyway! Go on in and git paid off, and let's git out of here. I've got our saddle horses tied over across the street, and I've got the hostler packin' up for us down at the corral. We can leave as soon as you're through. This jail keeper ain't had any calls come in about me here, has he?"

"He didn't mention any," I said. I had thrown away thirty-five dollars for him by not haggling down in the baggage room, but there was no use going into that. It wouldn't have made him feel any better to know that he had taken a scorching on both ends. "He said you'd been in this afternoon, that was all. You might as well come on in, as long as you're this close."

He wouldn't do it, explaining that he had better watch the saddle horses. There had been nothing to tie them to except an old hen coop, and the prospect of getting out on the road again was making them restive. He went across to them, and I went back in the office and counted eighty-five dollars into a cast-off patent-medicine envelope while Cap Burgess opened the door to the tank. Estéban was humped on a wooden stool in the far corner, pale and grimy and listless, resting his chin on his hands and staring at the blank wall, though the sight of it must have been worn a little threadbare after all the contemplation he had put in on it. He got up when we called him, without appearing particularly glad to see me, and picked his way to the door between the prisoners spread out asleep or brooding on the concrete floor. They were an average assortment for the town at that season—hoboes hauled in for staying on the freight train too long; a Chinaman and two Filipinos caught fighting over a fan-tan game; two Japanese truck gardeners who had smelled up their neighborhood distilling *saki* in the toolshed; a sprinkling of drunk Indians; some back-country sheep herders in for being drunk and disorderly according to their standard pattern for such splurges, first staving around a dozen times bigger than life, and then dwindling down infinitely smaller; a man who had been the Big Missouri River on a rampage; one who had claimed he was old Mount

Vesuvius getting all fixed to belch boiling lava; one who had acted out Mountain Locomotive Number 38 with its whistle tied down; and a little sandy-mustached man with glasses who had been telling around that he was from a country where people used rusty barbed-wire for toilet paper and the canary birds sang bass, and that he had been run out of it for being too tough—all stretched out on the floor limp and subdued, sleeping it off as meek as mown flowers in a meadow. There were no Greeks among them. Drunkenness was not one of the Greeks' failings, but gambling was, and it was a relief that none of them had got picked up for that while Estéban was in. I gave old Burgess the envelope with the money, and steered Estéban across the street to the saddle horses. Old Hendricks had them untied, and stood fidgeting with the reins like a remount jockey in a round-track relay race. It was too dark to make out faces, but he didn't light matches or ask questions. He handed me a set of reins and swung Estéban's horse sideways for him to mount.

"You took long enough at it," he said. We had taken less than five minutes. "Well, load him on if he needs it, so we can move."

The night hostler had the pack horses all roped and the herd bunched at the gate for us. He accepted five dollars from old Hendricks for his help, remarking with gloomy relish that it was too late to do any good but that it might help him to forget for a while, and drove the herd out into the street by flapping a saddle blanket against the light. We rode ahead to turn them at the cross street, and I turned and looked back, wondering whether he really had sobered up any. Old Hendricks misguessed what the look was for.

"This is hurryin' you out of here faster than I'd planned,"

he said. "You ain't had time to see any of the town, I guess. Maybe you'll git back before the rush gits over with."

"I'd as soon not," I said. "I've seen all of it I need to."

THE horses were hard to manage for the first few minutes, confused by the cross streets and lights moving and blinking out at them. Then the leaders worked ahead to their old places, we got them turned away from the railroad, and when the tail-enders had dropped back where they belonged and the fighting and jostling had ended; a wind across the open fields made them lift their heads and step out as briskly as if they were turning into a stretch that pointed straight for home. Nobody said anything till they were crowding along in the shadows under the scarred and half-dead old shade trees in the old section of town. When we rode into the shadow after them, old Hendricks spoke up.

"This young roundhead here might as well git it settled that he's comin' with us, whether it suits him or not," he said. "Tryin' to rein away from me all the time won't git him anywhere. I can rein as fast as he can, and if he tries much more of it I'll put a lead rope on his horse and take his reins away from him. I want him where I can keep tab on him, and that's where he's goin' to stay. Tell him that."

"I don't need to," I said. "He can understand English. The railroad bull said he talked a streak of it when he got pulled off the train."

We rode a few yards without saying anything. Then old Hendricks reached out and shook Estéban by the shoulder. "Well, let's hear from you!" he said. "Can you talk English, or can't you?"

It appeared that he could, though he didn't do it. "*Sí, tantito*," he said, on a sort of indrawn gulp. "*Unas palabras, sí.*"

That was all we could get out of him. He was willing to admit it, but we couldn't make him demonstrate it. A little sweating might have loosened him up, but old Hendricks forbade that.

"If he's told the truth, that's enough," he said. "We don't have to make him prove it. Here's that pistol of yours, while I think of it. I won't have any more use for it, I guess."

He unfastened the shoulder strap and handed it across to me. It was awkward to put on, so I buckled it to loop over the saddle horn. "It feels like there was something smeared on the grip," I said. "The checkering's filled up with grease, or something. It wasn't like that when I gave it to you."

"Hair pomade, I expect," old Hendricks said. "I had to use it a little over in that red-light house. It wasn't anything serious—some squallin' and hollerin', that was all. One of them young bond salesmen from out of town started it. He was workin' on the old woman that run the place, tryin' to git her drunk. He made some joke or other about it, so I used the gun to rub his ears down a little. I can't stand to see one of them fast-talkin' little slick heads tryin' to take advantage of a woman old enough to be his mother. He won't do any more of it for a while, anyway."

"I don't know what kind of advantage he could take of that old hellcat," I said. It explained our hurry to get out of town, at least. "She's been through more cussedness in her time than either of us ever heard of. He was the one that needed looking out for, if anybody did."

"That wasn't what he was after," old Hendricks said. "If it had been, he'd have done better to leave her sober and git drunk himself. He was tryin' to git her drunk so he could sell her some of his bonds. A man couldn't set there and see her swindled out of her money. If she's got any, she ain't had any easy time makin' it. It's cost her enough; you can see that to look at her."

Maybe it had. She wasn't much for looks, that was the truth. "How do you know there was any swindle about it?" I asked. "The bonds might have been good. Maybe you beat her out of a valuable investment."

"If they'd been any good, he wouldn't have had to git her drunk to sell 'em," old Hendricks said. "And there was his makin' jokes about her out of the side of his mouth, and the way he looked. . . . The main thing was that I took a dislike to him, I guess. I didn't hurt him much—scuffed him up a little, that was all. You'd have thought he was dyin', the way he caved around and hollered about it, but it wasn't anything much. . . ." He reached out and yanked Estéban's bridle. "You come on here! I've been through enough tonight on your account. You try any hangin' back on me, and I'll kick you off and drag you! Damn that town! I got some of them women's perfumery stuck onto me somewhere, and I reek to hell with it. Can you smell it?"

There was a perfume in the air, and it did seem for a minute to be coming from him. Then something white glimmered out of the shadow in front of a dilapidated house, and I knew what it was. A little locust sapling growing through a break in the old board sidewalk had come into bloom since I had ridden past it earlier in the evening. The perfume was coming from it. It was arguable whether we had complimented the girls by mistaking their slathered-on fragrance for spring locust blossoms, or whether it was a comedown for the locust to confuse its scent with hookshop perfumery. Old Hendricks was all for the comedown theory.

"It's like everything else in this place," he said. "Even the flowers smells trashy. By God, you walk around it and think you recognize somebody you used to know, and it ain't him at all. It's his son, or maybe his grandson. And the man you thought it was turns out to be some humpbacked old whistle-breeches with his eyes bleared and his mouth wobblin' and his knees knockin' his chin when he walks. Hell, I'm as old as any of 'em, and I don't look like they do! Or talk like 'em, either. . . ." He shifted his tone to imitate a senile cackle. "Heh-heh, I don't reckon any of you young fellers would know this country if you could see it like it was back in eighty-two. Yes, sir, heh-heh-heh, that was right after the big snow, and there wasn't a mark of man here except a hoss blanket on a couple of sticks and a strand of barbed wire to keep off the animals, heh-heh, nary thing in sight except bear and deer and antelope and bighorn sheep and prairie chicken and wild swans and geese and quail and grouse plumb to the skyline. The only road in them days was a little old squirrel trail through the weeds, heh-heh-heh, and now look at it. Brick buildings and cement sidewalks and big machine-graded bullyvards a-spranglin' out every which way from here like the testicles of an octopus, and nothing but people as fur as you can look. Well, it's a great thing. We've made something out of this country. Wrested it from the wilderness, that's what we've done. The old pioneer sperrit, heh-heh-heh!"

"You meant tentacles," I said. "I don't think octopuses have got testicles."

"People have, so there's still too many," he said, and dropped into his senile imitation again. "Well, sir, heh-heh, a lot of these high-flyin' young folks a-rippin' around in their big cars don't have any idea of the hardships we went through to build this into a land of opportunity for 'em like we done, a-ridin' in them covered wagons like it shows in the movin' pictures, and haulin' forty-cent wheat a hundred and twenty miles to market, and gittin' shot at by Indians when we run off a few of their horses that they didn't have any use for and we did. It was all to give our children a better chance in life than we'd had, and mine's made out mighty well, I'll say that for 'em, heh-heh, mighty well. Six of 'em a-workin' for the government regular; one a-holdin' down three full-time jobs and drawin' pay for all of 'em, and his wife a-teachin' school to help out; and another one with right onto eighty thousand dollars put away that'll be his free and clear when he gits out of the federal penitentiary so he can go dig it up; and the girls, they're a-doin' well, too. One of 'em's a-drawin' alimony from eight different husbands as steady as a clock, and another one got promoted to trusty down at the home for the feeble-minded last month. It's all been worth it. Yes, sir, it's paid out, heh-heh. Healthy home life and new country to start out in; that's what does it. Yes, sir. Yup. Heh-heh-heh. . . . By God, that's exactly how the rickety-headed old fools sounded, I'll swear to it! Damn such a place!"

"This was all your idea," I said. "We wouldn't have come over here if it hadn't been for your family responsibilities."

"I know it," he said. The town was behind us, an aimless cluster of lights that shuttled on and off as the wind moved the leafless shade trees in front of them. The horses moved between open wheat fields, reaching out at every step as if they had winded a waterhole in the middle of an alkali desert. "I got us into it, I know that. It's a good thing, the way it's worked out, but this is all. I wanted to do something for 'em, and I've done a blamed sight more than they'd have any right to expect from anybody, but enough's plenty. Money can't do everything. Some things takes time. They've got a damned sight more of that left than I have."

They had more money, too, probably, though not in the right place at the right time. "You don't want to see 'em at all?" I said. "Not any of 'em?"

"No," he said, and rode past a couple of dozen fence posts in silence. "No, I don't. I might be sorry we'd done this much. You helped with it more than I did. I couldn't have done anything if you hadn't showed up."

"Leave me out of it," I said. "If there's anything to feel sorry about, you can blame it on yourself. No South Junction, then?"

"I said no," he said. He toned it down a little, after a dozen more fence posts. "I never did want to go there. At first it was because I didn't want her to see what I'd got to look like. Now it's changed around. I don't want to see her. I don't want to look at her. Not now."

That was final enough. It settled several things. He was not avoiding the Farrand woman because of any grudge, any sense of enmity, any moral condemnation. It was because he loved her. There was no longer any reason for him to love her, and so many reasons against it that he was ashamed of it, but he did. That was what he was afraid of, not her. We rode on for the open country beyond the wheat fields. The wind dropped and a white frost began falling as we drew clear of them, the sharp frost crystals flashing blue and orange and blinding white in the starlight as they came floating down through the darkness like incandescent flakes of diamond; like threads raveled from a star; like streaks of pain lightening a last agony of loneliness; like a man's gloom of knowledge lit and tormented into restlessness by shreds of love. It was no wonder that old Hendricks had not fallen into the cackling senility of the old men he had been mimicking. His conscience had kept him prodded out of it.

We kept moving until the town and the wheat fields were completely dropped out of sight, and camped at an old haystack on a ridge overlooking the headwaters of a little creek, overgrown with thorn brush except in a few places where it had been widened for hay wagons to cross or stock to water. It was chilly, and the horses kept stirring around uneasily instead of going to sleep as they usually did toward morning. I went out about daylight to see what was disturbing them, and discovered a strange horse wandering among them, dragging a broken set of hobbles. He had come up from the creek; there were wild plum petals spattered on his head and withers and in his mane, and there were no wild plum bushes anywhere except the creek canyon. He dodged when I tried to catch him, but I managed by throwing rocks to work him away from the herd and start him back where he belonged, and followed him to keep him from circling up the ridge again. Halfway down it, he jumped the trail and took cover in a stand of giant sagebrush higher than a man's head. I angled uphill to keep him in sight, and met Calanthe coming up through the frost with a rope, looking for him. She was only half-dressed, and hurrying because of the cold, and she had been crying. Her hair kept tapping against the tear stains on her cheeks as she walked. She looked up and saw me, and pushed it back from her face with the end of the rope, staring doubtfully. There was always reason to look twice at any new thing in that country, where half the shapes and colors seemed some transitory effect of light rather than solid substance. People were deceived by its mirages sometimes, not because any mirage ever looked much like the real thing, but because the real thing did frequently look like a mirage.

"I was bringing your horse back," I said. "I didn't know whose it was, but I thought . . . He's down there in the brush."

She didn't look to see where. She kept staring, turning the rope end around her forearm and letting it unwind again. "I'd started out to look for him," she said. "It's good enough for me, I guess. I ought to have staked him, but I was in a hurry, and so many things happening . . ." She put her hand against her eyes, looked at it, and wiped it on her dress. "I saw your camp on the ridge, and I hoped it would be you. I knew I'd find you somewhere. There had to be somebody I could talk to. I was scared you might be somebody else. And then the horse got loose, and I was afraid I'd be left out here afoot, and my father . . ."

"Your father's not here with you?" I said. It was a foolish question. She wouldn't be out looking for a stray horse if he had been. She looked down at the rope, and dropped it in a coil on the frosty grass and sat on it. "He's not here; he won't be, either," she said, and pressed her hand to her eyes again. "He's at South Junction with that low-down slut of a Farrand woman, the no-good old . . . He's as bad as she is. They're both low-down, they're lower than—than a snake's belly-button; I don't want anything more to do with either one of 'em! I don't know where I can go or what I can do, but I won't go back there, not if they kill me! They've done worse, too! That's what I wanted to talk to somebody about. Only now . . ."

"You can talk about it now, can't you?" I said.

She rested her chin on her knees and stared down at the first streaks of sun beginning to burn the hoarfrost into whitish mist down the creek. "To you?" she said. "And have you know what kind of people I've got, when I thought we could . . . I wanted you to love me, that's the truth about it. Why couldn't you have been somebody that didn't matter? Oh, damn their dirty souls to hell, I hate 'em!"

She began to cry again. There was only one way to stop her that I could think of, not a very good one, but it was a case where anything was better than acting helpless. It was anger in her more than hurt. The hurt must have come first, but the anger had taken the harder hold on her, and crying was apt to make it worse instead of easing it. She cried so bitterly that I was afraid old Hendricks might hear it in camp and think she was being mistreated.

chapter twelve

SHE was easier to quiet than I had expected, at that. There was no long tapering-off process with relapses into more crying, and no run of unsteady-voiced questions carrying her from rage to petulance, like, What do you keep telling me not to cry for? I guess I've got a right to cry if I want to; what's it to you whether I cry or not? You don't care; what difference does it make to you; why should you; why should anybody? Well, if you do, what do you just sit there for? And so on, down a narrowing spiral with no way to back up, like Uncle Ben Shouns getting his whiskers caught in the feed belt of a threshing machine and running himself clear through it because he was too proud to admit his mistake by flagging it down. Calanthe's anger went too deep for such jockeying. She moved over and made room beside herself on the coil of rope, scrubbed the tears from her face on my coat, and then sat back and began telling about her father and the Farrand woman at South Junction—the things she had seen and overheard and guessed at that had led to her leaving.

Some of the things she told struck close to what I had already worked out with old Hendricks, but they were mostly guesses. She had no proof of them, any more than we had. It was what she had seen and overheard and caught hints of that opened up new territory in the case. Some of them cleared up points I had wondered about and had to leave in the air because there seemed no explanation for them. Her father had known about the Farrand killing before any reports of it got out, even to the sheriff's office. He had known about it when he drove over to Piute Charlie's camp on his dog-killing expedition—where it had happened, who was implicated in it, what the truth about it was, all the circumstances that had been reported on it afterward and a few that hadn't. He had come down across the Farrand place on the night of the shooting, bringing a string of Tunison's pack horses laden with whisky for the Indian reservation, and he had been lying in the rye grass below the house waiting for the lights to go out so he could cross by the railroad bridge, where the Indian police had no watch posted. Instead of the lights going out, there had been the shooting. He hadn't seen it himself, since he was a hundred feet from the house, but he had seen enough to know that it was nothing like the account the Farrand woman gave of it afterwards. It was impossible to make out from their hints and scraps of hurried conversation exactly how much he had seen, but it was something she had been willing to pay him to keep still about. Hiring him as manager for the estate property had been her way of buying him off. It was blackmail, there was nothing else to it, and she was in deep, or she wouldn't have paid that high merely to keep his mouth shut.

"She did it herself, that's what I think, and then she made up somebody to blame it on," Calanthe said, and sat for a moment watching the mist moving down the creek. The trees were so gray with frost that it was hard to tell where they stopped and the mist started. "She could, easy enough. She'd do anything, that woman."

Maybe she would, but I doubted if she had done that much. To imagine that she could have killed her husband and then invented a murderer and a whole string of corroborative evidence out of thin air, all in a single evening, sounded like stretching the probabilities a little too far. And Estéban jumping the Greek track gang without collecting his wages had something more back of it than restlessness. He had been in it with her. That much of her story had been the truth. So had her description of him, possibly because she had run short of imagination when it came time to furnish one. "It's a wonder she didn't try to blame it on your father," I said. "He'd have had a hard time clearing himself, if he was hiding outside the house when it happened, and it would have been a good way to get rid of him."

"She would have, I guess, but he was too smart for her," Calanthe said, and dabbed her face against my coat again. In spite of herself, she sounded a little proud of his smartness. "My eyes must look like fried eggs, with all the squalling I've done—all the way over here yesterday, and again this morning. It wasn't about them so much. It was everything. And having to watch them together, lallygagging and thinking they were making fools of each other. . . . He was too smart for her to begin with, anyway. I found where he'd pegged down a piece of paper with his name on it to mark the place in the grass he'd watched from. That was to prove he hadn't gone to the house. The grass would have showed his trail if he had, and it wasn't trampled past the place where he'd left the paper. And he didn't let on anything about it till she'd come out with her description of the Greek that was supposed to have done it. He waited till that got spread around so she couldn't change it or take back any of it, and then he dropped on her, and she had to give in. If there'd been any way for her to turn it against him, she'd have done it. I heard her tell him so once, when they'd slipped out together where her folks couldn't see them. That's the way she works it on him. She tells a little dab of the truth to start off with—something anybody else would be ashamed to admit, generally. He'll believe anything she feeds him after that. It works because he's not used to it, I guess. When I think how she leans her head against him and smirks, and how he leers down at her, when they're both as . . ."

She moved away from me a little, and smoothed down her skirt. "You said something about her folks," I said, to turn her mind from chance comparisons. "Are they still out there with her?"

"The Asbills left," she said. "That son of theirs is hurt, and in the hospital in town. He's that big-ended lunkhead with the spotted mouth that you saw down at the old ferry. Somebody shot him. It was supposed to be an accident, but I'll bet it wasn't. They got worried for fear he'd run up a big hospital bill on them, anyway, so they left to see about it. They're the only ones gone; the rest of 'em are all still there, stronger than . . . They're there, anyway. The women bunch up in the kitchen and take digs at each other about their housekeeping and their families, and the men sit out on the porch and brag about what they'd do with the property if they had the running of it. They all think they're going to get it turned over to them. They try to order my father around to show how much they know about running it, and he argues back at them, and you ought to see them. He thinks that woman's going to turn it over to him. He won't admit it to anybody, but he thinks she's going to marry him. Marry him, and her own husband not dead a month! That's how much of a fool she's made of him, the damned idiotic fool!"

She looked down the creek canyon again. The sun was reaching lower in it, melting the frost on the uppermost clumps of sagebrush into scatterings of rainbow-colored lights as it touched them. It was impossible to tell how much truth there was in what she had told, because her anger against the Farrand woman was too deep to make any exact allowances for. It was deeper than any ordinary moral condemnation, and different. She hadn't shown any indignation with her father for concealing the truth about the shooting; merely pride that he had turned it to his advantage. But telling how the Farrand woman was taking him in weighed her voice with anger so heavy it hurt to carry.

"Maybe she will marry him," I said. "There's nothing to stop her. It would fix him so he couldn't testify against her, and it would give him hold of the property. She's got to have somebody to run it, and it might as well be him as anybody else. Maybe you ought to have stayed."

"And had to watch 'em, and have everybody in the country snickering and whispering about 'em behind their backs?" she said. "I had all I could stand of that. If she marries him, it'll be worse. I wouldn't stay around 'em for everything she's got. She won't do it unless she has to. It would make a laughing stock of her, and him too; yes, and me along with them, and she knows it. She's got that much sense, anyway. He wouldn't get hold of the property even if she did marry him. She's only got a life interest in it. Then it goes back to the estate. That's what the men said."

"He'd have it to run while she was alive, and that ought to be something," I said. "She don't sound pindling, exactly. It's worth a quarter of a million dollars, and it'll clear twenty per cent a year with any kind of handling. You could buy three or four houses in town on that, and have enough left to live high on."

"On money from them, the way they've been acting with each other?" she said. "I wouldn't pick it up if they left it in the road! I'd live in a fence corner under a gunnysack and pull wool off rotten winter-killed sheep for a living before I'd take anything from them to keep them from throwing it away! Letting on they're in love with one another! In love, when they don't know any more about what it is than a hog does about Sunday! My father never loved anybody in his life! The trouble with him is that he hates anybody that's better than he is, and she's the first woman he ever struck that was worse! I know him, yes, and her too! She's already killed one husband, and she'd do the same thing to him as quick as look at him, and she will, too, before she's through! Her in love! If the alum factory ever burned down, she'd be forty miles up the . . . she'd . . . I can't stand her. I don't have to, either."

It was uncomfortable for a minute, wondering where she had found out about the connection between feminine intimacies and alum factories, and not wanting to let on that there could be any, but it didn't matter much. The other things she had let out were what really counted. It was not any wrongdoing or complicity in wickedness that had turned her against her father and the Farrand woman. What had been too much for her was their pretence of being in love when they were not capable of feeling love as she understood it, or of knowing anything about it, and still went on acting at it, clawing it lower, degrading it into a cover for their smallness and sordidness, their fear, guilt, covetousness, distrust, suspicion, plastering greasy finger marks on something that was worthless when dragged that low, something that was only worth having when people had to lift themselves up to it—cautiously and within limits, probably, but still up. They had been like a sheep herder using a branch of mock orange blossoms to flog a flock of greasy old ewes into a dipping tank. No wonder she had run away where she wouldn't have to watch them, no wonder her anger against them ran so deep. She had not been around much.

"What if your father comes out looking for you?" I said. "Does he know you've pulled out on him?"

"He does now, I guess," she said. "He'd gone to take some lambers over to one of the line camps when I left. That was how I got the horses sneaked out and harnessed. He was to be back about dark, so he's probably got it figured out by now. He'll be out after me, I knew that to begin with. There's all those people around, and he'll do anything he thinks they expect him to, so they'll think he's respectable. I don't care. Nobody saw me leave, and I kept away from the roads. It'll take him three or four days to find out which way I went, and I can keep moving. If he catches up with me, he'll have to work at it. I don't care much, anyway. I don't have to stand around for him any longer."

Separating him from the Farrand woman didn't seem to

count with her at all. It was not what he had done that angered her, it was what it had shown up about him, and that was hard to explain, too. This couldn't have been the first time he had wandered from her notions of grace and rectitude. Maybe the other times had been before her notions were formed.

"He might think something had happened to you, and report you in to the sheriff as missing," I said. "You'd have a hard time dodging him with the whole country on the lookout for you, and you'd get hauled back to him whether it suited you or not."

"He'll know well enough what's happened when he finds out the horses and camp wagon are gone," she said. "He wouldn't go to the sheriff about that or anything else unless somebody drove him. You mustn't let on to anybody that you saw me out here like this. It might get to him, and he'd think you'd . . . If he thought you had any hand in it, he might start out after you. There's nothing you can do to help, and I'm not afraid of him, not any more. He's not the only one that can tell things on people. I could tell a few on him if I wanted to, and he knows it, but it'll be better for you to stay away from him and pretend you don't know anything. He's mad enough at you already."

"I'll stay as far away from him as he stays from me," I said. "I won't tell anybody else about this if you'd sooner I didn't, but I'd better tell old Hendricks you've been down here. He's camped right up above us, and he's liable to come poking down here to see who you are if I don't tell him something. Where do you intend to go when you leave here?"

She inched away a little, and drew lines on the ground with her fingers. "I haven't decided, exactly. Or yes, I have, but it's . . . I'd sooner not tell you; not after what we've been talking about, not now. . . . Go ahead and tell that old Hendricks I've been here if you think he can keep it to himself. I don't want him to come down here; not by himself, anyway. I'd sooner he didn't come at all. I don't know what it is about him, but I'd sooner he didn't."

"I'll keep him headed back," I said. He had troubles enough piling up on him without mixing in any of hers, so it wasn't likely that he would need much heading. "Somebody ought to know where you expect to be. You might get hurt and need help. What kind of a fix would you be in with a broken leg or a sprained ankle, if nobody knew where to look for you?"

"I'll leave word somewhere," she said. "I don't mind people knowing where I am, if they'll keep it to themselves. I wouldn't mind you knowing, if it wasn't for some of the things I've told you. I shouldn't have done it."

It was plain enough what she was thinking of. "You don't mind people knowing where to find you as long as you don't care anything about them, then," I said. "If it's anybody that . . . If it's anybody like me, you want to get lost from him. Is there any sense in that?"

She said yes, and got up. The mist along the creek was lifting, curling up in grayish little plumes that writhed and splayed out into nothing like feathers dropped on a hot rock. "People don't talk about you when they know there's nobody around you but some frowsy old sheep herders. Everybody knows they don't matter, and they know it too. But if people found out that I'd run away and left word with you where to find me, they'd think there was something back of it, and they'd tattle it all over the country. You know what they can make things sound like. . . . There's my horse, down where the brush thins out. I'll have to go down and catch him. Remember, you're not to tell this to anybody."

"I'll have to tell old Hendricks something," I said. "It won't need to be much more than he knows already. Your horse acts like he had his hobble chain caught in a bush, or something. I'll wait here to turn him back if he tries to dodge on you."

She picked up her rope and went down the trail with it. The trailers of mist drifted across her as she entered the stand of trees along the creek, and then drew aside and disappeared completely as she came into the open where the horse was. He backed and circled when she shook out the rope, but I was right about his hobble chain being fouled on something. It took her a couple of minutes to get it untangled after she got the rope on him, and he followed along after her dragging a dead greasewood in it and shying back at every other step, but without any balkiness. She had gone to some trouble pulling her camp wagon in among the trees where it wouldn't attract notice. It was hard to make out more than its outline through the gray tangle of branches, even when she led the horse up to it and tied him to one of the wheels. Some of our herd horses came poking down from the ridge as the frost began to burn off in the sun. I threw a few rocks to drive them back, and looked down at the camp wagon again, but there was nothing in sight around it except the horse. So it had ended. She had told everything that had happened as near as she knew it. Part of it was her guesswork colored by prejudice, but she had told some things that filled in gaps I had given up as unfillable, and nevertheless there was a feeling about it of incompleteness, of something left hanging in the air to dry up and blow away; of evasiveness and fumbling; of failure. Failure ordinarily meant falling short of some intention or some hope, and

I hadn't had any, but the feeling held on, like the tingling that holds onto a man's nerves for an instant after he wakes out of a dream of being branded.

THE trees down the creek had been whitish and misty with the hoarfrost covering them. The sun melting it off changed them back to their own shapes and colors: the willows to crocus yellow; the mountain mahogany to a steel-gray tangle spotted in places with blackish oblong accumulations of dead sticks that were last year's magpies' nests; the clumps of wild plum trees in blossom to a white so dazzling that even the sunlight looked tarnished beside them. A big hawk sailed over, keeping watch on the horses up the ridge, and the blossoms where his shadow crossed looked a more blinding white than those in the full sunlight, strong as it was. There was a stick fire going in our camp when I got back up the ridge, and the sunlight on it was so powerful that the flame was invisible—the sticks changed from gray to black as if some creeping disease was eating through them. They looked so still and innocent that old Hendricks took hold of one to shift it nearer the center, and then yanked back and looked up, muttering something about needing to be bored for the simples.

"You don't need to make up any rigmarole about what you've been up to," he said, flapping his hand back and forth to cool it. "I know who you was talkin' to down there. I could have heard her bawlin' a mile off before you got her settled down. You kind of fell off with her right at the last, it sounded like. She ain't got herself in any trouble, has she?"

"She's got herself out of some, the way she tells it," I said, and told him the part of her story about what Busick had seen on the night of the Farrand shooting, and the use he had made of it. I had expected a few questions and side remarks while the recital was going on, but old Hendricks listened in silence, staring at the ground and waving his scorched hand back and forth absently.

"That's as much as she could find out for sure, but she's worked up some ideas of her own about it," I ended, to rest him a little before unloading the rest of it on him. "She thinks the woman did the whole thing all by herself, the shooting and trampling around in the grass outside the house and the story about it and the whole works. She thinks there wasn't anybody else in it at all. That might be her own notion, though. She was so mad at the woman she couldn't see straight. That was what she was crying about."

Old Hendricks spread his burned hand on the ground and studied it as if it was something he had picked off his saddle blanket, and then laid it against the water bucket and took a long breath. "That might be it," he said. "Yes, it might be. Shootin' sounds a little bit heavy for a woman like that to take on all by herself. I don't know, though. It sounds like too much for that Mexican kid, too. Still, he did git himself into one shootin' that we know of. It was my fault for puttin' him up to it, but she could have put him up to it as easy. Maybe easier. . . . What are you flaggin' out yonder by the horses?"

"Him," I said. The Mexican youth was only a couple of hundred yards away, keeping watch on the horses from a rock a few steps down the side of the ridge. He got up and reached for his bridle reins when he saw that he was being signaled. "There's no sense arguing with yourself over something he knows all about. We'll ask him."

Old Hendricks blew on his burned hand, stirred the fire together with the lid of a tin can, and frowned, showing his usual resistance to sound counsel. "What good will it do to ask him? Suppose he did do it; do you think he'll admit it when he's been keepin' it to himself ever since we started out? Do you think anybody'd tell you the truth about a thing like that? All right, then, go on and ask him and to hell with what the old man thinks; but you can count me out. I don't want to hear anything more about it."

"You don't want to know anything more about it, either, do you?" I said.

He got up and picked up one of the canvas pack-alforjas, watching Estéban prodding his rope-bridled old herd horse down the ridge toward us. "I guess I don't, when you come right down to it," he said. "I already know a damned sight more about it than I know what to do with, and any more would make it worse. We've done what we could to help out with it. Findin' out the straight of the whole thing won't make it any easier for anybody. It won't make it any easier for me, either. The best thing to do now is to keep away from it, as near as I can see. Go on and find out anything you want to, if it'll make you feel any better, but don't come around me hullabalooin' about it afterwards. I don't want to hear it."

He did a curious thing as Estéban came riding into the camping place. He dragged a couple of pack-alforjas a couple of hundred feet down the ridge to a patch of bare ground, propped them up about six feet apart, and sat down between them, leaning back against one and staring straight at the other so that it shut out everything except the sky overhead and the coarse gravel under him. From a distance, it looked as if he had started to put up a lean-to shelter and was testing it out for size, but he did nothing more to it, merely sat staring at the blank canvas with his back to us and his burned hand held out stiffly where the stir of wind could cool it. Estéban stared at it as he pulled his horse up.

"*Puede que está un jacalito?*" he said.

"He wouldn't put up a hut in a place like this, I guess," I said. "He wants out of the sun awhile, maybe. I want you to tell me something, and I want you to tell the truth about it. You will, if you know what's good for you. Over across the hills yonder there's a place on the river named South Junction. You worked there on the railroad with some Greeks a few weeks ago, didn't you?"

He blanked down to his expression of knocked-in-the-head limpness instantly. It was like watching chalk marks being shaken out of a blanket. He did answer, at least. "*Sí, Grecos,*" he said. "*Hace unas semanas, sí.*"

"There was a woman there," I said, taking him into it easy. "You know which one I mean. Somebody killed her husband; shot him in his house at night. Was it you, or was it the woman?"

His limpness may have been a good thing, I thought. It did keep him from turning panicky. "*Era yo,*" he said, in his vacant-sounding mumble. "*Yo, sí.*"

It was something, but not nearly enough. It sounded too much like a worn-down child owning up to something to escape being heckled by its elders. I tried again, hoping to draw him out a little farther. "Did you want to do it, or did somebody else put you up to it? Was it because the woman told you to?"

For a second it looked hopeful. He frowned as if trying honestly to recollect which it had been, but it turned up blank again. He shook his head. "*No. Ella no. Yo, no más.*"

That left it worse than it had been to begin with. It would have been actually clearer if he had done a little lying about it. "Well, what in the name of hell did you do it for, then?" I said. "Did you want to scare the woman into coming across with something, or did you just want to see how high he'd bounce when you dropped him, or what?"

Giving way to impatience was a mistake. He shut down blanker than ever. "*No sé,*" he said. "*Habían cosas que . . . No. No sé. Lo merecía, nada más.*"

That was the most I could get out of him. Arguing and threatening, instead of being any help, merely put him to edging his horse back and fidgeting with his reins as if he had half a notion to take out for the skyline, so I sent him back to his herding and went to work skirmishing up something to eat. Old Hendricks came back before I had finished, dragging the two pack-alforjas behind him. He started bunching cooking utensils to pack in them while I ate, and kept at it for a long time without a word being spoken. Finally, he couldn't hold in any longer.

"Name of God, how long does that guzzlin' have to keep up?" he said, and slapped a skillet against a dead sagebrush to clean it. "You can talk, can't you? What did he have to say?"

"Not much," I said. It was no use throwing it up to him that he hadn't wanted to hear anything about it. Knowing he would want to was why he had objected to my trying to find out anything, probably. "He said the woman didn't have anything to do with the shooting. He did it himself, he said. He wouldn't even admit that she put him up to it, and he wouldn't give any reason for it except that her husband deserved it. That was all. You said he'd lie. Maybe he did."

"If he did, he picked a damned poor direction to do it in," old Hendricks said. He bunched some plates into a stack without looking at them. "I don't know. Deserved it, hey? That ain't much of an excuse. He ain't any streak of lightning, but

I took him for better than that. Them feather-assed little pizzles that knows what everybody deserves ain't worth the axle grease it would take to haul 'em out and drown 'em. Maybe he did lie. Everybody does that's had anything to do with this, it looks like. Maybe that girl lied, too. By what you told, she swore the woman done the shootin'."

"She was madder than a hornet, that was all," I said. "She didn't claim to know anything about it except what she'd pieced together out of guesswork and bad temper. She's mad about the way the Farrand woman and her father have been carrying on together. They think they're in love, she says, or they're trying to make each other think so, or something. They're talking about getting married."

Old Hendricks put one hand on the ground behind him, and tried to put the stack of plates into a packsack that wasn't open. "Married? Them two? To each other?"

"It ain't happened yet," I said hastily. He looked so wrung and shaken that some kind of tempering down seemed needed as a restorative. "She said they'd been talking about it. That was why she pulled out and left. She swears she won't go back, not even if they try to drag her."

It helped a little. He opened the packsack and stowed the plates in it, looking a little steadier. "They're liable to try worse than that, if they catch her. She's a good girl. It's funny how they turn out. We ought to find out if she needs anything before we pull camp. You'd better run in the pack horses and tell the kid to git the rest of 'em bunched so we can start. I'll finish shovelin' things together here."

"They ought to graze a couple of hours longer," I said. "We pushed 'em hard last night, and they didn't get much out of the grass with the frost in it. There's no great big hurry, is there?"

He roped a bedroll and pushed it alongside the packsacks. "We've got some travelin' to do, that's all," he said. "It's around twenty miles north across the rock patches to the river, and we'll have to let 'em rest if we strike any grass. We want to git in reach of the Indian reservation by afternoon, so they can rest up to drive across it early tomorrow morning. We've got to git 'em across to the river by daylight, so them Indians won't try to slap a pasture charge on us. Then we'll have to swim 'em across the river, and they'll need to rest from that, and we'll still have about fifteen miles to make with 'em. It don't leave us much time to trigger around."

His line of travel had an odd sound of resignation about it; something he had given in to after a long struggle against it, a flag being hauled down. . . . "South Junction?" I said. "You switch around fast, don't you?"

He roped another bedroll and kicked it over beside the first one. "That's it. You ought to be a little more respectful about it. Maybe you ain't heard it yet, but you're talkin' to a man that's come into some sense. Yes, sir, redeemed and transfigured, that's me. I've been so I didn't know enough to pour piss out of a boot with the directions printed on the heel. Now I can do it right off the bat, if the print ain't too fine. I've changed. I've felt the witness. I've got ahold of a few brains for a change. You don't need to let 'em scare you, though. I ain't goin' to act high-toned about 'em. I'm a hell of a lot too democratic to let a little thing like brains go to my head. . . . It's South Junction, yes."

"On account of what Estéban told me?" I said. There had been nothing good-humored about his running on. It was all harsh, bitter, self-accusing. It was a relief to have him drop from it to a more matter-of-fact tone.

"On account of everything, most likely," he said. "It's all

been buildin' up on me since last night. Now I can see that I've got to go there. There ain't any way out of it. I'd been thinkin' all along that there was. I had it in my head when we started out with the horses that it wouldn't matter where we went, that we could go about our own business and let people git themselves out of their trouble the same way they got in. Then I thought maybe we could straighten 'em out a little with money and what help we could give 'em at long range, and then ride on and not have any more to do with 'em. A man could do it that way back in the old days. That was what fooled me; not a hell of a lot, I guess, but some. Now I know there wasn't anything to it. There's things you can't buy out of with money, no matter how much of it you've got. There's things you can't ride away from and be shut of, no matter how hard you whip. You've got to face 'em out for yourself, all the way to the end. Then you're done with 'em, and you can go on to something new. If you try to dodge or buy your way around one of 'em, you'll have it gougin' into you all the rest of your life. You can't take the pretty part of anything and leave the bad. If you do, it'll dog you clear to the middle of hell. I've tried it now, and enough's plenty. I've got to go see it out to some kind of an end, no matter what it takes, and by God, if I ain't glad of it!"

He may have been, but he didn't look it. There was not much elation in reflecting that he was falling right in with the sheriff's orders to take him to his relatives, either. He kept his hand up over his mouth and chin to keep them from drawing out of shape on him.

"It might work out a lot better than it looks," I said. "We don't know anything about it for sure: a lot of secondhand guesses, mostly. Maybe what Estéban told was the truth. Maybe he did do the whole thing himself."

Old Hendricks got up and began laying out pack ropes. "We'll find out, anyway," he said. "You'd better take word out to him that we're leavin', and then you can bring in the string horses. If I ain't here when you git back, I'll be down across the creek."

Coming at it so unexpectedly didn't leave much room for tact to operate in. "If you mean down where that girl's camp wagon is, I wouldn't," I said. "She's all by herself, and she's been under a strain, and she's upset and nervous, and she . . . She asked me to keep you away from there, that's the truth about it. She didn't say why, but you did act short with her that day we pulled her truck out of the mud, and she don't feel much like company after what she's been through. She's been under . . ."

"You don't have to go through that all over again," old Hendricks said. He didn't seem to mind being headed off, especially. "If she'd sooner not see anybody, she's got a right to say so, I guess. You don't have to haggle around and apologize all to hell about it. It sounds like she'd told you close to everything there was to tell about herself. I knowed she would, if you give her a chance. Where does she plan to go, or ain't that any of my damned business?"

"She didn't leave out much," I said. It was close enough to the truth, though not it exactly, but then some streak of fatuousness slewed me off into something not far from plain misrepresentation. She hadn't told me where she was going. I pretended that she had. "She'd sooner not have people know where she's headed for," I said. After all, it was easy enough to figure that it would be one of her father's old camps down in the sand hills where I had first seen her. There was nowhere else she could go and be let alone. "It wouldn't hurt anything if I told you, but she was afraid her old man would get wind of it if I told anybody, so I promised her I wouldn't. It might not mean much, anyway. She may have to keep on the move for a while, to stay clear of him."

He took that as equably as he had her bias against seeing him. "Well, you and her for it, then," he said. "Go bring in the horses. You might flank down along the creek yourself on the way back. Some of 'em might be strayed down into the brush, and there's something you can leave with her on the way past. Here."

He held it out and I took it. It was one of the unused bundles of bills he had made up to buy Estéban out of jail with. "I don't know how she'll feel about taking anything like this," I said. "She might turn it down. You can't tell what kind of notions she'll have about it, the way she's feeling. It might make her mad."

"Give it to her anyway," he said. "She ain't been particular about makin' me mad, so to hell with how mad it makes her. If she turns it down, scatter it on the ground and leave. She'll pick it up to keep it from goin' to waste when she sees that we're pullin' out and not payin' any attention to her."

It sounded like an idea, and it was his money. I put it away and, on the way out of camp, picked up an empty grain sack to toll the string horses in with. It was an ordinary jute bag, with the fiber broken in several places and some holes in it, but taking it along turned out to be the most important thing I had done since the day started.

THE clumps of plum blossom along the creek had not dimmed from their whiteness at all, but the ground behind them had lightened so they looked less dazzling against it. Earlier, it had been a sort of blackish-purple, powdered in spots with dark gold from the first long streaks of sunlight, and spotted with dark patches of naked sagebrush that seemed scarcely more than shadows against it. Now with the sun higher, it had dried out to a grayish-yellow; the sagebrush had turned a bleached whitish-gray like old bones; and the creek water had changed from gleaming black to a vague nothing-color that looked pale against the dark tree roots and dark against the gray stones that stood out of it in the shallows. Calanthe had changed, too. She had put on stockings and pulled her skirt around straight, and her hair was combed down smooth and tied at the back with a ribbon. She sat on a folded-up coat with a mirror propped against a tree, swabbing cold water on her eyes for the tear marks, and she was cool and standoffish. It was not only about taking old Hendricks' money, though that started it. She refused to touch it.

"I don't know anything about him, and I don't know what it's for, and I don't want it," she said. "I don't take money from people unless I know what it's for, and plenty of times not then, and you can take it back to him and tell him so. He don't need to think I'm any relief case. I didn't ask for any of his help, and I don't need any of it. If I do, there's other people I can get it from, plenty of 'em. I'm not a waif or a foundling, or whatever they call it. If you told him I was, you told him wrong."

"I didn't tell him anything about it," I said. "He could see there was a camp down here, and I had to tell him whose it was. That was all, except some things he knew about already. He thought you might have left in too much of a hurry to get things together, and he thought this would help out till you got squared around a little, and he . . . What other people can you get help from? Who are they?"

"There's plenty of 'em," she said. "Never mind who they are. You wouldn't know them, anyway."

"Ross Tunison?" I said.

"He'd be one," she said. "I could get help from him if I needed it. What of it? I know him. I've known him longer than I have you."

"He'd be a fine one to go to for any help you needed, too, wouldn't he?" I said. "He'd help you, all right, and you wouldn't be the first one, either. It ain't how long you've known him; it's how much you know about him."

She took the mirror from the tree root and laid it face down beside her. "I know as much about him as I do about you."

"So do a lot of people that won't have anything to do with him," I said. A loose horse splashed across the creek and edged close, eyeing the grain sack in my hand. He was one of the sheriff's horses, the leader in our pack string, and a chronic pet from a long time back. I folded the sack on the ground and sat on it to keep him from making a nuisance of himself about it. "Some things about a man don't count much. Some do. Have you ever let him kiss you?"

She turned the mirror over, looked at herself in it, and dabbed her eyes. "You would throw that up to me, wouldn't you?" she said.

Her voice was low, with a curious dull quality in it that sounded ominous. "I didn't throw anything up to you," I said hastily. "I didn't say anything except . . ."

"You did, too!" she said. "I know what you meant! I know what you thought, too, and what you let that old man think when you told him about it! You figured it out that I was some slut starting out to work the road camps for enough to live on, or something like that. Didn't you?"

"I didn't think anything of the kind," I said. "Neither did

the old man. I didn't tell him anything about that. He likes you. He thinks you're all right. He said so before I started down here. He said you was a good girl. You can ask him if you don't believe it."

She rested her chin on her hand, thinking it over. The pack horse tried to pull the sack out from under me, and I pushed him away and threw a stick at him. He trotted a few steps away and then began edging back again.

"I don't need to ask him," she said. "It's all right, I guess. There was something I said; one or two things. I was afraid you'd think something about them. You pick things up from men around a lambing camp, and sometimes you forget whether they're dirty or not. Mostly I remember. I will from now on, if it . . . There's that horse behind you!"

The pack horse tried to reach the sack again, and then nudged me with his muzzle so hard I almost fell over. I slapped him across the nose and picked up a rock. He backed off, thinking it was a game we had played together sometimes when things were dull, and laid back his ears and bared his teeth with pretended viciousness. I tossed the rock at him, and he kicked wildly at nothing and galloped away into the brush. Then, seeing that we paid no further attention to him, he came back and began grazing close to us, watching me out of the corner of his eye to see if anything was the matter.

"I don't remember that you said anything dirty," I said. "Maybe I didn't notice."

"Maybe you didn't," she said absently. "It doesn't matter, I guess. . . . I know what it means when a horse tries to play games with you like that. It means you've been lonesome a lot. You have, haven't you?"

"Not any more than anybody else, I guess," I said. "He's a

kind of a pet, and he's been spoiled, that's all. None of the other horses do it."

"You don't need to tell me," she said. "Horses don't get up games with you if you've got people to talk to or things to do. It's only when you're lonesome. They know it sometimes before you know it yourself. They can tell."

"They can be wrong sometimes, too," I said. "We've been talking here, and he came poking around us anyway. Maybe it does mean I've been lonesome, but it works both ways. You've been lonesome, too, or you wouldn't know so much about it."

"Yes, I have," she said. "A good many times, and long ones. There's not much about it that I don't know, I guess. That was why I let you kiss me, mostly. When I got back here and saw what a scarecrow I looked like, I was ashamed. I look better now, that's one thing, if you . . ."

She moved the mirror out of the way and shifted close and leaned her head back, as she had done on the sidehill earlier in the morning, and I kissed her again. It was not very much different from what it had been earlier, to tell the truth. It might have been if it had lasted longer, but the pack horse broke into it by putting his nose down and snorting wet grass seed all over us. She drew away and began brushing it off her dress, and I got up and picked up the grain sack, thinking what old Hendricks had said about having to see a thing through to the end once it was started. Some ends could be fierce and tragic. I thought of that, and wondered that it did not seem frightening. Then I thought that it might be because nothing had really started, after all. Kissing a girl didn't need to mean anything irrevocable. That might be it. Calanthe finished brushing her dress, and began dabbing at the wet places in her hair.

"I wondered if you meant it," she said. "I feel better now. You've got grass seed spattered all over you. I didn't tell you where I'd planned to go, and I still can't. You know why, though. It wouldn't look right, and if you run into my father and he asks about me, you can tell him you don't know and it'll be the truth. But you can find me if you want to. There'll be people that know where I am. All you'll need to do is ask around. Some of them will know."

"I'll find out from somebody," I said. "You'd better take this money the old man sent you. It's for some horses he sold, and you helped to trail them down from the brush to the river, so you're entitled to it. Have you got enough to live on without it?"

She laughed, and beat out the ends of her hair against her hand. "I haven't got anything," she said. "I was so mad when I left that I forgot all about that. Give it here; I'll take it. I can make it last. I've done it before. It'll only be till my father stops looking for me."

She didn't say what she expected to happen then, but she didn't need to. She had already laid that out, plain and clear, the first two times I had seen her, and there was nothing to add to it. I went up the hill to camp, carrying the grain sack, with the pack horse following and trying to pull it away from me.

chapter thirteen

THE trail north across the rock patches was old and not used much, and the horses, knowing they were entitled to a day off after their long night's traveling, took their time at it, pausing to poke into crevices and under loose rocks for new sprouts, and wandering off into swales and gullies so persistently that it was hard to tell half the time whether they were moving in any direction at all, unless it was around and around with a slight drift sideways. There was not much to look at—a few wood doves where the waterholes still held out; two or three lanky jackrabbits; a cock pheasant that flushed almost under the horses' noses and came near stampeding them with the blast of his wings and the odd jingling sound he made in flight; and once, when we had pulled up at a waterhole to rest the saddle horses, a hummingbird came and flitted back and forth within a foot of old Hendricks' face for several minutes, as if prospecting him for lichens to decorate its nest with. Spring was forwarder among the rocks than it had been back along the creek. There were black and red bird bills out on the high ground, and some patches of blue foxgloves opening, and a few mountain mahogany thickets that looked as if they were in bloom—not because of the flowers, which were too insignificant to see at any distance, but because of an odd restive effect about them like looking at something across a flame, which could have been bees at work among them.

At the edge of the rock patches there was a new sheep camp, with the herder's tent up and a lambing ground all laid out and marked at the corners with white flags, which we skirted around without finding out whose it was, and beyond it was a long swell of old plow land, sodded over and run to weeds and littered in places with the wreckage of broken-down sheds and windmills, over which there had been some fighting back in the old Indian wars. A Polack family named Ryczek had owned it then, and some Indians killed the old man and his half-grown son one morning for running a herd of hogs on a camas meadow that they claimed was public property. It happened within a quarter-mile of the house, with the old lady watching from the back window and not daring to venture out till it was all over and the Indians had ridden away. She refused to identify any of them on oath when the reservation police hauled them in to be tried for murder, but afterwards, when they were waiting handcuffed in a wagon to be taken to jail, she went out with the family shotgun and blew them all to pieces before anybody could get out and stop her. She was cleared for it later, on a plea of extreme mental and emotional strain, with no explanations offered for the strange distinction she had set up for herself between perjury and homicide, so that the place represented a cost of eight or nine human lives in addition to its ordinary expenses of upkeep, labor, improvements, and appurtenances thereunto appertaining. It seemed a considerable investment for a property that was being left completely unused and neglected, but there were reasons for it. A town doctor had taken it over in payment for his services in keeping the old lady alive and hale during her declining years, and he had taken out a federal farm mortgage on it, not having time to operate it himself. So it had to lie idle till the federal foreclosure went through, after which the title would revert to the government, which was where the dead Indians had been so ill-advised as to think it belonged to start with.

Beyond the Ryczek place was another swell of grassed-over plow land, also ownerless. It had belonged for years to a couple of old Welshmen, who had come out to live on it with their father back in the earliest days, when the whole country was wild and they were only around seven and nine years old. He started for town to bring back some supplies along in their first fall, and got drowned in an arm of the slough down the river without anybody knowing what had become of him, so they went through the winter all alone, with only a half-roofed cabin to live in and nothing to eat except what they were able to pick up for themselves—grouse and rabbits under the snow, cottonwood bark and dried service berries, part of a deer carcass that they scared a cougar away from, a few frost-killed fish. It was a hard winter, and everybody agreed when they were discovered the next spring that they had shown extraordinary heroism and resourcefulness in getting through it alive, but they must have used up all their afflatus in one splurge, for they never again showed any. They lived together on the place all the rest of their lives without ever going anywhere or seeing anybody or making anything beyond the same bare living they had managed to scratch out during their first winter on it, and people used to maintain that when they finally died, they did it at exactly the same instant, and then got up and buried each other to avoid having to depend on the community for even their last obsequies. Their land had some mineral springs on it that might have been useful for something, but they had no heirs, so it was taken over by the state and left unused, except as a camp ground for herds of sheep heading for their summer pasture in the mountains, and as a place where Indians and crop migrants sometimes came to steal boards from the old buildings for firewood and tent flooring.

One thing about those abandoned places was that the dense stands of sagebrush interspersed with patches of rye grass between the strips of old plow land made good cover for small game. The horses jumped one or two cottontail rabbits and several sage rats in moving through the dead grass at the edge of the rough ground, and then a big chicken hawk dropped down low and coasted along a little behind us, watching out for more. He paid no attention to us, though he was so close overhead that we could see the gray rims of his eyes and the tufts of down at the base of his wing feathers. At long intervals, he would flap once, drift ahead over the herd horses, and then drop back again exactly over our shadows. The monotony wouldn't have been so hard to stand if he had struck at game when the horses jumped it for him, but after he had let a couple of ground squirrels get safely to cover without even turning his head to see where they went, I got tired of his high-tonedness and took a shot at him with the pistol to shake him up a little. The bullet must have tipped him somewhere, for he tilted sideways so sharply that one wing almost raked the ground before he caught his balance and flapped haughtily away to the rockbreaks where he belonged.

It was a break in the monotony, at least, and when we came in sight of the old homestead buildings we discovered that it had been a two-way one. A small campfire was smoldering in front of the dilapidated toolshed, eight or ten or a dozen children of all sizes were knocking shingles off the barn roof with a pole and fighting over a dead porcupine, and a big flabby-fronted woman with a red face was screaming at Estéban that her husband had finally done it; that he had slipped away somewhere and shot himself; he had been threatening and brooding to himself about doing it almost the entire night; and now he was lying dead in his life's blood out in some weed patch and it was somebody's responsibility to hunt out the corpse and bring it in and notify the authorities, because she didn't feel able to bear the thought of it. We managed finally to get her quieted down and beat it through her head that the shot had been our doing, and that her husband had probably sneaked out behind a bush to sleep where the children couldn't bother him. She let go the suicide theory with reluctance, though she did admit, under pressure, that the only firearm he owned was an old single-barreled shotgun, and he would have had some trouble shooting himself with that, because it was leaning against the wall of the toolshed in plain sight behind her.

She refused to tell what had turned him to brooding about self-destruction overnight, but she did volunteer that he was a man of strong feelings, and liable to take it hard when anything hindered him in them, so it wasn't hard to guess what his trouble was. One of the chemical springs near the homestead buildings was what the old settlers called an anti-polygamy spring. Men who drank from it for as much as half a day usually discovered that their masculinity had dwindled to little more than an uncomfortable memory, and the longer they kept at it the more uncomfortable it got. He had probably been bringing water from it to avoid hauling the old well bucket up and down on its rusty pulley, which would have been safer, but more like work. Since his wife was too modest to lift the veil on their marital tribulations, we left her to work her way out of them herself, and rode on for the river across a long spread of open bench land with nothing on it except a few scattered spears of tickle grass, some half-dead clumps of sagebrush, and a long chain of dried-up ponds crowded full of wild blue and white lobelia, like lake water reflecting a deep sky when the air was still and as if breaking into little swells and ripples when the wind caught it. The shadows of the horses crossing one of the lobelia patches made no change in its color at all, but the hawk's shadow passing over it darkened the blue almost to black, and brought the white spots out so blazingly that they looked like sparkles of quartz.

The trail turned down from the bench land through a shallow gully broken by some half-dry mudholes and thickets of dwarf willow and wild gooseberry, the willows beginning to leaf out and the gooseberry bushes shedding dried petals to show green berries, no bigger yet than the head of a pin, but sharper to taste. Farther down, there was a steep gravel slope overgrown with little brick-red wild hollyhocks, and beyond it a long field of scrawny alfalfa where a hundred or so hogs were pasturing, with red-winged blackbirds perched on their backs hunting for ticks among their neck bristles where they couldn't reach. At the far end of the alfalfa field, close to the river, there was an old picket fence enclosing half a dozen gnarled old apple trees spotted with a few half-open blossoms, and behind them a small unpainted house where the owners of the place lived.

Strictly speaking, only one of them was the actual record owner of the place, but they had lived on it together so long that nobody knew for sure which of their names belonged to which of them, or whether they even had separate names. One was blind and the other a half-helpless cripple, so they had to handle the work together, the cripple pointing out what needed to be done and the blind man doing it under his direction. The old story about them was that when they were young and brisk, the crippled man had been a hired hand on the place, and had got into a love affair with the blind man's wife; and that they had hit on the idea of slipping some Indian knockout decoction into his coffee every evening to keep him from lying awake worrying about what they were up to.

It was supposed to be impossible to detect and temporary in its effects, but it ended by making him blind, and he finally got suspicious and used his last glimmer of sight to open up on both of them with a gun. The hired man got shot up so unmercifully that he remained crippled for life. The woman got off without much damage, but her feelings were so outraged that she left and never came back, so the two men settled down to run the place by themselves, each filling in what the other lacked, which was probably not far from the arrangement she had worked out for them to start with, if they had been willing to let well enough alone. It was a sight to watch them come out together into the alfalfa patch to feed the hogs of an evening—the blind man stalking cautiously along with a hundred-pound sack of grain balanced on his shoulder; the cripple hobbling behind and guiding him by touching his legs with a stick, like a child steering a hoop; the hogs galloping frantically for the feed ground through the greenish-brown clumps of alfalfa, with blackbirds swarming overhead and some still clinging to their backs, teetering back and forth and leaning wide on the turns like jockeys rounding into the home stretch in a driving finish. Men, hogs, birds. Their chances to make something of their lives had been as unequal as a homemade picket fence to begin with, but they seemed to be all finishing about even, with the blackbirds appearing to hold a shade the best of it.

Beyond the hog pasture, the trail struck uphill through a long greasewood thicket, still gray and dead-looking, and then leveled off into sparse pine timber, with bird bills and buttercups scattered among the underbrush, and wild sunflowers and blue lupin and scarlet bull pecker coming into bloom in the places that lay open to the sun. The pines were almost within sight of the Indian reservation, and old Hendricks' plan had been to camp somewhere among them for the night and dodge trespass charges by driving on across to the river before daylight the next morning. But there was no water anywhere close, and not much chance of finding any in pine timber, and since the reservation boundary didn't appear to be under any guard, we pushed across it another ten miles to one of the high creek headwaters to camp. Estéban was uneasy about Indian police, and refused to come in and eat if we kept a fire burning; so we spread down without one, and sat in the dark watching the night swallows skimming over the still stretches of creek water, and little slants and slicks of water gleaming through the lacework of naked willow and dogwood and rock maple and wild raspberry, as the blue-white beams of starlight glanced back from it.

THE silence was deeper because of the peaceful sounds that contrasted with it—horses eating; a horse snorting grass pollen out of his nostrils or a loose rock clattering; a grouse clucking along the creek; a little cat owl letting out a high-pitched snarl from a wind-twisted fir tree back of us; a rain crow calling a long way off like a gong striking faintly; the sound of water moving; a splash.

"That sounded like a salmon," old Hendricks said. "It's early for 'em to be runnin' this high up, ain't it?"

"They have to guess and risk it, probably," I said. It meant nothing to him. He was trying to skirt around thinking where we were headed. "They have to start from the ocean, and they have to keep going once they get started. They usually make it before the snow water's out of the ground. Maybe it wasn't a salmon. A marten makes a splash like that."

He said it had been too far out in the water for a marten, and too heavy. "These damned little shoestring creeks that one of them big Chinook salmon can't swim in without scrapin' its belly on the bottom, and they keep on at it every spring. All the way up from the ocean. To a place like this. How much time do you reckon we'll need to git the horses down to the river and across it?"

"It'll take about an hour and a half to trail 'em from here to the old crossing, and about twenty minutes to swim 'em across, maybe," I said. "They'll handle easy enough once they're started, but they're not used to water and it'll be colder than whaley, so it may take time to get 'em hazed into it—an hour, anyway. Longer, maybe. I don't see what you're so set on taking them along for. Why can't you leave 'em over here, and come back and pick 'em up afterwards? What use will they be to you?"

"Use?" he said. It appeared to be something he hadn't taken time to figure out. All his plans had been slapped together in the first few moments back in the ridge camp after he had heard the news about Calanthe, and his thinking about it since had consisted mostly in worrying over what he was going to the Farrand place for, not about any of the practical details. "I don't expect they'll be any use at all. I never thought they'd be. We've got to do something with 'em, that's all. They can't run loose out here without somebody to keep tab on 'em, and there's nobody to do that except the kid. We couldn't leave him."

"Why not?" I asked. "You won't get him near the Farrand place unless you drag him. There's nothing you need him along for, is there?"

He said doubtfully that he guessed there wasn't; nothing that mattered, anyway. "We'd be in a hell of a fix if there was. You can't depend on him for a damned thing, the way he is. I'd as soon not have him along to bother with, as far as that goes. The hell of it is, we can't depend on him if we leave him alone with the horses, either. We tried that once, and look what happened: he got himself into a shootin' and then sloped out on us and landed himself in the cooler. We'd be damned fools to risk anything like that again. We can't leave the horses here, anyway. Them Indians is liable to hit us with a pasture bill if we do; or a trespass warrant. If we take 'em back across the line, they'll drift back here to git water. The kid couldn't hold 'em all by himself. It would be too risky all the way round."

"You've got to take a few risks somewhere," I said. It was doubtful if he had thought about any risks when he decided on his change of plan back in the ridge camp. He appeared to be thinking them up as he went along. They were not points in a reasoned argument, so much as random excuses for something he had rawhided himself into on impulse. "Swimming loose horses across the river before daylight won't be any game of spit-at-a-crack in the back of a country grocery, either. We might lose some of 'em. There's a main road close, and we might run into a trespass warrant before we can get 'em into the water. They could stay here without being noticed. It's waste land, and there's no trails close, and there's grass enough for another day or two."

"They'll have to be herded," old Hendricks said. He was still turning over excuses, as if determined that something among them would still turn out to be the right one. "The kid's as liable as not to slope out on us the minute we git out of sight. He'd have done it a couple of times on the way out from town if I hadn't kept my eye on him. Leave him, and I'll stand to lose three ways: one on him and one on the horses and one over at the Farrand place. I'll lose there anyway. Damn it, I don't know."

"He's more apt to stay around here than he would be if you got him in range of that Farrand outfit again," I said. "He's got nothing to run away from here, and he's scared to move around much for fear some of the Indian police might nab him. He might work up nerve enough to do it, but you've got to play the percentage. It's better here than it would be on the other side of the river. If you stand to lose anything over at the Farrand place, what do you want to go there for? You still don't have to."

He sat without answering for a couple of dozen breaths. The horses ate rhythmically, and moved a little. The creek made a quiet sound in the dark: nothing that could be likened to anything except water moving. He finally spoke, in a sort of defiant blurt, as if trying to scare the place into silence. "I don't want to. I thought you knew that, after all the times I've dinged it at you. I've got to go there."

"What good do you think it'll do?" I said. "You don't expect the woman to own up to anything after she's got this far into the clear, do you? And if she did, what could you do about it?"

"I don't give a damn whether she owns up to anything or not," he said. "If that was all there was to it, I could sweat the whole business out of the kid right here. I don't want to. I know as much about it as I need to already. So do you. There's three of us here that know about it, and she don't know there's anybody around that does. She thinks the kid's skipped the country, probably, so she'll figure she's safe on all sides except one. That's the point, I guess. . . . There used to be an old Indian back in the hills below here once, and he got hold of an almanac and figured out how to foretell eclipses of the moon from it, and then set himself up for a big medicine man. The other Indians thought it was spirits workin' for him, and they was all scared to death of him. He could point his finger at anything he wanted, and they'd pack it over to his wickiup and leave it there for him—a horse or a woman or anything else. Along in the summer, eight or ten wagonloads of settlers come up through the reservation from Starveout Prairie with a half a dozen almanacs amongst 'em, and they could predict eclipses from them as fast as he could. So the Indians turned on him and made him give back all their presents, and then they run him off the reservation for good. It wasn't that he hadn't told 'em the truth about eclipses, but he'd run it up on 'em higher than he could live up to. He'd claimed to be the only one that could predict eclipses, and it turned out there was a whole pack of settlers that could do it. So the whole tribe turned against him. They like to beat him to death before he got across the line from 'em."

He was thinking of the Farrand woman and Busick, that was clear enough. "The trouble is that your medicine man over at the Farrand place ain't been predicting eclipses from an almanac," I said. "He's been threatening to bring one on. He might take a notion to tell what he knows about her, if you crowd him."

"You've got to take a few risks," old Hendricks said absently. He didn't appear to recall that I had already offered him the same counsel. "It ain't much of one. He won't start anything if he knows when he's well off, and I guess he does, or he wouldn't have stayed out of jail this long. He could git hauled in on that shootin' himself if he done too much talkin' about it. And there's laws against blackmail in this country, and we've got that girl of his to hold over him if we need her. If you know where she's gone to and she's still mad at him, like you said."

"I can find her if I need to," I said. There seemed no sense in telling him all about it. "I don't know whether she's still mad at him or not. She was when she left, and she's stubborn. Maybe there's enough on him so you won't need her. If you've got it all figured out what you're going to do across the river and how you're going to do it, I don't see how you can lose much by going there. You said you stood to lose on it."

"I do," he said. "There's no way around it. I'd lose if I stayed away, too, I guess. I'm like a man backed into a fence corner with a pocketful of money watchin' two bill collectors fight over which one'll take it away from him. He's well-to-do as long as the fight lasts, and when it's over he'll be broke.

The hell of it is that it drags out too long, and a man gits to wishin' it would git over with so he could fork over his money and go about his business. There's two things I was wrong about, though. I said I didn't want to go over there. That was wrong. I've got to go and I can't git out of it, but I'm glad of it. The other thing is that we can't leave the horses here. We've got to take 'em along, like I planned to begin with. There's another place over there I want to go when I'm finished with this, and I might not want to come all the way back here afterwards. It might be a kind of a long trip for you, but it's something I ought to tend to. What I ain't figured out is how we're to git the packs across the river. We can't swim pack horses loaded."

He was right, we couldn't. Letting him worry about it might have held him back from some of his projects long enough to decide whether there was any use in them or not. I didn't do it. "There's a duck boat hid in the willows on this side of the crossing, unless somebody's stole it," I said. "If it's gone, we can swipe some loose ties from the railroad and make a float out of 'em. I can last out your trip, if you have to take it. You might have said something about it to start with, instead of all that arguing and haggling around with yourself about horse herding and trespass warrants."

"I wasn't sure about it for a while," he said. "I was at first, I guess, before we pulled camp back on the ridge. I knowed then what we had to do, but I hadn't figured out the reasons for all of it, and then it looked like there might not be much sense to it. Maybe there won't be, but I've got it laid out to do, and I might as well do it. It'll be a kind of a clean sweep. You asked me once what I'd left this country for. I said I'd tell you someday, when things got straightened around so you could believe me."

"You don't need to," I said. He had me halfway scared, for some reason; maybe for fear he was about to let out something that wouldn't match up with what he had become. "It's none of my business what you left for. I'd as soon not hear it."

"You may not need to," he said. "You'll know more about it in the next couple of days, and maybe I won't need to tell you anything. If there's anything about it that needs to be filled in, I'll do it. If we're to make that crossing before daylight, we'd better roll in and git some sleep."

It was cold going to bed without a fire, but sleep came easy enough with the sound of the horses grazing—their rhythmic chewing, a step or two jarring the ground sometimes, a rock scraping, the soft rippling sound of bunch grass being twitched from the dry tufts. The disturbing thing was not the sounds, but the silence that fell when the horses all stopped eating and went to sleep. Being used to open country, they didn't lie down to sleep. They merely stood still, shifted onto three legs, and shut their eyes. Usually they did it at the same time every night, and always at exactly the same instant. First there would be the regular sound of their moving, scraping and clopping hoofs, pulling grass, and then nothing. The stillness brought me awake, listening without anything to listen to. The cold made it hard to get back to sleep, so I tried to put it out of mind by thinking of other things—a wheat field with headers moving in it; hunting quail in an oak canyon with sun drooping the dusty leaves; a grass fire on some stretch of railroad I couldn't identify, though everything about it was clear to the minutest detail, even to the bright snail tracks on the rock ballast and the date nails in the ties.

The scenes took to shifting too fast to keep track of, and I let them flit past without paying much attention to them. They were only scenes; no people in them, except at a distance as part of the landscape. In old Hendricks' younger days, there had been more value set on people. Nature had been the enemy then, and people had to stand together against it. Now all its wickedness and menace had been taken away; the thing to be feared now was people, and nature figured mostly as a safe and reassuring refuge against their underhandedness and skullduggery. It was the great healer: the hydrophobia skunk that had been turned into a household pet by sterilization and surgery where it would do the most good. Some day humanity would have to undergo a similar transfiguring operation, and it would follow the same upward course on which nature had preceded it. There would be hymns written booming vast sweeps of people as restorers of peace and faith to perplexed spirits; God's first temples, if only they would live up to it. Human beings. The scenes went on flitting past, but more dimly, and there began to be voices—a confused clatter of them at first, and then one at a time. . . .

—Yes, sir, doctor, I know as well as anybody that you're a mighty busy man and you've got all this big grist of payin' patients a-waitin' for you to cure 'em, but this here business about that husband of mine a-losin' his manhood is life or death, that's all there is to it. I ought to git one of them papers from the county about it, and I will when I can git a minute to do it in and somebody to keep the children from playin' around them powder cars down on the railroad, but this can't wait ary minute longer, or he's liable to do something desperated to himself. He ain't the kind of a man that can take a thing like that like it was a plain ordinary misery somewhere in him, no, sir. He's always been broody and headstrong, and the way he sets around a-mutterin' to himself and a-glarin' at the gun over against the wall and a-pindlin' away like he's a-doin', I'm scared to be around him; there ain't any tellin' what he might take it into his head to do. He's as liable as not to grab the gun and turn loose into the children and kill eight or nine of 'em before I can git ahold of him, or mangle himself, or something. You ain't got any notion how deep a thing like this takes ahold on him. Yes, sir, impotency. Well, the first time we noticed it was along yesterday afternoon, and then a couple of times last night, and again this morning; and it's come to the point now that he's . . .

—Yes, sir, judge, it's another one. In about three months, I reckon, and it looks like there'd have to be some kind of a court order so it can be took care of. Yes, sir, I knowed you wouldn't think too well of it, when you'd wrote out them separation papers and everything, but it wasn't anything I could help. I showed him the papers and made him read 'em out, and I told him what you said about how he'd have to go to work or stay away, and then he come at me and there wasn't a thing I could do, or that anybody could have done, no, sir. No, sir, I said there wasn't, and there wasn't, and I'd like to know how you'd figure out to handle it if a big lout like that had you backed into a corner with your rectum buttoned over the door knob so you couldn't . . .

—No, sir, Mr. Sheriff, I don't want to have anything settled with him. I'm a taxpayer here, even if I am a comparatively young woman, and I want that no-account plug-ugly arrested and throwed into jail and sent to the penitentiary; and I want an attachment for damages on whatever he's got in his name, and if there's any protection for law-abiding citizens that tends to their own business I'll have . . . For damages, yes, sir. He assaulted me and then he damaged me, and he occasioned me financial loss and bodily harm and mental anguish, and . . . Over at the dance in the Chicken Springs schoolhouse last Saturday, yes, sir; and I didn't do anything to him to start it. I was a-leanin' out of the window to git a breath of air between dances, that was all, and he come past and made some slighting remark, and then he hauled off and kicked me square in the stride so hard it give me the nosebleed, and I had to go to bed for four days and have a doctor, and it might have crippled me permanently, and besides that, it busted three of the hired man's fingers right in the middle of hayin' when we needed every hand we could . . .

The voices ran together and faded. The scenes had gone on flitting past, one after another, too fast to register. Now, either because they had come to a stopping place or because things happening in sleep bring on their opposites, as a red light in the dark will bring a green dazzle into a man's eyes when it goes out, they stopped on a scene of a hillside in cold sunlight, with clumps of scrub oak shaking in the flaws of wind, and some wild crab apple saplings in blossom around an old watering trough, dry and empty and weather-checked so the light shone through some of the cracks in it. Calanthe stood beside it, her hair lifting and settling as the wind moved and dropped, looking at me questioningly, holding something clutched tight in one hand. She had asked something; I didn't know what it was and couldn't hear what I answered, but she held out her closed hand, looking at me half-doubtfully, and spread it open, palm up. A small dark bird flew out from it into one of the oak clumps. She didn't watch to see where it went. She kept on watching me, picking aimlessly at a little tuft of the bird's down that was stuck between her fingers.

That was all. There was no way of telling what species of

bird it had been, or what the dream meant or whether it meant anything, or even what Calanthe had looked like in it. She had been clear enough, but trying to remember her got nowhere. I gave it up and slept, and woke up toward morning to the sound of horses moving. It was still pitch-dark, and colder than an icicle's backbone. Estéban had roused up the horses, and they were shifting around restlessly in the dark, bunched close together to keep warm. Breakfast would have taken too long to cook, so we let it go and saddled up and left, pointing the horses for the river and then letting them work it out for themselves, since it was too dark to have seen a trail even if there had been one.

They moved along confidently, and when the sky began to bleach out a little we saw that they had found a set of old wagon tracks and were following them down past some abandoned hayfields. Afterward, topping a rise of ground, we could see the river gleaming out of the shadows not over half a mile ahead, and some pole corrals patterned against it where the old stock crossing had been. The horses saw it too, and brisked up, which was a good sign. When horses are convinced that the trail they are on is going somewhere, they will follow it through worse things than a cold river crossing rather than lose it. I took the pack horses ahead at a trot, to find the old duck boat and get them unpacked in time to cross with the rest of the herd.

It could have worked out better. I had the pack horses all cleaned down and the packs piled in the boat when the first herd horses came in sight, with old Hendricks riding flank on the leaders and Estéban loitering somewhere back in the rear. They moved down to the water without even breaking step, but then they saw me waiting beside the boat, and began to edge off and sniff at the ground, so there was nothing for it but to go in with them and leave the boat for Estéban to try his hand with when he caught up. It fetched the leaders, which was the important thing with trail-broken horses. They shoved out into the current behind me, breathing a little sharply when the cold water struck their bellies, for which they couldn't be blamed much, and the rest of the herd came splashing in behind them without any urging, probably on the principle that whatever the leaders could stand must be good for all of them, and that any temporary discomfort was better than the fatigue of thinking up some way around it, and more companionable. Estéban's saddle horse came in with the tail-enders, so I knew he had taken over getting the boat across with the packs; not work he was used to, but easy enough, since the set of the current would carry the boat quartering across to a gravel bar on the opposite side if he merely sat still and let it alone.

The crossing was at a place where the river spread out instead of running deep and swift as it did through most of its course. It was about two hundred yards straight across, but not much over half of that was swimming depth for a horse, and the rest was solid gravel bottom, with no snags or sand pockets, and no great danger anywhere if a man took it easy and didn't let the cold and the white water scare him into hurrying. The cold did bear down. It felt like being run over by an iron-tired wagon by the time I pulled out into shallow water, but it was a sight to look back and watch the horses coming, the white-topped riffles racing past their heads out in midstream, the gray water lifting and parting as one of them touched ground and came up out of it, gleaming in the hard glare of dawn like a seal. Estéban and the boat were nowhere in sight, but old Hendricks was wallowing along with the horses still out in the rough water, and having trouble without appearing to know it. His horse had got scared of being carried downstream so fast, and was trying to hold against it by heading up into the current. Some of the nearby horses had noted the shift of direction and changed theirs to conform to it, so they were all holding themselves to a course straight across, wearing themselves out at it without actually getting anywhere. I yelled, but the water kept old Hendricks from hearing me. I couldn't swim out to him, for fear some of the horses might turn around and follow, so I picked up some hunks of old driftwood and rode back into the shallow water and started throwing them, trying to land one close enough so the splash would attract his attention.

The first was completely wasted. It fell far too short for him to see. The second would have been better, but it hit one of the loose horses and slid off without any splash at all. The third came close to being an almost perfect throw, except that his horse lunged at exactly the wrong moment, so that instead of slapping the water a couple of feet from him it hit him in the side of the head, end on, with a thump like heading a barrel. He tipped sideways, clutched at his hat and put his horse completely underwater, and then washed loose from the saddle and went under himself. It looked for a second as if he was gone for good, but then he hauled himself up by the saddle horn, scraped the water out of his eyes with one finger, and saw me. I waved and pointed, hurting to think what the cold must be doing to him, and he shifted his hold to the horse's mane and turned it downstream by slapping water in its face. All the horses turned, and all broke gleaming out of the water around him as he came ashore, one hand still on his hat and the other holding his shirt carefully away from the pit of his stomach, lurching heavily forward at each step as I had once seen a man do who had been shot through the bowels.

He passed me without speaking, his lips gray and his eyes half-shut, breathing short and raucously. His hat was pulled down tight, so I couldn't see what damage the hunk of driftwood had done to him, but there was enough without it. I hurried after him and held him by one arm as far as the old stock corral, and broke up some of the old poles for a fire and hung his saddle blanket up so it would reflect the heat on him. Our blankets were all with Estéban in the boat somewhere, so there was nothing to spread down for him to lie on, but the grass was at least dry, and I got his wet clothes off and rubbed him down with handfuls of it, like grooming a race horse, till he came uncramped and began to breathe regularly. There was a steep bump on the side of his head where the driftwood had landed, and a shallow gash that bled a little, but there was not much that could be done about it till we got the packs, and he insisted that there was no time to fool with it anyway.

"I ought to have had sense enough to turn them horses myself, so it's good enough for me," he said. "That's the only way some people can learn anything. There ain't any use sloppin' a lot of water on my head. I've had water enough to do me for a while, and my hat'll cover it, and there's too many other things we've got to tend to. We've got to find out what's happened to that kid. You'd better pace down and see if there's any sign of him. I'll be down to help look as soon as my clothes gits dry enough to put on."

"You'd better stay where you are," I said. "I don't know what good it'll do to look for him. He can find us easier than we can find him, if he's anywhere around. He must have the boat across by now, if he's ever going to, and he knows about this old corral. He could see the horses around it a mile away. Maybe he's skedaddled on us again. I told you he might."

Old Hendricks reached for his shirt, and held it in front of the fire to steam. "I know you did," he said. "I'd think he might have done it, only he's got them packs with him. He wouldn't lose them for us. Remember down at the old ferry when he skipped out on us, how he brung the rifle back and put it under the blankets where he'd got it?"

"What difference would the packs make if he's taken it into his head to leave?" I said. "He won't expect ever to see us again, and maybe this time he won't. What would he care whether the packs get lost or not? Maybe he's helped himself to the things in them. This is getting close to scary country for him. I told you he might pull out if we got him too deep into it."

Old Hendricks flapped his undershirt at the fire and put it on. "He wouldn't leave them packs without tellin' us," he said. "There's plenty of things I wouldn't trust him for as far as I could spit, but I'll trust him for that. He wouldn't do it. If he's had time to cross the boat and ain't done it, he's in trouble somewhere. Maybe it tipped over with him. Hand me them socks."

We argued it, but he won, and put his clothes on half-wet and put the wet saddle back on his old plug of a horse and climbed into it, with something of an effort. He won all the way round, as it turned out, for he found Estéban finally, armpit-deep in the river, struggling to wrestle the boat into slack water through a stand of dwarf willows a couple of hundred yards below the gravel bar where it would have beached itself if it had been merely pushed off and let run. It was a ticklish place to attempt any salvage job on a waterlogged plank boat full of packs. Estéban was so numb he could barely keep his hold on it, and spray from the swift water downstream beat past us like rain while we worked to get ropes on it so the horses could haul it clear of the current. We managed to drag it in through the willows and ground it, after sending him up to the corral to thaw out at the fire. Then we picked out a packsack with the groceries in it, and rode back to get breakfast. We were too tired and cold to talk much. Old Hendricks could have rubbed it in about having won his argument, but he let it go.

"Yonder comes the sun," he said. "This is one time I'm glad to see the blamed thing. I like to froze workin' on that damned boat, and I didn't notice how cold I was till it was over. By God, it was tightass and popcorn there in them willows for a few minutes, wasn't it? Well, now we've got to eat and git started. Nobody'll bother the kid if we leave him here with the horses, will they?"

"He'll have to keep 'em away from the railroad right-of-way," I said. It was about half a mile away across the flat. The sun caught a stretch of steel and a red switch target as the shadows drew back from the river canyon. There is beauty about a bright red switch target across an expanse of colorless sagebrush—a feeling that a vein of the world has reached out even into the wastes, or something of the kind. "You can take time to get your clothes dried out before we start. Your saddle blanket could stand a little of it, too. You're not trying to get yourself sick, are you?"

He did rub it in a little then, but only fleetingly. "I guess we can trust the kid not to steal anything and skip out if we git back before dark," he said. "We'll dry out what we can, but I want to git this over with. I ain't tryin' to git sick. I'm tryin' to git well."

THE ride to the old Farrand freight station was all gray hills, except for one creek crossing where there was a black cherry thicket and a small camas meadow. The horses were tired, the saddles were wet and heavy, and there was nothing to look at or talk about. A man could have shut his eyes and opened them again after half an hour's steady riding without being able to swear that he had moved a foot. The sun was almost straight overhead when we turned down from a long table land patched with scrawny greasewood and looked across at the Farrand place. It was not over a quarter of a mile from us; we could make out all the buildings plainly, all the landmarks we had been hearing about for so many days in so many places—the house where the shooting had happened, with a cluster of automobiles parked outside it, the rye grass patch outside the gate, the railroad track past it, the small white and yellow railroad station a mile in the distance with two or three freight cars standing on the siding where the Greek outfit train had been on the night of the shooting. We pulled up. Old Hendricks pulled up first, and sat looking without speaking.

"We've got here," I said. "Yonder it sets. That's the place."

He backed his horse a little, and stopped back of a tall sagebrush. "So I notice," he said. "Yes. Them cars outside . . . I was thinkin'. I don't want to see the whole pack of 'em right at first. You go on down and talk to 'em. I'll come along after you when they're at dinner. Tell 'em you're on office business. Git the woman out by herself, and tell her there's somebody to see her. Out by the bunkhouse, tell her. I'll wait for her there."

"What if she balks?" I said. "What if they won't let her come? They'll see your horse if you ride down, so they'll know there's some stranger around."

"I'll leave the horse out behind the corrals," he said. "Tell her something that'll make her come. You can think of something. Tell her you've got the man that done the shootin', and you want her to identify him. That ought to fetch her, if we've got this figured out anywhere near right."

"It'll fetch her, I expect," I said. "Hadn't you better take this pistol again? She might fall for it too hard, and send somebody out to bushwhack you. What if she sends Busick?"

He motioned the pistol away. "She won't send anybody, if she thinks it's the kid. She can handle him, and she knows it. Busick'll be out after that girl of his. You don't know this kind of an outfit as well as I do. Go on down and do as I tell you. When they're all at dinner, remember."

chapter fourteen

THE old freight road dropped down to the Farrand place along a dry creek bed where there were two or three boxed-in springs overgrown with alder and choke cherry, and then turned past its old hitching yard, flanked on either side by rickety one-story buildings that had once been blacksmith and harness and wagon repair shops, hay and grain storehouses, a commissary, a place for salting and baling hides, and even an assay office, if the faded board sign leaning against the broken front window meant what it still faintly said. There was a long wooden watering trough in the middle of the hitching yard, dry and warped and scarred along the rim with whittling. At the far end adjoining the main house there was an overwooded and half-dead apple orchard, with which the elder Farrand was supposed to have laid the foundations of the family fortune back in the gold-mining days. Fruit had been scarce along the old freight road then, and his apples had sold readily to homesick wayfarers at a dollar and a quarter apiece. It must have taken him some hard work in the beginning to get the trees planted and the freight-station buildings planned and put up, but the only thing anybody living could remember about him was that he spent all the working months of the year lying on a bull hide under his apple trees, reading the novels of Alexander Dumas, with an old Basque attendant standing by to pull the hide around into the shade when the sun moved onto him. It may have shown something about the changing times that while he had made all the money and accumulated all the property the estate had, the younger Farrand, by working feverishly during every waking hour and never thinking of anything else, had merely managed to keep from losing it.

The main house stood a little back of the old apple orchard, facing the river and the railroad across the field of coarse dead rye grass that had occupied so prominent a spot in the Farrand woman's account of the shooting. It was a big three-story wooden structure full of gangling windows, mostly boarded up, with a roof that sagged in places from too many heavy snows and a veranda that went all the way around and was cluttered with wooden crates, dry sheep pelts, pieces of broken harness and discarded automobile parts, and several spare piles of cordwood. As in most such places of the period, the kitchen was built separate from the house and connected with it by a roofed-over passageway with a big old-fashioned school bell swung from a scaffolding at one side to call guests and hired hands at mealtime. A couple of women were talking in one of the storerooms as I passed, taking the hide off various people they had known when they were younger—somebody named Lit Brummett, who had embezzled money from a farmers' cooperative, corked stacks at a gambling table, chased little girls up alleys after dark, and would have gone to the penitentiary a dozen times over except that his wife had been fool enough to go on her knees to the district attorney and get him let off; some girl they had known who was a kleptomaniac and had given her trusting husband a painful social disease three times hand running, and persuaded him every time that it was something in the drinking water; somebody else who had got divorced from and married back to a couple of sisters three times apiece, six times in all, so their successive babies would be born in wedlock, he being apparently unable to beget children except on the sister he wasn't married to, whichever it happened to be.

"It's nice to talk over old times like this," one of them said, after a moment of silence. "Well, there's some right in this house that ain't much better, I guess. That Peeny, out in the living room with that man of hers. A section hand that can't hardly talk English, and she's had six children out of him, and slobbers over him like he was something she'd packed home on a chip. I'll swear, if it don't make me embarrassed to watch her at it."

"Anybody can tell what her trouble is," the other one said. "She can't help it, I guess. Everybody notices it; the children, too. They try to sound brassy about it, and I think it's bad for 'em. They was playin' out back of the wash house the other morning, and I asked what their ma was doin' that kept her upstairs so late. What do you think that oldest little girl said?"

She told what the oldest little girl's reply had been. It didn't leave much to the imagination. They both took a shocked breath, and then tittered. "Well, if she's got what she wants, it's her for it," the first one said. "She ain't the only one that could stand straightenin' out. You know who I mean."

"I wouldn't talk about it too much," the second one said. "We don't know."

"She claims she can't eat or face people," the first one said. "She eats, all right. There's things gone from the pantry every morning that I've put away at night myself. And that man she's got. She ought to be able to face anybody if she can stand him."

"I wouldn't say too much about it," the second one said. "There's too much that we don't know. He's gone now, anyway. . . . Well, there's the coleslaw all fixed. I guess there'll be enough of it to go around, if they . . ."

It was all that seemed likely to be worth listening in on, at least. I backed away and went around to the living room where the men were. There were four or five of them all told, and the woman I had heard referred to as Peeny, with a free character reading thrown in. She was high-jointed and thin, with a dead-white face and strained colorless eyes, and sat close to her husband, a big loutish-looking roundhead who was holding up patiently under the double strain of following a conversation he didn't more than half understand and trying to look dignified when she rubbed against him or squeezed his leg. The other men were from places in the wheat country—a loan adjuster for one of the banks, with considerable to say about how he had rearranged various wheat ranches on a sound economic footing by eliminating waste and insisting on a limit of three automobiles per family unit; a quarter-section wheat rancher, very deaf, who kept interrupting the loan adjuster's recital of financial reforms with some savage and irrelevant staving about banks and railroads taking the bread out of working people's mouths; a baldish man from an insurance company, looking a little as old Hendricks might have if he had been stuffed with sawdust, who filled in the lulls by telling what somebody had got off down at the office; a heavy-built man with a dust-colored complexion and huge hands, evidently some son-in-law, who wandered about the room picking things up and glaring around challengingly as if for some explanation of them, which he never got. They sat back when they saw me standing in the doorway, and they all exchanged uneasy looks when I explained what I had come for.

"Nobody can see Mrs. Farrand," the loan adjuster said. "Not yet, that is. Not alone. It's doctor's orders. She's been through a severe shock, a trying experience, and we don't know how long it may take her to get over it. We're here to be what help we can to her, but we don't know. She can't see anybody." He raised his voice and yelled in the rancher's ear. "He says he wants to see Mrs. Farrand!"

"Well, we can't allow that," the rancher said. "She can't see anybody. You know that yourself." He turned on me as if I hadn't heard a word he had said. "You can't see her. What do you want to see her for, anyway?"

I explained that it had to do with identifying a material witness, and showed my badge. The loan adjuster bawled a keyed-up rendering into the rancher's ear, and said they couldn't take the responsibility.

"None of us could take it without the doctor's orders," he said. "It's—it's not an arrest, or anything like that, is it?"

"It sounds mighty peculiar to me," the rancher put in, before I could answer. "Talkin' about witnesses when he's all by himself, and comin' all the way out here a-horseback." He turned on me again. "What did you come plumb out here a-horseback for, if it's so important? Why couldn't you come on the train?"

"She'll get herself worse upset than she's been, if she hears all this yellin'," the woman called Peeny said. She nodded at me as if his questions didn't count anyway, and laid her hands self-consciously in her lap. "Her whole nervous system's all tied up in knots inside of her, that's the trouble. She's got her nerves tightened up, and people around her tighten 'em worse. The doctor said it might last a long time; he wouldn't say how long. She can't cry, that's the worst of it. She ain't cried once since all this started. Not once. She wants to, and she's tried to over and over again, but she can't. She didn't even at the funeral, or out at the graveside, or anywhere. She tried, but she couldn't drop a tear. If she could, she'd ease down and be all right again. That's what I think, anyway. . . . Was that her upstairs? I'll bet she's heard us down here. I'd better go see."

She went, ignoring the men's protests against disturbing the patient needlessly. It sounded a little as if they were trying to caution her against telling too much, but she gave no sign that she had caught the overtone, if it was one. We waited for several minutes, with the loan adjuster picking lightly at me in an effort to find out exactly what it was that I wanted, and the rancher shouldering in on him with rumblings about legal authority and credentials. Then she came back, hurrying and stumbling over a small rug on the hall floor at the foot of the stairs, spread there to cover the marks of the shooting, probably. It looked new. She halted in the door without noticing her husband, who looked first surprised and then relieved.

"She heard you down here," she said, in a sharp sickroom murmur. "Somebody left her door open, and she could tell there was some stranger here, and it's made her worse again. She don't want to eat anything now, and it's right onto dinner-time, and she hardly touched her breakfast, either. She can't see anybody; not any of us, either. Is that your horse tied out back of the orchard?"

I said it was, and that I might as well be going. It didn't look as if there was anything to stay around for. Old Hendricks always made things sound easier than they turned out to be. The deaf rancher suggested staying for dinner, but Peeny put her foot down on that.

"He can invite people to his own house all he wants to, but this one's got a sick woman in it," she said. "She could see your horse out of her bedroom window, and she made me leave her door open so she could tell when you'd gone. You'd be welcome if it wasn't for that, but it's her house. She ain't afraid of anything; it ain't that, but she's not well."

I invented some story about being due somewhere else anyway, and left. One thing that struck me, going back through the old orchard, was the discrepancy between their account of the Farrand woman's condition and what Calanthe had said about her. It would have been hard for all of them to hold together in lying about it on such short notice, and the woman called Peeny hadn't sounded as if she was making anything up. Still, Calanthe had no reason to lie about it, either, and she had sounded even less as if she was making anything up. The things she had told weren't the kind that anybody could have made up. I climbed the old orchard fence, wondering how to break it to old Hendricks. As I was untying the reins, the woman called Peeny came hurrying down the path through the old apple trees, catching her hair in the dead lower branches and motioning me to wait.

"I was afraid you'd get away before I could flag you, and I didn't dare to call to you for fear they'd hear me back at the house," she said, and held onto the fence for a minute to get her breath. She was not far from being a case for the doctor herself, I thought—a bright scarlet patch on each cheek, and the skin drawn so tight on her forehead that it must have hurt her eyes. "This thing you wanted to see her about, this witness business. She wants to know about it. She wants to know if he's someplace close where she can see him, and whether there'd have to be anybody else there. She wants to know who you think he is."

There it was, then, right in my lap when I had been about to give up. All it needed was handling. Old Hendricks did know them, after all. "We think it may be the man she's accused of the shooting," I said. "I can have him around back of the bunkhouse as soon as everybody's at dinner. If she can identify him, all right, but she won't have to swear to anything. There won't have to be anybody else there. He's safe enough, I guess, if you think it won't make her worse."

"It might make her better," she said. It struck me that old Hendricks had said something to the same effect down at the river crossing. "Back of the bunkhouse, when everybody's at dinner. I'll tell her. This side of the house is the safest to bring him in on. The orchard covers the downstairs windows, and the upstairs ones are all boarded up. If she can't identify him, what will you do with him? Take him away with you?"

"If he wants to go," I said. "There's nothing else to hold him for."

She turned away from the fence, and then turned back. A man would almost have sworn that she was enjoying herself. "I'll tell her, then," she said. "I can tell her for sure that there won't have to be anybody else there?"

THE back door of the old bunkhouse was propped open by a long wooden bench, worn glossy with years of use and carved full of initials that had long since shed what little meaning they had to begin with. There was nothing inside except a rickety pine table, a pile of worn-out clothing and a couple of broken sheep-herder rifles, and a double row of plank bunks holding some piles of empty grain sacks and a broken bale of straw. Old Hendricks sat in the doorway, looking out across the dry creek bed at the gashes of naked earth up the hillside where the old freight road had been, and the weathered remains of an old wagon strung out below it where some early-day freighter had gone to sleep on a bad turn. A beam stuck out from the eaves almost over his head, with an iron hook and a pulley dangling down from the end and a joist bracing it to the wall. It was intended for hanging beef to be dressed, but it did look considerably like a gallows. He looked up sharply when I came around the house, and then went back to contemplating the hillside and digging dried mud out of his boot welt with a stick.

"She'll be here," I said. "She don't want the rest of 'em to know about it, so she'll wait till they're at dinner. They think she's sick, or pretending it. Or else they're pretending they think it."

His stick broke. He studied the broken end and rubbed it on a rock to repoint it. The bump on his head where the drift-wood had tagged him looked painful, but he paid no attention to it. "Couldn't you tell whether she was sick or not? You didn't let on to her who was out here, did you?"

"I didn't let on anything except what I had to," I said. "She thinks it's somebody we're holding on suspicion, and that she's supposed to identify him. I didn't see her. It's against the doctor's orders, they said. I had to send word to her by one of the women. Peeny, I heard them call her."

"Pheemy," he said. "Her name's Euphemia. She'd help stretch a man out to be crucified if there was any excitement to it. You didn't have to come out and tell something that wasn't so, did you? She'll think we've lied to her."

"I did what you said to do," I said. "You wanted her out here, didn't you? All right, she'll be here."

He dug at his boot sole with the stick, and threw it away. "You have to take what you can git, I guess. Well, it don't cost anything to wait. . . . I helped build part of this old station back when I was new out here. Over yonder past the gully is where some Willow Creek Snakes jumped us one night. We ducked down into the gully to stand 'em off, and they set fire to the rye grass back of us. They could see us against the light when we raised up to shoot at 'em, and the smoke like to choked us. It was a long time ago."

"Did anybody get killed?" I said.

The dinner bell tolled from the house. He sat looking at his hands till it stopped. "A couple, and most of us hurt," he said, and leaned his head back against the wall to hold it still. Gravel crunched faintly around the corner of the house. The bump on his head fluttered visibly. "Well. Here's where henshit freezes. Don't tell her who I am. See if she knows. I wish to God . . ."

SHE had lipstick on. She had put it on hurriedly, maybe when her color was high, and it stood out in irregular scarlet blotches against the bleached gray of her lips. The effect was more abandoned and tragic than if she had left her mouth in its nakedness. She was tall and dark-haired, with pale gray eyes that looked prominent because of their pallor, though actually they were deep-set. It was impossible to guess how old she was. Some women only begin to come into their looks at around forty, and she could have been more. There was not much expression in her face—a sort of blank haughtiness, with an emphasis about all her features like a piece of formal sculpture, or the contemplative steadiness of a captive hawk. She glanced first at old Hendricks and then at me. Then she turned back to him. Her voice was disappointingly flat and ordinary.

"If this is the man you've brought for me to identify, you can take him away again," she said. "He's not the one. He's nothing like the description I gave out. I don't see why, when I have to stay in bed and take medicine and have a doctor all the time, that you people from the sheriff's office have to keep bothering around me with your . . ."

There was no use letting her run on. Old Hendricks showed no signs of stopping her, so I did it for him.

"He's not from the sheriff's office," I said. "I am. I sent the message in to you. It wasn't what we wanted to see you about. We've got the man that did the shooting. We know he did it, so you don't need to identify him. What we wanted with you was something else. He'll tell you."

She stared at me, her mouth sharpening. "You mean you've got the man that I . . . How do you know he's the one? How do you know anything about it? You haven't been around here; where could you find out anything about it? Where is he?"

It was an opening for old Hendricks, if he had wanted one, but he still didn't take it. He merely moved from the wall a little, studying her.

"We've got him in a camp a few miles from here," I said. There was a helpless feeling about having nothing to depend on except the truth, but it seemed safest. "He's close enough so we can find him if we need to. We know he's the one that did it, because he said he was. He wouldn't have had any reason to lie about it."

"If you believe him, why don't you take him to jail?" she said. "What would hinder him from lying about anything, after what he did and what he tried to do here? What do you bring a man like that around here for, and what do you come around here telling about him for? I don't want to talk about him or think about him. You must know what he did here."

It sounded a little as if she was trying to blur issues, or maybe her mind blurred them for her. Old Hendricks put in before she could carry it any farther.

"We heard something about it," he said. "I didn't need to hear much. I'd heard most of it before, a long time ago. It's what you accused me of once, when I wouldn't give you your head about something. It looks like you could have got up a new one to use, in all the years you've had to work on it."

It may have been the angry-looking gash on his head that had kept her from recognizing him sooner. She looked at it first, and then at him. He looked back at her without moving. She turned her eyes away and put the back of her hand against her face.

"It is," she said, half to herself. "It's you; you're finally back. I might have known you would be when it got around about this estate. And you've been working around finding out a lot of old women's gabble and making up things so you could be bought off. There's been some others that have tried that. You won't do any better at it than they have. I don't know what worthless tramp you've got hold of that you think you can scare me with, but you'll have him on your hands. I'm not afraid. Not of him or you either. Have you got anything to live on?"

"Enough," old Hendricks said. He had steadied down considerably; enough to be aware for the first time of the bump on his head. He put his fingers cautiously up to feel it, and drew a sharp breath with the pain. "I ain't worked to find out anything about you, or made up anything. You don't have to be afraid of anything. You are, though. What have you got in your coat pocket where your hand is? Take it out and let's see."

She tried to stare him down, and then looked away and took her hand from the coat pocket. She didn't show what was in it, but it tipped open so we could see the butt-end of a short-barreled automatic pistol. "I've got right enough to have it in a place like this, I guess," she said. "How did I know what you might have fixed up out here, or anything about you? I don't know much yet, and after what's happened . . . If you don't want to be bought off and you don't need anything to live on, what do you want?"

It looked as if it might be heading towards some discussion of family matters. I got up to leave so they could have it to themselves. Old Hendricks stopped me. "You'd better stay and see us through this," he said. "Somebody's got to, or we won't git anywhere. There's things I might know about her, or she thinks there is, and she's got that gun that she could use on me. Or she might do worse. She has before."

She took the pistol from her pocket and tossed it on the ground at his feet. We both flinched back when it hit. The safety was on, which meant that it was cocked, and the things did jar off sometimes, when the sear was worn a little. "That's how much afraid of you I am," she said. "If you've been around digging up anything you think you can scare me with, let's hear what it is. We'll see."

"Your father hasn't been digging up anything on you," I said, to keep her from harping on it. "The kid from that Greek track gang walked into his camp down in the sand hills on the river one night and started working for his keep. Neither of us knew who he was or that he'd done anything. We found out about him afterwards, by accident. There's more people know about this than you'd think."

"That Calanthe," she said. "I thought there was something back of her flouncing out of here the way she did. She went straight to you with everything she could think up, did she? Where is she now?"

"He ain't supposed to tell where she is," old Hendricks said. It wasn't quite the way he should have put it, but it seemed close enough to do. "He promised her he wouldn't. He wouldn't even tell me, and I don't blame him. She didn't tell any more than some others did, anyway. The kid would have told us the whole thing if we'd worked on him. I didn't want to hear about it. Not from him or anybody else. Not from you, either. Too many people knows about it already, and it's costin' you more than it'll ever be worth."

She started to say something defiant, and changed her mind. "I know what she must have told you," she said. "I know what she did it for, too. All right, her father's been working here. He's out hunting for her now, but he'll be back. We've got to have somebody. What do you want me to do?"

"You know as well as I do what you've got to do," old Hendricks said. "You've got to git rid of him when he gits back, and you've got to do it honest and aboveboard, instead of workin' on it like you've been doin'. You've got to git over bein' afraid of him or what he can do. He can't do any more than a half a dozen other people could, if they took a notion. What if they all come down on you to be bought off? The longer you drag along tryin' to keep things covered up, the worse off you'll be. You're bad off enough now."

"He might not want to go," she said. "He might threaten something."

"There's men in the house that can help you move him, if he needs it," old Hendricks said. "If he's got any threatenin' to do, send him to me. I'll be back towards the mountains, along the old freight road. He can find me easy enough, if he wants to argue. You've got to do it. You'll never git out of this unless you start now. There's talk about you and him already, and there'll be more, and anything you do to stop it will git you in deeper."

She sat down on the bench, and touched the pistol on the ground with her foot. "Nobody can help much. There'll be trouble. Most of it will come on me, no matter what anybody else does. That's what I'm afraid of. I've been trying to keep from having any till all this trouble clears up a little. It's been a strain. I don't know whether I could stand much more of it. I wouldn't want to try. I don't have to. There's nothing you could do if I said I wouldn't."

"I could do as much as he's threatened to, and more than he'll dare to," he said. "Either of us here could. That girl of his could. The boss of that Greek track gang could. The kid could, if we wanted to turn him in. That's five witnesses we could line up against you if we wanted to, and there might be more. You've got to do it, no matter what it brings on you. It'll git you out of worse. You might as well make up your mind to it."

"I don't know how I can," she said. "After all that's happened, I don't know. I don't know. I could lie to you and say I would, but I'm not going to. I'm afraid of him and of what he'll do, and I can't help it. I can't help what I'm afraid of. I don't know why you expect me to, or what difference it makes to you, or why you had to come all the way out here to lay down the law to me about it, after so long and after what happened. . . . I did tell people things about you that weren't so. None of the other girls would have done that; nobody would have believed them if they had. You wouldn't do a thing like this for any of them."

"They wouldn't ever need a thing like this done for 'em," old Hendricks said. "No, I guess I wouldn't. There's some kind of a difference. I don't know what it is, but there's always been one. It's been ever since you was born. We was on the homestead up in the mountains when you was born, and there was a Chinook wind that took the snow off and raised the creeks so the doctor couldn't git through. I got an old squaw from across the ridge to help out, and part of it I tended to myself. When it was over, I took you out on the back porch and washed you. There was still some snow patches on the hills, and a warm wind. I held you in it and thought to myself, this one's started different from the rest of 'em, and she'll stay different. There'll be something to her that they ain't got, and I'll see that she keeps it. That ain't all of it, but that was the way it started, I guess. I loved you. A man can't help things like that, any more than you can help what you're afraid of. It sets a hold on him."

"So that's what you think it is, do you?" she said, and drew her shoulders forward under her coat as if against the cold. "The others don't mean much to you; not as much as I do, so they can go on doing anything they please, and you don't care whether it's good or bad for them or what they amount to. But I'm different, you love me, so you have to come trailing out here and pry and lie and browbeat and threaten and lay down orders about something I don't want to do; something that'll hurt people and make trouble and be so dangerous it scares me to think about it; and I've got to do it because I'm not like they are, because you love me more than you ever did them! That's what you call love, is it?"

"That's it," he agreed gloomily. "You can call it anything you please. That's what it is."

"How can you love anybody you haven't seen for years and don't know anything about any more?" she demanded. "How do you know what I am, or what's happened to me since you left? Do you think I've got any better than I was then, and was that anything you could love? How do you know but what I did kill my husband? Some people think so, and maybe I did, maybe I got sick of his puttering and piddling and smallness, having to sleep in a little third-floor back room with half a window and a sheet-iron stove because he'd slept in it since he was little and couldn't stand to change; having to live in a place like this that's falling to pieces and rotting, and away from everything, and nothing in it except dust and dead people's initials and the smell of sheep! Maybe I got so sick of it that I thought I'd have to kill myself, and when he tried to stop me I killed him! How do you know that wasn't it? Would it make a difference to you if it was? Would it make you let me alone?"

"I'd have to try it and see." he said. "I don't believe so. You didn't do it, though."

"What makes you so sure?" she said. "What if everybody else thought I did; and what if your witnesses all thought so and could prove it on me? How do you know I haven't done worse than that? What if I had; what if I'd lied to everybody about it, and to you, too? How would you feel about me then?"

She was trying to draw herself clear of his feeling about her, it seemed; trying to find where its limit was so she could step over it and be safe from the gougings of responsibility, self-consciousness, doubt, humiliation and desperate restlessness that went with being loved. He refused to set any limit for her. He merely studied her thoughtfully, and flipped a pebble at the pistol on the ground.

"I'd feel the same as now, I expect," he said calmly. "If you'd lied, it wouldn't be the first time. You didn't kill him, anyway. If you'd been tryin' to kill yourself, you'd have used that pistol. He was shot with a rifle. Besides that, the kid we've got down the river says he done it."

She turned to that with sudden interest, though she had let it pass almost unnoticed when it had first come up. "You really have got him, then," she said. "Are you . . . Has he been arrested for it yet?"

"We brought him out here so he wouldn't be," old Hendricks said. "He's come close to it a time or two, and we had to buy him out of jail in town for fear somebody'd recognize him from that description of yours, or that he'd give himself away. You oughtn't to have described him so close."

"I had to tell something that was so," she said. "You can't help it sometimes. . . . Do you want to know how it happened, or has he told you?"

"All he told us was that he'd done it," old Hendricks said. "I didn't ask him anything about it, and I'd as soon not have heard that. If you want to tell about it, you might as well. Maybe you'll feel better afterwards. Have you talked about it to anybody else?"

She looked past him, her face blank and immovable, thinking where to begin. "How could I around here?" she said, as if that had been part of the tragedy. Maybe it had been. She began telling about her acquaintance with Estéban. It had been nothing much to begin with. He was working with the Greek track gang, and its camp was at the South Junction station only a mile away. Some of the men worked for a while surfacing the track across the rye grass field from the house, and she noticed that he was young and scared-looking, and that the other men always put him to work somewhere by himself and left him out of their conversations and arguments. Afterwards, they took to sending him up to the house to fill their water bucket two or three times during the day, and then he began dropping down of evenings after work, and her husband got suspicious of his hanging around so much and ordered him to stay away. It didn't mean what it sounded like. Her husband never liked strangers loitering around the place, for fear they might be planning to steal something. He was always rough with them, and he was rougher with Estéban than there was any need for, and rough with her when she tried to intercede for him. That and maybe a few other things led Estéban to think she was being mistreated.

"You told him so, I expect," old Hendricks said. "You must have, or you couldn't have got it through his head."

She agreed that maybe she had, once or twice. He was somebody to talk to, and it helped him to think that he wasn't alone in his forlornness. He kept coming, anyway, of evenings when young Farrand was working out somewhere, and sometimes he would walk down past the house after dark, merely to make sure that everything was all right and that she was not in need of any help. He never came close or bothered around, and usually completed his inspection and left without anybody knowing he had been there; but she knew that he was in the habit of doing it when he couldn't sleep sometimes. So, on the night of the shooting, when young Farrand heard somebody prowling outside and went downstairs to turn the lights on, she hurried down after him to see for herself who it was, or whether it was anybody. He was always imagining sounds outside that turned out to be nothing more than the old house sagging apart.

The rest was almost as she had told it to the sheriff and the station master, except that she had told merely what happened, and had left out all the contributing circumstances. Young Farrand was standing in the hall when she got downstairs, listening. He ordered her sharply to be still and not to move or say anything, because he could hear something moving. She insisted on opening the front door to see, and managed to get it unlocked before he could pull her away from it. He tried to relock it and she pulled him away, and she tried to open it and he pulled her away and wrung her arm back till she screamed to make him stop. She couldn't remember what she had screamed—maybe for help, or that he was killing her, she wasn't sure. It didn't mean anything, whatever it was, and he ordered her to shut up. Then she saw the door opening, and screamed because of that, and he tried to hold her and stop her mouth. There was a sound like slapping boards together. It blinded her and made her throat ache. She felt his hold loosen, and then saw him on the floor and saw Estéban coming toward her with one of the sheep-herding rifles from the saddle shed. She saw blood on the floor and smoke coming from the rifle barrel and the door standing open, and she ran. The rest of it was the same as she had told it before, except that people had drawn their own conclusions from it, and she had let them. He saw that she was scared when she ran past him out into the rye grass, and he tried to find her to bring her back to the house and get her quieted. At least, she supposed that was it. Since she hadn't said so, people had taken it for granted that it must be something else. That was it, as near as she remembered it. She had been trying not to think of it for so long that it was almost as if it had happened to somebody else.

"You wanted to tell this and git it off your mind, didn't you?" old Hendricks said. "The way it was, everything about it?"

"I've told you what I remember," she said. "I wanted to, yes. I didn't have to."

"The two of you scuffled, and he twisted your arm back till you screamed, and then you saw the door open and screamed again, you don't remember what," he said. "He tried to hold your mouth shut, and the next thing you knew there was a shot and he was on the floor. Then you saw the kid comin' at you, and you dodged him and run outside. That was all of it."

"It's all I remember," she said. "If there'd been anything else, I'd have told you. You can't see everything that goes on at a time like that."

"You was pinned so you couldn't git loose, and then you saw the door open," he said. "You screamed again, and you still couldn't git loose. You couldn't have turned around. You couldn't have turned your head, if he was tryin' to hold your mouth shut. But you didn't see anybody come through it. You didn't see anything else till after the shot. And neither did he, or he'd have let go of you."

She drew back and took a long breath. I expected some kind of outburst, but her voice when she spoke was lower than it had been, almost muffled. "I told you everything there was to tell. I wanted to tell it to you, and I told it as near right as I could remember. All you see about it is something to pick holes in, something to catch me up on, something you can turn against me to prove that I've lied, that I . . ."

He waited for her to finish, but she sat silent, watching him.

For once, he didn't stare her down. He leaned his head back against the wall and looked past her.

"You saw the kid come in the door before he shot, didn't you?" he said. "You let on to be worse hurt than you was, so he'd think he had to do something to save you. Didn't you?"

"You think that about me?" she said, still low. "You call that love, I suppose?"

"It's the same as it was," he said. "The truth ain't ever hurt it yet. Did you?"

She looked at his face a long time. Her chin drew down and her mouth began to twitch. She put one hand up vaguely, and then laid it back in her lap and put the other hand over it. "I don't know what happened; I don't remember. I don't know what came over me. I'd told him some things, and I didn't want him to think I'd . . . I don't know what I said to him. How could I, when it was all . . . Yes. Yes, I did. I don't know why. I've tried to remember why, I've tried to think . . ."

She didn't cover her eyes to cry, as Calanthe had done. She sat with her mouth wrung out of shape and tears falling on the backs of her hands, her face turned to him as if to let him see for himself that it was real crying. Then she turned away and began to sob, letting her voice go in and out with her breath in a dreary monotone. He came over and sat down beside her, drawing her face against him, and she began to weep fiercely, as if something was breaking in her, clutching him with all her strength, grinding her eyes and mouth into his coat as if to punish herself with it. It lasted a long time. Finally she relaxed her hands and drew away a little, letting her voice trail in and out meaninglessly, like a man worn out at the end of a long race, as if holding it in took more strength than she had. Old

Hendricks got up, still holding her, and saw me. He appeared to have forgotten that there was anybody else there.

"She'll be better now, I guess," he said. "It's too bad it had to happen like this. There wasn't any way around it."

"You'd better take her to the house, if she can stand it," I said. "I'll help you. Here's the pistol she dropped."

He dropped it in his coat pocket without looking at it, and helped her up. She still held to him a little, and there were still tears trailing down past the corners of her mouth, but her breathing had quieted, and she put up her hand to straighten her hair.

"I feel better," she said. "I'm not like this much. I'll be all right now."

She took a step, as if to prove it, but he kept one arm around her. "I'll take her to the house," he said. He looked white and old. There was a dead sound to everything that was said, like after a burying when there was nothing left for voices to do except comment on what was already done and over with. "I might as well, anyway. I ought to see who's there, as long as I'm this close. You can bring the horses while you're waitin', if you want to. Mine's tied in the cottonwoods down the gully. I'm liable to need him when I git back. I'll need something."

THE trail back to the river crossing was as gray and monotonous as it had been earlier, but the morning haze was gone from the air so we could see the black-timbered sawtooth line of mountains hoisting against the sky to the west and south, and the little scrawls of pale-green willow and alder brush where creeks wandered down through the open sagebrush toward the river canyon: Fish Creek, Wagonwheel Creek, Wicky Creek, Deadhorse Creek, Crane Creek. Old Hendricks sat up in his saddle for a minute and pointed at one of them with his bridle reins, and then put his hand back on his saddle horn as if its weight was too much to hold up.

"There's your open country," he said. "That's where you was supposed to head for when we started, and that's where we'll be by tomorrow night. We oughtn't to have any trouble makin' it. They don't waste fences on this sagebrush much any more."

"They fence it so they can plow it up and mortgage it to the federal land bank for farm land sometimes," I said. "You'd better plan on taking tomorrow off. We don't have to run on any time card, and you could stand to take it easy for a day or two."

"When we git up there I will," he said. "I can stand it that much farther. There's places you can rest, and places you can't. I homesteaded up there when I first come out here. That girl you saw was born up there."

"Is she all right?" I said.

"She's better," he said. "She needed something to break her up a little, so it helped. I don't know how long it'll last. . . . I used to look down across this country and over at the mountains, and think how long it would take a man to find out about everything in it. All his life, more than likely, and the things he found out would always be new to him. He'd never know whether he'd found all of 'em or not, and there wouldn't be time for him to git used to 'em. Things change around here faster than a cat can lick its trigger end. I used to think that if a man could raise his children out here all the way from the beginning, without anything else to look back to, it would be better for 'em. They'd be used to everything before they even knew it, I thought. They'd know enough about it to know what it was apt to change to next. They wouldn't have to stumble over something new to git used to every other minute. They'd have it all off their minds, and they could go on to something else."

"What?" I said.

"How could I tell anything about that?" he said impatiently. "All I could do was open the ground for 'em, and then leave 'em to figure the way out past it for themselves. It didn't work. Startin' 'em off used to everything didn't help any. It left 'em without anything to think about, that was all. They didn't know what to do with it. They didn't try to do much of anything with it that I could ever see. Make some money. Tend to other people's business for 'em. Pick at themselves. Raise kids to do it all over again. You seen 'em. I had hopes of that girl once. Well, she knows it, for all the good it'll do her. Maybe it'll do her some."

Maybe it already had, I thought, if crying was what she had needed. And it was the consciousness of being loved that had finally started her to crying: not guilt or remorse or fear, but being made to see how far she had fallen short of what she had been loved for to begin with: the failure, the waste, the desecration. There had been some hint of earlier trouble with her that hadn't been followed out far enough to be understandable.

"You said that when this was over I'd probably know something about why you left the country when you did," I said. "You said if I didn't you'd tell me. There wasn't much about it."

"Not as much as I'd expected there'd be," he said. "It was after we'd moved down to Burnt Ridge. Land went up, and they thought it would be a good time to sell out so we could move down to town and start a store or something. They was mostly grown then. She was about thirteen, I guess. We had a row about it, and she tried to run away one night. I caught her and brought her back, and the rest of 'em got her to write out a deposition that I'd been tryin' to rape her. Maybe she made 'em believe it, I don't know. She was always headstrong, and she'd do anything when she was mad enough."

That was what the sheriff had remembered about him, then. A man's past did follow him, changing but hanging on, like a tin bucket full of rocks fastened to a bull's tail to keep him moving. Knowing the case made it seem ridiculous.

"They'd have had to prove it," I said. "How could they have done it?"

"They couldn't have, I guess," he said. "They proved that they wouldn't stop at anything to git what they wanted, though, and that was all they needed. They wouldn't have tried it if she hadn't been in with 'em. They knew what I thought of her, and how I'd take it when she come out with a thing like that against me. A man don't have to be afraid of people he don't care much about, or of people he don't like. They can't do anything to you. But when it's somebody you love, you're laid wide open for her to work on. She don't have to do anything to you. She can twist you in two with what she does to herself. There ain't a thing you can do about it. That was what I left for. There was more to it than that, but it don't matter. I'm through with it now."

"She's going to get rid of Busick?" I said.

"She told the men at the house she would, and they'll keep her reminded of it," he said. "And help her if she needs it, I guess, and glad to do it. I don't know how he'll take it. I don't care much. Maybe we'll hear from him later on."

"I ought to arrest him," I said. "It would get rid of him, and he's done enough to deserve it. Maybe this time we could make it stick."

"If you arrest him, you'll have to arrest her," he said. "And you'll have to arrest the kid along with 'em, and if you do that, he'll git hung. He's in it deeper than both of 'em put together. He wouldn't stand a chance. I don't want to tell you your business, but sometimes them things turn out to be more harm than help. Think it over first. You've got time enough."

"You're against anything that might land her in trouble," I said. "He will, if he's left loose. What if he tells this on her? He's threatened to."

"She's in trouble enough, no matter what happens," he said, though he skirted around any denials. "She always will be, I can see that, and it wouldn't help any to arrest him. He can talk as fast inside of a jail as out, only what can he tell that anybody will listen to? We know more on her than he ever has. He made out all right threatenin' her when he had her scared, but he couldn't do it now. You can't blackmail anybody with something that other people know more about than you do."

He was right, except that there was an unsettled feeling about it. Something did need to be done about Estéban, for one thing. Two shootings, one involving homicide, were a little too much to leave hanging in the air. There was always danger of a blowoff on anything like that, and aiding a fugitive from justice to evade arrest was a little too serious to risk being let in for on the strength of a few small arguments. Still, being hanged by the neck till dead was serious, too, and arresting him would mean heading him for it as straight as a stretched gut. I decided to let it go, for lack of anything that looked better. Nothing could happen for a few days, at least. Busick could be put off for a while, too. He was out hunting for Calanthe, and when he got back from that he might not feel like coming after us; and when he did come, it would take him some time to find us; and even then it wouldn't be all one-sided. He could be argued with, one way or another. "If he comes bothering around us, I will arrest him, I don't care what for," I said. "I'll haul him in for vagrancy, or violating the herd laws, or something."

"Suit yourself about it," old Hendricks said. "He ain't bothered us yet, so don't pull all the stretch out of your suspenders ahead of time. . . . Yonder's the crossing, and yonder's the kid with the horses, and I'm glad of it. This has been a long day."

We turned in early, but the jarring of the river through the ground made it hard to get to sleep, and a wind strengthening about midnight struck cold through the blankets like light leaking through an old barn. When I fell back on the game of letting scenes flit past that had some feeling of warmth about them, they stopped on one of a long open ridge with a dark shadow moving across the grass, and a girl running. She was in the middle of the shadow, and it appeared to move with her, turning when she turned and picking up speed when she ran harder. It was too far away to make out whether she was trying to escape from it or stay in it, or to make out who she was. There was no meaning to it that I could figure out. It seemed to be merely memories overlapping—Calanthe running to head us off when we had ridden up from the old ferry to help pull her truck out of the mud; a hawk's shadow drifting along with us on our way up the river, or maybe somewhere else.

We broke camp a little after daylight and moved out for the mountains. Old Hendricks still looked grayish and tired, but he refused to admit that anything was wrong with him, so we shoved ahead through the sagebrush flat and into scattering juniper, and then into a belt of yellow pine bordered with lupin, and from that to the edge of the fir timber where there had been an old supply station in the days before sheepmen took to tending their mountain herding camps with trucks. It was not much of a place—some broken-down sheds; a couple of caved-in cabins with dead flower gardens in front; a huge empty store building with a long loading platform facing the road and a watering trough at one side; a small graveyard with old lilac bushes and white iris and vine maple and thimbleberry crowding each other for the upper hand in it. We camped beside the old store building because it was handy to water, and turned the horses out in a long meadow a couple of hundred yards away, with a mat of dried pea vine and stone clover and afilerilla between a scattering of half-burned stumps and old boulders. There were not many signs of spring that far up in the mountains. Even the sunlight seemed cold.

chapter fifteen

It was the graveyard that old Hendricks had come there to rake through, it turned out, but he was worn out when we got in, and the wind roaring in the firs kept him awake so much of the night that he stayed in his blankets the next morning, doctoring himself for a tightness in his breathing by applying a cone of sunflower pith to his chest, touching a match to it, and letting it smoulder, surrounded by damp cloths to make the heat strike in where it was needed. He insisted that it helped him, and maybe it did, as a counter-irritant against congestion, though the fire end of a cigarette would probably have got the same results if he had put the same devoutness of belief into scorching himself with it. The horses always stayed close enough to a new camp not to need much herding, so I left Estéban to see that he didn't set fire to his bedding with his muzzle-loading therapy, and rode out past the stump meadow to see what the country looked like.

The trails through the deep timber were still mud-bound and cluttered with the wreckage of winter—dripping earth slides, unmelted snowbanks, uprooted trees, raw clay gullies choked with soggy leaves and broken tree limbs, slopes of huckleberry bushes stripped and broken and beaten flat to the ground by the trees dumping snow on them after some heavy storm. There was nothing green except the firs. They were putting out new buds overhead, and a few blue grouse were clucking among the high branches, feeding on them, but there was nothing worth fighting mud and chill to look at. The soul and body rived not more in parting than a fir forest trying to pull loose from its lifeless dreariness after a hard winter.

The burned-over flats below the stump meadow had come ahead faster. There were a few spots of old snow still showing along the edges of the deep timber, but there were dogwoods in bloom between them, and rhododendrons, and even a few spotted lilies showing above the dead bracken, and the bone-white and gleaming black of the old burned-out stumps trailing crimson-leaved blackberry runners down into the gray-green mat of grass was as beautiful as any flowers could have been if they had stayed up nights working at it. There were some printed signs, mostly faded and weatherbeaten, scattered among the stumps. An old one proclaimed the area to be a part of the Prickettville municipal water district, and carried a caution against trespassing that didn't appear to have had much effect, since it was shot full of holes. A newer one from the government printing office stated that the territory thereto adjacent had been stocked with poisoned bait against predatory animals, and advised against permitting sheep dogs to run loose on it, which, since the buzzards always ate all government poisoned bait and scattered it over half the sheep ranches in the country before the predatory animals got near it, was a way of insuring that there would be enough to go around among the sheep dogs, and that they could all poison themselves right at home instead of having to walk miles out into the timber to do it. There were smaller signs of varying ages forbidding hunting, fishing, camping or building fires without a suitable permit, cutting trees or pulling wild flowers, or picking huckleberries except in duly posted and assigned areas and under properly authorized supervision. None of them were supposed to mean anything till summer. They were put up to draw city vacationists, to whom such things gave a pleasantly excited feeling of being the objects of somebody's attention.

The signs were all within a few hundred yards of the road. In the meadows farther down where there were none, there were signs of wild horses—trails leading back from the waterholes along the edge of the timber, and a few bare places where they had worn the grass off to roll in the dust. None of the signs were fresh; all the tracks had been rained on, and there were no signs of horses hiding anywhere near. A saddle horse would usually point them, if they were in winding distance. There were some bones scattered back of a hazel thicket that looked as if they might have some bearing on the problem, and where one of the trails turned close to some half-burned logs undergrown with alder and mountain cherry there was a wallowed-down place in the dead weeds that cleared it all up. It was where a mountain lion had bedded. He had knocked over one of the horses—an old one, by the size and color of the bones—and the others had dropped down to some lower meadow to stay clear of him. I searched the undergrowth back and forth in search of other tracks, but there was nothing. It was impossible to still-hunt mountain lions; they were too alert and cautious. He had probably been drilling a hole in the atmosphere a couple of miles over the skyline before I even knew he was there.

There was no great cause for uneasiness about it. Mountain lions never bothered people in that country, whatever their reputation elsewhere, but if he had managed to gather in and finish off a horse from a wild range herd, there was a chance that old Hendricks' horses wandering loose in the upper meadow might be more of a temptation than he could resist. I rode back to camp, to warn Estéban and arrange for close-herding the horses at night, when the temptation was apt to be strongest. Old Hendricks had improved so fast under his sunflower-pith medication that he had spent most of the day building himself a fir-bough bed, chopping down a thirty-foot tree, fitting the logs together into a rectangle, and packing the fir tips into it end up, like rose cuttings set in a garden, till it was completely filled with them, and so springy that a man could fall on it and bounce three feet in the air. One advantage about such a bed, he said, was that when properly built its springiness lasted forever. It would have seemed more worth talking up if he had expected to need it that long. In spite of his claims about feeling better, he didn't look much as if he would.

We arranged to keep up a guard fire out in the stump pasture, in case the mountain lion did decide to come nosing around after dark, and we tore down a couple of old sheds for fuel so it would throw out enough light to shoot by. Then we rolled boulders into a vague circle about thirty feet away for a blind to shoot from, hoping that the lion would be too busy watching the fire to notice any small improvements in the scenery around it. The circle of boulders was a little over two hundred yards from our camp beside the old store building. It looked farther, but I stepped it off afterward and made sure.

We took old Hendricks' rifle out to stand guard with because it shot farther and aimed better against the firelight than the pistol, and we spent the night keeping the fire up and glaring hopefully into the darkness without seeing anything to shoot at except a couple of owls and a porcupine. As a protection for the horses, the arrangement worked so well as to cast doubts on whether there was any need for it, but we left the rifle in the blind for stubbornness, and Estéban carried his blankets out to sleep in it the next morning, explaining that it rested him to be near the horses and away from the road. I spent the morning carrying old boards for the next night's fire, and then went to help old Hendricks with his work in the graveyard. He was clearing some of the old headboards from the grass and old leaves and vines that had piled completely over even the ones that were still standing. He had only his hands to work with, and the grass was so close-matted and heavy with snow water that it took him a long time and several rests to clear even a small space in it.

A GRAVEYARD in one of those old back-country communities was never anywhere near a cross-section of the people who had lived in it. It had always been the custom for the families who could afford it to ship their dead out to be buried in one of the bigger towns, where the undertaking equipment was more up-to-date, the funeral arrangements more elaborate, and the cemeteries cleaner and better-kept and farther from what nature had intended. What the rural graveyards caught was the people who had been too poor to afford anything better, or too unlettered to know that there were distinctions in such things, or too mulish or preoccupied to care. Most of the names on the headboards we uncovered were of people old Hendricks couldn't remember ever having heard of—floaters, sheep-herders found frozen to death after a storm, friendless men to whom the place they died in made little difference, and dying probably not much more. We uncovered a dozen of their graves before we found the one he was looking for. It had a plain wooden headboard like the rest of them, but the name had been put on by sandblasting over a stencil, so it still stood out plain and legible—Mahala Damron Hendricks. There had been a date lettered underneath in paint, but the damp had flaked it off so it was impossible to make out.

We cleared the grass mat away from the grave in layers—first the dead stalks of late-come weeds, wild sunflower and mullein and sweetbrier and wild morning glory; then a layer of tickle grass and broomstraw that had spread in from the abandoned plow land after the homesteaders proved up and moved out; then bunches of old garden flowers with pieces of blackened string still clinging to them, and some broken glass jars where they had been kept watered. Under them were scraps of wire and tinfoil from the old funeral wreaths, and then the bare ground, with a couple of sluggish pinch beetles struggling dazedly across it to get out of the light. Old Hendricks sat for a long time looking at the ground without paying any attention to them.

"Maybe you'd sooner have this to yourself for a while," I said, to break the stillness. "There's some other things I could tend to, if you would. I want to see that Estéban gets that herd fire laid before dark, and drag out more wood for it."

He went on looking at the rectangle of bare earth without touching it, like a man gazing into a pool of water. "I'd as soon you stayed," he said. "For a while, anyway. I've had this on my mind for a long time. This is the way it was to begin with.

They had the headboard leaned against that rock yonder so the dirt wouldn't scatter on it, and they'd laid some of their shovels on an old grave to one side of it. I stood over there at the edge of the grass, back of where you are, and thought how they'd used a place where somebody else was buried to lay shovels on, and about puttin' people into the ground, and about things I could have done different. Some of 'em had done more hurt than I'd expected, and the good they'd done didn't matter as much as I expected it would. That's as near as I remember it. It ain't the same as it was. These weeds wasn't here then, and the ground wasn't black like this. It was red clay."

"People at a time like that generally think about things they could have done different," I said. That much nobody needed to tell me. "You can't tell whether they'd have turned out any better, though. Nothing ever turns out the way you thought it would."

"No, it don't," he agreed. "I thought about things like that because everybody else always does, I expect. They wasn't what I had in the back of my mind. There was something else there, and I didn't want to think about it. It kept sawin' at me all the time I stood over there at the edge of the grass, and I kept tryin' to hold it back. I know it now. I know what it was. It was, Well, they've got to put her down into that red clay now, and, my God, what if we loved each other?"

"I'd think that much stood to reason," I said. "You got married, didn't you?"

"Sometimes them things git so they don't count much," he said. "Sometimes it gits so it don't matter much. Sometimes you think it don't and then find out it did. There's people you come to know less and less about the longer you live with 'em. You may know all about 'em to start with, but then they branch off and grow away from you underground, or something. You can't always tell whether you're to blame for it or not. There wasn't any change about her that you could put your finger on, she talked and acted the same as she always had, but she didn't have her mind on it as much. She'd be workin' or lookin' out of the window, and all of a sudden she'd tell one of the kids to go bring her some paper and a pencil; she'd had a new kind of bird come into her mind, and she wanted to draw a picture of it while she remembered what it looked like. If she let it go, she'd worry about it for a month, and sometimes not talk to anybody. So she'd drop everything when one come to her, and set down and draw it off. She acted like she had to; she couldn't help it."

"Did the pictures look like anything?" I asked.

"She never showed 'em to anybody," he said. "If she had, I wouldn't have thought much about it, but she always put 'em away somewhere when she got 'em done, and that was the last of 'em. We never found any of 'em. Something has to happen to a woman to make her like that. Something had, I guess."

"Anybody's bound to get hurt a few times," I said. "Most people get over it. They have to."

He broke an old sunflower leaf in his fingers, and went on as if I hadn't spoken. "Hers happened a long time back, if that was it. We was up here tryin' to git started, and we both wanted to git ahead. We had the homestead and some cattle, and there come a bad winter. The grass all got froze under four feet of hard snow and the feed run out, and hay went up to ninety dollars a ton and no way to haul it in. Everybody's cattle was starvin' to death, and nobody knew anything to do but let 'em. There was a camp of Indians that had some land allotments over at Hot Creek Meadows on the reservation. The creek spread out where they was, and it run warm enough through the winter to keep the grass open, and they wasn't doin' anything with it. They couldn't sell it, and they didn't want to lease it because the money would have gone to the agency and they wouldn't have got any of it. So I took up with one of the young squaws, and she got 'em to help move our cattle over onto it, and they wintered out as slick as moles. We didn't lose a one. Most people lost every head they owned that winter, and went broke tryin' to keep 'em alive besides. I kept it up after that for a long time, off and on; almost till we bought in down at Burnt Ridge and moved from here, I guess. It's hard to stop with Indians, once you're started, and it worked all right. They couldn't have sold their grass anywhere, and they didn't need it. They always wintered their ponies on cottonwood bark. It looked like everybody was ahead on it. I couldn't see how it hurt anybody much."

"You can't tell what will hurt people sometimes," I said. It might explain something, at that. Having it on his conscience may have been why he had left Burnt Ridge because of his children's impudent fourflushing, instead of staying and having it out with them.

"She'd have got hurt either way," he said. "If I hadn't done it, we'd have gone broke. That would have hurt her, too. The cattle was all we had, and she'd put as much into 'em as I had. I thought she'd sooner keep 'em than be cleaned out and have to start all over again. I didn't think . . . I thought she felt the same way about it that I did, I guess. Nobody wants to be broke and have to depend on other people. I done the only thing I could that would head it off. I didn't think anything else counted for much. She never said anything about it, that was one thing."

"What about the squaw?" I asked.

"She got married," he said. "To some Siwash or other, about

the time I left Burnt Ridge, or maybe a little before then. She was all right. I've seen worse. She's dead now, one of them bucks down on the river told me. A long time ago . . . Well, we'll cover this back the way we found it."

He didn't start raking the dead grass back over the grave, though. He merely sat looking at it.

"We could trim it up a little, if you want to leave it cleaned off," I said. "There's flowers down along the edge of the horse pasture; wild ones, but they'd look like something."

"It wouldn't make up for anything," he said. "You can't make up for what you've done. When you do it, it stands against you. You pay for it, no matter what you do afterwards. Good and bad don't cancel each other out. It don't lighten a twenty-pound load on one end of a pole to hang twenty-one pounds on the other end. The pole's got to carry 'em both. Well, there's this grass to rake back. It'll look better put back where it was. This is a grave, the same as the rest of 'em. It's been through the same as they have, and it might as well show it. I'll tend to it. You go in and help the kid with that herd fire of yours. I'll be along in a few minutes."

He was entitled to be left alone awhile. It was getting late. The shadows were lengthening, the air was clotting up with night damp, and a top wind was begining to roar in the firs. "Don't stay out here too long," I said. "You'll give yourself another chill, and it won't do any good. It don't help to sit out here beating yourself around a stump about things that are all over with."

"I know that better than you do," he said. "Some of the things may not be all over with, that's the only thing. A man can't tell what's layin' around inside of him. There's too many corners, and things reach out from 'em sometimes that you'd thought was all dead and buried. I want to git some kind of a count on 'em if I can, so I can start on something else. A man don't want to traipse around the same stump all his life."

Going down across the road to camp, I thought of a huge old fir stump that a family of new homesteaders had tried to burn out of their hayfield once, in the mountains back of Thief Creek. They prepared for it by boring auger holes in the top of the stump and filling them with turpentine. They plugged them and allowed a year for the turpentine to soak in well, and then they piled brush over the stump and set it afire. The fire followed the turpentine down into all the roots and clear out through their dips, spurs and angles to the extreme tip ends. It was still burning underground eight months afterward. A man wouldn't have believed how many of them there were, or how far they reached. It was dangerous to ride a horse anywhere on the place, for fear of breaking through into one of the burned-out tunnels where a root had been, and places in the hayfield and under the house were still cracking open and emitting striddles of smoke even after there was a foot of snow on the ground. A man's thoughts could spread a hundred times farther than a tree's root system could, and take more than a hundred times longer to burn out. There was no kind of turpentine that could penetrate down into them to make it easier. It took time, and there was no way to tell whether they were all out or not. It was better not to have too many of them, maybe. Some people managed fairly well without any.

There was a plank bench nailed against the wall on one side of the old store platform that we had turned into a wash stand because it was the right height and open to the sun in the morning. The old grass in the graveyard had been heavy with dirt, so I stopped and slopped some water into the tin basin to clean some of it off. Then I decided to be a little more systematic about it, and tend to all the dirty chores first, so that one washing would do for all of them. I split kindling and built up the campfire for old Hendricks to warm up by when he came in, and tore off a load of old shed boards and roped them into a bundle for our herd fire after dark, and saddled up the camp horse to drag them out with. There was a faint rattling audible above the wind in the timber when I went back to the loading platform to wash up, but the air was beginning to stir up little dust whirls along the road in front of the store, so I decided that it was a loose window frame rattling somewhere, and peeled down to wash without paying any more attention to it, folding my coat and shirt together on the far end of the bench and shoving the pistol under them out of sight for safe-keeping. As usually happens, I discovered when the soap was beginning to sting my eyes that I had forgotten to bring a towel out, and had to go groping half-blind around the store and fumble one out of the packsacks behind the watering trough. There was no sound of anything except the wind while I was busy digging for it, but when I got back to the platform and had started scrubbing my eyes and splattering clean water on them to get rid of the sting, I saw that there was a wagon coming. It drew even with the platform and pulled to a stop as I finished with the towel and laid it across the bench to dry. The man in it nodded, leaned down and wrapped his lines around the brake, and reached a rifle from behind him: a .250-3000 coyote gun. I had seen it before, and handled it, and seen a sample of its work. I recognized it a fraction of a second before it dawned on me that the man holding it was Busick.

He didn't look altogether as I had remembered him. I had only seen him after the shooting down of Piute Charlie's camp on the river, and part of the impression I got of him then may have been sand glare and dust and excitement, but I remembered him as leaner, paler, higher-keyed and unsteadier of temper than he looked to be as he sat sizing me up from the wagon seat with his rifle laid in his lap and trained carelessly somewhere around the third button of my undershirt. He shifted his eyes from me to our camp, and then to the horses out in the pasture, with such sluggish-looking indifference that I tried shifting a couple of steps to see if the rifle pointed at me was intentional. He glanced around and moved it to cover me again.

"Stay where you are," he said, and settled his hand on the stock so the barrel moved up and down like a sort of cautioning finger. "This here's a gun. It shoots bullets. You've seen 'em. You've got yourselves all fixed around to make a stay of it here, it looks like. Horses all out on pasture, and wood piled up, and beds laid, and everything. You didn't expect I'd git your trail run out this far for quite a spell yet, did you? Where's the old man? He's around someplace, so don't try to lie about it. Yonder's his bed quilts."

It was not only his bed quilts that were in plain sight. So was his saddle. It limited me a little, but it would have been idiotic to tell the truth about where he was, with the cemetery in easy rifle range.

"He went down to look over some of the meadows below here," I said. "There's logs across some of the trail, so he went afoot. He said he might be late getting back."

It wasn't a very creditable effort. I could see several flaws in it before I had finished telling it, but it worked. He glanced around again, and said it was late already. "It'll be dark in another hour, or close to it. He won't stay out any later than that, I guess, if he's afoot. Where's that kid you had with you, the one you had camped down the river before you come up here?"

He had talked to the Farrand woman, then, and she must have kept her agreement about getting rid of him. That explained his tone, and the rifle pointed at me. It made lying to him a little precarious, because I didn't know what she might have told him and couldn't remember exactly what we had told her. "He's been night herding, and he went out in the brush somewhere to sleep," I said. "That's where he said he was going, anyway. He always sleeps away from camp, because it makes him uneasy to have anybody around him."

"He'll have to git over that," Busick said, and studied on it, frowning; not weighing any probabilities, it seemed, but trying to think what was the next thing he had to find out about. He thought of it. "You've got a gun somewhere around. You're supposed to pack one when you're workin', and it ain't on you. Where's it at?"

It didn't take much work to get up an answer for that. Anything was all right, as long as it stayed far enough from the facts. "Old Hendricks took it with him," I said. "There's been a mountain lion around the horses, and he thought he might jump it somewhere down in the logs."

He filed that away, and then took it under advisement again. "He had a gun of his own, one of them old eight-square rifles. Why didn't he take that? Where is it?"

"It's hard to carry in the brush, and he wanted to save weight," I said. That much of it was easy. I could think up answers to questions like that as fast as he could think them up to ask. The rest of it needed a little more careful treatment, and an idea struck me. If I could draw him into climbing down from the wagon, and make a break for the pistol at the end of the wash bench while he was off balance . . . It was only three steps, and he needed both hands to climb down. "I didn't notice where he left it. It's around camp somewhere. Under his blankets, maybe. That's where he generally keeps it."

For a minute it looked as if it might work. He looked over at the blankets, shifted his rifle to one hand, and put his foot out on the wheel. I must have moved or looked eager, or something, for he drew back and laid the rifle back across his knees again.

"All right, it can stay there, if that's where it is," he said. "You stay where you are. Don't you try any break on me. If you do, I'll shoot you in your tracks. I can do it as easy as wait. I've took about enough off of you, anyway. Haulin' me to jail. Runnin' off horses that belonged to me. Gittin' me throwed out of a contract at the Farrand place. Puttin' that girl of mine up to run away and git me talked about all over the country. You've got enough piled up to answer for. You'll answer for it, too. I told you that once before, and I meant it. Where's she gone to?"

That was something else he had got from the Farrand woman. Old Hendricks had made some mention of it to her, I remembered—not an accurate one. She hadn't held much back, evidently. "I don't know," I said. "She didn't tell me."

"So you seen her, then, did you?" he said. "You knew she was runnin' away from me, too, didn't you? She told you a lot of truck about what she was doin' it for, didn't she? What did she tell you?"

"That's her business," I said. "It didn't amount to much. It's for her to tell you, though, if she wants to."

He debated the point of etiquette with himself, and let it pass. "I've got a right to know where she is, anyway," he said. "I'll git it out of you before I'm through with you, too. The quicker you puke up, the easier it'll be on you. Where's she at?"

There was a dented tin pan standing at the edge of the platform, almost opposite his horses and about ten feet away from them. Two steps would reach it. If I could kick it at them, I thought, they would jump. It might upset him long enough to . . . I edged a couple of inches towards it, and he tightened his hand on the rifle breech and scowled warningly. I let it go.

"I told you I didn't know where she was," I said. For some reason, I couldn't feel that he was angry, in spite of his trying to sound like it. I couldn't even feel that the list of grudges he had reeled off against me counted for much with him. He was too deliberate, too controlled. He seemed to be trying to work up a state of emotion, and not quite making it. "She didn't tell me, so I don't know. I don't know; can you get that through your head?"

"You could guess close enough to it," he said. "She'd have seen to that. You seen which way she headed when she left you, didn't you? You know which way she was from the Farrand place when you seen her, don't you? Was it towards the reservation, or down towards the river? Stand still, or I'm liable to git tired of tellin' you to. I don't need to keep you here arguin', anyway. I can track down the kid and the old man if I have to. I don't need to hold out any bait for 'em."

Bait? It began to dawn on me what was in his mind; what he was there for; why he was holding his gun on me so long; why he wanted to bring Calanthe back when she was determined not to be brought. There was no emotion about it, no sentimentality, no sense of vengefulness or injured feelings. It was all severely practical and business-like. I had been right in feeling that his anger didn't run as deep as he tried to let on. There were four people who knew something of the truth about the Farrand shooting and his blackmailing the Farrand woman afterwards. He had three of them within rifle range of him. If he could leave two planted deep and out of his way, and haul Estéban back to hold over the Farrand woman as we had held him over her, he would be set up in business all over again, better and solider than ever. Calanthe, who was the other one of the four, he could tend to later. We had picked an ideal place for him to operate in: lonely, secluded, miles from any main road, with a cemetery within easy walking distance that had been left completely undisturbed for years. The only drawback was the quiet. If he shot, old Hendricks and Estéban would know by the sound that it was a strange gun, and it might make them suspicious. They might decide to stay out till after dark, when it would be hard for him to handle them; they might decide not to come in at all. I shifted a little, to see if I had worked it out right. He half-lifted the rifle and settled the stock under his armpit, and I stood still again. He didn't want to shoot yet, but he could be induced. I thought how Piute Charlie's arm had looked, stuck stiffly out of his blankets with grains of sand glittering in the wrinkles of his hand, and his wrist showing the faded blue tattoo lines that the old-time Indians wore to measure off shell money on. It was cold standing in the damp wind with no shirt on. The cemetery would be colder. I looked up at it, and saw old Hendricks lifting the gate open. He came through it, looking back behind him, and lifted it shut and stooped down to retwist the wire fastening around it.

"That's him, by God!" Busick said, in a low voice. He moved his rifle and glanced across it at me. "Stand right there. Keep your mouth shut. I'll . . ."

He threw the rifle to his shoulder and drew down on old Hendricks. I took a long step towards the tin pan at the edge of the platform, and he swung it back at me. Then he flinched sharply, and there was a crunching whack, like a butcher cutting bony meat with a dull cleaver, and then a whop and a clatter, like windmill paddles breaking in a storm. It sounded as if something had broken inside him. He let the rifle fall into the front of the wagon, and leaned forward as if to reach for it. I kicked the pan at the horses, and they jumped, throwing him out over the wheel, and ran away up the road. Old Hendricks came hurrying down the hill and caught them. The brake was still on, so they were not hard to hold. He tied them to a stump and came running to where Busick lay as I came to the edge of the platform with the pistol. There was no longer any use for firearms, but I had set myself to go for it as soon as I kicked the pan, and it had meant too much to give up on such short notice. Old Hendricks was kneeling over Busick. He looked up at me, and I could see blood on one of his hands.

"Why, he's hurt!" I said, as if he needed to be told. "Why, it looks like he'd been shot! Why, there's . . ."

"He is shot, damn it!" old Hendricks said sharply. "It's that kid again, can't you see that? He went and bushwhacked him from that rock blind of yours out in the pasture! Git out there and see what he's up to, and hurry up about it! He may be runnin' away on us again!"

I ran for the saddle horse and headed for the pasture at a canter. Estéban had left the rifle lying across the rock where he had rested it to shoot, and was dodging through some arrowwood bushes at the opening of the lower meadow. He made for the edge of the timber when he saw me, but I went after him at a run, and finally headed him back and got him by the collar. He tried to pull away, and then went limp so that I had to hold his full weight one-handed. I dropped him, and he sat up and looked back at the rock blind, and then down at the ground. He didn't look at me at all.

"*Otro*," he said, half-whispering it as if to scare himself. He was out of breath from running. "*Ahorita son tres. Yo que no tenía enemistades, yo que . . . Gente humilde yo, nada más. Y á morir ahorcado, como . . . No hubo remedio. Lo que hice . . .*"

"It's all right," I said. It did look like piling it up on him a little—to be completely alone in a strange country, obscure and timid and friendless and inoffensive, without even nerve enough to collect the wages he had coming to him from the railroad company, and to be rawhided somehow into three shootings. "Settle down, and come on back. Nobody's going to hang you. Nobody's going to bother you at all. If anybody tries to when I'm around, he'll get some of his fingers stepped on. Come on."

There was more to him than his timidity and inoffensiveness, though. He wouldn't look at the rock blind when I rode over to it to bring in old Hendricks' rifle, but he remembered what it had been built for, shootings or no shootings. He refused to go on into camp until we had started our herd fire for the night, to keep the mountain lion away from the horses.

OLD Hendricks had considerable first-aid work done on Busick when we got back—his shirt split down, and the wound in his shoulder cleaned out and bandages wrapped on to stop the bleeding. He was able to talk, though too weak and shaken to move much. His manners had undergone a startling improvement, but his pulse was steady and there were no other unusual symptoms, so we decided that it was nothing to be alarmed about. We carried him over to the fire and fixed a lean-to out of old boards so the heat would reflect on him, and went out with a jack light and collected fir pitch to calk his shoulder. There were red firs at the edge of the timber along the horse pasture, with pitch blisters that held half a cupful apiece, and except for its stickiness there is no better disinfectant for a wound than fir pitch. The wound was a bad one, and hard to work on, but it showed something about Estéban's hand with a rifle. He had shot from two hundred yards away, with a waning light and a target in motion, and he had to allow for a cross wind and a bullet drop of nearly a foot and a half. He had hit three inches below the point of Busick's shoulder, and the bullet had ranged back and come out in the middle of the shoulder blade. Busick told us while we were working on him that he hadn't felt it hit at all; there had been merely a twinge, as if a pin had stuck him, and then he saw his rifle slipping out of his hands and discovered that he couldn't make his muscles work to keep hold of it. Those old-fashioned bullets lumbered along at approximately the same speed as sound, so the impact and the report of the rifle had come so nearly together that neither of us had been sure for a minute or two what had happened. He dropped off to sleep after we had finished pitching and bandaging him. Estéban went out to his night herding. Old Hendricks sat down on his fir-bough bed and looked around him—the camp, the herd fire out in the pasture, the line of dark trees against the stars.

"This is all, I guess," he said. "You was supposed to turn the horses loose in open country. This is as open as you'll find. We can't let you auger around takin' care of an outfit like this all the rest of your life. You've done enough of it already; more than you had any business to, I expect. If there was any way to pay you back, I'd do it, but you've got work of your own to do. There's people down below that ought to know about this shootin' business. You'll have to make some kind of a report on it to some of 'em. Some of it, anyway."

"The sheriff won't care much what it was, as long as it's straightened out," I said. He hadn't been thinking of the sheriff much, probably. He was right about one thing—it was time for me to pull loose and go back to work serving divorce papers and chasing down hobo herds of sheep to put attachments on. "I'll see that word gets to whoever needs to know about it. I don't know whether I can send out anybody to help you with Busick unless I arrest him."

"We won't need any help with him, if he stays on the mend like this," old Hendricks said. "If he don't, we can sell off some of the horses and have a doctor out for him. Or take him in to the hospital like we done down on the river. We'll make out, one way or another."

"I'll have to take the pack saddles and pack horses in with me," I said. "They're county property. You'll need some way to move your camp when you get ready to pull out, and you can't keep a herd of horses here more than a few weeks. What do you plan to do?"

He looked out at the herd fire. "Move, move," he said. "We'll shove on down this chain of meadows and pick up a road somewhere. Maybe we can run in a few of them wild horses below here. These wheat ranches will be draggin' summer fallow in another week or two, so there'll be a market for 'em. We'll move on somewhere else after that, and keep on at it. It's the best thing for us. Shut a grass horse up in a stall for four or five months, and he'll turn vicious on you every time. Turn him out to run loose for a while, and he gits all right again. You've seen it. I've got everything settled now, and there's nothing more to stay here for. A man's got to find out what he's good for, and then do it. If people want it, that's all the better, but you've got to do it, whether anybody wants it or not, if you know what it is. It's took me a long time to find out. We won't need any pack horses. We've got a wagon to move camp in now."

"You mean that wagon of Busick's?" I said. "What if he don't want you to . . . You mean you're planning to make him go along with you? What if he don't want to go? How do you expect to make him behave himself? What if he lands in trouble somewhere?"

"He'll go, whether he wants to or not," old Hendricks said. "He'll behave himself, too. It may not set very well with him, but he can learn, and he'll be out of people's way, anyway. I'll tend to that. I might as well. He's my son."

I sat with my mouth dangling open. Things he had said and done and left unexplained all the way back to the time I had first seen him began to clear up and take on sense and relevance. It was like picking a loose end out of a mass of old wires and coupling it to a storage battery, and watching it begin to glow in and out through the tangle. "The Indian woman you . . ."

"She was the one," he said. "It's my turn at him. She went through hers. I was out to pile up money in them days. Gittin' ahead in the world was what we called it. Nobody ever figured out what they was gittin' ahead of, I guess. There's more things than that for a man to git ahead in, anyway. It's took me a hell of a long time to find it out, but I've found it out good. Here's him and the kid—two men that can't stay out of trouble when they're left to themselves. When they're with me, they can. I can keep 'em out of it. That's one thing I'm still good for. . . . Well, git to bed. You'll want to start out early tomorrow morning, and you've got your packs to straighten out."

There was still one thing. It was a little foolish, but I had to ask it. "He don't know about this, does he? What you've told me?"

"No," he said. "Maybe I'll tell him one of these times. I don't know. It might not help any. Sometimes it don't. You've seen how it works out with some of 'em, and you never know. Git to bed."

THE next morning was the last time I talked to him. It was not long after daylight, and he was still in bed. It was cold, with a fine gray dew covering everything, and he had gone back to his home remedy of burning sunflower pith on his chest to relieve the congestion. Estéban had come in from night herding to fix breakfast and attend to the camp chores. Three men, I thought, and the most helpless and dependent and unenterprising of them was having to do the work for the other two because they had attempted more than they were equal to. Old Hendricks put his hand out from under the blankets and said good-bye, and swore because some smoke from the sunflower pith drifted into his gullet.

"We might see each other again somewhere," I said, to fill in. "People do sometimes."

"We might," he agreed, and blew on the sunflower pith to keep it smoldering. "I'd be halfway uneasy if I thought we would. It might turn out that you hadn't amounted to as much as you ought to. I don't know whether I could stand that or not. You'll take word down about—about what happened yesterday? As much as you need to tell, and how he's gittin' along, and what he'll be doin' when he's straightened out."

"I'll get word to her," I said. "Maybe I'll see her. If I don't, I'll send somebody."

"Either way'll do," he said. "It would be better to tell her yourself, but I won't blame you if you don't, after what you've been through. A man sees how other people has made out together, and he knows he ain't any smarter than they was. Do the best you can."

"I will," I said. "There's nothing you need?"

"Nothing except that," he said. "Whichever way you feel about it, play it straight through. Anything a man does takes nerve. The more you put in, the more you take out. Well, good-bye."

The last I saw of him was when I looked back from a stand of elders coming into bloom at the bend of the road, turning down toward the long sagebrush flat. He had sat up in his blankets to watch the pack horses out of sight. He put up his hand, and then lowered his head and blew on his sunflower pith again. The sun came up, and its light on him made him look almost as gray as if the dew had settled on him, as it had on everything else. The mist from the grass shut him out, and I stirred up the horses and rode on down toward the open flat.

The last I heard about him was from some horse dealers at a livestock auction over in Nevada, in 1937 or 1938, after he was dead. They had bought grass horses from him, they said, when he had his outfit at work among the wild bunch grass herds around the edge of the Piute reservation at Walker Lake, down in the south. He had been working out some trails in rough country, and his horse fell on a sidehill and rolled on him. A younger man might have got over it, but he was too far past his youth for doctoring by the time help reached him. He hung on for about a week after they got him to the doctor in town, and some of his children went down to comfort his last hours and find out what disposition he had made of his accumulated profits, in case there were any. The horse dealers didn't know how that part of it had come out, but they had heard that toward the last he turned kindly and mellow, and expressed his earnest regret for anything he had done to them, and asked them to forgive him and let bygones be bygones, and forgave them for anything they might unthinkingly have done to injure him. He lay still for a long time after that, and they got up to leave, thinking he might have dropped off to sleep. He roused up and called them back before they got to the door.

"There's only one thing about this forgiveness business that I want you all to remember," he said. "If I git well, it don't count."

Estéban had taken it hard, they said, and had to be kept under watch for several weeks afterward for fear he might try to do away with himself. He had gone back to Mexico, they thought, when he finally steadied down enough to be turned loose. They didn't know what had become of Busick; drifted down into the mining country, maybe, but they didn't know for sure. Nobody ever heard from him again.

chapter sixteen

SPRING always moves against the rivers. Trailing the horse herd all the way up to the edge of the timber had kept us moving through country where it was always only beginning. Riding back through it with the two pack horses meant going through all the stages we had kept ahead of—one near the old river crossing, where the thornberry thickets were flowered out in patches so heavy the branches dragged the ground, and the gullies had run full of white poppies and little orange-colored wild hollyhocks; one along the rockbreaks beyond Crosskeys, where the perfume from masses of greasewood and blue lupin in blossom was so heavy that it made a man dizzy to ride through it; one around a cattle-branding corral at the edge of the wheat fields, where there were islands of pink grass flowers wider across than a horse could jump, and where the branding season looked to be about to start, because several dozen magpies were waiting in some new-leafed cottonwoods to be ready for it. Magpies followed calf brandings, it being their practice to tear meat from the raw brands to carry home to their grateful nestlings. The shade trees across the flat in Crosskeys were leafed out so the town was hardly visible through them, though the few glints of it that showed when the wind stirred looked almost too shy and innocent and peaceful to live.

Down the rolling country below Crosskeys, the winter wheat was stooled out heavy enough to run full of long white ripples when the wind swooped through it, and a few places were at work harrowing summer fallow. It was a lonely occupation. The ingredients were a spike-tooth harrow weighed down with rocks, a dozen or fifteen scrub horses lined up abreast dragging it across a half-mile or so of ash-colored plowed ground, scratching a black track behind them as they moved, and a driver, who rode a saddle horse on the flank farthest from the dust cloud, with a sackful of rocks at his saddle horn to throw at them when they showed signs of lagging or ignoring him. Farther down, the old scurf-colored strips of winter-killed wheat had all been plowed up to reseed, though there were still no drill marks in most of them.

The plowed ground ran all the way down to the river breaks, empty, lifeless, too dark to show cloud shadows blowing across it except where shallow patches drying out in the wind gave it a mottled effect, like roils of mud welling up from the bottom of a deep pond. The wind was driving up from the river hard and cold, as it usually did after the first few weeks of spring growing weather. It was tiring to ride against, and having to keep up a constant pressure against the horses' wanting to drift sideways away from it made it worse. For a long time there was nothing in sight that looked like any possible shelter from it, but in the late afternoon, working along the edge of a plowed field within sight of the river breaks, I found an old board shanty planted down in a shallow draw where some plowing crew had camped, and pulled in for the night. It was not much of a place; there were cracks in the floor, the window was broken and rattly, and every hard blast of wind made it feel as if it was about to pull loose and take off across the plowed ground at a gallop, but there was a stock pond, and a corral for the horses, and some hay left over from the plowing crew's beds. I carried it out and turned them into the corral to work on it, and then ate and spread down to rest.

A man never knows where his mind will take him when he is too tired to hold it in. Going to sleep to the sound of shingles flapping and the window clattering, I tried to think something about Busick and old Hendricks, what they must be talking about with the wind roaring in the firs and the night chill crimping down, and of what would happen at the Farrand place and what might have happened if old Hendricks had kept away from it, but it was merely turning over names. I went to sleep without thinking anything about them, and began to flit through pictures of how the sweep of plowed ground around the shanty would look later in the year—the green wheat with birds swooping over it; the ripe wheat with the harvest in full swing and the headers moving in echelon through it, their fan arms turning against the sky; the stubble after harvest, with straw piles scattered in it to be burned, and a pile of straw burning in sunlight so intense that the flame was invisible except as a black charred spot that spread out toward the edges and fell into white ashes in the middle. After it had eaten deep into the pile, Calanthe came and stood watching, and held her hand out between it and the sun. Where the shadow of her hand fell, the flame became visible. It was clear white and patterned exactly to the shadow of her hand, like a hand of fire hanging in midair—a narrow strip of white fire for each of her fingers, and a broader one for her wrist and palm.

As with the two earlier dreams about her, there was no meaning to it, but it settled one thing. It would be useless to send anybody else to tell her about her father. I had to see her myself. It was the only way to keep some vague uneasiness of conscience from dogging me with meaningless dreams at night. Old Hendricks had been right—a man didn't escape from anything by skirting around it. The way to end it was to go straight through it and have it over with, for good or bad. I would sooner have got out of it, but the dreams were no easier to stand and they could keep coming, so it had to be done. It might be simpler than it looked, when I thought it over. I didn't love her. I wouldn't have minded not seeing her again at all. She was not especially pretty; not as pretty as she imagined, at least. I had been sorry for her, mostly. She didn't love me, either. Her trouble had been loneliness and desperation, with maybe a certain tinge of stubbornness. And love itself would have been nothing to count very high, from what I had seen of its effects, and I didn't want any of the things she had set her head on having. I remembered too well what wanting them had done to my father. Somebody else might want them as much as she did, or at least not care enough to mind her wanting them. It could be worked out to an understanding, with courage and honesty and common sense. She was courageous enough, and she could be sensible. I wished it was over with. I spent the rest of the night haggling it over with myself, and got up and started on down to the river before daylight the next morning, to have it over with quicker.

THE wind was still tearing across the river breaks for all it was worth. Two or three dead tumbleweeds were hovering a hundred feet in the air, like stray kites, and at the edge of the plowed fields where the old trail led down into the canyon the furrows were blown full of mock-orange and fruit-tree petals in long white stripes, like the start of a zero blizzard, though there were no mock-orange bushes or fruit trees nearer than the bottom of the canyon, ten miles away on a slant and eight or nine hundred feet down. It blew so savagely where the trail turned down into the canyon that it was hard to breathe facing it, and the horses had to be kept headed into it by main strength, like steering a boat crossways in a river rapid. Halfway down, at a box spring where somebody in the early days had made a start at a flower garden, the daffodils and bleeding heart and love-in-a-mist were flaxing themselves to a pulp in the flattened saw grass, and broken sprays of lilac were banked against the old picket fence so it swelled and strained in the wind like a sail.

There was some shelter for the horses among the willow thickets at the bottom of the canyon, but the sand and river spray driving across the open places would have rasped sawdust from an oak plank, and I had trouble finding anybody to ask for directions. A couple of Indians guarding a wagonload of salmon in the lee of a rockbreak denied knowing anything about any girl with a camp wagon, and tried to pump information about her out of me; a flagman in a dismounted boxcar at one of the railroad crossings thought he had seen a girl driving past in a wagon, but hadn't noticed much about her, because he had been busy at the time running off a Sunday's supply of whisky on his kerosene stove; an old French sheep herder huddled behind some boulders on a sidehill had seen her, and thought she was camped somewhere down the river, but couldn't describe the place clearly enough to be of any use. Finally I found an Indian salmon-drying camp in the rocks close to the river, and cornered a half-dozen squaws who had actually talked to her and knew where her camp was, though they were too fluttered and embarrassed at first to let out much information about it. Two of them were the squaws who had brought word to me about Piute Charlie's shooting in the sand hills down the river, and two or three of the others had sworn in court afterward that they were unable to speak a word of English. They loosened up when I told them that there had been no harm done, and described the place for me without much trouble. It was the horse camp where I had first found old Hendricks. One thing it proved was the value of building things to last. The old Greek bread ovens where the trail turned up to it had done their last baking years before, but their usefulness as landmarks hadn't dwindled a particle.

The wind tore hard against us all the way down, but it was easier traveling, because the horses began to recognize where they were, and to hurry along without having to be prodded. Turning up into the draw, I took one look back at the river, so as to remember how it had looked to a clear conscience. The sand dunes were dazzling white, fogged at the edges with sand blowing across them. There were some red boxcars on a railroad siding that flinched when the wind struck them broadside, and a play of light in the telegraph wires like a huge electric spark jumping back and forth across them. The river was black like wet slate, and the whitecaps breaking out on it tore into spray and went whipping away across the sand before they could move across the water at all. It was the way the first phase of our spring always ended—strong, harsh, not leaving any room for doubt that it really was ending.

THE draw had not changed much, except that there were new leaves and grass in it for the wind to hammer at. The fence panels that Estéban had put up to keep the horses in were still lying where he had laid them when we drove through to leave, with red-seeded grass blown flat over the crooked old posts and rusty wires. It was impossible to tell whether the road had been used recently, because all the tracks were blown out of it, but at the place where it turned across the creek bed it was closed by a pole hung between two cottonwoods and wired down. There was no other way across the creek except through the tangle of trees and underbrush, so I dropped the reins and got down to untwist one of the wires. The wind was louder than it had been in the open, because of the trees catching it, and it was full of torn leaves and dead grass stems and flower petals, dried locust blossoms and catkins of willow and cottonwood; all the wreckage of spring being driven out to make room for the entering streaks of summer. I climbed up the creek bank to get clear of it for a minute, and saw Calanthe's camp wagon standing between the board shack where old Hendricks had slept and the stock pond where the horses had come down to water. The old rosebush that had half-buried it had come into full bloom, and the wind was tearing yellow petals from it and driving them past the wagon wheels and across the surface of the pond in a cloud.

There was no sign of anybody around, and no smoke in the

camp wagon stovepipe. For a minute I went through a cross pull of opposing feelings, hoping on one side that she might have left everything and gone somewhere else, and being afraid on the other that something might have happened to her. Then the door opened and she climbed down into the cloud of petals and dead stems and wreckage and stood shading her eyes against it, and then she came running through it, laughing and letting it beat on her face. When she got close, I saw that the wind was spattering tears across her cheekbones. I had intended to go back to the horses before telling her anything, but I ran to her and caught her and bent her head back, and let all that old Hendricks had taught me blow away with the loose petals and dried locust blossoms and shed catkins that were ending to make room for a beginning.

THE END

About the Author

Oregon's only Pulitzer Prize winner for literature, **H. L. DAVIS** was born in 1894. His first novel was *Honey in the Horn,* for which he received the Harper Prize for the best first novel of 1935. Over the next ten years, he published four novels, a collection of earlier short stories, and a number of shorter pieces, including movie scripts. His fourth novel, *Winds of Morning,* was highly acclaimed and became a selection of the Book-of-the-Month Club. He died in 1960.